W

MW01713330

Book Three

Jasyn Turley

JHH III

Remember, Sometimes
a fool's Chance is your only
Chance.

Jasyn Turley

Scripture quotations are taken from the Holy Bible, New Living Translation, copyright © 1996, 2004, 2007. Used by permission of Tyndale House Publishers, Inc., Carol Stream, Illinois 60188. All rights reserved.

Professional Edits by Dr. Michael from firstediting.com
Book cover (front, spiral & back) design by Jelena Gajic
Book cover (front, Spiral & back) Intellectual Property Rights owned by Jasyn Turley via design transfer pursuant 2021.
Author Photograph by Megan Teeuwen, owner of Megnificent Designs & Photography

Characters and events portrayed in his book are fictitious. Any similarity to any real persons, living or dead, is coincidental and not intended by the author.

Copyright © 2009 Jasyn Turley
Self-Published by the Author, Jasyn Turley, March 25th, 2023

All rights reserved. No part of this book may be reproduced, stored in a retrieval system, or transmitted in any form or by any means, electronic, mechanical, photocopying, recording or otherwise nor used in any manner without written permission of the copyright owner except for the use of quotations in a book review.

481 Pages in total length: 169,787 words total

ISBN- 978-1-7334027-6-7

Table of Contents

For you, Grandma Bonnie.
I remember all the times on your backyard patio. You, mom, dad, and Nea with your homemade tea while I and Atley had grape soda.
We miss you, Grandma.

Prologue

Night before 'Retribution'

-October 17th, 2030-

Cold air swept across Autumn from the AC window unit in her room. The apartment didn't need the extra help to cool anything, not with the sudden temperature drop. She just enjoyed the cold that much. The only drawback was that the window unit took up the bottom half of the only window in the room. The blinds were raised to permit the sight of an overcast yet bright sundown. The smell of the AC's cold air was soothing, and the unit's sound was drowned out only by her little box TV playing *Fairytale*, her favorite anime on an old DVD player.

Her room was small, like the rest of their apartment, but it was comfortable, and she was happy where she was. Between her bed and TV stand and a closet, holding the rest of her belongings, was a table-part bookshelf and part makeup station, currently buried under homework: Gen Ed courses, weapon safety, and handling, along with a dumbed-down version of the Alyeskan militaries SERE. On top of the mundane studies, she had her own pursuits-old hardback copies of *The Iliad* and *The Odyssey* and a copy of *History of the Archbishop of Hamburg-Bremen.*

She was closing in on fifteen, and sixteen marked her adulthood, requiring military service for up to five years. All things considered, the future seemed dim, lacking excitement and the bliss of her simple and joyful existence with dear Uncle Richie. Just one year left to enjoy the "now" before it became "what once was."

Then came the knock at her door: Lieutenant Igor Petrov was waiting patiently, decked in full kit as if ready for war. He and the rest of his team, Wolf Pack, came to her with a request that she saw as an early crossing over the threshold of adulthood that she desperately wanted to push back against. It caused a nauseating uncertainty and anxiety about the future, suddenly nearer than it should've been. Adventure was calling to her, and she wanted to refuse it with everything in her, save for one caveat: Thomas, her only real friend.

She was looking out her bedroom window now, down at a good view at a cluster of apartment buildings and small sheds with a haphazard path for vehicles to maneuver. She was taken aback by her thoughts about the others who lived around her. What were they doing, and what were their goals in life? How often did things go the way they were supposed to? Was there ever enough time?

She couldn't imagine what it must feel like to be left in harsh wastelands outside the country. She knew it wouldn't be anything like her typical stroll into the woods. Now she wondered what it would be like to go out to her little tree stump, only to never see her friend again. Someone else would be sent to find her, someone who wouldn't understand her or care.

She found within herself a wanting to go that contrasted with her trepidation. It felt like it was only right to go and help bring her friend back home. How many times had he done the same for her? How many times had they stopped at a little diner and grabbed some coffee for him and hot coco for her to warm up as they chatted? And then there were the many hospital visits he took her to, just in case she caught a cold or something else during her explorations into the freezing wilderness.

There was no debate; her heart had already decided, and her chaos of a conscious was catching up. She worried about leaving her uncle, but this Lieutenant Igor Petrov promised she'd be back soon, and he'd explain everything to Richie.

Still, though, the worry wouldn't leave.

There was another knock on her open bedroom door. Lt. Petrov was patient—holding back the urgency of their quest. The rest of his comrades were waiting in the living room. Something lurked deep within the man, something he kept tightly reined in. Calm and collected. She knew this look from Thomas, who seldom said much in response to any inquiry. There was a sadness to these men that dwelled underneath.

"Devushka." Igor gently broke the silence, pulling the knuckles of his fingers from the door. "Ve must leave now, and I need your answer."

She took a deep breath and nodded, staring out another window. She often explored the forest beyond, and the urge to get lost in the trees came upon her. That curious nature came to the fore and played tug of war with her indecision.

"What will I be doing again?"

"I vill tell you, zere's unidentified person in Colorado. Ve tink it is Sergeant Nilges. If so, familiar face may coax him into lettin us take him home."

"And if it's not Thomas?"

"Dva, zere are risks." He nodded.

She took in a quick, deep breath and blinked many times over. It sounded like they already had their answer. Why would Thomas not jump at the chance to return home? Unless it was someone else; there was that slight chance. Heart pounding, Autumn softly replied, "Okay." There was no going back now. She reached over to grab a bag. "Can you give me a couple of minutes?"

"Dva." Igor held up two fingers. "Two. Once lost, time is gone. No getting back." She liked how Igor spoke. It held a classical vibe; he seemed both a scholar and a gentleman.

Her heart thrashed in her chest as she grabbed her bag. *I'm really doing this.* It didn't feel real, but her knees trembled, and every time she took in a breath, it was like gravity disappeared. She felt faint as she packed her copies of *The Iliad*, *The Odyssey*, and *The History of the Archbishop of Hamburg-Bremen.*

She added spare clothing, a compass, hygiene supplies, and most importantly a Leatherman tool; she made sure this was safely stored inside her bag. Her knees shook as she walked to the door, sparing a look over her shoulder, back out the window to the forest beyond.

Her mind was made up, and she was ready to repay Thomas. This time she'd be the one to venture into the forest and bring him back.

Part I – Fallout

Chapter One – By the Sword

-October 18th, 2030-

Autumn stared at the mangled, butchered carcasses of the two pilots. Gone were the memories of yesterday; the night when Igor and Wolf Pack showed up at her door felt like a lifetime ago. One pilot lay in a contorted state, his broken bones twisted in ways they were not designed to be. She was transfixed on the other pilot, whose bare back had been flayed open. He was left hunched over one of the back seats in the bird as blood pooled and dried down around him. The interior walls were splashed in the thick red substance, and crimson handprints smeared across the splatters in thicker strokes. Protruding from the flayed open back, the man's spine arched outwards as if the killer had yanked and pulled on it with great force, the back ends of his ribs seeped through the sinews and flesh.

The sight of the two pilots screamed at her, a silent corruption of innocence, a resonating crescendo of horror and violence. It dug through her eyes, carving a permanent place in her memory, tainting and staining her like an old busted pipe dripping crimson over white sheets. Her soul mourned what once was, now lost.

Her front teeth clenching over her bottom lip, quivering sobs escaped in heaving gasps of weeping and panic from the corners of her lips. Covering her mouth with her hands, a sudden urge to vomit swept over her with the cold push of the storm's wind. A welcoming discomfort, a distraction that, albeit brief, pulled her away from the sacrilegious disregard for human life. She stepped back, her eyes pulling away, chest heaving as she looked to and fro, lost. A *boom* of thunder sent shivers up her spine and a nervous twitch through her fingers. The torrential downpour mingled with the tears streaking her mascara down her face as she pulled her hand back to see the black makeup on her fingers.

Igor had told her about the chances of encountering a madman in the wastes. A man was reported to have attacked Thomas in the wilderness. Like a flashing strobe across her mind in tune with storm, the next flicker of lightning illuminated the charred cinders of the city and the crater, and she remembered this man's name: *Sergei Cultivascú!*

It seemed mythical to her now, as if the very mention of the name would invoke the killer. While calling out Bloody Marry from the mirror required three incantations, Sergei needed only one. As if it would conjure him like some malevolent spirit. There was no other person it could be. That fifty-fifty shot in the dark they had taken, hoping on a prayer to find Thomas, instead ended in their ruin.

She looked around; the crater in which the helicopter was situated felt like an emptied lake, a gateway into Tartarus where darkness consumed her, and the Wastelands robbed her of any sense of rescue. The flicker of lightning offered a brief illumination of the void, revealing the ruins of the once city. Skeletal structure of buildings rimmed this dent in the earth like broken teeth; the crater was a giant mouth ready to swallow her whole.

A hand grabbed her from behind, and her mind flared with fears of what would come. She looked up over her shoulder at the dark figure—another silhouette, in the form of a man, veiled in the helicopter's shadows and the storm's darkness. A shadow figure conjured forth by the very invoking of his name. Her thoughts had betrayed her and summoned him to her doom. She grabbed his hand in a vain attempt to free herself, but he pushed down on the top of her head, forcing her to her knees as she splashed into a puddle of mud.

Set in his other hand, swaying in a lethargic rhythm of movements mirroring his labored breathing, was the twisted rust of a metal blade on an unnaturally crude scythe. The old wooden shaft appeared twisted just a bit more than usual, with a jagged bend where rusted metal met twisted wood coated in blood. The rain dripping from it was transparent crimson.

"Please, don't." Autumn sobbed, gasped, and then wept.

Her thoughts spiraled into the chaotic discord of a typhoon, along with her breathing. Unfocused, she fell back on the only instinct she could focus on: to survive. Her extremities were numb and shaken by the adrenaline that only added to her hysteria.

She expected a strike, maybe a stab with that rusted blade, or perhaps a simple bullet to the head; that would be quicker. As long as she wasn't awake or alive to remember what he would do to her. But the man didn't do anything, just shushed her as Uncle Richard would do when she was young and sickly. A soft lulling, as if he wanted to comfort her but didn't know how, and she certainly didn't understand why.

Madman, Igor had called him.

He jammed his scythe down into the mud, letting the blade stick into the slippery floor of the crater and splash brown splotches over her face that were quickly washed away by the rain. He pushed her chin up to look at him, loosening his grip on her head while staring down at her. She wondered if he could see her at all or just wanted her to listen.

"Scarecrows don't get to pick their faces, child." There was a certain semblance of an accent to the man. Yet his voice rasped, dry, as if running a five-kilometer dash with no water. There was a faintness, almost weakness, to his tone, and she noticed his breathing was labored. His hand now vacant of the scythe's twisted handle, he held his side as if in pain. There was vulnerability. "And this. This is not my face." His words faded into another cold burst of the storm's wind.

Scarecrows? Her mind shouted, looking back at the butchered and mangled pilots. *What do you mean scarecrows? These are human beings!*

Then came splashing footfalls in the form of a hard limp and heavy heaving. Sergei's hand lowered to the back of her neck, making her feel almost like the runt of a litter. Much like how a momma cat would pick up her young up by the scruffs of their necks to move them where she saw fit.

Autumn's hands tightened on his wrist, resisting his will as her feet and knees dragged around in the mud, searching for a foothold. But as with every other course of action, her efforts yielded no fruit.

But even as weak as he was, she was still weaker, unable to pry off a finger of his. His stance shifted, and his other arm moved rough and fast, grabbing at her just above the elbow and enforcing his decree. She swayed in the air, almost effortlessly, coming to a gentle splash in the mud behind him. She landed on her hands and knees, catching herself as the mud puddle rose over her wrists, looking up to see Sergei's back to her.

The sight of another figure came through the gape of his left arm and side, emerging from the darkness as more lightning illuminated the crater for a millisecond. Just long enough for her to see Igor aiming a rifle at the "madman," his weakened stance coming to a halt. There was an animal within the Wolf Pack warrior, revealed through his hardened expression. She envisioned a wolf snarling, revealing teeth ready to rip and tear.

"Igor." Her voice cried out in a distorted whimper. Her thoughts knew the words, but they were incomprehensible to her ears. Her lips quivered in the rain, her tears unyielding like a gushing geyser spewing water from all the pressure built within. Her bangs stuck around her face in clumps as Igor looked at her and then at the assailant.

"You let her go!" Igor projected his voice in a booming rage with an undertone of pain flaring. Despite the mangled left leg and the pants torn midway up, soaking from his bleeding calf and shin, he stood. There was a calm and steadiness to him as he held the assailant at gunpoint.

Lightning flashed and gave Autumn her first clear look at the man's backside: red and black checkered flannel, blue jeans and boots tattered, torn, and ragged. He looked like he had walked through a paper shredder. The man didn't move, separating her from Igor like a shield. His rifle hung by a strap at his side, and on his hip rested a revolver in its holster. He had a giant knife at his other side and another knife sheathed at his calf by his left foot.

The flash of lightning disappeared just as fast as it had arrived; when her heaving stopped, she looked back to Igor. The once stoic and rock-solid warrior paused. Terrified recognition locked his face in a state of shock.

"You!" Igor hissed. Anger, hatred, and a loathing rumble in his voice shook and trembled in matrimony with sorrow and grief.

Autumn didn't miss a beat, registering the tone of familiarity in the Russian's voice. "What?" she tried to cry out, but she managed only a distorted whimper ending in a cough. *You know each other?* She leaned over on her shins, hands still in the mud, to hold herself up.

A second followed before a bright flash split the sky, like the Red Sea separating as the Israelites escaped from the Egyptians. Out from this gaping split of lighting, the audible weight of a thunderclap fell over them like a meteor. It rumbled in its descent before shattering and cracking open the air in a deafening thunderclap. In that moment of clarity, she saw hesitance in Igor's face. In that brief second, she noticed Igor's shaking despite his eyes narrowing. The difference between them was immense; if only she could stand and fight like him and not remain a helpless runt on all fours, whimpering in freezing fear.

"Igor," she begged, just wanting to be out of this hell, this Seventh Circle of Dante's Inferno.

His eyes crossed to hers, that sympathy veiling something behind a thick curtain of the present circumstances. Then came the quick movements of the killer, synced with the flicker of lightning and that same booming thunderclap. He yanked out his revolver and hip-fired before Igor could react. The bullet zipped through the rain, ending in a fleshy splash in Igor's chest: just like that, the last Knight—the last Wolf—had fallen.

A moist grunt splattered from Igor as his left leg gave out. As she watched Igor fall to his knees, Autumn didn't realize her hands were covering her mouth. His weight and gravity pulled him back, but he didn't hit the ground; he remained erect, sitting on the back of his legs in a slump. Igor's breathing was now a bloodied wheeze that whistled through the rain as his eyes fell to the hole in his chest.

The killer closed the distance, and Igor didn't move, waiting like Autumn in a paralyzed state, save for slow movements of his head. Each of Sergei's steps fell in rhythm with nearby thunder, like the tolling of bells as the world seemed to silence itself, calming with the deed done. Evil stood with its victory as the rain lightened and the wind was soothed to a moan, rain transitioning into a gentle shower.

Igor's face lifted, and he looked at her again, blood covering his clenched teeth—but not enough to seep through his lips. He grimaced when he shifted his gaze to the assailant now stepping towards him.

"Please!" she wanted to scream, but her voice couldn't find its way out of her lips. Instead, her breaths escaped in dry heaves, pressure building in her head. Forgetting how to breathe, she felt light and numbness take over.

Igor's face turned back to her, bearing the same apologetic look. Uttering a sincere apology for the hell he had brought her to, he spoke with a weak voice pounded by the rain before delivery: "Tysyacha Izvineniy, Devushka."

Though she knew not what he said, his face expressed it all. "Forgive me." She thought he may have been shedding tears of his own.

"There's no forgiveness for you!" Sergei's voice thundered in a raging bellow. His voice was hoarse and rattled in shaken hatred as each step moved through the air in hastened aggression. Thunder felt as if it were rumbling in tune with his movements. His voice carried such weight that it seemed to add to the gravity anchoring her in place.

"Please." Autumn cried in a desperate plea, clenching her teeth, wreathing in her sobs as the madman's splashing footfalls thundered in her ears. The sound stopped as his feet halted in a stance, and she dared a look to see the man's grip over his revolver adjust.

Igor managed to raise one hand, his eyes still and stern, a cautionary hand, and a genuine plea of remorse, urging for the killer to wait. "Radzi Bogha… Please," Igor slurred and coughed with the effort to speak. Blood now dripped down the left corner of his bottom lip. "Prostit'."

There was a pause, a delay, and the world seemed to slow when the killer himself stood as still as the dead world around them. Autumn didn't notice her sobs coming to an end as the rhythm of her breathing eased. Hope reared its taunting head, like a bird ready for takeoff: there was no guarantee it would stay.

Igor held his eyes to the killer, and some unspoken exchange went between the two; she was a third wheel thrown in the mix.

Igor broke the silence, his wheezing voice like one a broken man apologizing on his deathbed. However, the look of hate didn't leave the Russian's eyes, nor the remorse that was just as present in his voice, spelling heartache: "Ya Nadeyus', Shto ty smezhesh prostit' Menya."

Sergei paused briefly, giving Igor time to speak his peace. His fist had a cold rigor mortis grip around the handle of his revolver. She noticed his index finger twitching over the trigger in an impatient need to pull it. Then she heard it, easy enough to miss in the pouring rain and rattling thunder—a snivel of the madman's sobbing.

Panting now as her mind seemed to settle, the storm inside passed as she looked around. Her eyes fell onto the sight of the crude scythe, its shaft sticking out of the muddy earth like the twisted limb of the undead crawling from the ground. Then she glared over at the madman, her breaths rising and falling in heavy heaves as she pushed herself to her feet. Both hands latched around the twisted shaft; the fuzziness of mold covered it as she plucked it out from the earth.

Looking now at Igor and the attacker, she started towards the assailant, holding onto the handles and rearing the farming tool back. Closing the distance, the barrel of the antiqued weapon kissed Igor's forehead. She gave the weapon a brutal swipe at the man's back one second too soon.

He was faster, head twisting to look at her at a mechanical speed that stopped her attack mid-swing. Grabbing the shaft of her weapon, the blade came to a stiff but sudden stop an inch from his face. He didn't flinch or recoil; his eyes glimmered in a beady glare at her through the darkness. He stepped forward, his leg passing between hers in a quick motion that swapped her behind her left ankle and dropped her instantly.

Falling to her left knee, she didn't have time to comprehend the speed with which he twisted her arms and used his as leverage to push the rusted, bloodied blade down upon her. Her right leg sank and slipped as the assailant weighed over her. The rotten metal was inches from her neck as she pushed back in futile defiance against an unstoppable force. She looked to Igor for aid, but he was now on his back, blood from his injuries diluting in the rainwater.

She could smell the man's breathe. Her pants turned to seethes as she glared at him. "Do it." A muffled grunt escaped her lips; her body was light and numb, and more than anything, she felt the need for the night to just end. Either in defiance or longing for the chaos to cease. "DO IT!"

Instead, Sergei pulled back on the weapon, and Autumn was yanked upwards with it, closer to him. His hand gripping the scythe shot it forwards, sending the wooden center to her face. Her hands let go of the weapon, and she fell. Landing on her back in a blurred state, the next thing she saw was the tread of his boot stomping down on her head, rendering her unconscious.

Chapter Two – Reunion

-Twenty-Six Years Ago-

Being inside the bus bore the same shock he recalled from high school—a feeling of displacement, not belonging when leaving his assigned classroom and walking into another. Fellow students, he knew, but they weren't his classmates, nor was the teacher his own. That feeling of not belonging, of feeling so foreign, outside the comfort of the known, was a similar feeling. Now among the many recruits; such recollections were minuscule in comparison.

The bus driver stopped for a few minutes at a gas station down the interstate, where he did a quick shave of the stubble on his face. There hadn't been enough time to shave before he left home. His hair was a bit longer, but his recruiter had advised him to "leave it as it is, we'll give you your first buzz when you arrive. It's better to receive your buzz cut than to show up with one. A sort of a rite of passage."

Tim wasn't one to turn down advice, so he did just that. He remembered his big bro, his homie, his idol as a kid—Rufus—who had first left home with a short afro and came back bald. Well, why not do the same? Maybe seeing him as a full-fledged Marine would change his mother's disapproval.

If you walk out that door, I won't let you back in, you'll be dead to me! Those had been his momma's final words to him.

She'll come around, she has to, Tim had thought, shaking away the thoughts before they could take hold, sink their claws in deep, and anchor themselves like a thorn in his side. Constant mental bleeding.

But the sight of leaving his childhood home with its front door shut and locked as he walked off to the bus station weighed heavily. Heavier still when he had looked back to see no one outside to wave him off or hug him goodbye. Nothing. But she'd come around eventually.

Tim hadn't been sure of what to expect. He only knew that Rufus had gone through the same experience years prior. He would've done it sooner, but with high school in the way and his mom's disapproval, he had to wait to sign that dotted line until he could speak for himself. He was following a path paved but not lit; his one goal was to become a Marine, honor Rufus Morse, and make his older brother proud.

The bus came to a slow stop as they pulled into the Marine Corps Recruit Depot in Parris Island, South Carolina. The driver opened the doors, and that feeling of foreign uncertainty became like a cup overfilled with water. Right on the dot, at one-thirty in the morning, one of the drill instructors was through the door no sooner than it had opened. Dressed in blue bottoms and sleeves rolled up, a hat rested on his bald head. Tim imagined at that moment old cartoons with the stereotypical military guy but with protrusive veins from his neck and temples.

He glanced outside to see other instructors waiting while "Sergeant Guy" shouted a brief introduction before pacing up and down the bus, shouting Lord knew what else that he couldn't understand. The man's instructions or introductions were too fast and loud to comprehend. Already the fog of chaos was upon Tim, and he felt more lost than ever before.

"Stand up!" Sergeant Guy barked in a loud command. Tim had missed the man's name in the process. All the young men on the bus shouted in a chorus, "Aye, Sir."

Tim joined in and stood with his fellow passengers. Sergeant Guy didn't seem satisfied and yelled at them to sit down again. "Aye, Sir," Tim said in rhythm with the others this time, taking his seat.

Rinse and repeat, standing and sitting, until the message was engraved in their psyches. Life was simple at that moment. If Sergeant Guy or any instructor said "Jump," Tim and the others were to ask, "How high?"

They all stood for the last time, and Sergeant Guy gave the disembark command, simply put: "Now get off my bus!"

All together, they roared, "AYE, SIR!"

Leaving their seats and walking down the aisle in an orderly fashion, they stepped down and out of the bus into the warm, dry South Carolina spring night. The first day of thirteen weeks—the start of the transformation from civilian to US Marine. Tim understood that not all the recruits would make it. But somehow, he knew he would; it was already set in stone, carved in his mind. He wouldn't be one of the failures.

Outside on the pavement, several rows of yellow footprints were painted, four pairs to a row. Tim found his feet planted over a pair somewhere in the center, furthest from the bus. He hoped, with a sense of awe, that he was standing on the same ones his older brother had several years ago. He looked down as if the steps themselves were knighting him his armiger. As if the yellow footprints wielded sentience and recognized him as Rufus Morse's younger brother. As if his late older brother was there knighting him from the great beyond. The sword of destiny had passed from the late older sibling to the younger.

These have to be the ones. He thought, looking down at the yellow prints under his feet; he needed them to be. But standing on the yellow prints didn't make him a Marine—not yet. That moment became a priceless heirloom. Then and there, he decided for himself that these were indeed the same prints Rufus had once stood upon. Tim felt pride, forgetting the absent father at his brother's funeral, and the mother who refused to wave him off.

Pride and grief mixed into a concoction that simmered into bitterness, leaving an aftertaste of anger inside. Tim stood waiting for the next set of garbled and hard-to-understand instructions. When he eventually passed through recruit training and received his right to be called a Marine, his cousin Crystal would be on the other side waiting for him. She had walked him through the process, the medical screening, and everything else. But she couldn't be there to hold his hand during the transformation.

"Are you listening to me!" yelled an instructor, snapping him back to reality; the man was half an inch from his face. A wave of goosebumps traveled up Tim's spine, enforcing his straight posture.

"Aye, Sir," Tim yelled.

The instructor nodded and yelled out through a reddening face, making Tim's ears ring as he shouted another "Aye, Sir" in reply once more, and then the instructor ran down the line to some other poor recruit.

Amongst the chaos of all the instructors' chorus of yelling and shouting as they ran amok around him and the other recruits, Tim tried once more to shove the thoughts away. Fresh scars that would heal on their own by the time he returned home a full-blooded Marine. The world felt lighter; he could feel his blood pumping at an all-time high, and his senses were on high alert despite his racing mind.

"AYE, SIR!" They screamed after one of the drill instructors finished shouting his next line of dialogue. Tim felt like hitting himself. While lost in his thoughts, he had missed whatever speech or instructions were given by the instructors.

The recruits in front of him started moving as instructed, rows moving in neat lines to the front doors of the processing center? Barracks? Whatever they were, they were the first threshold, and he was just glad to start moving. Mimicking what he saw the others do.

Out of nowhere, one of the instructors stood not an inch from Tim's face yet again after shouting something. A nervous spike traveled up Tim's back as his fists clenched. Walking with two men yelling in his face, he was only able to shout "Aye, Sir!" He dared not strike either, lest he wanted to eat the tiled floor they were walking on.

That concoction of anger came to a pressurized boil as his fists shook. The instructor's voice was loud enough to ring a nervous flare through Tim as he straightened his back and kept his eyes forward. This was it, all gas, and no brakes.

"Aye, Sir!" Tim yelled back, keeping his eyes forward on the doors, throwing all the sudden hatred that conjured in his thoughts at the door. He let that carry him forwards like riding out a storm, going wherever it took him.

This was confusion at its finest, and he already felt himself breaking down—like the falling of pebbles that precedes a rockslide. So began the breaking down of the civilian, so that he could be rebuilt as one of the few.

-Present Day, October 19th, 2030-

The memories echoed in the back of Tim's mind in rapid succession. A flash memory skid as he stood looking at his mother and father stepping out of Colonel Winston's Buick. Uncertainty crept its ugly mug once more as Tim stared at the two people who brought him into this world. Hope that had invigorated him, expecting to see Phil step out, deflated as suddenly as it had emerged. Left in its place were longing, grief, and confusion.

"Mom? Dad?" The words escaped his lips unwittingly, as the initial spurs of joy from his early childhood were quickly drowned out by the sorrows of adulthood. Scars that had never really healed, only scabbed over, were now freshly picked, allowing them to bleed again.

Monika and Dereck. He corrected himself.

To his side, he could see Dakota's bloodshot, sorrow-stricken eyes looking at him. Her arms raised in a slow, cautious manner as though facing a vicious dog. "Tim." Her voice shook in lingering grief, a soft plea, reading him like he was an open book.

"Timmy," Dakota spoke again, lost for words, taking one slow step to him. Her tear streaks from redden eyes were drying. There was a 'brace for impact' look upon her face.

Looking at Dakota was like looking in a mirror. Seeing her caution prompted his mind to catch up; he came to realize that the same feelings of hatred and anger were now building inside him like pressurized gas inside the pistons of an engine block, right before exploding and shoving that piston downwards. Causing havoc and destruction, whether to the self or others, didn't matter—as long as the pressure was lifted. He felt himself starting to combust.

First, we lose Phil, and now this? he thought, his good hand shaking from a bottom pit of simmering hatred. He could feel the right corner of his upper lip fidget as he held back the tears building at the corners of his eyes.

Monika stood with her hands clasped around her mouth; she had aged a great deal since the last time he saw her. For a moment, he wondered where life had taken her and what hardships she had encountered since their last meeting.

As he remembered Rufus returning home from his first deployment, it felt like an age ago. Tim had been a young kid, not even thirteen, and he had jumped out the front door and wrapped his arms around his brother. Momma joined in a weeping embrace, and Daddy had stood waiting for his chance to hug his boy. Did his mother expect the same reception, coming to his front door, after what she had done to him?

It was all clear in memory, coming home after the war. He knocked, and his mother's face gave him a cold reception when she opened the door. Instead of being his mother, instead of loving her son when he needed her most, she slammed the door in his face. From behind the wooden barrier, her last words to him had been, "Both my sons are dead."

He looked at Dereck. The man he once knew as "Dad" had aged considerably. His salt and pepper goatee stood at least three weeks unshaven, with at least a week's worth of growth on his cheeks. His fro was a centimeter high and cut to a flat top with the sides shaved. But the man still had that same *DAMNED* hard and callous exterior Tim and Rufus grew up knowing.

At Dereck's core, there had always been something of a good heart; but a mantle of jaded bitterness surrounded it. Still, very much present here and now, just by looking at the man, Tim thought Dereck hadn't changed at all. The whole world may have changed, but old dogs were hard-pressed to.

Somehow, someway, Dereck was there beside his mother. Like he should've been when the military vehicle pulled up to their front door. When two soldiers stood from that black SUV and walked up to the front steps to notify them. The father who should've been there when Tim was left to comfort a weeping, broken mother as an empty casket was lowered into the ground and a flag was folded and given to her.

Where the fuck were you then?

His last memory of Dereck was taking off to the bar for a drink at the sight of the Death Notification Team. He just up and left, then and there, never returning. And Tim thought as he looked at the man now, he'd be fine if Dereck just left again—but this time, he could take that woman with him.

Tim couldn't help but look at Monika and Dereck with anything short of bitter hatred and clenched fists. Two people who were happy to see him, and yet he wished they had never visited.

"Hey, son." Dereck offered a weak smile.

Tim's eyes welled as he glared at the man, *Son?* And though it was weird, a part of him wanted to embrace that. Still, he just clenched his front teeth down as the corners of his mouth cracked open. He reeled in that weird part of him like a disobedient dog on a leash, yanking it back and smiting its nose for even entertaining the idea.

Dakota now grabbed his good arm; an aura of yellow about her spelled caution as she tried to get between him and them. But he pulled his arm free from her and shook his head.

"Don't," he hissed at Dereck as he looked at Colonel Winston. "Why would you bring them here?" he tried to ask, but his voice was cracking too much to get the words across.

"Timmy, please," Monika said, taking a step forward, a hand stretched out.

Before she could close the distance, Tim took a step back, stabbing the air at her with his finger. Grimacing at the sudden pain in his body from the movement of his avoidance, he glared at the woman. Dakota took another step forward, hands pressed against his chest and shoulders.

His broken arm and leg made her attempts to keep him back easy. He dared not resist his sister too much, seeing the discomfort on her face as she barred him from his parents. The flinch of her left eye and the wince of her lips brought his attention to the sight of her broken arm in its brace, the medical wrap that covered her upper chest and lower neck, and the bandage over her right eye. For her sake, he forced the animal back.

That is, until Monika dared to again call him by his name and take another step forward, her hand now clenched over her heart, something in him broke. He shook his head at her again, a warning to *stay the fuck back.*

His bottom lip quivered before setting into a snarl.

"She's the only person who gets to call me that," he snapped at the woman, pointing at Dakota. His sister now looked like a deer in the headlights. All her efforts to hold back a huge, rolling ball of snow, with too much momentum to stop, failed.

"That's your mother you're talking to," Dereck shot at Tim as he took a step forward, his voice hard and firm as if he were speaking to Tim when he was younger.

Wrong move MOTHERFUCKER! Tim's mind blazed as he took a step toward the man. He was ready to smash his casted arm across the old dawg's face. His lips twitched in a snarl, slurring his words with heavy ventilation of breaths. All he saw in his mind was red.

"Who the fuck are you?" Tim barked as spit went airborne with his voice, and a tear escaped the corner of his eye, mixing with the drainage from his nose. He stabbed the man with a cold finger, jaded in his own right. "You are not my father!" he yelled at Dereck and then pointed back at Monika. "And you! You sure as fuck ain't my momma."

"Tim." Dakota grabbed his shoulder, but before she could try anything, Tim grabbed her hand and eased her forward, a gentle prompt to stand beside him. That middle space once occupied by Phil was now closed.

"This is Dakota, my sister, and she's the only family I need. Don't you dare talk to me like I'm your son. Don't presume anything from me." Tim sneered feeling his upper lip twitching.

He could see it. The moment when a person who knows their mistakes stands and accepts whatever inevitability comes from them. Like how most deer just lie in wait when they know the end is nigh. Like when a judge slams down his gavel and the sentencing is made final. Monika and Dereck grew quiet, solemn, as they held their mouths shut, accepting whatever came, and he—the judge—dealt the only sentence he could.

Except, he felt no satisfaction from it—not satisfaction like he wanted to feel, or the feeling of a weight lifting. He just felt hurt.

"You." Tim pointed at Dereck. "You left, right after Rufus died. We didn't even have you there when we buried that empty fucking box." That did send tears down his cheeks, the memory of his brother's funeral picking those scabs open just a little more.

"And you." Tim pointed at Monika. His face was now riddled with tears, his breathing coming in fits as he heaved so hard he thought he might pass out. The adrenaline throbbing throughout his body brought pain to his broken limbs with each pulse. His temples pounded like war drums beating behind his eyes.

It was easy to forget that Inimicus has crushed his larynx. His breathing was suddenly labored as if the monster was choking him in the present. His voice hoarsened in a dry rasp under the phlegm congesting his throat.

He could see the guilt in the woman, and she couldn't hide it or the shame on her face. The wretched woman knew what was coming, and she stood there accepting her fate as his words cut through her like a guillotine; he was the headsman.

"After all we had been through, without that man standing next to you. Burying Rufus. And when I came back home…" His bottom lip fidgeted as memories of England emerged from that dark pit within himself, memories he seldom revisited. He saw the mother with her dead baby cradled in her arms, begging for help, and it broke him even more. "When I needed you the most, you..." His eyes welled, his breathing now laborious.

"I'm sorry, baby," Monika cried out, but it was too little. Too late.

"You abandoned me," he whimpered in a pitiful croak, his vision blurred in tears.

Tim's bottom lip quivered as he shook the tears away, shoving the pain back inside that pit. Where it belonged. He let the heat of anger swell his mind.

He noticed Dakota holding a hand to his chest. Her mediating attempts transitioned to imitating panting maneuvers. Maneuvers that would help when breathing became difficult. But he wouldn't give his parents the satisfaction of seeing him in a more pitiful state than he already was.

He followed the maneuvers and slowed his breath. Tears dried under his eyes as he cleared his throat, looking at his parents.

"As far as I am concerned, you two should've died when the world did. And I'm not hiding behind a door when I say it. Fuck you both," Tim simply said.

He turned and crutched his way back to the house. As he opened the door without a yank and closed it without a slam, all was quiet. He left in his departure a weeping Monika, being held by a defeated Dereck. He took a deep breath, opened his mouth with his tongue sticking out for an exhale, and repeated, practicing the panting maneuver Laura had taught him.

Leaning against the wall as he tried to regulate his breathing, Tim looked for Phil, scanning the living room and the kitchen. Phil would know what to do; his brother could fix this, but Tim couldn't find him. Then he remembered and fell into bitter weeping.

Monika's face was buried in her hands as Dereck draped an arm around her. There were cracks in his demeanor, cracks through that calloused exterior that allowed some glimpses into the inside. Dakota could see sorrow underneath, no matter how well the man hid it. He didn't cry, but his face was so flushed he might as well have been sobbing convulsively. He refused to let it show as he needed to hold his wife together. Just like Phil, Dakota assumed the man would weep in private.

"Is there anything you can say?" Dereck asked, looking at Dakota.

Tears were still rolling down her face; she could taste their salt through her gaped mouth. Dakota shrugged, shaking her head. She was speechless, looking to her right, where she expected to see Phil standing. She expected him to have the answer, calm and collected, but he wasn't there. There was only that same empty space, and she didn't know what to do. Phil was gone. The world that felt like it had stopped on its axis when she lost him now felt as if it had turned upside down.

She wiped her eyes, wondering what she could do. She knew the story, knew Tim's demons, and judging by his parent's reaction, the story wasn't one-sided. So, she took in a deep breath, her flushed face now calming as she shrugged.

"I think he said all he wanted to," she mumbled. *I'm sorry.*

"This was a mistake," Winston said, opening the back door of the Buick.

"No," Monika sniveled, laying a hand on Dereck's shoulder. "We expected this. We knew. But just seeing him alive made it worth it."

"I'll take you back to your quarters then," Winston said as Dereck nodded a "thank you" and followed his wife into the back seat of the old Buick.

Dakota watched as Tim's parents climbed into the car and the colonel closed the door gently before turning back to her. A heavy sigh escaped through clenched teeth as he walked up to her. She could feel his eyes gauge her, studying the brace on her left arm, the bandaging across her upper chest that was visible through the neck hole of her shirt. He noticed her shy breathing and reddened eyes burning in the salt of her tears.

"He's going to need some time," Dakota uttered, her voice little more than a dried-out croak as she looked over her shoulder back at the house. She wiped her eyes dry with the sleeve around the cuff of her sleeve before looking back to the colonel.

"I know." Winston rested his hands on his hips, looking off to the road. The second he looked away felt like a long, awkward minute before he looked back at her. "The President wants to meet with you two, personally," he said.

"Tonight?"

"No, I talked him out of it. But tomorrow. I'll be back at 1600 hours. Think you'll be ready?"

"Yeah, we'll be ready."

Winston reached his hand up, presumably to her shoulder, but he thought better of it and lowered it. She nodded her thanks, and the colonel just shook his head, breathing in through pursed lips. "The moment I learn anything about Phil's status, or sending more men there, I'll inform you two."

She nodded, expecting as much. "But you are gonna send someone, right?"

"You both verified yourselves. He was motionless at Inimicus's feet." Winston sighed, eyes dropping. "And his remains were carried off with the monster. I don't need to explain to you what occurred next."

"No," she uttered in a bare wisp of breath, hollow and void of life. She wiped the palm of her hand across both eyes, drying them. "I guess not."

"For now, just rest," Winston said, rotating the green beret in his hands, lost in his thoughts, before motioning to take his leave in a single step to the Buick's passenger door.

"Thank you, colonel," she mumbled.

Dakota went back inside after the Buick reached the highway. Closing the door behind her, she was careful not to disturb the silence, save for the panting rhythms of Tim's breathing. The blinds were all closed, blotting out the sunlight, creating the familiar atmosphere of all the decrepit and decaying houses they had searched over the last twelve years in the Wastes—houses that belonged to the Old World.

Her brother was on the floor, broken leg outstretched, busted arm held in a sling. His good arm and leg crumpled up to his face, where he tried to burrow his head. He had made it no more than five feet inside before collapsing. He was sobbing into the sleeve of his good arm, unable to hide his face from the world.

It took considerable effort to lower herself to the floor next to him. Her whole body burned and ached as she sat down against the wall. The blood rushed to her head when getting down, making the laceration on her forehead throb. But she managed the journey down to the floor and reached her hand to Tim's chin, lifting his face to hers.

"We're gonna be okay." Dakota's voice broke as his head fell on her shoulder.

She rested her face on the top of his head, the fabric over her right shoulder wet from his tears. She reached her arm up and around Tim's back, pulling him closer to her in a tight hug, stroking her thumb left and right over his shoulder. It was much like what he had done for her on the Kootenay River.

"I hate 'em," Tim cried, his whole body shaking violently in her tight grip. "I hate 'em, and Phil's not here to tell me not to."

She didn't speak or say anything; her breath came out in a steady, shaky stream. Without knowing what to say, sometimes silence was the best answer.

God. She mouthed without speaking, too shaken to even support Tim. She looked up at the ceiling, crying out. Lost for words, she asked the Holy Spirit within her to finish the prayer on her behalf as tears dropped from her cheeks onto the top of Tim's head.

Chapter Three – Checkup

A loud series of knocks came from the front door in the fashion of musical notes, bearing a youthful rhythm. The rhythm reminded him of "Rock of Ages" by Def Leppard. His eyelids fluttered open, groggy, and crusted in sleep; he didn't remember feeling so tired before. His index finger instinctively thumped to the melody even as the knocks died down, the song playing from memory.

He rolled over to look at the analog clock across the room by his window. Open curtains gave a view of a brewing storm coming in from the northwest. The clock read 1714 hours. He sighed, wishing the day had just breezed by and that his reunion with his parents earlier had been a fluke—a bad day that would just wither and fade away. But he knew better. Both hands clenched into fists, he rubbed the crust off his eyes, then sighed as he tossed his blanket off with his right hand. His left lay useless as his leg, and he grunted and huffed as he came to sit up.

Outside his door, he could hear the squeaking of Dakota's door hinges and then her feet softly falling on the old carpet towards his room and the stairs. The knocking came to a cease-fire only for a few seconds before picking up again. He couldn't recall the climb up the stairs but vaguely remembered Dakota tucking him in before he passed out.

A soft rake of knuckles came outside his door as his sister opened it and poked her head through, a robe draped in one arm. She looked like she had barely slept; her eyes were red and burdened with bags. What made it worse was his inability to get up and comfort her. Deep down, he knew, selfishly, he just didn't have it in him to get up. If not for the repeated, rhythmic "Rock of Ages" knocking, neither of them would have gotten out of bed.

"I'll get it," she said. "You need help getting down?"

"I'm busted up, not helpless," he grunted.

A tired smile pulled at her lips, absent of joy. She stepped in and held out a hand to him anyways. He exhaled through his nostrils, accepting the gesture as she helped him to his feet. When he got his crutches under him, she stepped out and disappeared down the steps to the relentless barrage of knocking. Tim looked at himself, dressed in jogging pants and a simple green tee. Presentable enough.

Tim paused at his door and looked down at the bottle of painkillers for his arm and leg next to his lamp, along with his migraine medicine and a glass of water. All the bottles still had seals around the lids; despite the doctor's insistence that he take them, he left them there sealed and would ignore Dakota's encouragement to follow the doctor's orders. Instead, he downed the water and braved the throbbing pain still coursing through his mind and body. He set the glass down, half-emptied.

The sound of the front door opening, followed by a very lively greeting, contrasted with the silence. The voice was familiar: Olivia Blundell. Two more familiar voices joined in at the door. Second Lieutenant Bracket and Doctor Laura Ellis.

That can't be good, he thought, though he felt a measure of excitement for the company.

It was an odd place to be, but the more he heard that first youthful, lively voice downstairs, the more drawn he felt to the joy in her voice. Her joyful voice seemed to brighten up the whole house despite being muffled and inaudible.

The descent downstairs was slow. When he reached the bottom, standing in the living room were Laura, Bracket, and Olivia. Laura was dressed in her typical doctor's blue scrubs and a white coat. Bracket wore his usual outfit—a dark, solid gray tee, coyote cargo pants, boots, and a pistol at his thigh with extra magazine pouches at his belt. There was nothing out of the ordinary here, and Tim found comfort in the routine and predictability.

It was Olivia who never wore the same outfit more than once a week. Today, she sported cut-up denim pants and a short-sleeved shirt of many colors under a denim vest. Her hair was held in check by a beanie, boots rose over her ankles but tied below them, and a chain dangled from a back pocket to a front. Her wrist was decked out in bracelets up to her elbows.

The diva smiled when Tim crutched down, her grin brightened the room. "Hey, you," she greeted, looking at his arm and leg. "I thought you were supposed to give the beat-downs, not receive 'em."

Tim grunted a fake laugh. "Funny."

"Still uptight as ever there, Sergeant Soldier, Sir?" She gave a quick and firm salute.

It was received but ignored.

Afternoon light shone through the closed blinds behind Olivia and Laura. Bracket remained in the shadows of the door and Tim shook his hand.

"How are you, Sir?" Bracket asked.

"Kicking," Tim replied.

"I hope you don't mind. I was on my way to check in on you two when…" Laura started, then Olivia jumped in.

"I told Captain Shillings I wanted to come by and check up on you," the diva mumbled, rubbing her hands together. She didn't look him in the eye, but her gaze looked to Dakota and then to him. "Either that or I make her job a lot harder. The other day, we found out that I can outrun her."

"Thank you." Dakota offered her hand, her other folded under her armpit to keep her fingers warm.

"Alice, right?" Olivia asked, shaking Dakota's hand, "Tyrese Anal Wart here has told me about you. Nice to put a face to the name now."

"I get why you're here," Tim said, looking to Laura, then back to Olivia and Bracket. "But what are you two doing here?"

"To be frank," Olivia said, "I just wanted to come by and tell you how sorry I am." She mumbled, rubbing her hands together as she looked at the coffee table before looking back up at them.

"Who told you? The colonel or captain?" Tim asked.

"Well, neither. At least not directly. I was eavesdropping on Captain Shillings speaking with the colonel. I was trying to figure out when the hospital would let visitors in, but you were already sent back home. Well, they mentioned Thomas, and I knew… Look, I'm trying to..." She sighed, and the words appeared to have escaped her thoughts.

"Thank you." Dakota smiled at her, but not even a smile could hide the pain that still lingered, and Tim saw it.

Over the last two years, he felt a rift between himself and Olivia. There had always been a point of contention between them. She wanted to mingle with her fans during and after a concert, while he would not allow such things. He wanted to keep her safe; she had been targeted by a group of domestic human traffickers, and for that reason alone he had to prioritize her security. That was his job.

It never seemed to him that she liked him or cared. She certainly never made his job easy, and to be frank about it, he didn't think she noticed the efforts it took to keep her safe over the last two years. But now, maybe he was wrong. Maybe she did understand, and perhaps she appreciated what he was doing. Yet, here she was, on her own accord, and that alone was hard to put into words—just what it meant for him and for Dakota as well.

A moment of silence settled, harbingering the awkwardness to follow. Then Olivia started again, yammering on with small talk about a deer she saw crossing the street on her way to visit. She then jumped straight to how much she hated Bambi and somehow got on the topic of old Godzilla films, to which Tim just laughed.

"What?" Olivia asked as he pinched his forehead with his thumb and middle finger, feeling a migraine start to set in, but he didn't mind this one.

"Nothing." Tim shook his head. "I think I might make something. You hungry?" he asked.

Olivia didn't get a chance to answer as Dakota stayed Tim with her hand. "You're on bed rest, technically. You two chat; I'll put something together." She headed into the kitchen. Tim sighed and took a seat as Olivia sat down next to him. Laura followed Dakota into the kitchen. Out of Tim's periphery, he saw the doctor checking up on Dakota, whose constant movements made the doctor's job difficult.

He sensed Olivia staring at him and saw her picking up a marker from the coffee table, wanting to sign his cast. *Why not.* Tim sighed and offered his casted arm. "Go ahead."

"I know you're older than I am," she said, her eyes focused on the air cast over his arm. "But the pain does pass, after a while. I thought, maybe I could remind you on that."

He raised a brow as she leaned over, and, lifting the pen she smiled at her work, satisfied. She dropped the pen and leaned over, elbows on her knees, rubbing her hands together. Her eyes locked elsewhere in the room, staring at nothing, just avoiding eye contact.

"I barely remember when I was younger." The corner of her mouth flinched her eyes fell to the floor. "I must've been four… five maybe? It was just me and my brother, Aldrin. I called him Al. Our parents died in the explosions…" Olivia's face fell as she rubbed one of her wrists, both decorated with assorted bracelets jingling over her sleeves. Her face grew flushed and her eyes moistened. "He didn't make it, but he made sure I did."

"I'm sorry," Tim said, nodding at her. "Is he why you wear so many bracelets?"

"No." She shook her head; any traces of her smile were gone. She started rubbing her forearms. "Not directly at least." She now looked Tim in the eye. "I'm sorry to hear about your brother."

"I'm sorry, too. Five is too young to grow up." Tim's eyes fell to his arm in its cast.

Bracket stepped forwards, tapping his watch, and Olivia sighed, dropping her head. She looked over to Tim. "I am glad you made it back and… I know I can be a pain, but I am grateful." She offered a fist bump, and Tim smirked, huffing out his nostrils as he returned the gesture. He looked at Bracket, who gave him a two-finger salute. "Be seeing you, First Lieutenant," Bracket said, and he escorted Olivia out the door.

Laura stepped in from the kitchen and sat next to Tim. Her stethoscope was draped around her shoulders, and she set her doctor's bag on the cushion next to her. She looked at him with an expectant flat line of her lips, barely a smile. A "You know what comes next," kind of smile and he did know. When she was done examining his injuries and assessing his health, she asked him if he was taking the prescribed medicine. Tim simply replied "no," and what followed was a bombardment of berating.

He sat straight, his breathing made shallow with the effort. Laura, seeing this, pressed her index finger under his chin, lifting his face to hers.

"Remember," she said, gaping her mouth with her tongue just a little past her bottom lip. She sniffed a series of quick inhales before panting her exhales through her gaped lips.

Tim followed her lead; maybe today he'd be spared from the verbal reproaches that only Dakota and Laura were permitted to give him. He didn't remember the specifics of how this maneuver was supposed to help him, only that it worked. It had something to do with the "straightening of the airway, relaxing the muscles," or something of that nature that he couldn't recall.

The hard breathing wasn't the only issue; perhaps the biggest problem was that on the onset of each episode, he'd forget this panting maneuver. Because every time, *every damn time* that his breathing started to choke up, he saw Inimicus. He felt the fiend's hand around his neck, constricting him as if five snakes were constricting around his neck. He could feel his feet dangling feet over the ground as the fiend held him raised. He would begin to panic, looking for something to grab or kick on—anything to help free him.

Then he would hear Dakota's or Laura's voice, whoever was around him at the time, speaking to him. It sounded like a gentle wind fluttering over the decimated landscape where the fiend had almost killed him. The voice pulled him back to the present with each pant. His vision would clear, and he'd see either his sister or the doctor helping him from both the nightmare and its suffocation.

But the effects of each episode would linger. Like a gas stove's heat turned down, allowing a boiling pot to simmer, he was left a brooding mixture—forced back to the sight of the fiend kicking Phil's limp body. After that, it was Dagger and Slug keeping him and Dakota stable, pumping air into his lugs, until they got back to higher care in Bonner's Ferry.

His eyes watered, hating the last week. Hating that they ever agreed to their last deep recon operation. Leaving as seven and coming back as six. He felt Laura's hand, in the present, offer a comforting hold on his left shoulder, and anchor him steady as the episode rode its course. Coming back to the present, he blinked until his eyes dried. He hated what he came back to: a broken home and would-be parents who thought just because the Old World had ended all slates were magically wiped clean. Worse than that, Dakota bore all that weight on her already tired shoulders.

He saw his sister in the kitchen, standing before the coffee pot, arms folded as she waited for the dripping brew, and his eyes watered again. *I'm sorry.*

He sniffed hard, between pants, blinking away more tears and following Laura's lead. The doctor truly was a good friend, and he thanked God that there were good people to come back home to.

"She's right," Laura mumbled, eyes focused on him as he panted. "I know it's hard, but it'll pass."

"I know," Tim uttered between pants. God, did he know, but that didn't make it any less painful.

Chapter Four – Preparatory Matters

-October 14th, 2030-

Winston wiped his dried, chapped hand over his eyes, pinching the bridge of his nose. He wiped away the crust of sleep that had survived from the morning, before letting his hand fall, hovering over his chest to check his watch. The time was 1559, and Frank was pulling the old Buick into the front drive of SRT-Alpha's house.

By now, most of the other SRT units had already caught up, completing their first objectives after Alpha and Bravo had finished theirs. Besides The Calamity that occurred in Colorado Springs, Seattle, and Portland were found to be epicenters of BR-Hostile activities. *No surprise there.* But what was a surprise was the confirmation that four Spirals had been encountered in the Oregon countryside by SRT-Charlie, Whiskey, Lima, and Mike.

The casualties that amounted to their efforts were stacking up. Of all the 26 SRT units, spanning the whole alphabet, 10 casualties had been sustained and twice that number wounded. The only solace in their preliminary efforts for *Operation Apocatastasis*—the restoration of the United States—was that all the primary objectives had been fulfilled. They now had a detailed report on the condition of the interstates, bridges, and railroads, along with a general idea as to the force numbers of BR-Hostiles in the northwestern corridor.

Most essential were the interstates: I-5, that spanned the Western seaboard from Northern Washington to Southern California; I-90, spanning Seattle into Idaho and Montana; I-84, coming out of Portland and into Idaho all the way to the Utah border; and I-82, connecting the former two—all these interstates were still intact and serviceable. There were a few notable locations along overpasses and rivers where Launch Bridges would be needed. Everything the logistics department needed was provided, and the pieces were falling into place for the next phase, *Vine and Branch.*

In the wake of the SRTs fulfilling their duties, there were holes in just about every team. Alpha was that one hole to hit him the hardest. The SRTs had been formed and put together for such a massive undertaking, and there was more to go: the Northern states, the Midwest, and Southern states, until eventually the East Coast. Those holes would need filling soon, but he didn't think he could replace that space Phil left.

Being the director of such an ensemble of events meant he hardly slept. But Winston found some comfort in that as well, knowing many of his soldiers hardly slept either. If the hands and feet didn't get enough rest, then why should the brain?

He looked down at his watch again, pleased when he saw they were arriving on time as he had expected. *1600 hours, on the dot.*

Not a minute later nor sooner. Frank pulled them up to the driveway and put the Buick in park, and the driver then leaned his head against the headrest and rubbed his eyes. Winston leaned forwards and patted the old man's shoulder.

"Are you going to be able to make it?" he asked.

"Yeah, just out of coffee and on fumes now. I'll be fine, catch a cat nap while you round up those two," Frank replied, with an assuring look behind worn eyes and a tired voice. He was up there in age, like Winston, pushing seventy. They were both old enough to remember when Vietnam was all over the news.

"I won't be long," Winston assured him, then opened his door and stepped out, closing it behind him.

He walked around the car and to the front porch steps, looking at the chairs and table. For a moment, he remembered all the times he had been greeted by Phil, who had sat in the same chair every morning, staring out at the trees beyond.

He and Phil, two US Special Forces operatives, had first-hand experiences from the First Cold War. There was a kinship he found in Phil more than anyone else. The Special Forces—Green Berets to others—were few and far between. Since the 2017 Calamity, he had met only one other survivor who shared the same heritage. Perhaps that was why he felt so stricken over Phil's "MIA" status, though, in all honesty, from the reports, he believed Phil was KIA.

Maybe it was the feeling of being the last one of his kind, the aloneness, that felt both heavy and thick in the air. It was alleviated when he had first met Phil and now as freshly potent as before. He didn't show it; he wouldn't allow it through the cracks of his exterior.

He looked from the empty seats, hearing shouting from inside the house. It wasn't a full-fledged hollering and screaming match, but

Their CO stepped in as Tim crutched back towards the couch. "Is it time already, colonel?" he asked.

"It is," Winston replied, catching both his and Dakota's look. "We need to be in Juneau by 1700 and in the President's Office by 1730."

A frown crossed over Dakota, her back to the colonel, as she looked at Tim. Tim shrugged as they headed to the steps. They'd have to wear a more formal uniform, and the Alyeskan Army Service Uniform required woman to dress in a skirt, which Dakota didn't like.

A few hours and several checkpoints later, complete with pat downs, Tim and Dakota stood side by side in their Army Service Uniforms before President Solyom. It was their second time meeting the man, who sensed their formal welcome into the state. Solyom sat behind his large red oak desk. The contents there displayed a chaotic mess of hours of work, along with a contradiction of professionalism that came with Solyom knowing every piece of paperwork's location.

Time appeared to be both lacking and a commodity; organization just wasn't in the cards. The windows flanking the big bookshelf behind Solyom didn't shine with bright rays of sun, but instead offered a view of the gloomy overcast sky rolling down over distant mountains. The four rows of filing cabinets to the right were left half-open. The couch off to the side of the room held tossed covers and pillows, and the coffee pot behind the President's desk was freshly brewed, the smell permeating the air and masking the unkempt smell of a man who lived to work.

Despite it all, Solyom still maintained a calm and professional demeanor, waving a hand for Tim and Dakota to sit down. But Tim elected to remain standing. It was hard to get back up with a broken arm and leg, and standing helped keep his mind straight. The physical stress of simply standing was more of a focal point, keeping him in check behind his display of professionality. Dakota remained standing as well: all for one and one for all.

It was then that President Solyom elected to stand himself, meeting them where they were. This was a gesture that Tim felt some measure of appreciation for as Winston stood to the President's left, their right, and Colonel Stacey opposite. Solyom stepped around his desk and gave both of them a firm shake. Then he leaned back, sitting against the edge of the red oak; the two colonels stepped forwards to his flanks.

The President's cordial demeanor shifted, and his shoulders slumped slightly as he folded his hands across his lap.

"It was my decision that has rendered you two in your current condition." Solyom's smirk had inverted, the corners of his lips turning downwards as the folds at the sides of his mouth receded.

Tim couldn't tell if the admission was genuine or not; there was a hiatus in eye contact, and the President's eyes shook as they dropped for only a millisecond before returning to his and Dakota's. A faint smirk followed, one of remorse. Tim felt himself breathe in deep for the next order of business. *Formal condolences.*

"I am sorry about your comrade."

"Thank you, Sir," Tim said.

"We appreciate it, Mr. President," Dakota replied, voice stoic by force.

"I won't waste your time, and I assume you'd like me to… cut to the chase, yes?" asked Solyom with a wave of a hand. "That is why I've asked Colonel Winston to bring you two here today," he said, turning at his waist and reaching back over his desk to retrieve two envelopes.

"You see, your mission was a success. Colorado Springs is to be our furthest reach in the near future, except now it's just a stretch of scorched earth, given recent events. Considering such, and your history with the two BR-Weapons, I thought it best to inform you we have confirmed that Inimicus and the Jackle are still alive and at large."

The President paused, assessing and gauging.

Tim felt a twist in his stomach. His eyes watered, his insides feeling as if they were being scraped out with a shovel. If anyone could have survived Inimicus, it would've been Phil, and now reports of the fiend's survival nearly sent him falling to the chair. Hope had become a withering candle flame, now snuffed, and gone. He felt Dakota's hand on his back, supporting him.

He looked at Dakota, and she shook her head with a frown, still forcing a stoic response, now cracking with a twitch of an eye and the corner of her lip. "We're not surprised, Sir." There was a scratchiness to her voice. She raised her left arm, the brace covering more of the left side of her face for a scratch. But Tim saw the sleight-of-hand maneuver with her index finger, the wiping of a tear.

"How do you know they survived?" Tim asked.

"After you were Medevacked, a recovery team was sent in. Finding both monsters unaccounted for. Followed by a Search and Recovery Team to look for Sergeant Nilges. That team has now gone MIA."

"Thank you for telling us in person, Mr. President," Tim breathed out, "But I'm sure you have more pressing matters to contend with?"

"In fact, I do, which is the reason I've summoned you both," Solyom said, raising the two envelopes to them.

Tim's brows raised, and he accepted the envelope at the same time Dakota did. Both looked down at the sealed paper casing with faint curiosity.

"As promised. Retirement of Active duty from the Alyeskan Army." Colonel Winston spoke up this time.

"Sorry?" Dakota asked, leaning her head in.

Tim's heart ached as he turned his head to look at her, tugged at her arm, and leaned closer to her. "Retirement," he said, and it felt like he had just delivered her a gut punch.

The world was a hungry place; it wasn't the zombies taking pieces of them little by little—but the constant and spaced-out encounters with Inimicus, or the Jackle. The need to survive the behemoths slowly chipping away at their beings. Remembering the Garden of the Gods and the repetitive bang of the flash grenades. Dakota's last interaction with the Jackle had taken some of her hearing with it. Just another piece of themselves, a keepsake, taken by the behemoths.

Dakota, despite being right next to Tim, suddenly felt four feet away. That space where Phil should have been, that vacant ground where he too should be accepting that which they had strived for twelve years to achieve—that was another piece of their soul taken away as a keepsake as well.

They were getting up there in age; Phil was already up there, and their fight with monsters was now to be over with. Done. The military and Alyeska's first native generation would keep up the fight. But for Tim and Dakota, their ordeals with the macabre and malevolent forces of the Wastelands would finally be over. The dawn of their bright future was now reduced to a dim dusk before the night. In the end, two out of three was just a fraction and not a whole number.

A moment of silence fell as Tim felt the emotions pass. Dakota maintained a stoic front. People like Solyom wouldn't be able to see the conflict underneath, but Tim saw it clearly, and he felt it just as heavy. Neither of them spoke, just passed a cursory look over the sealed paperwork stamped with the Alyeskan Army Seal and looked back to the president and the colonels.

"One caveat," Solyom said, looking at them and raising a finger. "You are correct that I do have pressing matters—such as what we're about to discuss." He looked over at Colonel Stacey, who stepped forwards. He held up a pen and two pages titled 'Confidentiality Agreement.'

"Your activities in Bellingham, while executed brilliantly, were an unintentional crossing of jurisdiction into matters of national secrecy."

"You're referring to those younger draugrs we encountered?" Tim asked. The sound of the sirens of Bellingham flooding the whole city in unyielding cycles of rising and lowering pitch suddenly haunted his thoughts. The terror was still freshly etched, the younger zombies ripping apart and feasting on the older ones.

Tim's head started to hurt, the growing pains of his migraine irritated him, and anger burned in his belly. The frustration came out in flinches and twitches that he tried to clench down and repress through slow breaths. But he couldn't. The signs were picked up easily by Winston although Solyom and Stacey seemed oblivious.

"Even in the first days of the fallout and the dead rising, was it common to see fresh zombies munch on one another?" Stacey asked. Then, she shook her head. "No, they never did. These are not draugrs, or satyrs, and certainly not wraiths. They're a new breed we've engineered ourselves and have come to call Revenants."

"To eat older BR-Hostiles… How is dat even," Dakota stammered, shaking her head.

"Our understanding of UF-Radiation has drastically expanded over the last twelve years." Solyom replied. "Advances have been made such as radiation treatment in the medical field."

"And Biological-Radioactive-Weapons." Tim nodded, restraining a snicker that came out in a huff. "It worked out so well for the US," he almost added but bit his tongue.

Winston's lips parted to respond but were intercepted by Colonel Stacey, who pointed at the paper in Tim's hand. "The purpose of these weapons is to eradicate pre-existing BR-Hostiles and weapons. The forms below are just a formality that the two of you will keep what you experienced that day in Bellingham secret."

Tim looked from the paper to Dakota; there was the proverbial "And if we don't?" right behind his mouth, wanting to part his lips. But the answer was rhetorical, they both knew. *Then though shalt be deemed traitors to the Republic, imprisoned, and executed by firing squad*, he thought. *Or something along those lines.*

It felt like he had been given two vials of poison. One vial contained retirement papers for a future that the three of them had, struggled, bled, cried, and fought for—and only now received in the absence of one. The other vial was filled with the poison of secrecy and contempt in the pursuit of mad ambitions. Making monsters fight monsters. But the latter was a story they had seen, read, and experienced before. Tim thought it was hubris and would ultimately end in disaster.

Dakota's eyes were heavy with thoughts much like his own; there was fatigue in them. A yearning to be done fighting. *What can we do?* her face asked, and he supposed there was nothing that could be done.

Winston still stood behind the President, though a bit more in front of Stacey. His placement felt like guidance through indecision. He had once asked them to trust him, and now they were without Phil, but there he still stood as if to ask them, "Trust me just once more."

Tim sighed, and it was Dakota who took the initiative, accepting the pen. Tim ceded and took the other paper. He signed his when Dakota passed him the pen. Colonel Stacey accepted both agreements, and Solyom handed forth the two envelopes.

"We're gonna need some time on these," Tim said, taking the two envelopes.

"Of course." Solyom nodded, "But in a few days, I've asked Colonel Winston to rope you both into your retirement duties. Of course, you'll be on light duty until you make a full recovery."

"Just point it out, and we'll see that the work gets done, Sir."

Tim and Dakota were excused to the main lobby; there were other, more "confidential," matters to discuss. Both colonels sat before the President's desk, and Solyom had a dossier thick enough to be a novella in his hands. It was a coalition of reports from SRT-Alpha and Bravo, mission reports from the first Siberian recovery team, reports of Inimicus and Jackle's survival, a report of the sighting of an unidentified person, and the last report detailing Colonel Stacey's deployment of Wolf Pack—who as of 24 hours after their last communication went "Black on Comms and MIA."

"What elements do have present in the region now?" Solyom finally broke the silence, looking first to Stacey, dropping the thick dossier flat over some papers. Other loose papers fluttered but were held in place by paperweights.

"None, after Wolf Pack went MIA. I've arranged Special Purpose Center Alpha Group for Search and Rescue. But I've yet to give them clearance for deployment."

"Good." Solyom nodded, but there was a stern flatness to his tone. It was not one of satisfaction, but the same tone expected when a parent was ready to berate their children. It was the same flatness found in a boss separating two feuding coworkers.

"Colonel Winston?" the President asked, now looking at him.

Winston shrugged, waving his hands, before lacing his fingers together on his lap. "I have no assets present in the region for the time being," he said, "but I do have plans prepared for Search and Rescue via SRT-Juliet, along with myself."

"This, right here," Solyom waved his finger at them in a circular fashion, "is why this mess is the way it is. No communication, no sharing of intel, no joint-operational comradery between the two of you. Charles, friend," He shook his head, "Your S&R is denied. Colonel Stacey will handle all future operation in Colorado."

Colonel Winston remained silent, sensing the same from his counterpart to his left.

"Furthermore," Solyom's voice deepened, taking in a deep breath as he shook his head. "Any clandestine or covert operations that have been scheduled and executed must be communicated and properly understood by me and your counterpart. Such as investigating a city being used for BR-Weapon testing, when I've handed over jurisdiction of said city to Miss Stacey." Solyom now looked at Winston.

"Yes, Sir." Winston bowed his head, "I merely wanted AILA to be fully aware of the situation. It was an error in judgment on my part."

"Our Logistics and Intelligence Agency is meant to keep the status quo of the Mainland Republic, Judiciary, and National Council. It has no bearing on our Siberian territories and other counterparts. I'll make sure Colonel Stacey sends you a list of these black sites, but they are to remain off-limits to you, AILA, and your SRT units. Understand?"

"Understood." Winston agreed.

Solyom then looked to Colonel Stacey, a bit more gravel in his tone as his eyes stabbed at her. "Furthermore, all intel that may be essential is to be shared if it is in relation to or influences present and future operations. Especially when I gave you direct orders to share said intel that would've prevented our losses here." He held up a list of names belonging to soldiers now MIA: Sergeant Nilges, AKA Philip Shurlan, being at top followed by the ten men of Wolf Pack and two pilots. "This is on you, Colonel Stacey, regardless of Colonel Winston overstepping his boundaries. You cost us these men."

"I was wrong, Sir." Stacey's face fell in a slow nod.

"The two of you are to be allies, partners. Not bickering children. There's a reason I delegated the two of you with the highest authority over our generals and the secretary of defense." Solyom gave the list of names a jerking wave. "Men like these are hard to come by these days, not to mention the two who just left this room, now crippled beyond serviceable use. I will not tolerate any meddling or negligence. Too much is at stake here!"

"Understood," both colonels replied, for the first time in unison with one another.

"Okay," Solyom said. That alone seemed to offer some satisfaction, but there was more bothering the man. More irons in the fire needed hashing out, and Winston shook his head in anticipation. The fact that the GFOAB's main objective was a failure prompted the President's frown to remain, and it was news that troubled them all.

Then there was the financial and resource consumption loss that went into making a bomb that ended in utter failure. Not just the one, but the many prototypes and tests conducted, the efforts and fuel spent to get the missile into space, and the manpower required to attach it to the satellite's weapon attachment. Such resource use was not acceptable unless it yielded great rewards or prevented greater consequences. Now they had only two missiles left, with no more scheduled to be produced anytime soon.

"Colorado will be our back door once our forces move into the Northwestern States. We can't have these two things still active when we get there."

"What do you propose then, Sir?" asked Colonel Stacey.

"In a minute," Solyom sighed, giving a slight shake of his head while biting down on a thumbnail.

A quick inhale followed, and the President snapped his attention back to the present discussion. Winston watched in interest as an apparent line of verbal communication passed between the president and Colonel Stacey—some kind of subtextual message that he knew nothing about and that he didn't like. Nothing short of complete informed awareness was his standard with the Alyeskan Intelligence and Logistic Agency. Winston held down his displeasure and waited for the President to continue.

"The Zombie Crisis out East in Canada takes immediate priority on my end," Solyom mumbled. "For now, I want you two to remain on course. Winston with the SRT finishing on paving the way into the Northwestern States. Stacey with your duties maintaining the aforementioned black sites and remaining liaison with our Siberian neighbors." He concluded, pointing his finger down at the report.

"With everything working on schedule, Mr. President, Phase Vine and Branch will be ready on your command. Should I give General Patton the go-ahead to establish supply caches for our expeditionary forces?"

Solyom's face sparked with pleasure, an excitement held on a tight leash behind his eyes as he leaned back into his chair. "Yes. That would be great. Colonel Winston, you may be excused now, but keep me updated on Phase Vine and Branch."

Winston nodded and pushed up on the armrests to take his leave.

"Colonel Stacey, I do have more business to discuss with you."

"Yes, Mr. President." Winston nodded.

Winston left the room, closing the door behind him as Stacey remained seated. Walking with the stealth of a mouse, his dress shoes fell over the red rug-lined wooden floor in silence. Passing by stands with vases upon them at every panel of the wall, the paintings from the Old World and of Juneau's early days back in the late nineteenth century—there was a rich history of the natives, Russian influence, and the subsequent American influence.

Winston pulled out a square plastic capsule, where inside two blue-tooth ear devices were neatly stored. He took one and placed it into his ear, giving the impression that he was taking a pill to the camera monitoring the hall. He set the capsule back in his pocket and removed a cellular device, unlocking the screen and connecting his device. Together they had just one purpose to it: providing audio feed on a bugged device within twenty yards.

Winston avoided facial contact with the security cameras; opening an app on his device brought to his screen a list of bugs he kept. None were labeled with names that anyone could make inferences about, just numbers that he memorized, the top two being his most used ones. 1, or *President Solyom's office*, and 2, or *Colonel Stacey's Office.*

He tapped on 1 and listened in on President Solyom and Colonel Stacey's discussion as he took slow strides down the hall.

"The Revenant prototypes in Bellingham have proved to be a success so far, correct?" came Solyom's voice.

"Yes, Sir," came Stacey's. "My men are working on rounding up and storing the remaining Revenants in Bellingham for transport to the Sahtu Region, per your request. The first batch of assets has been loaded and shipped already. Captain Brecken is waiting with his ship at the docks for the second and final shipment; he was adamant about a manifest, though. And is still pressing for one."

"More and more of the undead are flooding into Eastern Canada as we speak. We need those Revenants there, and any hesitation from the captain or his crew will just delay the colonies' rescue."

Winston pictured Solyom shaking his head.

"He's better off not knowing what we're shipping on his vessel."

Winston reached the steps, and the audio feed started to cut out. He stopped, eyeing another camera monitoring the stairs. Per his design, the Capitol Building didn't have one nook or cranny that wasn't under constant observation. He stopped, holding his hand on his chest. In his old age, it wouldn't be uncommon for him to appear to have shortness of breath. Or need a break, especially if he knew how to play it out.

"Contact Major General Petrov and have him speed up Project Dreadnought and Project Hydra."

"Consider it done, Mr. President. However, I spoke with Major General Petrov, and he said they've hit a stump on Project Hydra and are—"

Solyom cut her off.

"Our Siberian forces are en route to reinforce the Canadian Confederacy, but it's only a temporary measure. Whatever Major General Petrov needs to do, tell him to do it."

"Yes, Sir."

Winston couldn't wait any longer, and he descended the steps. Taking out the earpiece, he feigned the actions of picking ear wax out from his ears. He held the little pill-shaped device in his hand as he reached the bottom steps and stowed it in his pocket. There at the bottom, he met Tim and Dakota, sitting in the lounge. His two golden soldiers stood up to meet him, Tim hitching a thumb over his shoulder.

"You are aware that homeboy over there thinks he's blending in but is really a sore thumb, right?" Tim asked. The tone of his voice, sounding like a passing thought, came more from a place of melancholy than concern.

Winston looked over Tim at the man he was pointing at. Over by a secretary's desk sat a man, one of Colonel Stacey's undercover security detail. As Winston had seen over the many years, and, like Tim and Dakota, the detail stood out; they were the only people in the main lobby dressed in solid gray tops, tucked into coyote cargo pants that were bloused to their boots. He donned an overshirt, presumably to hide his side arm in a shoulder holster.

Winston let loose a half-assed laugh, shaking his head and motioning to the door. “That’s not my department, I’m afraid.”

Chapter Five – Rough Waters

Captain Brecken and his crew of forty-five men had long since departed Bellingham, their "heading" being northwest, to the recovered and restored city of Prince Rupert. The town had once been a transportation hub and place of industry, among many other things. It was the pre-existing port and railroads that traveled through the city that marked it as a major settlement of British Columbia, Alyeska. Now Prince Rupert stood, resurrected, as an Alyeskan Naval Base.

All of that was fine and dandy; Captain Brecken had been stationed in Prince Rupert since the city's annexation nearly two years prior. What the captain didn't think was fine, and dandy was the sudden, out of the blue orders to make port in Bellingham, Washington—a city no one knew was under Alyeskan Domain. That revelation could have been ignored as a failure of the ship's crew to keep up on news, but any chance of that was drained by the lack of the cargo manifest they had been sent to pick up.

Colonel Stacey had answered his "insistent requests" for a manifest before departing Bellingham with a simple: "The contents of your cargo are on a need-to-know basis."

A simple "No" would've sufficed, Brecken mused as he rubbed his nose, thinking about how Colonel Stacey's "No" was emphasized by coming straight from President Ivanov himself.

Then there were the interactions of working with a city unmanned by American-Canadian military personnel, but rather by Siberian personnel. These forces had no jurisdiction here on the North American side of the state. 300-some shipping containers, pre-measured and calculated to not exceed the ANS Odysseus' limitations later, and they were off.

It wasn't just Captain Brecken who felt edgy. Silence filled the space between orders and the standard formality of addressing one another—a space usually occupied by the ball-busting antics and casual chatter of his men.

Brecken knew that it wasn't just the strange encounter with Bellingham that had everyone's nerves tightened. No, there was more. They were close, too close for comfort, to the longitude—right smack dab, in fact—on the Alyeskan Naval Submarine Net. It was a net whose sole design was to monitor the southern edge of Alyeskan-controlled waters and to keep the Northern Pacific clear of all Biological-Radioactive-Sea-Hostiles.

Orders directly from the President himself couldn't be neglected. They stemmed straight down the chain of command to the Admiral and to him. In the end, Brecken couldn't say "no, Sir." That would be tantamount to treason.

The row of square windows across the front of the bridge gave a view of the storm outside. Clouds darkened the sky, and the waters swayed in enlarging waves that the ship plowed. Rain fell in intervals of heavy sheets and light mist. Down below on the ship's deck, he saw the shipping containers, chained, and anchored in place. None were moving, and not one was lost in the roughing storm. He didn't think the situation was ideal for the container ship to sail in, even if all the cargo was held in place. He felt more and more like treason was the best choice with the ever-increasing fury and strength of the ocean's might bearing against them.

His men were seasoned and well-trained sailors; most hailed from the US Navy. So, he was allotted some comfort in their competence—that is, until the signal bridge's commanding officer's words came in sync with Communication Officer Ross's in a duet of ill-met news. Captain Brecken looked first to the CO of the Signal Bridge, holding a patient index finger to the comms officer.

"Captain. We can't find the coast; the storm is blocking us from any visual," he said, in response to Brecken's previous orders for frequent updates. Their compass and satellite trajectory had been compromised earlier, and they were forced to resort to visual navigation. The navigation officer and his subordinates had been working tirelessly to pinpoint a heading for land.

"What side was the last visual of land seen?" Brecken asked.

"Starboard, Captain."

"Then operate with that for the time being," Brecken ordered. The officer nodded and returned to his post.

"Any updates from Juneau?" Brecken looked to his comms officer.

Communication Officer Ross held a speaker of a headphone over one ear; his eyes were saucers, staring back at him. "No, Sir. The last weather update we got was of Typhoon Samson's trajectory shifting eastbound, Captain. But now, I don't know where we are with respect to the storm."

"My God," Brecken mumbled, covering his mouth with his hand, his other resting on his hip. He looked due west out the row of windows; the storm made more sense, and he felt in his gut he knew where they were in line with Samson.

It offered some theories as to why their satellite assets were down, but not the compass. The captain then found himself praying to a God he wasn't sure was listening. Lost adrift at sea with no clear heading, and no visual of the coastline they had been traveling parallel to, he didn't want to travel too far eastwards, less he risk running the ship aground in the shallow waters near the coast.

The waves were escalating far past the point of concern, and with each rise and fall, the container ship plummeted downwards, almost nose first, into the ocean's surface. It created the illusion of falling straight down from the sky, towards the unknown watery depths. The view wasn't so uncommon. But somewhere in the deep recesses of the captain's subconscious was fear, suppressed by years of experience and conditioning. Being so near the edge of Alyeskan charted waters only added to the fear rising out of the depths of his subconscious.

Sea monsters of epic proportions existed: their numbers and diversity were unknown, with only a few sightings and sonar detections to prove their existence and fuel people's imaginations about the mythic beasts. For the most part, such beings stayed south of the submarine net, a red dotted line at 115 degrees longitude between North America and Asia.

The captain suddenly had a sickening feeling while standing next to Executive Officer Montgomery, who manned the helm. Older than most of the men on deck, but still younger than Brecken, Montgomery steered the helm while idly murmuring self-made hymns to old Lovecraftian works.

"We live on a placid island of ignorance…" Montgomery's words added to nauseating feelings that subtracted from Brecken's stillness.

"Enough of that." Brecken snapped his fingers, a loud and sharp snap that could cut the tension in the air like butter. "We don't need to be hearing that right now." He bit on his cheeks, trying to suppress the dread the Executive Officer's songs elicited; the man had an odd attraction to the macabre. An attraction that Brecken couldn't appreciate.

Maintaining his composure for the sake of his crew was the best he could do as their captain. He was a focal point for his men, a source of calm in the storm despite the growing fear and throbbing dumps of adrenaline his heart was sending out. He was a stress ball secured inside a shell of rock.

Lightning struck, and the thunder rattled the glass as the darkening clouds of the storm pushed aside the overcast sky, lit by the bright sun behind it. Brecken looked over at Ross, still trying to contact Juneau. But his Communications Officer just shook his head in response.

"Keep trying, son," Captain Brecken ordered departing from Ross's gaze back to the helm.

Lightning flickered outside. The panels of glass rattled from the thunder. The nose of the ship dipped once more into the sea, spewing forth a flood over the deck. He looked out over the waves. This time, the signal bridge outside was flooded, and several of his sailors were nearly dragged over the safety rail and into the waters. A quick order later, and all were ushered into the bridge as all doors were sealed.

Then a voice he didn't want to hear shouted: it was Sonar Technician Brown, seated near the helm. "Uh, Captain!" Brown's voice trembled. "Sonar has picked something up."

Brecken walked around the bridge and down a short set of three steps to the lower bridge and Sonar Technician Brown. He patted the young man's trembling shoulders. The shaking, without a doubt, was aided by Montgomery's resumed singing of macabre themes.

"Lemme see," Brecken said as Brown moved, giving him a full view of the sonar screen.

Brecken felt that stony shell he kept on for his men start to crack. Even the hardiest man he ever knew, his father, trembled at the sight of the dead rising 12 years ago. He looked down at the sonar screen and couldn't believe what he was seeing: a large figure bearing towards their location.

"What category?" he asked, holding his tone steady and calm.

Brown fumbled with a measuring tool on the radar and did some quick mental math in his head as he looked at a handbook mounted on a stand next to the sonar. He came to a single page with very limited intel on Biological-Radioactive-Sea-Hostiles. Brecken didn't know the specifics, that was what Brown was for, but he knew the results. Sea monsters were categorized just like storms were. Category One was the least and lowest threat but still warranted enough caution to steer clear.

"Four, sir." Brown's voice trembled in hollow terror.

Brecken stood away from the sonar screen and saw Comms Officer Ross looking over at him, waiting for orders. "Relay SOS to Juneau. I don't care if we can't receive word back, but maybe we can send word. Inform them the submarine net has been breached somewhere northwest of Bellingham. We have incoming BRS-Hostile Category Four converging on our location. And keep relaying that message 'til I say otherwise."

"Yessir," came a shout from Ross.

Brecken climbed back up to the helm. The ever-darkening horizon, with its spiking and rolling torrential sea waves, had all but blotted out the bright, cloudy morning they had started with. Typhoon Samson was somewhere in that dark rising chaos, and he found it understandable that older civilizations would personify such things as sea deities. Poseidon didn't like Odysseus after all.

Montgomery's singing only added to the repressed hysteria tipping Brecken's resolve into trepidation. The storm appeared omnipotent, with a malevolent disposition to terrestrial creatures. The absence of a horizon, spelled with the jagged waves of coiling liquid teeth, surrounded them in the endless abyss like a watery mouth ready to consume them.

"The Dreamer wakes," Montgomery mumbled to Brecken.

"You're an odd duck. Have I ever told you that?" Brecken looked over to the man.

Montgomery replied with a slight huff of a laugh to the old joke that was long worn-out, like a broken record. "Every day, Captain. Orders, Sir?"

"Gimme the helm," Brecken said as Montgomery released the wheel to him.

In absence of assurance and outside aide, he made the best call he could. Freezing up would spell only doom for his men. A decision had to be made, and they would course correct along the way as he steered the ship towards the storm. It was a gamble, and if it should end in their demise, then Brecken believed the responsibility should fall upon their captain. Let the cargo be damned as long as his men had a chance to survive.

Brecken then had to holler at his navigation crew to shut up. Fortune favored the bold, and without a naval escort, they couldn't face a category four threat. Hell, a category one would've been bad enough. But perhaps the chaos above water would repel the threats below. Ross spoke into the ship's intercom system, ordering all crew to "batten the hatches, prepare for potential exterior damage" and for the boatswains to get inside. All bulkheads were to be sealed, and anyone of faith was asked to pray.

Brecken's outer shell continued to crack, and Montgomery's singing picked up a few minutes later. Fear spiked up in him as he had seen it do in his father over a decade ago. But he hardened himself, hardened his heart, tethering all those emotions to his shaking, trembling core. He clenched his teeth as if the action itself held the fragments of his breaking outer shell together. Glaring out at the darkness before his beloved ship and crew, Brecken found himself praying to a God he hoped was real and who was listening.

Colonel Stacey was in her office, the phone at her ear dialing as she looked at her computer screen. The screen was black with the green words of the clone bug copying a report being emailed to Colonel Winston. She frowned, though, as she read the green wording on her screen:

Sergeant Merlow [Morse] head of security duty in Operation Lure and Hair; authorized by Colonel Winston. Olivia Blundell primary objective... Sergeant Sousa [Jones] on escort duty to improve diplomatic relations with Canada; authorized by Colonel Winston. Bobby Wheeler primary objective.

The line picked up on the other side. “Major General Petrov here, vat do you need, Colonel Stacey?” Major General Petrov asked.

“Yes, Major General. President Solyom has given you clearance to execute any needs essential to completing Project Hydra. Emphasizing ‘in all haste.’" She heard the Major General clear his throat over the line.

“Understood, I’ll contact Mr. Maximus…”

“I’m better off not knowing the details, Major General. Just see that it gets done, and soon.”

“Understood, colonel.”

As soon as Major General Petrov got off the phone with Colonel Stacey, he dialed a number. It wasn’t saved to his phone, and any call history to said number was immediately wiped off the record after communications were made. It went without saying that he rarely made calls, for all the trouble they could be. But if Project Hydra was to continue with its progress, then the possible trouble was worth the cost.

There were over ten million people in Alyeska—a sizable enough gene pool for some of them to have what was needed for Project Hydra. There had to be at least more than a few needles in that giant haystack.

A *click* sounded over the line, the one that signaled a call answered, not going to voice mail. The ever-polite Mr. McArthur answered his call: “Ah, my friend. What may I do for you at this late hour?”

“Ve are running on clock now ‘friend’.” Petrov replied. On his desk was a picture of a civilian inside mainland Alyeska. Blundell, Olivia was her name, and out of all those plausible needles that existed, so far she was the only one they had found who had what he needed. The only issue had been McArthur’s people’s failures to capture her. “Ve need the target. Do whatever you have to do.”

"We've spoken about this," said McArthur. "Her protector has made acquiring her more challenging over these last few years. I'm not prone to just throwing my men like bones to a dog. Any of them get captured, then they get traced back to me. Then they'll trace me to you. We're both at risk."

"I'm not vorried about the risks," Petrov remarked. "Get the girl, and I'll give you fifty more names of people who you don't want in mainland of State."

There came a pause, before McArthur replied, "I'll be in touch."

Chapter Six – Pestilence

Autumn saw nothing upon waking, but she could feel the bare skin of her back resting on a soft, sagging surface. It let out a crackling sound with every small movement. Rows and columns of stiff spots poked up at her small form, like springs from a sagging mattress. Tingles of pain throbbed over her right eye and forehead. She lifted her hand and felt around her sore eye, jolting her fingers back from the tender spot and wincing as she did.

She smelled must, dust, and the stale odors of rotting textiles and molding wood. She could taste putrid bile and snot in the back of her sore throat. Her throat seemed to inflate in swelling protest as she tried to swallow her spit.

She tuned in to her hearing last, and she was convinced she had fallen into a nightmare. That had to be the explanation for why everything hurt and ached, the sick feeling she had, and the absence of light. But she couldn't recall ever having a dream where the roaring wails of agony were so crisp and clear—lucid, even—set in proper tune with the grinding sound of metal teeth sawing through wood. Only, it didn't sound like wood. The wailing cries—harmonizing horrifically with that ungodly sawing—told her what was being sawed.

Maybe it's an amputation to stop gangrene or something, she tried to reason, tried to hope. But the wails didn't just sound like pain. They sounded like terror.

No, this wasn't a nightmare. This dream was reality. She sat up, fast at first—too fast, as her head spun. She sat there, dazed, completely disoriented. Her brain felt like it was beating against the insides of her skull. She felt hot and cold, and in the darkness she couldn't tell if her eyes were open or not. A sudden fear gripped her. Had her eyes been gouged out? Had she been given painkillers to not feel the pain?

Weak, shaky fingers reached up to her face, rubbing the skin of her cheeks up to her eyes, expecting to feel the empty sockets. Her eyes started to tear and burn at the gentle probe of her fingertips.

Then she noticed it, from her right periphery, a faint glimmer from behind what she guessed was a curtain over a window. It was a contrast between the dark inside and the nocturnal darkness outside.

She leaned over the bed and pulled back at the fabrics, old and stiff with a musty smell released upon their movement. Rusted metal loops grinded in squeals of protest over a rusted rod above the window frame. That contrast between inner and outer sharpened into a beautiful view. The moonlight washed over the wall of the Rocky Mountains, splashing silver light over a pine forest that stretched as far as the mountainous wall would let her see. The inside was now illuminated, the contrast blurred in a silver ingot of light that made a smoother transition between dark and darker. She could now make out a bed, dresser, nightstand, and other furnishings in silhouette forms, shadowy polygonal figures in the dark.

The wailing cries and sawing noises were now replaced with guttural "umphs." From the outside darkness came high-pitched cries of coyotes, godawful shrieks that rose to a spine-tingling high and fell in a *yip* with each "umph" of the poor soul being tortured, as if in sequence. As if nature itself was slowly consuming the dying man in a tortuous ritual with coyote spectators. Those "umphs" slowly receded and died with the striking of what she imagined to be a hammer upon flesh. The rising cries crescendoed before falling into a *yip* in tune with each "umph," continuing without end.

Beads of sweat coated Autumn's face. Her whole body was heating up to a sweat, and tears dampened her eyes. Cold seeped through the cracks of the wall and window frame, stabbing at her sweat-soaked arms. The invasive chill brought a heaving fit upon her as she pulled back and covered herself under the blankets, back in the warmth of the bed. The crinkling sound from underneath her permeated the room, and she felt the bare skin of her legs, back, and sides slide across the surface. She realized then that she had no clothes on; it felt like she was lying over a tarp, completely wet from her sweat, the spot she had lain now suddenly made cold by that invasive chill.

Her mind, already a pulsating mess, suddenly flared in fear as she clenched her thighs together, squeezing her eyes shut, and panicked through the tears streaking down her cheeks. She feared the implications of all this. Had she been raped? Had that psycho done more to her than that? She didn't feel as if she had been violated, but then again, she didn't know what it would feel like either.

She wanted nothing more at that moment than her uncle—wanted the safety and warmth of his embrace to comfort her as he always did, like when she'd fall ill or wake up in the middle of the night scared. Over her entire 15 years of living, Richard was always there in such moments. Her place of refuge and unwavering love, he was more than her uncle. He was her father. Only now, he was too far away to offer any of that. Instead of comfort, she was allotted the pained wails of a dying man.

Soon the "umphs" came to an end, replaced by the distinct sound of metal dragging against a cement floor that echoed through the halls, drowning out the wheezing gasps of breath. The coyote spectators outside continued their *hoots* and *yips*. A heavy and violent heave then rose over the crescendo of the canine cries outside, the gruff sound of a man lifting an ax to chop wood. Only instead, came a bloody impact before the cries finally ended.

Autumn scrunched her ears under her hands, the fleshy sound of impact bubbling her stomach into heaves. Clenching her eyes shut, she screamed internally for the man to just *SHUT UP, SHUT UP, SHUT UP!* She hoped death would soon follow the source, for the sake of her sanity, as tears poured out effortlessly through her sealed eyes. Never had she ever wished such ill on someone, especially for such a cause as her sanity. But the heaves didn't stop, and she leaned over the tarp expecting to puke but only dry gagging.

Then came another loud pitch of crying from those nocturnal animals; several more joined, but in lower barks, following the man's death. She leaned over the bed, the blankets falling off her, and the instant registering of icy-cold air passing over her bare skin made her shiver down into her core. She pulled the covers up to block out the cold.

She closed her eyes, as if the simple desire to be back in the safety her uncle provided her would somehow allow her to wake up back home. As if this was some awful movie she was dreaming about. But she found wishful thinking to be just that, and only that. Opening her eyes, she saw the same dark, dead world outside her window.

Out of the corner of her eyes, she saw a brief sparkle in the moonlight. There, in the corner of the room, was a rope traversing vertically in a tight line. Enough tension was in the rope to support her clothes that were hanging there.

She leaned over the bed and lowered her feet to the ground. The simple sensation of the bottom of her bare feet contacting the frigid floor made the urge to vomit greater. A chill shivered up to her knees and her whole body trembled, spiking in goosebumps as she tried to rub warmth into her arms. The putrid taste of bile rose to her throat; there was nothing in her stomach, so just the acid alone burned up her throat and left behind that acidic taste. Legs clamping together, arms clenching at her shoulders, she was cold and frantic in the isolating darkness as she rushed over to her clothes.

Her breathing rattled when her feet touched the wet ground underneath her hanging leggings and skirt. She reached for her shirt, but it was damp, icy-cold like snow from where the wind had dried the soaked fabric. All her clothing was stiff, close to being frosted over. Her jaws jittered as she scooped up her clothing and hugged it against her. The convection of her body heat warmed them. In all haste, she dressed.

Fully clothed, but not warm, she retreated to the bed where the residual heat of her presence still lingered. Rubbing warmth into her arms under the blankets, she waited for her body heat to build. All the while, the coyotes outside did not relent in their chorus.

It felt like hours passed until she felt some measure of warmth; her head pulsed and was bogged down more than before. Sitting back up, she draped one of the blankets around her, tying it like a cloak, a shield from the cold. Next to the foot of her bed, she found her boots had been set upside down and small pools were under them. The leather was damp. *Better than wet.* She shrugged and slipped her feet into them. Pulling the boots up to her knees and setting the many buckles in place up the side, her toes soon numbed inside the frozen leather.

She faintly recalled when Igor had recommended she not wear her favorite two-inch heel boots before leaving. She now saw the wisdom in his advice, for the pair she had on were more suitable for hiking, with a thinner sole than her others. It had been the very same advice Thomas had given her countless times during their many hangouts at that tree stump. "If you're gonna continue to come out here and get lost so I have to come find you should at least wear the proper footwear, kiddo," he had said. And she had followed his instructions.

She used a nightstand to lean on as she stood up, one hand holding her cloak in place. She looked back at her bed as if it were a campfire, offering warmth and protection. It was just her, and she didn't know what good she could offer. What could she do for Thomas, especially now, in her current state? Was her quest, her journey, even still active? Without Wolf Pack to protect her, wasn't she just a liability? It felt like it was over, her quest ending in disastrous failure.

She nearly collapsed back down to rest then and there, but in the bog of slurry thoughts and dizzied movements, a simple thought provoked her to keep standing. Thomas, she hoped, was still out there. He needed help, and if there was even a sliver of hope left, then that didn't mean it was hopeless, right? Autumn felt as if she owed her friend that much.

Some strength was finding its way back inside her, along with the warm acidic taste rising again at the back of her throat. *Keep it simple, keep it simple,* Uncle Richard had always told her. *Life will make things complicated. When you find yourself overwhelmed, make your next goal simple. Keep it simple, honey.*

Simple, Right... Get away from psycho. Find Thomas.

Following her decision-making, she fell into a heaving fit, hunching over in a violent retch, but nothing came out. The force her body heaves nearly caused her to fall her to her hands and knees had the nightstand not been there to catch her. It wouldn't end until the heaving and retching ran its course, becoming two minutes of freezing agony.

After a quick inhale when the spell subsided, she held her breath for a moment before releasing it. With shaking knees, she moved, slow and weak, using all the fortitude she had to take the next step. At that moment, reaching the door first became her life's goal.

She reached the door, hands feeling for a handle or press bar, resting her head against the old wood, her eyes closed. Each breath became a solution of meticulous rhythm and quantity, carefully measured, and slowly executed, lest she fall victim to another heaving fit. The coyotes yelping outside spurred some speed to her hands. Finding the door handle, her fingers constricted around it. Her thumb found a latching lever over the handle to disengage the lock, pushing it down and releasing the locking mechanism. In the silence of the darkness, the metal workings moving sounded like a gunshot that ricocheted down the corridors—a loud yell to wake the dead.

The pounding of her heart brought her to a still after the door opened on its crowing hinges. Waiting for a response to the disturbance of the silence, her pulse throbbed in her ears. She stared down into the empty abyss of the hall beyond. The silence remained, and nothing stirred from the metallic workings of the latch. The coyotes outside fell silent.

A long, dark hall extended down until the darkness created a pitch-black square at the end. It was a straight-edge mouth with a black hole of a throat leading to an endless pit. Her mind voyaged off to her studies of Tartarus in Greek Mythology or Hel's kingdom in Norse mythology: abysmal places of the dead, undesirable after-life abodes, and hellish fates.

Rapid pitches of cries and yelps from the coyotes picked back up so abruptly that she was riddled with goosebumps and pushed out the door in flight. The soles of her boots sank into a mushy floor, the same feeling when stepping into the mud. She pressed through the top layer until she stopped over something flat underneath, slippery from the slightest of movements. Her face and shoulders breached into a mess of what felt like snakes and vines dangling down from the ceiling. Her breathing quickened, panicking at the thought of walking in a tar pit while serpentine predators descended upon her from above.

Only when her stomach threatened another heaving fit did she realize there came no hissing, nor conscious movement of snakes, and just as quickly she understood the cords and wires that dangled from the ceiling. She swatted and brushed through them with one hand; her other hand held a death grip over her rumbling belly. She grunted and whimpered through the dangling coils.

A faintness swept over her, and that turbulent rumble of bile at her throat remained, ready for the moment when her resistance waned, and release was imminent. Her stomach shriveled like a raisin as if trying to force itself out, and she leaned against a metal obstruction in the hall, fingers falling over a depression at waist height and feeling the form of a padlock. She leaned completely against the locker. Calming herself in that meticulous solution of breathing before continuing onwards, she took one slow shuffling step at a time in the dark abyss.

The lockers came to an end, transitioning to two cinderblock squares of the wall before ending completely. A rail came to her waist, to which she latched on for guidance, until she found where it ended—at the top landing to a stairwell. She nearly fell down the first step but caught herself on the railing and sat down after her near accident. Both arms cradled her stomach that rumbled and growled. She rested her head against the railing, calming herself.

Her nerves would never settle, not when the yelping cries of coyotes shot through the halls in a violent echo. Her heart pounded harder in her chest, and she took a moment to settle her fright. The dark cold of the building seeped out what little warmth her body and clothes had. The darkness was vampiric, shapeless, and void of sentience: starving not for blood, but for warmth, sucking and draining the meager measures of heat she could produce. Just like the primordial forces of chaos and the void in the mythologies she read, a hungry void leeched onto her; she felt drained of it all.

A loud bang that sounded like a hammer strike against wood echoed through the halls. It traveled like a ripple across the water from the floor underneath, jolting her in place as she wiped her eyes dry and listened. Another loud bang, this time sounding more like a thud, shot through the stillness of the building. But it didn't come to a full end, like the sound of a piece of wood bouncing on the floor from being dropped.

Thomas! She needed to find Thomas that was her focal point and before that, she had to get away from this madman.

She sniffed hard, and the sound of hammering pounded through the hall and up the stairs. Sitting on her rump, she climbed down the steps one at a time. She descended only a few steps before her feet encountered something metal. She moved around, looking for a way around the obstruction, finding the next landing completely blocked off. Thinking of a bottle with a cork in it, she sighed. Muffled coughs escaped her mouth as those godforsaken hammer strikes continued in merciless prejudice against her nerves.

Seeing nothing but shades of black in front of a backdrop of darkness, she could barely distinguish the silhouettes of tables, chairs, desks, filing cabinets, and other items before her. Her right foot then fell through a gap in the barricade, and, feeling around that gap, she thought she found a little crawl space she could squeeze through. Leaning forwards, face-first, she burrowed down through it.

The knot of her cloak pulled against her neck, stopping her before she made it even a meter down through the gap. She pulled at the blanket, trying from every angle, but it wouldn't come free. Not wanting to waste what little energy she had in backing up, she untied the knot and the blanket fell off. She instantly felt the cold drape over her as she burrowed onwards.

Coming to the stair landing, she felt a sharp edge cut through her sweater, shirt, and arm. A burning sensation throbbed at her arm, and warm blood soaked into the fabric of her sleeve and dripped down her arm. She held back her cry in a tearful moan as she hurried down to the landing. A spill of bile nearly came up to the roof of her mouth as she leaned against a metal desk and held her arm as the initial high of pain lingered.

The thought of turning back stalled her. The warmth of the bed and blankets was still a lure, a strong lure that felt like a trap: lying back down to rest and get better before daring any kind of escape. *It's not too late.* An intoxicating thought found its way to the front of her mind.

The scraping sound of sawing reverberated from down the stairs. Her stomach was churning, now in unease, as the echoes bounced through the many objects surrounding her: an unending chorus of unholy butchery. The idea of getting closer to that sound was about as exciting as coming out into the Wastelands in the first place.

Taking in slow deep breaths, the sawing came to an end, replaced by stroking rhythms of hammering.

Down the next flight of steps, she could see another little gap in the clutter, more narrow and twisted than the first. She looked back the way she came, feeling blood soaking through her fingers as she held the gash. Then, she thought of Thomas and looked back onward.

She removed her belt, sniveling, while moving her arms in the tight nook she was in. She wrapped it above the gash at her arm and silently screamed as she tightened it and secured it in place and leaned into the twisted narrow gap, burrowing downwards through the contorted crawl space.

Her hands and arms pressed down into the mushy floor, feeling the cold hard tile underneath, as her head and body squeezed through the last of the barricades. The musty old air was fresh from the tight confines. Her right hand found the drawer side of a desk, the contents spewed across the ground. It was not covered in dust, nor were the drawers laying scattered over the floor. Her right index finger pressed to something hard, metallic. It glimmered, sparkling in the darkness from the dim light of the moon out a nearby window. She picked it up and felt the top flip over, revealing the teethed grooves of the switch to a lighter.

Finally, she grimaced thought. *Some luck.*

Finding the wall to help stand up and lean against, she paused as her belly threatened to upheave. But she was quickly drawn away by the slithering and tickling feeling at the back of her neck from the dangling cords.

Dust particles sparkled like Perl in the ambient moonlight reflecting down the hall. The floor, walls, and roof ended in a black square of darkness beyond. A hungry mouth ready to consume.

She stroked the lighter several times, and with every attempt came nothing. She struck it faster with a sudden curse at the old contraption. Eventually, the warmth of an orange spark shot up, and she stroked it faster, not realizing her tongue escaped the corner of her mouth and her eyes were squinting; she was completely absorbed in getting that lighter lit.

Finally, a yellow flame flickered and didn't wither, but stayed as it illuminated a few feet around her with a warm glow. There was a little heat around her fingers, radiating over her clenched fist and fading up to her arm. The light itself made her feel warm: a trick of the mind? She didn’t care.

She faced the long, dark, hungry mouth of the hall with her meager torch; her breathing was steady but faint with heavy eyes. The hammering again came to an abrupt stop and was replaced by the grating sound of metal teeth sawing away at flesh. That sawing sound vibrated from down the long dark she faced. She cried as she stepped forwards.

The yellow glow of the lighter was her guide with every step, a guardian angel that kept the darkness around her at bay. Her other hand was raised, pressed against her chest as if able to hold in all the warmth her body had left and favor the now numbing limb. The belt felt like it was constricting tighter, until all the feeling in her arm was suppressed by those heavy beating throbs preceding the numbness of feeling.

Taking a turn down a hall, she looked down to see that the mushy floor was now occupied by old, ragged remains of clothes and boots, rusted old guns, and melee weapons left behind. She realized that the old school building was now a tomb where the Old World had perished. Here the dead lingered, and she felt the darkness and wrong of the place seep into her. It was like a bog, a marsh pit of tar that soaked into her being, slowly marring her bones. The white canvas was now stained in crimson red and black darkness.

Weaving in and around the cords dangling from the frames of a suspended ceiling, like vines through a jungle. Autumn stopped when she came across piles of shredded and torn clothes and dusty old shoes and boots. The final resting place, a mass grave, had more souls to grieve and mourn for.

The dark gave way to her lighter like the road passing underneath headlights. Along the way came the sight of the stump to a right femur bone, a mangled mess of skeletal remains tangled in the vines of wires high above her.

She covered her mouth to muffle her scream, holding back another heaving fit. Raising the lighter to get a better view, she saw that the poor soul above could have been no older than herself. Left in his desperate escape from the undead, he was just withered old skin draped over dusty old bones under the tattered remains of clothing in a place out of arm's reach. His right leg up past the knee had been eaten, and where the rest was out of reach she figured he had probably bled to death in his entanglement.

She sniffed, sidestepping around the ill-fated person, and came to a stop at the skull. She aimed the light closer to see the absence of skin and a bottom jaw. She reached up and cupped her hand over where its left cheek would've been, and she stared into the endless shadows of the void eye sockets.

"I'm so sorry," she said before continuing.

Down the hall, she found more signs mounted on the wall, offering some guidance, until eventually finding one that said 'EXIT,' pointing her left at a 'T' intersection. Yet, that same long, dark corridor birthed the dreadful sawing, banging, and thudding in the deep. She had followed the source of the noise, figuring the way out was closest to the one who needed it.

No windows lit her way; the ambient light faded into the dark, swallowing it and her, until she was completely submerged save for her little warm flame to shine on the path. Gently, she crept onwards. The hall came to another T intersection, she leaned against the corner. The sounds of sawing, a hammer striking, and wood grinding against metal came thicker and louder as she looked around the corner where the exit sign prompted her to go.

Midway down the hall, a door was propped open by a kickstand, and an ingot of copper light shone outwards, illuminating specks of dust floating about the corridor. As gentle as she could, she closed her lighter; the sound of the metallic *click* felt comparable to a foghorn blaring through port. She waited a good several seconds, panting hard, as she watched the wall of light. She was waiting for any kind of figure to emerge forth and investigate that soft metallic noise disturbing the silence.

But no demon, no monster, emerged; no person silhouetted themselves in the light in search of her. There was only the sounds of the wretched sawing, each push and pull of the tool chipping away the poor soul as it did her sanity.

Autumn crept close to the door like a cat on the prowl, stopping just before the line of warm light emerged in the black darkness of the hall. Leaning to the edge of the door frame and around the corner, she peered into the school's old woodshop, illuminated by a couple of wick lanterns. The room was large, with many square worktables of wood set standing with lockers underneath. Bench vises were anchored around the workbenches' sides. A series of tool racks lined the wall, and beyond, large, heavy machinery spanned deeper into the shop. A classroom was offset to the left. Glass panels lined a wall separating the classroom from the shop room, giving a view to three more bodies hanging from the ceiling by bound feet. They dangled in slow movements from the outside wind. The corpse's fingertips barely touched the tops of the student desks under them.

Straight inside the room, her eyes locked, frozen in place. With his back turned to her, at one of the workbenches, stood Sergei. Spread out to his right was a pair of legs, and to his left the arms and head of Lossif. She covered her mouth with her blood-dried hand, tears instantly meeting her index finger. Lossif's arms and legs were held in place between the bench vises. Blood dripped over the table sides as Sergei worked on whatever sacrilegious project he was making. Other tables were lined with the bodies of Wolf Pack, one with an ax sticking out of the man's chest, the wooden shaft leveled with the corpse and the metal head firmly embedded dead center in his chest.

Sergei pulled back, setting down a rusty old wooden saw in his hands, the metal teeth was dripping with blood. He wiped his hands and stepped around the worktable, giving revelation to the purpose of the hammerings and sawing. A wooden frame held in place the upper portion of a mask composed of bone tissue. Sinew-like wires hung down in a sewing pattern to a bottom piece, waiting to be pulled in place by a simple tightening of a wire. Two small, thin plates hung at each jaw to secure the bottom jaw in place.

Halfway to the tool rack, Sergei fell, and favoring his right side, he landed on his left knee. Coughing so much that he didn't have time to breathe, he was left wheezing when the coughing fit came to an end. Still holding his side, he pulled himself back up with his left hand on the tool rack and changed his course over to the furthest worktable. There, he stopped at a pile of Wolf Pack's looted plunder.

Autumn noticed that the tables not occupied by bodies were organized by the plunder: weapons, gear, food, water, and so on. Sergei was at the table holding medical first aid kits. Taking out an auto-injector from a container, he stuck it into his thigh. Suddenly, he stood, invigorated with fresh yet weak breaths that faded into a persistent wheeze.

Autumn seized the moment, moving, in mouse-like silence, through the ingot of copper light and across the room into the concealing safety the darkness had become. She stopped and listened, using the wall to keep herself still, expecting to hear stomping across the room to the door—or the grunts and curses from whatever frustrations he'd have of her roaming about. But what followed was the ceasing of his coughing fit, followed by the sounds of him continuing his work.

Autumn released her held breath and continued down the hall with mouse-like movements. Coming to another junction of corridors, another 'EXIT' arrow now pointed right. There, she found a set of double metal doors with sections of panels on the top and bottom halves. Ingress/egress points.

She struck at her lighter furiously to get the flame back; several times it *flicked*, but nothing. Cursing at the old thing seemed to prompt the device as the warm flame returned, illuminating the exit doors. She looked and recognized the clear welding line fusing the entire exit shut—what had been her hope of escape from Hel was a dead end. The top and bottom glass panels were covered by wood panels, with large bolt heads sticking out the center.

She clawed and pried at the sides, one barely budging without much sight through. What she did see was the rest of the bolt going through another wooden panel outside, where the nut must have been. Her strength gave out to the pressure of the wood pulling back at her as she let go. Wood clattered in a rattling stop against the metal, a loud signal that echoed down the hall.

She heard tools being set down, single thuds that struck her heart in a sudden surge of adrenaline. Panic overtook her focus at the onset of distinct *THUMPINGS* against the floor departing the woodshop room.

Her stomach receded, and her head jerked forward in a violent retch sending her to all fours. The lighter was still in her hand—now light in the darkness that gave her location away. She heaved and retched, on and on, and there wasn't time to breathe; stars filled her vision at the peripheries, flanking her left and right with obscure visuals. A recess in the heaving gave her a chance to cry and gasp for air, but after a few rapid breaths came another heave before stomach acid shot up and out her mouth. The bile spewed forth on the mushy floor underneath. Tears stressed out her eyes and her face felt as if it were swelling like a balloon with too much pressure before popping.

Autumn's body jerked with the upheaval; those *THUMPINGS* were now moving down the hall like heavy bricks. His breathing and pace gave the impression of him moving in laboring limps. She cried the closer he got, unable to move, until finally, amid her fit, she saw out her periphery. Through starry vision emerged the form of the madman, now walking straight towards her.

Her vomiting came to a cease, her belly now void of stomach acid, as she fell from her hands to her elbows in fatigued tremors. The retching didn't end; the motion of vomiting continued. She couldn't breathe, and her vision now darkened. Her face tingled as if poked with needles. The stench and steam of her bile rose under her chin and infested her nostrils.

The warm glow of her lighter allowed her to see the bottom half of the man, coming up to a stop just a foot beside her. A pair of blue jeans and boots: she looked up as the warm glow of the lighter showed his pants topped by a red and black checkered flannel. She looked up to his neck and saw him pulling his now-finished mask over his face. That same mask stared down at her, eyes reflecting the firelight through the blackness within the eye holes.

"Please," she gasped, her head swaying in the fatigue now taking over.

Sergei didn't respond; his chest rose and fell with his heavy breathing. One hand held an injured side, as the warmth of his exhales fumed out the jagged and contorted mouthpiece like smoke from a Chimera bellowing through its nostrils. She didn't know what to do; her head pounded, and her eyes had never felt heavier.

She gave in, hopeless and helpless. Perdition was all around her, though she was never a believer to begin with. But here and now, she truly felt that if there was a God, he had abandoned her. She did the only thing she could do, not wanting to be awake for what came next. She gave up, gave into the faintness, as if floating into a sea of apnea, and she allowed herself to pass out. Sergei's face was the last thing she saw as he knelt and reached out to her.

Chapter Seven – Purgatory

-October 21st, 2030-

Tim noticed the house was empty when Laura pulled them into the driveway of his home. The little old sedan was still gone, taken by Dakota to her escort ops. The house looked like one empty box, less than a home: just a place of broken dreams where he could crash for the night.

He was ready to sleep back at the safe house where they were keeping Olivia. But Second Lieutenant Bracket had forced his hand to take the night off by calling Laura. “What are you, my mother?” Tim had asked, but the comment was received by his second-in-command in jest. The last week had been grueling and tiresome, and that was how he liked it; it kept his mind busy, distracted.

The last week had been met by three concerts in the local districts. Though his duties were light, they were equally met with busted limbs. Mostly he stayed put in a security console trailer observing cameras and delegating to his team’s Second Lieutenant Bracket running interference.

As far as gigs went, it was easy and sometimes boring; he resorted to a dependency on the foul-tasting coffee that Dakota and Phil enjoyed. For him, it was a necessary price to keep awake and alert. Even when there was no concert, Tim busied himself with patrols around the amphitheaters, checking for security breaches and planning logistics for the event.

But now the next concert was a few days out; a gap in the busy schedule allowed for some R&R. But where he could’ve been getting a head start on the amphitheater in Anchorage, he was back at this broken place: a hollow tree, dead of its beauty and in slow decomposition, like the world outside. Tim grabbed the passenger door handle and opened it; the cab lights came on with the *chiming* of the alarm.

“Would you like some company while you wait for Dakota?” Laura had asked. There was a fatigue to her that hadn’t yet taken root, and she did well to hide the bags under her eyes. Tim knew he hadn’t been the only one racking up hours late at night. But Laura’s state worried him; she lived to work, and sooner or later fatigue would take hold.

Tim moved the muscles of his face, contorting a forced smile. "Nah, I'll be fine," he said, looking at the doctor's gray eyes. They were windows into another world, with its joys and sorrows. He could read the burnt-out weariness pulling down at her cheeks. "Thank you, though."

"Okay." She nodded, and Tim opened the door, starting to get out before the seat belt stopped him, digging into his neck. He leaned back and dropped his head against the headrest, a sigh fuming out his nostrils.

"My car, my rules. Safety first." Laura offered an impish jab.

Tim's eyes widened with a raised brow, a "Yeah, I know" response as he unbuckled the seat belt. "Safety an' shit."

The climb out of vehicles had gotten easier with practice over the last week—the twists and angles, when and where to put pressure to get his broken body out. It hadn't come without trial and error, and much to Laura's frustration, he refused pain meds. He denied them every time with a "give it to a serviceman who really needs it" response.

He closed the door, careful he didn't slam it, and settled into his crutches. Laura rolled down the window and leaned over, looking at him from under the passenger door window frame. "I'll be in Anchorage by the fortnight, and I'll stop by to check on you at the safe house there. What's the call sign again?"

"ACE. Hang on, lemme double check," Tim replied, picking up a folder he had folded into his cargo pocket. He opened it and ran his finger down until he got to the details of Anchorage's safe house. "Yeah, ACE."

"Then I'll see you there. Take care of that leg and arm, you hear me?" Laura pointed at him.

"Sounds good, doc." Tim offered a smirk. "I'll have Captain Shillings relay the coordinates to the colonel to give to you."

"You better." Her hand transitioned from pointing to a wave before falling over the shifter and placing her car into reverse. The sedan slowly backed out of the drive, and Tim returned a halfhearted wave.

Tim watched until her car disappeared down the road before crutching over to the front porch and up the short flight of steps. He sat down on the seat where Phil used to sit, and he stared off into the scenery across the highway. A far-spanning field that cut off at a dense thicket, and beyond, stretched the waters of the archipelago.

It had been Phil's scenery, a place his brother had frequently gotten lost in, a spectator mesmerized by the painting. "God is a great artist," Phil would say like a broken record. Tim stared too; he could admire the beauty of God's creation, but more than that, he lingered in melancholic nostalgia, wishing to just have Phil there.

For as much as Tim tried, he couldn't get away, even if he kept busy; there were still moments of lapse where his mind could catch up and the hurting picked up again. Now, sitting in his brother's favorite spot, he felt heavy. The air was thick like it was drowning him. *Grieving was proof that you loved someone.* He had read that somewhere long ago. He raised his hand to wipe his eyes dry.

-October 22nd, 2030-

It was 0230 When Dakota came home, the sun was already setting, and Tim was nowhere to be seen. From the bottom steps, she could see his door was closed, just barely left ajar. She had been looking forward to seeing him, maybe spending the evening with him to catch up on his last week. But the fact that he was resting set her at ease, slightly lifting the weight off her chest.

Walking to her chair, she looked at Phil's empty one, and sat her ruck down between the two. She removed her belt, unstrapped the hip holster from around her thigh, and sat it down on the coffee table, along with her pistol, still secured under the safety clip. On the table sat Phil's book, *Learning Hebrew*. The bookmark where he had left off, with the intent to continue when he came back. Now it was just collecting dust. She sat down in her chair, regarding the book, the windows facing her as she looked at the due date for the old book.

Reinstituted Alaska State Library, the sleeve read, with a card in the pocket, columns, and rows for renting information to be listed starting *January 1st, 2025*. But the table was empty, save for one single entry: *Thomas Nilges, Check-out date: September 1st, 2030. Due October 31st, 2030.*

She closed the book and laid it back in the clean square where the dust had collected around it. She changed her gaze to the window; out beyond she could see the setting sun over the field and dense thicket beyond. She propped her feet up. The sensation of her feet hanging in midair was a well-deserved reward for the last week. It had been non-stop escorting from Fort Liard to Whitehorse. Individuals with specialized skill sets, training, education, or experiences in different fields were being smuggled into the state, and it would pick up again at 1700 hours that day.

More than the driving, the silence was tiring; she had nothing to offer the individuals she was escorting, save for the common courtesy of greetings and simple, close-ended answers to questions. She didn't feel like talking to anyone, nor did she want to: there were only six people she felt a need to speak with. One was upstairs sleeping, the other was probably punching in long hours at the hospital, and the other four were probably integrating into their retirement.

She leaned on her good hand; over the right armrest, the lower fore of her hand rested under her chin. She didn't turn away from the sight of the sun disappearing behind Phil's trees, and dimming blue across the horizon, prickled with treetops that was darkening into silhouettes. In the last seventy-two hours, she had gotten around six hours of sleep. Now that she was winding down, rest felt like an unstoppable force—and she, a moveable object.

As her eyelids became heavier, she took the time to free her broken left arm of its brace, allowing the now whitened skin to breathe. Rested her head against the back of the chair, and set a pillow for her arm to rest on as she watched the sky turn black.

There was no dream to wake from, only an empty blackness of thought. Her last memory was sometime during the night; she had made the climb up to her room and dragged herself under her covers. Now she lay as the morning sun dawned on her from the window across the room. She was curled up on her twin mattress, the blanket tucked under her chin, and she remained staring off into nothingness. The soft warmth of the mattress and blanket touched her thighs, calves, feet, and arms, and she thought she'd rather stay there instead.

She had always been one to enjoy relaxing in bed before falling asleep or after waking. The silence, the comfort of the blankets' light compression, and the warmth had a way of making her feel as if everything was right—in place—and peaceful.

It wasn't one of those relaxing mornings where she could just lie in bed and relax. She stayed in bed simply because she didn't have anything to get her out. She would lie there and think about everything and everyone. She never got closure for her husband or baby girl, or her mother, father, siblings, aunts, uncles, and everyone else. It had gotten easier to bear over the years, with the occasional regression into her shell. The pain never went away; she just got more accustomed to it.

Being back home didn't help much; her control over her thoughts was lax, and soon she found herself reminiscing. She remembered all the times she could when, lying down in bed or waking up, she listened to her brother's casual chatter, or the two riled one another up. So, when her mind reached the thought of that last time those two idiots were arguing over a muffin, she let loose a chuckle, feeling the wet lines of tears drip over her nose and down her cheek. She buried her face in a pillow.

Warmth came with the light, warming her room. She heard ruffling and scuffling from Tim's room down the little stretch of hall between them. She could hear his door open, and she thought about getting up to help him, but figured it would end with rejection and dismissal. So, she just stayed put, listening to his door opening and his slow descent down the stairs. She counted the steps to make sure he made it down each one safely. There were fifteen in all. The sixteenth marked his safe arrival at the bottom. Then there was his scuffling and slow progress into the kitchen; attempts at being silent were made but failed. She heard the clatter of a pot, the pouring of water, the opening of a box, and, to her excitement, the brewing of the coffee maker.

It would be another two hours before her bladder forced her out of bed. The clock read 0903. Even if the sunlight warmed her room, it was still chilly at her fingers, neck, and cheeks: not the chill of morning, but that of summer's transition into winter, skipping over fall almost entirely.

They hadn't experienced snow or winter since the fallout. So, waking up in a pair of boxers and a tank top usually didn't cause much of a temperature change when getting out of bed. But, as she pulled off the covers, she found the alien sensation of cold shivering her body in the warm light.

Groggy movements turned to zipped urgency as she hurried into a pair of green jogging pants and an olive drab long-sleeved shirt. Rubbing warmth into her biceps, she made her way downstairs to the bathroom.

Closing the bathroom door behind hers, she stepped across the stairs. Her left periphery took note of the front door left open. Through the screen door, Tim's right shoulder and leg could be seen sitting on the front porch in Phil's chair. From the kitchen, her ears picked up the sound of the radio. Tuned to the weather station, the volume was kept low. Outside air seeped in through the screen door and stabbed at her feet and ankles, pricking her neck as she shivered. Drawn by the warm scent of fresh coffee, she went into the kitchen to a half-full coffee pot.

What a guy. A smile crested her lips, reaching to the dish-drying tray where, inside, she had left her mug before setting off on her week-long relay of escorts. Her left arm had a slight tingle; she usually kept it up over her chest, a constant reminder of how sensitive it was. The instinct to use it oftentimes threw her off. She paused and listened to the radio sitting next to the coffee maker. Pressing her broken arm to her chest, she was unable to hold back a grimace at the tingling turning into sharp pains. The voices coming from the radio were alert, with an unsettling worry to them.

"Amir Ahmadi, our newest chief meteorologist…"

Dakota got a chuckle out of that; she could recall the man in question from a year back. It had been her and Dagger who smuggled the meteorologist into the state.

"…believes he has confirmed the climate shifting. However, the sudden presence of cold storms and fronts has him more concerned that it may not be reverting to its original state, but bouncing like a pendulum from warm to cold in a manner of speaking. He expresses strong concerns for, start quote 'a severe winter not before endured by mankind since the end of the last Ice Age' end quote. National Councilman of Labor Naoyak, as well as National Councilwoman of Agriculture Dishta, have been making strong pushes for an increase in textiles for blankets and winterwear and have issued warnings to all…"

Dakota turned it off; she had heard what was needed. Curiously, she wondered if the powers that be already had reason to believe the world was getting colder. Had that been the reason why this Amir Ahmadi was chosen to bring into the state? Was there more thought to all the individuals being brought in? It was certainly plausible. The concept of "do this and don't ask why—good soldiers don't ask questions, they follow orders," and other cynical thoughts rooted inside her, flushing her head and chest in frustration at the thought.

Bellingham was one such case of intel being shared on a "need-to-know" basis, creating a distinct feeling of being just expendable assets, tools being used to meet ends. This brought her thoughts right back around to Phil, left behind, without word or promise of Search and Rescue. *Why? Because he was all used up and there was nothing else the higher-ups could get out of him.*

She believed thoughts controlled one's life and diving down into the rabbit hole of cynical pessimism had been a tough one to climb back out from during her time in Regiment. She knew she couldn't feed the thoughts, just cut the line of thinking off and let it wither. She repressed her wondering thoughts and instead focused on the simple act of getting her morning brew.

Just pour some damn coffee, girl.

Tim's act of consideration brought a soft smile to her face, a good point to focus on no matter how small. Normally, she'd split the pot with Phil, and when she looked back at the pot, half-full, the smell and warmth weren't the same. His mug was sitting upside down on the drying rack where he had left it the last time he had used it. Her frown came back. The sharp pain in her left arm persisted, and she considered getting her brace back on.

Next to the coffee pot were two bowls, one clean and the other full of oatmeal. She hardly ate, less than normal now. The oatmeal would be cold and needed to be reheated, but her stomach wasn't hungry. So, she just took Phil's mug, where he had left it, and poured the rest of the coffee into it.

She nudged the screen door open with her foot. The gentle swing of the hinges *creaked* as it did so, and she stepped out into the cold morning. Tim sat in the spot they would normally find Phil in, with an empty mug in hand.

"Here you go." Her voice was soft, congested, and she cleared her throat, lowering Phil's mug to Tim.

He accepted it, ribbons of steam floating up in the cold chill. Relief came to her left hand from the release of the mug's weight, leaving behind a tingling discomfort. Hearing Tim sip as she took the seat next to him, they were separated by the little table. Tim handed her back Phil's mug and she took it, feeling the hot beverage warming her hand.

Tim didn't look at her, just kept his eyes on the trees, barely blinking. He was more than distant; the lights were on, but no one was home. She joined him in awe of the sight: the trees lined up in such a way that when the sky was just the right shade of blue in the dawn, it was easy to forget they were on an archipelago. It could be deep mainland in Missouri or Arkansas.

It had always been a mesmerizing sight for Phil, like the twilight hours of dusk. There was something in it that drew him; perhaps it was the beauty of it all. God's creation was still breathtaking despite the 2017 Calamity.

"I don't know what to do." Tim finally broke the silence. His voice had no emotion or tone to it—just flat and tired; it broke her heart to hear Tim speaking with such a hollow voice.

She could feel him looking at her now, and she caught a hint of hope behind his vacant features: hope that she might have something to offer.

But she was more fixated on the bags that bogged down his reddened eyes. His pupils were far more contracted than what had to be normal; she wondered how long he had gone without sleep.

"Timmy?" she asked but stopped at his sudden inhale, the kind that was immediately followed by some spark of an irritable snapping.

"It's bullshit," he hissed through gritted teeth, looking back to Phil's trees. "He was in sight, he was so fucking close. I just couldn't..."

"When's the last time you had any sleep?" she asked, setting down her coffee.

"I mean…" Tim looked away as if she hadn't spoken, his eyes now out of her sight. "We were supposed to be here, the three of us. Safe, sound, doing fuck-else until we die. No more of the Wastelands.

It's not fair. No funeral, no fucking grave marker, they just wanna list him as KIA and expect us to move on with that?" His voice raised like he was in a shouting match without an opponent, leaving her the punching bag of it all. Pointing his finger out to nowhere particular, he looked now to her: "HE DOESN'T FUCKING DESERVE THAT!"

She leaned over and grabbed his shoulder. Her face flushed, heat rose in her cheeks and swelled into tears behind her eyes that took considerable effort to hold back. The gesture seemed to calm him some; it was the kind that pulled him back into reality while letting him know he wasn't alone nor among enemies or indifferent superiors—his sister was right there, and albeit calmer, she knew how he felt.

He stopped in a snivel, the outburst burnt out just as quick as it flared. Only now, he struggled to hold back his tears. She couldn't imagine how worse off he was. What happened to Phil was devastating on its own, but Tim had to deal with the added weight of baggage that came with his parents. She wasn't surprised that he looked like he hadn't been sleeping at all.

"He didn't deserve it," Tim spoke again, his voice choked at his throat as he wiped his nose. "He's supposed to be here, we were supposed to do this together."

"But he's not. We are... Buddy, you need to get some sleep." She could feel her voice choke in the back of her throat now.

"And you need to stop sleeping so much."

Ouch. She didn't respond to that, letting it slide. The space between them suddenly widened into a rift. Her grip on his shoulder tightened, and she now stabbed daggers at him for his attention.

"I meant you need to go to bed."

His eyes snapped at her, and in some tired haze he fumed: "When the fuck did you become master-fucking-drill-sergeant?"

That's it. She brushed her hair behind her ears and stood up. Walking back around to the front door and opening the screen, she said, "Timothy." Her voice leveled in such a way that she thought she might be scolding her late child Sara for some wrong behavior long forgotten. "Get your ass in bed, now."

He glared at her, eye to eye. But he soon ceded, his head tilted down in submission with heavy breaths before a careful rise back to his feet. But this time, he held his hand out, in need of aid, and she gave it without hesitation. Helping him to his feet, Dakota helped to post his crutches under his arms and held the screen door open for him.

Dakota stayed behind him during the slow crawl up the steps, ready to catch him should he fall backwards. At the top, she opened his door and helped him inside and down onto his bed. Croaks of pain escaped him during the process as he laid flat, and she took off his boots, leaving his socks on in case his feet got cold. She grabbed one of his pillows and positioned it under his broken leg. Then she covered him with his blanket. Despite him explaining he didn't need one, she tucked him in all the same.

Still, she felt heated when she turned to leave but stopped when Tim grabbed her hand. "I'm sorry." His voice was hollow and dry.

She saw the fatigue take him over, swallowing him as fast as though he fell into a pool. It consumed him the moment he lay down, like an engine going from 3000 to 100 RPMs in a second. Her heart felt heavier than her nerves pinched, a weight that cooled the heat and dissipated it. She got down to a knee, instant pain twisting at her side, coming out in a grunt, and she took his hand in hers, resting her chin over his fingers.

"Don't forget." Her voice remained soft. "We still have each other."

"That counts for…" he trailed off. 100 RPMs fell to 0 in the blink of an eye, and like that, the engine had shut off, and Tim passed out.

Something. She finished for him, resting his hand in the position she knew was most comfortable for him when he slept on his back: his hand face down, bent at the elbow. She pulled the blanket up over his shoulders and kissed his forehead before leaving, closing the door behind her.

She made it to the bottom of the steps, but once at the bottom she didn't feel like she could go any further. There she sat and rested her elbows on her knees before burying her head in her arms as if to shield herself from the world. She ignored the pain in her arm and chest; there was hardly a day she didn't feel discomfort. No, it was the pain of the soul that hurt worse, a busted spirit inside a broken shell.

Dakota supposed that was the new normal; something to adjust to like she had to do when she first started her periods as a young teenager. Life just continued to flow, and you could either sink or swim. But now, she was just floating through life and remained there on that bottom step, hiding, and weeping in silence.

All the while, Phil's coffee mug was left on the porch, growing cold with the world.

1600 hours came around and it was time to get ready. Tim was dressed in a button-up, olive drab shirt over a T-shirt of the same color. The latter tucked into his ACU bottoms. His pant legs bloused the elastic bands at the bottom, hooking between the second and third eyelet from the top of each boot. Each pant leg cuffed and tucked underneath the band as per Alyeskan Army standard dress code. Though now, he supposed they should be considered retired Army.

Tim crutched down the steps, where Dakota was sitting reading her Bible. She was already dressed in her ACUs, though she didn't wear the added button-top like Tim. She wore a regular olive drab short-sleeve shirt tucked into bottoms of the same color. In turn, her bottoms were bloused with her boots. She did have a coat, with a woodland camo design, resting over the back of her chair. She smiled as she looked his way with a "Morning."

Tim left his packed ruck by the steps and crutched over to the couch. "Hey, chica." He patted her arm as he passed her, crutching to the couch, and sat.

"I was just about to come wake you up." Her voice was dry with a quick cough to clear it.

"Yeah," Tim sighed, easing down onto the couch, prompting his leg up on the center cushion. "Thanks, by the way."

"Cu plăcere." Her remark came in a mumble. "You're welcome."

A sudden loud series of knocks at the front door interrupted them. In the fashion of an all too familiar beat, it had a pounding rhythm to it that ranged of youth. "Rock of Ages." Tim's thumb was tapping along instinctively as Dakota shot up to her feet and motioned for him to stay seated.

She opened, and the young woman jumped inside in greeting. Olivia was dressed in some kind of punk, military-themed design: a short-sleeved pink and green camo T-shirt with a hood under a woodland green bustier. She wore a pair of olive drab cargo pants, one leg cut at mid-thigh and the other full of holes left and right as it spanned down to her boots, which were tied at the ankles, the top portions dangling at the sides. The short side of her pants had socks rising over her knees. No bracelets this time—instead she sported black topless gloves that went up to her elbows, with spikes over the knuckles.

You look ridiculous, was Tim's first thought.

"Hello, Miss Blundell," Dakota greeted.

Olivia responded with the offer of a fist bump, and Dakota returned the gesture with an amused smirk.

"My friends call me Olive." Olivia smiled, then her smile fell, and she just shrugged. "Well, I don't really have any friends. But if I did, I'd want them to call me that." She asked, leaning closer to Dakota, "How is he by the way? Is he still an anal worry wart?"

"Uh." Dakota looked over at him for backup.

Tim heard it loud and clear and rested his head on his good hand as his index finger and thumb pinched the bridge of his nose. A headache came, and with it, the promise of a migraine.

Ignoring the comments, Tim asked, "I thought you were with Bracket until I got on post?"

"Well…" Olivia mumbled, grinding the tips of her shoes to the floor in a back-and-forth motion, "I just wanted to see how you were doing." She avoided all eye contact. "You left without saying goodbye, and I just want to make sure you're… well, not good. But, you know, at least managing, I guess."

"That's sweet." Dakota's amused smirk brightened into a smile as she looked at him. Raising her brows to Tim, she widened her eyes as if to say, "Aren't you gonna say thank you, Olive?"

The two women's smiles were shared, and Tim felt his lips start to rise in a smirk. Like a plant synthesizing sunlight, or the slight lifting of a burden, he feigned a chuckle to allow the short-lived smirk.

"Plus," Olivia interrupted, "I made a deal with Captain Shillings. The old bat didn't have a choice. I said I would stop running around if I got to see you sooner." Olivia smiled, no sooner than the captain stepped up to the porch and pulled at the girl's shoulder.

"Which, by the way, you're not making good on," Captain Shillings spoke, shaking her head. "Call me an ol' bat one more time, missy… I'm in my forties. Not sixties. I told you this already." She fumed.

"You thought I was listening?" Olivia asked sharply and with a shrug, hands stuffed in her pant pockets. "It's more like you do the discussing and expect me to listen. I never agreed to that part."

The captain rested a hand on her hip, and her other hand rubbed her forehead. It was the look of a frustrated and ready-for-a-break person; more specifically, a person ready to hand the diva off to Tim.

"I'm already set to go, just gotta grab my ruck," Tim offered the captain.

"No, that's fine. We'll wait out in the car. Give you both a minute," Captain Shillings replied.

"No, I'd like to wait in here." Olivia tried to step further inside but was stopped as the captain's hands caught the hood of her T-shirt and dragged her back outside, closing the screen door.

Tim heard Dakota chuckle as he craned his head to look out the window at the captain forcing the young woman back to the SUV parked out front. He got up, crutched over to the stairs, and picked up his ruck, stopping just beside his sister.

"It's gonna be a long turnaround," Tim mumbled, shaking his head and looking at her. "You gonna be okay on your own?"

"Always am." Dakota's shoulders rose, then fell in a slump. She wrapped her arms around him, and he wrapped his good arm around her.

He rested his chin over her head, which leaned into his chest. "You be careful out there."

She pulled away, and he felt her hands cupping his cheeks. Their foreheads met in one last moment of comfort and togetherness. Tim closed his eyes, wishing for more time.

"You as well, buddy."

"I love you, sis."

"I love you, too."

Part II – Jade "Autumn" Nector

Chapter One – On the Mend

-October 22nd, 2030-

Waking up felt like walking into the cold AC inside after playing outside on a hot summer day. That transition from hot to cold came to her like a flash of light before her eyes opened. The light of an overcast day shone dimly through the window, illuminating the murky room. She was sweating so much that her whole body was drenched, and she shivered. Her hand felt the blanket tucked around her. She threw it off and sat up to the familiar but now faint nauseating heaves from her belly. Her head was foggy and her eyes heavy; she found any attempts at movement to be slow and shaky.

Memories of the last several dark nights and rainy days came in blurred fragments. She had lain in bed, heaving and vomiting, with a gentle hand patting her back, holding her hair away from her mouth as the sickness ran its course. In the mornings, she had woken to canteen cups filled with an odd-looking soup and crackers left on the nightstand beside her bed, along with a cup of water, but no madman.

She couldn't tell if they were memories or memories of dreams, until she looked at the nightstand to see another canteen cup. No steam rose from the stew. She jogged backward in memory, back to the last lucid thing she could recall; digging like a mad grave robber, she excavated six feet down into her mind until she found that coffin. She opened it to the memory of her failed attempt at escape—to her surrender at the feet of the madman, on her hands and knees at Sergei's mercy.

The memory pulled at her, dragging her mouth into a shameful frown, and her eyes fell in disappointment. Autumn always fancied herself as someone with the ability to endure—not to win, but to keep going and "finish the race." Only she had never been trialed by fire, never cast into the crucible of life-or-death situations where you got a real good look at who you truly were. She saw now, from the night of Wolf Pack's Slaughter and her failed escape, that she was nothing. The way Sergei had moved her about, like a puppy by the scruff of her neck—she knew she wasn't a threat. But now, she saw that she came up lacking when it mattered.

Sergei's mercy perplexed her, and despite not knowing what it felt like to be raped, she didn't feel violated in any way. The only pain present was in her belly, over her eye, and at her arm. What she did know was that at some point Sergei had to have carried her back here, and he was attempting to nurture her and sit with her while she was sick.

From time to time, after many arguments with his friend Colonel Winston, Uncle Richie would tell her, "There are redeeming qualities in most people." She didn't want to give Sergei that much credit, but there was no arguing the facts. She was feeling better, and he hadn't hurt her, at least physically.

Save for knocking me out, she corrected herself, touching her black eye. Still tender but not as sensitive.

She looked down at herself, inspecting her body for any injuries, relieved that she was still in her clothes. On a chair at the foot of her bed, her boots sat upright. She reached for them, and a wave of fatigue swept over her and pulled at her heavy eyes. Before she knew it, she fell backward, head landing back into the depression left in her pillow. The warmth and comfort of the mattress tempted her back to sleep, and much to her added shame, she couldn't resist. There she remained in a state of half wakefulness, half sleep.

What felt like just a couple of minutes had been several hours. The constant intrusion of the cold air piercing through the holes of the wall pierced her clothes and made her shiver, keeping her from rest. They came like arrows, let loose by the moan of the wind. She envisioned ghastly spectres of transparent human forms, armed with bows and bombarding the outer walls in endless volleys.

She didn't hear the approaching footsteps or the soft metallic tinkering from the door handle. Only when she caught sight of the door opening did she teeter over the edge in a full panic. In a desperate effort to hide, she only got as far as falling off her bed, and she pushed back against the nightstand, watching the door. Tears fell down her face, and the wet streaks from her eyes chilled in the air. Waiting was always the worst, and the seconds passed as they would to a criminal walking to the gallows, the electric chair, the headsman's block, or the firing squad.

There was an old flagpole, the tapestry of America's heraldry, rolled up. She scrambled to her hands and feet, moving with mouse-like stealth. The sudden haste in movement nearly sent her spiraling into heaves, tasting bile at her throat. Standing up, she latched the flagpole in both hands before running behind the door. The old wood swung open, and the hinges groaned in soft protest. The glass panel above the door handles gave her sight of the madman limping into the room, still favoring his right side, a revolver raised as he entered. From the back of his head, she didn't see the straps of his mask.

The angle of his body and the trajectory of his movements as he scanned the room telegraphed his intent to look behind the door. Her chest was thrashing in rapid pumps of adrenaline, and she breathed quickly as she took the initiative herself. Some violent force in her erupted; she would not freeze up this time, she would not give up; there was a spark of an ember within her to fight. She swung hard, bringing down the flagpole upon the back of his head.

As with her efforts with the scythe, the man was fast. His insane reflexes struck her with both awe and fear. He grabbed the flagpole midair, his right leg stepped forward between hers, and in a quick motion, swept behind her left foot. Her balance was toppled, and the sensation of falling backward expelled any lingering drowsiness. The *thud* when her back met the floor was accompanied by a sickly cry.

The man stood over her, and she couldn't get words passed the dry rasps of her cries, holding a hand up to ward off the barrel of an antique revolver now aimed at her. But he didn't shoot.

"Jade?" A familiar voice, a lifeline, a wick of firelight in the darkness came to her. It seemed her soul registered the voice before her thoughts could, her eyes tearing and her lips quivering in as hope got down on one knee before her. His face came into focus. Out here, in the Wastelands, Thomas had found her, when she had been the one to come seeking him.

He rested the flagpole against the wall, sitting it upright, ensuring that the colors did not touch the floor. He holstered his revolver and reached out an open hand.

"You found me," she cried, taking his hand, and immediately wrapping her arms around him as he pulled her back to her feet.

Her head cradled against his chest, she felt his hand resting on the back of her head. A pained "oof" escaped when she more or less rammed into him with her embrace, and he took a couple of steps back.

Like a tree, however, he remained standing; she was just a flower, moved by the wind.

"Hey there, kiddo." Thomas's voice was a soothing and comforting anchor in her mind, one that chased away the fear and terror, leaving only the sickness behind. Suddenly, everything felt bearable. The monsters, Sergei, even fear and sickness. All of it would yield to him, and he would keep her safe.

"What are doing here?" he asked in a weakened gasp for breath.

Sniffing hard and taking a breath, she replied, "We came to find you," her voice fading off into whimpers and soft heaves. Her sweat, tears, snot, and spit soaked in his flannel. "I was so scared."

Thomas moved, backing up towards the bed where he pulled at her, and, reluctantly, she let go. She sat on the edge of the bed, and he sat next to her as if to take a break. Her left hand felt sticky with something wet and thick. Looking down at the crimson red coating her hand, it deepened in the cracks of her skin and arm.

"Tom?" The word murmured past her lips, joy and confidence disappearing as soon as they had arrived.

Thomas held his right side with ginger care, his red and black flannel wet around the afflicted area. He put most of his weight on his left side as he sat, grimacing with a shrug and a smirk. "Now don't get too worked up, I just took a beating is all." He waved it off before she had a chance to ask, but his efforts seemed strained and forced.

"Are you going to be okay?" she asked.

"Da, just a little scratch is all."

"How did that happen?"

"Fell down a fucking clock tower," he offered with a chuckle.

"Hunchback of Notre Clock Tower Dame, then?" She returned the laugh.

"That's funny," he huffed.

Looking at his right side, the injury looked more severe than he let on, but she understood he knew better than her. Wrapping her arms around his arm, she leaned on his shoulder, feeling his hand reach up to pat one of hers.

"You okay, kiddo?"

"I'm so scared."

Thomas sniffed hard, his head leaning on hers. "Da, I am, too."

"You don't seem scared."

"I'm used to it." He gave a brief chuckle, his voice ending in another strained grunt with a jerking motion as he leaned away.

She pulled back and watched him hold his side again; it was then she could see the rough patch of untreated skin behind his right ear, both charred and mangled like a grinding wheel had been taken to it. He looked like he hadn't eaten in weeks; his skin was sinking inwards, and his eyes, though reflecting light, appeared lifeless—like the sockets of a skull with a sparkling gimmer within. The comfort she felt in believing that any threat would yield to Thomas, she realized, was folly. He wasn't in any shape to do anything; if anything, she was.

Concern plagued her thoughts and must have apparent on her face. Thomas, reading her like an open book, patted her hand. "Don't worry about me," he said. There was some girth to his voice now, and he made a slow climb to his feet, using the bed as support. His right hand shook, and she didn't like the look of that. Her English teacher, Miss Hix, had Parkinson's, and she would shake much in the same way. Thomas's chest rose and fell in laborious breathing, like an asthmatic without his inhaler. He held out his left hand to her.

She smiled, a sympathetic smile at that, taking his hand, and she felt immediately lighter as he quickly lifted her to her feet. "I think we spent too much time here…" he said, looking her up and down with a perplexed look. "How about we get back home?"

"Yeah," she nodded, but felt that same sense of hopelessness. "But how?"

"I got an idea or two." He gave her a brief smirk, picking up a rifle she hadn't noticed he was carrying.

Back at the door, he turned to look at her; she hadn't moved but stood in place. The fear of what was outside that room still froze her. He smiled at her, resolute even in his own toil. "Be my shadow; I move you move. Okay?"

She nodded, tearing up, not wanting to face what was past that door. The room had become something of a panic room, a safe room. She trembled like her English teacher and grabbed onto the lower back of his flannel, which was coming untucked. A tether, Thomas was like her uncle's tugboat, towing a boat lost at sea to port.

"I'll get you back home," he said, grabbing her shoulder. "Whatever the cost, I promise you that."

Autumn only smiled in response, filled with doubt as he stood and faced the door. Taking the first step out, he towed her behind him. She wondered where had Sergei gone and when he would reveal himself? Why did he execute Wolf Pack with such prejudice? She moved like Thomas's shadow as he navigated the halls with some effortless fashion like he knew the place. Every fifteen meters, he would stop, look around and shush her protest to stopping so he could listen to the silence.

She studied his smooth and effortless transitions in movement with his revolver at the ready, how he pied each corner, scanning for threats. But there was one noticeable chink in her friend's steady rhythm of movement. He had a significant limp in his right leg, and he didn't, or couldn't, bend his right knee. Each stride forwards or backward was a stiff motion. Slow was steady, and steady was fast. For all that, Thomas didn't speak once. He must have possessed a well of absolute resolve, from which she felt inspired, as if drawing from those waters herself.

He moved with intent, a familiarity or some internal GPS guiding him to where they needed to go. She was already lost, the difference inside the old school between nighttime and daytime, as the saying went, and she chuckled at the redundancy of it: the difference was night and day.

The building was more illuminated, revealing to Autumn what had first given her an impression of Tartarus or Hel's Kingdom: a void of darkness and despair, the desolate remains of a high school. Now it was a tamed place of despair, a dormant gloom during the day that would turn back into a monster at night when the monsters and homicidal psychos came out. Old brick walls were painted red, white, and yellow, *the school colors*, which were now just faded and peeling, caked under thick dust and ash. Lockers were stripped of primer and paint, just metal boxes of rust lining the walls. Doors to classrooms were reduced to dry, rotten wood, to which a good kick may leave behind a hole. The mushy substance of the floor consisted of the ceiling tiles that had fallen from the lower ceiling.

It seemed to her that they weren't moving towards an exit to leave this building, this sanctuary of Sergei. Rather, they were ingressing further in without the intent of immediate egress. The building was a maze, and Autumn was lost; at every corner, she expected Sergei to emerge forth, like the Minotaur when hunting Theseus. Eventually, her concerns shot forth in a bare whisper that echoed in the deep of the labyrinth's dark: "Why aren't we leaving, Tom?"

"Sergei took something from me we'll need," was his response. "Without it, we won't be able to go home."

Understanding departed her lips in an exhale of despair, the air now thick like water; waiting was always the worst. She clenched harder to Thomas's shirt as the walls transitioned to brick, locker, and door, and the corridor intersected with another, ending in a fork. The way continued straight, while the split broke off to the right in a decline and disappeared around a bend. Thomas went right, his steps slowed, and she saw him canting his revolver to properly pie around the bend.

All the while, she couldn't stop her thoughts from wanting to move faster, as if she could will him to move faster. She was caught in a tug of war between her firm trust in his decision and the snail's pace at which they moved. "What is it you need?" she asked, when the tug of war became intolerable with the silence and their slow progress.

"My satellite phone," he replied, and there was a finality to his tone that signaled the conversation had ended. But not for her—she felt she may know where they could begin to look for it: the woodshop room, turned Sergei's workshop.

She was about to press the matter but became distracted when the old dusty walls and peeled paint transitioned into a wall of glass panels, one by two feet in dimension, set in one-inch-thick metal frames. Brown grime covered the glass, and Autumn tried to rub a clear spot with the sleeve of her hoodie, finding the grime to be on the other side of the glass. She was pulled forwards by Thomas, with her other hand still holding onto him. The brown grime was everywhere but thinner in some spots. The impression of splatters and smeared handprints that left behind a stain on the windows gave her a view of the dozens of folding tables and seats in a cafeteria long since turned into a tomb of slaughter.

Only articles of shredded and torn clothing, and dozens upon dozens of shoes, littered the floor, tables, and seats. The other sides of the cafeteria led to the outside, with broken barricades and breaches in the coils of concertina wire. She knew zombies didn't leave anything behind, not even the bones, and the age-old articles of textiles and shoes left memorialized the perished.

The window frames came to a depression for a set of double doors; a crowbar was set between the handles to keep the door closed with door jams at the bottom. *These poor souls had been locked in.* Autumn's hands rose to her face and covered her mouth, her other hand pressed over her heart as she stared at the memorial, mourning.

"Jade, grabă," Thomas's voice harkened her, low and flat.

"Thomas," she bleated, lips pressed in a frown that quivered at the corners. She felt as if she was going to break down. In school, you heard about the number of people that perished, but it taught in such a detached manner that she might as well have been learning about World War II. The tomb of the cafeteria now transformed those detached teachings into a great and terrible quantity of suffering that she couldn't comprehend.

"This isn't right." She looked at Thomas, expecting the same understanding he always offered. He didn't offer empathy, only a hint of sympathy as he took in a breath, and the skin of his cheeks moved from clenched teeth. After all, he had lived in places like this for ten years. *How can you believe in God?*

"There's nothing for it," he said, motioning for her to catch up. "C'mon now, grabă."

I'm so sorry this happened to you all, Autumn offered in silent mourn, turning away from the cafeteria as more brown stains coated the glass and obscured the tragedy within.

A door led them into a special education room, not the way out, puzzling her as Thomas went in first. The floor inside was a carpeted classroom, spanning down to a ten-foot corridor. A couple of doors offset to their left, and the little stretch of hall fed into a wide square room. The room came complete with a small kitchen, bathroom, and a bed to the far-left side; all no longer usable, save for the latter. Student chairs and desks sat before a teacher's to the right side of the room. At the furthest straight were tall windows that looked over the front of the school. Sandbags were stacked up waist-high behind the windows, with old machine guns stationed behind them, long since past their usage.

Thomas stepped over to the sandbags, leaning on them and panting as beads of sweat dripped down his face and neck. Taking a couple of seconds to breathe, one hand held his side and the other supported his weight as he leaned on the sandbags.

"I woke in here, cuffed to the bed. I didn't get much time to search when I heard footsteps outside, down the hall. See if you can't find a sat phone anywhere," he said.

Autumn scurried over to shelving on the wall, but when she pulled on it, the bolts gave, and the support faltered as the frail wood collapsed. The aged contents dispersed in a clatter on the ground. "How'd you get out of the cuffs? Was it Sergei you heard?" She looked over to her friend, blowing a loose strand of hair from her eyes, and waving freshly disturbed dust from her face.

"I know a few tricks." His face tightened, pulling his hand away from his side. There was fresh blood over the old that dried over his palm and fingers. "Though I did hear three pairs of feet, unless Sergei has friends…" He trailed off, done with the topic.

The light of hope shined in her thoughts as she thought that maybe there were survivors from Sergei's slaughter and the following torture she had heard on that delirious night. She knew a good deal of the team was deceased, immediately remembering Demitri falling over her, pinning her to the ground, and choking on his blood, and Michail shoving his friend off her. Next, she heard Michail's voice barking at her during his scuffle with Sergei, telling her to "Run!"

She'd seen Michail again, when his body came rolling down the crater's edge, that hole in the earth left behind by some colossal explosion. The man's body came to a stop right next to her, eyes gouged out and those empty sockets staring up at her, a knife firmly wedged into his chest. She had looked up the sloped hill to the edge of the crater, seeing the silhouette of the madman staring down at her.

"Jade." Thomas's voice brought her back as the silhouette faded, and the memories receded as she blinked her dried eyes.

She hugged herself as if to block out the cold, and her breathe quickened. Sat phone or not, she wanted to get the hell out of that place. "What?" she snipped, ready to move and forget the school.

Thomas jerked his head towards the windows as she stepped closer to look outside. The sky was still bright, and behind the stretched clouds a bright white spot showed where the sun was. It was bright enough to see the circular drive in front of the school, a bus rider pickup, largely cleared. Beyond that was a large parking lot, filled with cars belonging to students and faculty, perhaps. The EMP of the fallout giving them permanent residency until nature took them. How many other "tombs of suffering" were out there? Just how many people had died since 2017?

"What am I looking for?" she shrugged, hands falling at her sides. "I see a whole lot of nothing here."

Thomas pointed upwards, away from the parking lot and the neighborhoods. Past all the dilapidated houses and trees, up the side of the mountains and forest, his index finger was aimed at one mountain in particular—a peak, white as snow, that towered over the rest.

Autumn thought back to the stories, myths, and legends. Scaling a mountain was never a small ordeal but rather a large undertaking, one never taken lightly. She looked at the giant force of nature as it gloomed over the land, stuck in its shadow. It mocked them with its might; they were just ants in comparison. How did man go against nature? According to the story of Actaeon, you didn't.

In the gloom of the shadow of the mountains she felt only dread. The air outside was clear but thick, ominously crisp, like in the season when things either died or went into hibernation. A mist far off in the distance blurred the forest under the mountains, who were like giant spectators, sitting above in colosseum seats, watching, and waiting for them to make their move.

"The mountain?"

Thomas didn't answer her question, and she found herself hoping he wouldn't.

"That's your idea?"

"It's not as bad as you think." His voice had a measure of enthusiasm. *Humorous*, she thought, as he walked over to the teacher's desk and took a seat in an office chair. She walked around to the other side, grabbing a student chair as he unfolded a brochure detailing a hiking trail up the mountain. He removed a map from his cargo pocket and sat it all out.

"Our target objective is Pikes Peak, west of us, which we're facing. Also facing us, traveling up the mountain, is the Barr Trailhead. According to my calculations and this brochure, it's roughly a five-mile journey to the trailhead, about three to four hours. From the trailhead, it's around a thirteen-mile trek that can take six to eight hours up the mountain. All in all, with a nightly curfew, a two-day ordeal at best."

"Seriously?" she asked. "We could get up there today, then."

"Well, it is possible." His face went blank, eyes drifting off into thought, almost pessimistic as he bit down on his bottom lip, running mental calculations. "There's no telling how many BR-Hostiles are in the area, not to mention that two big fuckers are still active. I know that much. Then Sergei's just… gone! And Wolf Pack…"

"What if any of them survived? If we find them, they can help?"

"NU!" His voice instantly fell flat, without room for argument, shutting her down faster than she could think. Heated breaths fumed through his lips as if smoke from a fire-breathing creature. He raised a finger and pointed at her, his eyes digging through hers and demanding obedience. "Under no circumstance are you to ever be around those men."

"Why? They, we, came to rescue you."

"Nu." He shook his head.

She insisted, however, arguing that he was wrong, slowly breaking apart as she did so. Her voice choked and the words came without much pause or space between them. She cried every word and sniffed between each sentence, wiping her noise along the way. She told him about Igor and four other men going out to find Petr and Anton, and Lossif breaking off to help Igor. She told him about Michail and Demitri's attempts to get her back to the helicopter, ending with their deaths. Then the pilots! She stopped there, cuffing her hands over her mouth, remembering how they had been left, splayed open, as if she had just seen it then and there.

She broke down, and, when her tears ran out, she fell into a fit of heaving tears. Her breathing shallow and rapid, she exhaled as fast as she inhaled. Her nose ran, and she felt light-headed; she was no longer standing but leaning on Thomas. Her head was against his chest, and his hands held her. The soft "shhhs," soothed her thoughts.

She felt him pull away, and he lowered his eyes to hers when she had calmed down. "Nu," he repeated, and she saw the conviction and astute certainty in those tired brown eyes. "They would've executed me as soon as they had seen me. Then, Lord only knows what they would've done to you."

She felt the legs to a chair behind her and took a seat; it was a student's chair in front of the teacher's desk. Suddenly dizzy, her stomach both churned and growled as she held herself, drying her eyes with the sleeve of her coat. "What aren't you telling me?" She looked to him.

His jaws moved from his teeth, clenching behind sealed lips, shaking his head, eyes dead still.

There had never been a question he didn't answer, never a hint of a lie. With him, she always found open honesty. But then, nobody could be put on a pedestal, and she supposed it was only a matter of time before she found a line with Thomas.

"They've hurt you?" she asked, and she received only silence for her answer. She understood.

Some pains were too deep to bring to the light or to be spoken. She saw that Thomas didn't want to peel back that scar and let it bleed. Her uncle was very much the same way; she was only ever able to speak with him about hard topics when he was buzzed or occasionally drunk. Richie never got violent or belligerent, but he got mopey. Sometimes she'd encourage her uncle to keep drinking, bringing him another beer or pouring him another glass while he sat. It was the only way she ever got to hear about her parents. The liquor numbed the hurt and opened the storybooks of memory he kept under lock and key, buried deep.

She was seven years old at the time, on the 4th anniversary of the Great Calamity, properly termed the 2017 Calamity. Uncle Richard had some downtime and the idleness allowed him to stir in his demons. "An idle mind is the devil's workshop," she had heard before, and that night she believed there was some truth in it.

It started with her grabbing him another beer, and slowly, he opened up. Seeing a pattern, she kept the rounds coming for him until he got up and went for the whiskey instead. When he couldn't stand up on his own, he finally told her. How a dying mother handed her infant daughter off to her brother. How the father stayed with the mother, fighting against the odds to make it from the hordes of the undead, holding onto the slimmest chance of making it through. But they wouldn't, and they couldn't, gamble with what they loved most.

"Make sure she makes it," Richie quoted his long-deceased sister, the bottle missing his lips and spilling some whiskey down his stubbled face.

"And?" a seven-year-old Autumn asked.

There was a pause, and Richie stared off at the wall, building up the courage to say what he needed. The weight of it drowned him under the bottle, and he took another drink. His eyes fell with the lowering bottle to his lap.

"I made sure."

She saw the same turmoil in Thomas. Different as it was, it was still the same burden of weight. She reached her hand over and rested it over his clenched fist; she didn't like guilt-tripping others, but she needed to understand "why?" The men of Wolf Pack had treated her so kindly, and Lossif had taken an interest in her as she reminded him of his daughter. They had laid down their lives in a vain attempt to save her from Sergei.

"Why?"

She had always had the sense that he was holding something back, but she never pried. Usually, it wasn't a big deal to her—until now. Long ago, she had shared with him the story of her parents, perhaps the most painful story she could share so far. Since then, she allowed only two people to call her by the name her mother and father had given her. Thomas was one of them, and as he looked back at her, his bloodied hand patted hers. *Fair is fair.*

"Please?" she asked.

He pulled his hand back and scratched his nose, and she thought that he could use some numbing to open his locked storybook.

"Without getting too deep." He sighed, his face suddenly becoming pale, and he looked like he might faint. "My real name isn't Thomas. It's Philip." His eyes watched her, gauging and assessing her reaction.

She nodded along, body moving while her mind caught up. Everything felt like it could have flipped upside down, and she was held upright only by the idea of fairness. She had, after all, gone a year without telling him her real name, so she bit back her tongue and waited. *Fair is fair; it goes both ways.*

"Okay. You look more like a Phil." She offered a chuckle, and he replied with a soft smile.

"I was given the alias Thomas when I came to Alyeska because of people like Igor and his men."

He wiped his eyes dry and leaned back in the chair with a deep breath. "My past isn't clean or innocent. This much I know: the same goes for Igor and the others. I had dealings with them in the past, and believe me, they are anything but good."

Silence fell between them, and she fiddled with her fingers in her lap. She understood that this was as much as she was going to get out of him. It was enough of an answer, and she kept her mind open. Thomas's breathing became heavier, and his breaths rattled in a wheeze, his face wet with fresh sweat.

"You said your hands weren't clean, either." She fiddled wither her fingers, avoiding eye contact. "But I know you, 'Phil,' and you're a good man, now. What if Igor and the others were as you said, but then…"

"I won't take that chance." Phil shook his head, and Autumn could have sworn she saw a tear escape his left eye, but he turned to hide it. "If you were back home, safe and sound. Maybe. But I won't risk dragging you into the crossfire. You are my priority; do you understand that?"

She felt a sad smile as her eyes fell to the table, and she gave a nod.

"You need to understand, with that in mind, that I may have to do things to potentially 'repentant' men, as you suggest. Things that I will not be ashamed of if it means keeping you safe."

"Sergei already did that." She dropped her shoulders, "Where does he factor in?"

His eyes closed. It wasn't a blink, but a restful intermission.

"Phil?" she pressed, and his eyes fluttered open and back shut.

"I haven't the faintest idea." His shoulders slumped, and, shaking his head, he leaned back in his chair. He appeared asleep, and she stood up went around the desk, feeling his clammy forehead.

Fever. She understood and gave him a shake.

His eye's cracked open, "Prostit," he uttered, depleted.

"You're sick."

"Doesn't matter." He leaned forwards, ready to get back to the grind.

Phil's strength lasted only for a second before he nearly collapsed. His left hand caught the desk, while Autumn jolted to his right side to catch him. She tucked under his right arm just in time, but with his whole weight on her, they both nearly fell.

Groaning and grunting, she felt the strain on her back as she carried him ten feet to the bed tucked in the corner of the room. There wasn't much grace in sitting him down, for she wasn't strong enough, so he fell onto the bed.

She panted, stomach-churning and violent motions of retching threatening to send her into another vomiting spell. She calmed herself, resting her hands on her hips as she arched her body backward, relieving the lingering strain. Then she lifted Phil's legs and slid him up on the bed, adjusting him into a more restful position.

"Gotta find that sat phone and call in the Nine Line," Phil mumbled, his voice slurring in a state between half awake and half asleep. "Just need a minute to—" he started.

She looked around the room for a blanket but found none. One of the offset doors in the small corridor before the door was a closet, and inside, she found several brittle old plastic bins and storage containers. Inside one was a plethora of blankets, foul with a musty odor, but beggars couldn't be choosers. She grabbed a blanket and gave it a rough shake, sending a cloud of dust into the hall before she tucked Phil in.

"—catch my breath," he continued.

"You gotta break your fever first," she said, tucking the blanket under the arch of his back, up his arm, and up to his neck.

As best she could tell, it was the best way to get past a fever, like going through a brick wall. The windows were starting to frost over, and so she decided to play it safe, mummifying Phil under an additional four blankets. She felt his forehead again, in case the first time she had made a mistake. Using the back of her hand, she still felt the fever.

She looked at him wondering, *How?* How could he push himself so far? How did he look so calm and focused? Where did that strength come from? If he could do that much, then she felt she had no reason to give back any less, no matter how sick she felt, or how terrified. It was enough just knowing he was alive—alive and well, all things considered.

She stepped back over to the sandbags and looked out at Pikes Peak, her terrible sense of direction adding to the worry. But the mountain was a very prominent focal point to guide her, like a lighthouse guiding ships to shore. Surely, she had no excuse. *But I'm not you.* Doubt clawed at her, and she looked back over to Phil.

Her friend was out of commission, down, and inoperable. There was no one else to pick up the slack, and that terrified her. She stepped lightly over to the teacher's desk and sat in the teacher's chair. Pulling the map before her, she looked at a local map of the area. It was annotated with many abbreviations and markings whose meanings she couldn't discern. It came more like a foldable packet: maps of Idaho, Montana, and Wyoming were also included, with annotations along a route. They didn't matter to her, and she flipped back to Colorado and next, to Colorado Springs. To the margins were more annotations, one listing a Nine-Line MEDEVAC. Pikes Peak had been dotted with a sharpie, and under the mountain, the writing followed: *SRT-Bravo HMMWV/Viasat.*

Then she understood the importance of Phil's missing satellite phone—why they were still here in this hell hole of a school. She had to find it, reach the mountain, and make that call. *ET phone home*, she mused, in a chuckle that was more forced than natural.

She searched her memories, back to courses in school. Many classes were added to General Education to help prepare kids for required military service. One was Standard Operating Procedures 100, where they spent a whole lecture on Alyeska's use of the HMMWVs. Nodding along, she pieced it together, the objectives becoming clearer.

She had practically forgotten the whole class, which she had taken a year ago. Her memory was jogged by Phil's writing. Looking at the map, and reading the writing again, she kept digging deeper. It was Standard Operating Procedure for military units to keep a Broad-Spectrum Field Injection Kit, or BSFIK, in every vehicle; the Humvees were no exception. If there was an Alyeskan Humvee on that peak, then there might be medicine she could give Phil.

"Get to the Humvee on the mountain, contact home for rescue, give them this Nine Line. Get back with the medicine." Simple enough in thought but executing it would be another story.

The reality that this was happening dawned on her. An enigmatic fusion of excitement and anxiety gave her hesitance. Was this how Heracles, Sigurd, Lugh the Silver Arm, and other heroes felt in stories of old when facing their adventures? The longer she stood there, the more she toiled in anxiety.

Compartmentalize, she told herself. *Take it one step at a time.* Pulling away from the maps, her objectives were clear now. Looking back out the windows, she thought of the first step. She needed protection, equipment, and supplies if she was to make this journey. *Yes.* Her left index finger tapped the teacher's desk.

The same night when she failed to escape Sergei, when she had given up, she had seen Wolf Pack's supplies organized in the school's woodshop along with the madman's horrible projects. She knew where she could find what she needed, but then she looked at Phil. What would happen to him if Sergei found him in the same place he was cuffed? What if he was too sick to fend for himself?

With one last glance out the window and at the sky, she took in a deep, nauseated breath. *What could it hurt?* She folded her hands at her waist and shrugged.

"If you do exist…" she prayed. It felt silly, almost like talking to herself. "Don't let Sergei find Phil, please. See us through, and um…Amen, I guess. Oh, and uh if you could keep us alive that would be great." She looked back at the way they came in and gulped, studying the door. Back to the lion's den she would go.

Chapter Two – Sheol

Autumn dusted her hands off with several claps, stepping back and observing the special education room door. Student tables, chairs, and even a filing cabinet barricaded the door, wondering at a job she hoped was well done. For someone like Sergei, it would be a trivial effort to clear the obstructions although it had been laborious for her. There was no point of reference she had to determine if it would keep out zombies, and she found herself mumbling in idle prayer, “Please hold.”

Now her soles moved the muddy surface of the ceiling tile as she turned on her heels and started down the hall, using the tracks she and Phil left behind as her guide. Through the serpentine wires, tile frames, ceiling light covers, and fixtures they were attached to, the inside was a jungle of decay and rot. Their footsteps stopped at the door of the very same one she had woken up in.

It felt like a recent memory, the route she had taken that night when she had tried but failed to exit the building and escape Sergei. *No, not just failed. You gave up*, she reminded herself, following the tracks she had left behind. *A day ago? A week ago?* She had no sense of time to gauge how long it had been, wading through more mush and serpent coils of cords down the familiar corridor. Ambient light illuminated the way as she followed her footprints from before.

Her left hand rubbed against the wrapping over her bicep, staring down stairs corked with enough furniture to make a small junkyard. She breathed in through her nose, and her stomach rumbled and growled as her heart banged behind her chest. She could still hear the savage sawing and poundings from that night; the cruel ending to the poor soul sounded lucidly in her memories. She closed her eyes and held them there for several seconds, willing away the memories, and she attuned her hearing to the quiet noises of a large old structure.

Slower this time, she found the same jagged edge of a filing cabinet that had given her the laceration. She moved around the rusted piece of metal, and all other dangerous edges, as she reached the bottom of the steps. Like a prairie dog emerging from its hole, she climbed out on the ground floor of the building.

The path here was marked only by her footsteps, two sets from Sergei. It was not frequently traveled. The man's larger prints were to the left and right of hers. The mushy top layer over the floor tile disturbed by her first time coming hid her second. Standing up and making slow movements to keep her balance, she walked in Sergei's steps.

At the next junction, the traffic of disturbances in the mushy ceiling tile went back and forth, to and fro from the woodshop. The ingot of copper light no longer illuminated the hall, but a splash of cold gray from the shop's windows. Her steps could move more freely with the countless imprints left behind by the madman, and slower. Her chest ached from her pounding heart as she closed in on the door and peered inside, hearing the sawing, the hammering, and the splattering impact of an ax upon flesh.

The woodshop was empty, Sergei nowhere in sight: gone, and the bodies with him, none held in the vice grips on the tables. She dared a glance at the classroom to the left, seeing no cadavers hanging by their feet over the student tables. Blood coagulated into puddles on the tables and vice grips, soaking into the sawdust on the floor.

Did Sergei just up and leave, leaving her and Phil to their fate? Would he come back, or had he never left? Why did he spare me and Tom, er, Phil?

The only thing that had remained in the same location was the plunder of Wolf Pack, set and organized on worktables. On one table was the weapons, gear, and clothing, the guns neatly arranged, and clothes folded into stacks organized by size. Another table contained stacks of MREs and water canteens; it didn't look like much to feed the twelve men who brought her down here, but it seemed like enough to get her and Phil by while they waited for help to arrive. The third table was cluttered with chest rigs and plate carriers, padding attachments for joints, helmets, and an assortment of other items.

Ditching her gray hoodie for one of Wolf Pack's coats, she unfolded the garment and stopped when she read *Lossif* embroidered on the left side of the chest. She did the math; twelve pairs ten were identical: *Wolf Pack.* She understood. She had seen the pilots wearing the other two coats. She hoped some Wolf Pack men had survived, but in the end, she supposed it was a foolish hope to hold onto.

A frown crested her lips, the dots connecting in the likelihood of the man's death as she held the coat to her chest. No words came to her, only the motions of grief.

Lossif, out of all the others, had been the friendliest. He shared his food and water and he talked to her, allowing the conversation to meander in whatever direction it pleased. He had been a calming focal point on the way here when she was nervous and helplessly anxious. So, she thought, in an ironic way, it was only fitting that it would be his coat to keep her warm. The sleeves had to be rolled up until her hands poked out. By then, her wrists looked like pencils sticking out from a soup can. She grabbed a chest rig that fit over her new coat, and she pulled the straps to tighten it around her abdomen. She found that when all the straps were pulled to their tightest, the whole rig was still baggy on her.

Buried under a plate carrier was the bag she had brought with her, packed with her books, hygiene items and other things—but one item she wanted more than anything. She found it located inside a little pouch compartment inside, and she pulled out her Leatherman. It was a gift from her uncle, who received it as a birthday gift from his sister, her mother. "Always have it with you, these things come in handy in a pinch," he had told her, and she had done as he said and would continue to, securing her tool to her belt.

The plate carriers were heavy, and she didn't want the extra weight of the metal slowing her down, so she neglected to take one; she didn't expect to be shot at. Not by any survivor of Wolf Pack, or Sergei.

All the big guns looked as intimidating as they did heavy. She had never been the strongest nor fastest among her peers. In Gym or PT class, she barely ever ranked above the standard. So, it made sense to her to choose the smallest firearm from the plunder, one she remembered seeing secured between the pilot and co-pilot seats on the way down here.

It didn't look like a rifle or a machine gun, and it wasn't heavy. She took a knife and cut a slit in her skirt. It gave her more freedom of movement and doubled as a place where she could fit a holster for a pistol over her leggings. The holster was held up by the belt around her waist, and the straps circled her thigh. She took one of the pistols and walked over to the table holding the ammo.

All the pistol magazines were the same, and she loaded one into her pistol before holstering the weapon and clipping the safety strap over it. Then, she looked among the magazines until she found the one that fit her primary. Doubt gnawed at her, and she thought about when, or if by preference, she had to shoot, and if she had the right magazine and bullet loaded. She had been taught enough to know that shooting the wrong-sized caliber would be dangerous, disastrous, even.

There was no other magazine on the table that would fit inside her primary: process of elimination. She took the extra four magazines and loaded them into her chest rig, along with two for her pistol. Radio equipment sat with the magazines, and it all looked alike save for one item. It was similar in appearance to a radio, but it wasn't a radio. Closer examination revealed that it was the sat phone she needed.

She almost cried out in excitement; the high of completing an objective on her own filled her with pride. She tried to turn on the power, but the battery was drained. Figuring that there was a way to recharge it at the Humvee, she stowed the phone, along with a radio that still had some power. Now she had around a good 25 pounds on her.

That was when she heard noises from the outside hall. Picking up her primary, she tried to creep up to the door. But being unused to the added weight made silent movements a challenge, like trying to not make a sound while walking on glass. At the door, she could hear soft, steady footsteps—three sets of them. Worse, or not, she could sense a methodic rhythm to their movements, nearly silent. Sergei came to mind first, but then she had to wonder, *who are the other two?*

She wasn't even past the gate yet, and she froze. Panic brought her to indecision as her legs locked into place. That spurt of pride was a small flame, easily snuffed out under the galling weight of her inadequacies. She had failed her mission before it started, and, armed or not, she still found herself at the mercy of Sergei: when he captured her at the helicopter, when she froze at his feet from a failed escape… Her eyes teared and she thought she might cry, and all the while the footsteps got closer.

Then something sparked a sudden realization that came to her with a freeing breath. It lifted the weight of her indecision and guided her thoughts in a snowball effect. She now knew where Sergei was, and by proxy, *where he wasn't!*

The other two footsteps were a mystery, the owners were nobodies that didn't matter. What did matter was now she could lead the threat away from Phil—a small goal that would lead to the ultimate one, taking precedence.

Looking around for a way out, she found nothing. The shop itself was a dead end, the windows too high for her to reach. But on the table were grenades that she purposely neglected. Now, she appreciated their existence as she grabbed up two of each, unable to remember what they were called; all that she knew was one went *BOOM* and the other *BANG.*

She opted for the Banger, not wanting to kill or hurt anyone with the Boomer. She stowed three of the *BANGERS* in pouches on her chest rig. The fourth she kept in her hands, racing through memories from the Basic Firearms Safety and Handling course. She pulled the pen, held the safety lever in place, ran to the door, and tossed it out the hall. She was unsure if the threat was close enough or not, but when she heard the sudden alarm of a man's voice telegraphing the threat, it was too late. In a brief flash of light, an ear-piercing *BANG* traveled like a river current caught between the walls of the hall, gushing into the room and leaving a profound ringing in her ears.

The lividity of the moment sent her mind into flight mode with fresh dumps of adrenaline coursing through her shaky legs and arms. Veins and arteries pumped recklessly, faster than she could pant her breaths as she ran out the door and into the wall directly across. The fluid movement continued as she pushed off from the paint-peeling brick and ran away from the men.

She came to the dead end of the exit, where she had given up her flight to Sergei. Determined not to repeat her past failure, she looked away from the door, the light shining through the cracks illuminating a narrower hall that broke off to the right. Tucked away and easy to miss, it led elsewhere to uncharted territory, and she took it.

She heard the sound of her pursuers in full chase behind her while recovering from the disorienting concussion she dealt them.

In school back home, this was how she could best others: being faster or stronger didn't matter. Evasion and endurance to outlast them had been her strength, and it didn't always pull through when thrown into the spotlight among her peers. But sometimes, such a strategy was just enough to give her a small measure of confidence, and it worked. She was the last one who could still jog laps after the other boys and girls tired out. Here, she realized, outlasting wasn't going to work, as she listened to the closing-in, reckless beat of boot thumps and the panting breaths of her pursuers getting closer.

Her focus became clouded again, panic building up as she came to 'T' in the hall; she made a right turn that led past the library room and into the school courtyard. The once tamed and well-kept piece of nature within set boundaries was now a wild small forest of tall grass inside a thicket. A cement path, now covered in weeds and blades, with tall grass constricting it, led across to the other side of the school. Through the doors, she barely noticed, out of her periphery, a service hatch left open.

There was no time to consider; she looked down to see the tight confines of a cement tunnel and several rows of piping lining the walls. Flashlight in hand, she set her legs down and hopped into the tunnel. Shining her light forwards and backward, the light failed to reach an end both ways, and she was consumed in the black depths of the darkness. The pipes lining the sides gave it an industrial look, and prongs issued forth, or from, the dark pits at her front and back. Old fluorescent bulbs lined the roof with cords arching downwards, inoperable, to mock her in her need for light.

From above, she could hear the courtyard doors open. A voice called out the service hatch, and she took off crawling without pause. The direction of her light swayed and jerked left to up and right to down as dust particles floated like bodies down a river. The air thickened the deeper she went and sweat instantly beaded over her face, her clothes sticking to her skin as she came to a stop, catching her breath and wiping the salty sting from her eyes. She was blinking moisture back into her eyes when a man's voice echoed down and passed her— Russian, Romanian, she couldn't tell. Rolling over to look back, she saw lights and men still following her. The hysteria of her panic invigorated her with new strength as she squirmed and crawled in wild desperation to keep her lead.

She wondered how simple it would be if she just rolled over, aimed her gun, and tried to dispose of the men. They were just fish in a barrel; problem solved. Yet, despite having the means to end life, perfectly proportioned to the opportunity before her, she couldn't. Her heart felt heavy and sickened by the idea. Her thoughts ridiculed her for even thinking of such an option; she was a lover of life, not a taker of it.

Witnessing death and dealing it weren't the same for her, so she kept fleeing. The tunnel widened, and a transition to a declining slope came into view. Sitting on the top, before the decline, was a roller bed.

Thank God! Her soul rejoiced, lying down on the torn old leather cushion, teeth clenching down over her flashlight in sharp discomfort up through her gums and to the back of her neck as she tasted the metal, freeing her arms to grab onto the rusted pipes. The first pull came with resistance; the wheels wanted to spin but locked in place.

Her pursuers were closing the distance, nearly within arm's reach. She pushed back and pulled, feeling something break from the wheels. In a split second of despair, she imagined the wheels snapping off and her advantage now gone; she was proven wrong when she could feel all four wheels under her rolling in a loud, rusted squeal. She tried once more, and something gave—something else broke in yielding movements to the freedom of full spinning wheels. A hand reached for her boot, but the man's fingers failed to grab purchase, brushing along the sole. She cried out as she sent the wheeled bed down the decline, her pursuers falling far behind her.

The sting of salt burning her eyes didn't cease, and she sweated as if a pipe was busted, showering her while she crawled around like a giant rodent looking for food. Her hands and feet stroked the ground, and a stiff soreness brought aching pains to her biceps, lower back, and neck. Her ability to keep going, to keep pushing, came to fruition: deliverance from the threats. Her breaths seethed in and out between clenched teeth in hopes of filtering the musky air.

The tunnel came to a stop, the decline a smooth transition to a flat surface. All momentum burned off as the wheels came to a stop. The roof lifted with the pipes, offering enough space to stand in a small maintenance room. She held the wall, stretching her sore back, and rubbing out the stiffness from the lower part. Behind her, the lights of the men were small and far away. Ahead, stood a three-foot tall door leading out of the service area, and she pulled the door open and left the tunnel behind.

Autumn slammed the door shut; a handle lined up with the cement wall of the room she had entered. It was a perfect setup, and she rammed a nearby broomstick through the old wooden shaft to hold the door shut. At least for a little bit. The men nearing the end of the tunnel made her heart continue pounding. Brushing her hands through her greasy hair, she looked around to some kind of mechanical room.

A set of metal doors allowed outside light to bleed in, and she ran for them. Stepping up to her tippy toes, she looked out the glass of the doors, staring out into the back parking lot of the school. Although it was another way out, the only caveat was a herd of zombies, around fifty in number, moving about idly between rotten bodies of parked metal.

The door yanked back, stopped by the wooden broomstick. Again and again, the men tried to open it, their voices calling her by name, and her mind went back to panic-flight mode. Prolific *cracking* and *splitting* came from the broomstick with each battering attempt. Taking a step backward, the floor suddenly vanished as she nearly fell. Metal scraped up her left leg as her right knee nearly gave her chin an uppercut. Her hands spread out and caught on the floor, keeping her from falling into a drainage channel in the cement floor.

The broomstick broke into two.

She jumped the rest of the way down, her feet making a mushy splash as her head poked up out of the mechanical room floor. She was looking at the service door when the broomstick finally snapped in half, and the door swung inwards in an angry fashion. She ducked behind a round concrete pipe, just big enough to crawl through. Autumn took it as fast as she could, hunched over with bent knees.

There were signs of recent use throughout the drainage system as well: fresh disturbances through the wet leaves, soon to be reduced into a muddy surface with dirt and decayed trash—the plastic litter of bottles and boxes, brittle enough that they broke from the smallest contact, and murky puddles. This was as good as it would get. The trail had the impression of something being dragged. Some of the drag marks were straight, like from wood, and others wide, as if a bag of potatoes had been dragged through the murky collection of decaying trash. Enough so that she had a guide to follow, to good or ill she didn't know, and she thought she had found Sergei's points of entry and exit.

Her knees cramped, and a cramp in her neck formed, leaving her in a stiff posture that was hard to break when she came to a service ladder. Sore pains brought her to lean on the ladder as she straightened herself out, one arm leaning on a rusted crossbar, the other bent back to favor her back. Adrenaline had passed through her system, and now her body's cellular respiration ceased to fermentation. She felt like she was about to buckle, collapsed in a state of crippling paralysis, sweating and tired, as the sickness taking back its seat at the table was no longer repressed.

The drain system continued onwards, but the dragging depressions didn't. She returned to the intersection, seeing the lights of her pursuers down the circular wall of cement. Then, she started brushing all the debris and leaves until it looked somewhat undisturbed, covering her trail back to the ladder and out of view under the service lid.

She could hear the voices stop, a small and whispering conversation where the trail had gone cold. They were discussing among themselves what to do. Autumn held her breath and waited.

She felt stuck again—another dead end. Another hopeless moment, no matter how hard she tried. She'd only ever fail; she'd only get caught. Holding onto the ladder like a life preserver, the drainage system was but a torrential storm at sea. The voices became hushed, a resolute end, and she waited to pay witness to her deliverance or another failed attempt. She hoped and prayed that they took any other path but hers.

She didn't open her eyes until hearing their footfalls fade away in their search. Her body convulsed from her held breath, aching at her chest, and when she was close to fainting, she gasped and inhaled deeply. She exhaled and inhaled with fast repetition until the pressure in her head lowered. The men were gone, along with all audible cues of their presence: not even their echoes reached her, and the world became silent.

She scrunched up to the service lid, her upper back and lower neck against the chilling metal that complimented the stiff pains in her spine. Her feet pressed against the tallest bar of the ladder. The metal lid made a metallic thud, opening until she could slide it off to the side, and like Heracles she emerged forth from Hades, like Buldr freed the Kingdom of Hel she made it above ground, to the fresh outside air.

She climbed out, rolling over onto her back, her weapon clambering around her arms and legs from its strap as she lay on the flat surface of the sidewalk outside. The air was fresh and rejuvenating. Cracked, weed-infested cement offered a sturdy, nearly straight surface to lie on, and it was a straightening relief to her neck and back. Her body rejoiced as she stretched. Only when her mind had settled did her throbbing aches ease. She realized that the air, despite being outside, wasn't fresh at all. She was cold and free from the confines of Sergei's domain but not from his art.

A poignant smell lingered in the air, preserved by the cold with an intoxicating hint of dewy morning and fuel. The scent of putrefaction was heavy and overpowering. She opened her eyes, seeing first the red sun rising over a dreary sky, poked at by the bare, skeletal limbs of branches rising as black silhouettes between the rotten, sinking old roofs of houses and the hunched heads of scarecrows veiled in burlap sacks.

A gap in time came to her as she was lying amidst the silent spectators lining the cul-de-sac. They were just dark silhouettes in the rising sun watching her. The wind was a low moan, wisped through the dense, dead thicket surrounding the houses. Crows cawed around her, taking up residence in the skeletal limbs of the trees.

She counted nine bodies in all, and at the center end of the rounded dead-end street were three more posts: erect, but vacant. Autumn shook in silent understanding, accepting the implications; the cards lay where they fell. She counted a total of thirteen posts, ten men from Wolf Pack, and two pilots. The last spot, unlucky thirteen, was reserved for her friend—or was it for her?

Autumn turned away from the sight to the exit of the street. In the near distance, she saw the roof of the school, barely visible over a lake of tree branches and folding roofs of houses. Crows took flight; some landed in nests that gave knuckle-like bulges to the branches. A couple of ravens passed by and disappeared in the rising sun. Its warmth basked her, in contrast to the chilling wind.

She picked up her radio, recalling that Thomas had his set to channel seven, and squeezed the PTT button. She spoke, her voice sounding hollow and vacant to her ears, drained: "Ta, Thomas?"

No response came, save for the malevolence of the Wastelands sending forth another bone-chilling gust of wind blowing southeast. Not long after, came the low grumbles and gargling breaths against the wind that were too deliberate to be some concoction of the wasteland's symphony. With such guttural breaths came the sound of metallic scraping over cement—another threat coming closer. She never knew how to appreciate the dangers outside Alyeska, believing Sergei to be the worst that the world had to offer. Now she wasn't sure; when the ground shook in slight tremors, the quivering traveled across the ground in a limping rhythm that showed in ripples forming in the puddles of rain. The tremors reverberated up the bones of her legs and to her heart.

The wind blew once more and carried off towards the direction of the growls and scraping. Then, traveling once more against the wind, the growls boiled up in a roar that tore through the air.

Chapter Three – Fox Hunting

Autumn fled from that terrible roar, deeper into the dead world, into tall grass that limited her vision. She caught herself before face-planting into the walls of houses, over creeks, and through holes in rusted fencing too tall for her to climb. She didn't stop to think and didn't remember the lessons taught to her in school. She always thought the courses added into Alyeska's curriculum were for some distant feature Military Occupational Specialty, or MOS. Too far away to be important, and if she was lucky, never to be needed: until now. Perhaps, if she had time to stop and think, she'd recall her instructors in BR-Hostile 101, and how they dealt with zombies in open areas versus tight spaces and unseen sectors.

Life at the present became a simple matter of two things: the sound of the deathless monsters giving chase and the need to survive. She would have stuck to the road, more exposed to threats, yes, but with chances of being swarmed and cornered minimized. Instead, with her thoughts spiraling out of control, her instincts regressed to basic survival mentality; she looked for the nearest path of least resistance and continued.

She didn't see the monsters but knew they were after her. The great many bare, rotten feet slapping against old asphalt crunched over leaves and snapped twigs. Scratchy cries issued forth from decayed throats in hunger pangs. Their breathing was quickened into feral panting. Then there was the big one, his footfalls like meteors rocking the earth upon impact. Tremors rippled through the ground under her boots, and his breathing reverberated through the air. He sounded calm, a pleasing rhythm to his twisted breaths that permeated over the others.

She came out amidst a thick tree line that had consumed the backyard of a row of identical houses: suburban America in its urban decay. Past that, she came into a park that served as a junction between the suburb and a trailer park occupying a hill, traveling up a steep road. A hole in the perimeter chain-link fence allotted just enough space to crawl through, and a stray link nicked her right ear at an angle. The pain flared that side of her head in an odd, focalizing way. It was like being slapped back into focus from hysteria; the burning pain and warm blood traveled down her ear and neck.

Rushing back to her feet, her hands tossed up old mulch, grass, and rocks in her wake, and she looked back to see the threats now becoming visible. Like waves of water breaking on rock, the monsters rammed into the fence, but it held.

Alarm shouted, alarmed, and turned from the horrible sight of the lifeless husks of humans, whose silvery eyes latched onto her with ravenous hunger and apathetic malice. Turning forwards, she saw an old swing set an a body decayed into a skeleton draped in raggedy old garments; the upper body twisted and tangled in the metal links of the swing, leaning forwards, with its head missing. It was being consumed by nature. Vines and weeds constricted the dangling arms and hunched legs, and she jumped aside, running in grievous disgust.

Words from Petty Officer First Class Grant, former Navy Seal, and instructor for the PT class she took, came into focus. The first memory coming to the fore was when he did his first roll call. She stood in line with her classmates, reading the list: "Autumn, Nector?" he asked, looking at her with comically quaint interest.

"Ye-yes sir." She had nodded.

"You're Thomas's protégé?" he smirked, more of a statement of interest than a question, filling her with unexpected pride. Never had she considered herself anyone's protégé. Grant continued, "I was told to give you a hard time."

Then she started to dislike the surprise she felt.

A fond memory wasn't what her thoughts led to though, merely a catalyst; from that day forward, Petty Officer First Class Grant's PT course had become more personal. Resonating more, though she wasn't gifted in strength or speed, she learned she could keep going. Especially when Grant shared the forty percent rule.

"No. Matter. What. You're. Feeling." Autumn fumbled for Grant's words with every panting breath she took. The right side of her head burned and her bleeding ear throbbed; her left leg ached, and with each gasping inhale pain stabbed her right side. Her legs flared and burned, and her eyes felt heavy.

She breached a couple more decayed houses, one with fencing, the other decimated with what looked like bullet holes and old scorch marks. Coming to a city street that took her away from the neighborhood, Dead Traffic was cluttered here and there as she weaved in and around cars, the monsters soon flooding out from the housing behind her like a violent wave.

"I. Still. Have. Sixty. Percent. Left. In. The. Tank." She was now wheezing.

In PT, when doing their daily five-kilometer jog, Petty Officer Grant would clap his hands and cheer everyone on. But he gave special praise to the less physically gifted, and she had been no exception. Quiet and overlooked by many, he had given her special praise with every wheezing kilometer she made, even if her jogging turned into a fast walk with flailing arms to keep going as she was now.

Good job Nector, keep going girl. Keep going!

Her eyes watered, and she nodded to her PT instructor despite his absence.

"Sixty," she cried, ignoring the barks and hunger howls of the zombies behind her. Another nausea fit left her in a faint spell. "...ixty,"

The road turned and led straight to the fenced-off community of a trailer park. The hill rose tall like a small mountain, a great and terrible ordeal to scale. The gates were open, barely holding on to their rails at the sides. Arms flailing to keep her momentum going, her jogging became less and less as Grant's voice echoed through her thoughts: *Good job Nector. Keep going, girl. Keep going.*

Trees were blocking from view what she looked at with heavy dread and a frustrated cry that cost her more air than she could afford. The road split and branched off, but to dead ends or scenic routes around the main stretch traveling up that terrible hill. Gravity worked against her as she made her climb.

The trailers were but a cluster of old, decrypt structures far beyond use. Sidings had fallen off the pressboard walls, and they looked like soaked sawdust. Some barely held onto the old, rusted frames of the trailer themselves; others fell, lying in dilapidated piles of rot and gave a clear view into the homes of people from long ago. Their whole lives were left in place as they were forced to move or take their chances and stay when The Calamity struck.

The spaces between were clutters of obstacles: abandoned cars, yard ornaments, outside sheds, and some trailers fortified by their owners who chose to stay. Her fast pacing was failing to keep steady. She could take deep breaths, body jerking from the side with each attempt, and she resorted to shallow breaths instead. She didn't waste the energy to look behind her at the same ravenous pursuit she had heard the whole way.

The hill peaked, and she nearly toppled over, falling in wheezing pants, each breath accompanied by a sharp pain in right her side. Sweat fell in several beads, some that followed the bone structure of her face and coming to a burn in her eyes or leaving a salty taste in her mouth. She tried to blink the tears away and get a couple of good breaths in, at least as much as she could before suffering another stabbing pain at her side.

The splashing of rotten flesh against the pavement got closer; the zombies kept a steady pace behind her and flooded up the hill. She couldn't cry because her body and mind were too tired for that. Rolling over and pushing herself up with shaking arms, her running failed and turned into jogging. Her jogging soon failed back into the same tiresome pacing. She made it twenty yards before looking back to see the zombies finish their climb up the hill.

The end of trailer park came to an end at a thick thicket of underbrush between oaks and pines. She bolted inside, and after a few moments spared another cautionary look back. Fifteen yards away, the zombies' movements strobed between the trees. Vertical figures ran horizontally and diagonally between the pines and oaks. One moment they were there, then they disappeared, and they were back again.

Now she could see the big one. He became visible in that split second of looking back: a fiend if she ever saw one, reminding her of the Fomorians from Irish Myths, sea monsters with one arm, one leg, and one eye. He had one arm, but two legs and eyes, and a mass of faded, dark gray, linen-like skin. He paced towards her with a significant limp. His right arm and shoulder were completely missing in a gory display of mangled flesh, charred muscle, and bone tissue. His left arm stretched behind him, dragging something heavy. His gaze met hers, and through the scorched stretch of flesh where an upper lip was missing, she saw him grinning.

She yelped, crying out in terror. She faced forwards, not only to see the path ahead, but to look away from the terror. A pine tree came in fast, and she jumped around it, losing some speed and momentum, and plowed into a low-hanging branch. She was met with a face full of pine needles stabbing at her flesh. Her pace slowed as she cleared the branch and nearly fell over the sheer drop of a steep slope.

Her feet anchored in place, she stared down a nearly straight drop. The muddy embankment was spiked with bushes and trees sprouting upwards. Down below, she barely caught the sight of a crumbled old road, but without much guess of how to get there.

Grant spoke to her again from her memory bank—she was running through an obstacle course. The rope climbs always gave her pause; she had a fear of heights she now felt, staring down the long, rough terrain of the drop. *Just make a decision and follow through; never freeze up!*

But she had frozen up, like she always did, ridiculing herself. Looking back at the hunting party now within ten yards of her, the fiend glared back with a lively snarl of sadistic pleasure. She saw with clarity now the heavy object being dragged with his left hand. It was a mass of twisted rebar and an 'I' beam ending in a giant cluster of reinforced cement that held a form very similar to a Nordic hammer.

She gritted her teeth, wailed out a cry of woe, and took the leap. Her fall arching downwards, almost immediately, she missed the first tree. Disappearing through a wall of green pine, she fell to another tree. This time she landed against it, her chest ramming into the trunk, her lungs bereft of air upon impact with a thudding *oof*. But her arms and legs constricted around the bark, midway up the trunk, hidden and concealed. The bark prickled and poked at her arms and face.

There, five seconds felt like they spanned thirty minutes. Taking the time to catch her breath the best she could, shallow inhales stabbed at her sides. Her hands gripped the trunk so hard, her fingertips prickled to a state of numbness. All was silent, except for the wind blowing through the trees, an eerie composition in tune with her breaths. The sound of rocks falling came as ill-met news, joining in the tune; she looked down, frozen by the bizarreness of the macabre scene below. A river of bodies, not rocks, were falling and rolling passed underneath—

human husks smashing against rock, root, and tree; the River Styx formed under her en masse. Then came the giant brute. She didn't have time to react when the Fomorian came into view, sliding straight for her tree.

Time slowed as she watched. That one second before his crude weapon broke the base of her tree felt like a minute, and the monster rammed his whole being into the weakened trunk. The fiend slipped, spun, and soon joined in the current of flowing bodies. But the damage had been done; the tree creaked and moaned.

"No! No, no, no, no!" She cried in quick succession as if her voice could enchant the tree to keep it stable. It couldn't.

The tree fell towards the hill, catching on others, and soon came into a rolling collapse down the hill with the rest of the landslide the Fomorian had made. She held to the trunk like a hamster in a ball as the branches above and below her broke in the tumbling. She was trapped in a dwindling roll cage that chipped away with each collision from rock, branch, and earth.

Her vision faded into view, seeing first the sky. A white peak soon sprouted up in her vision, swaying with her head before fading back out. Then again, and this time her eyes opened with added ease, looking at the mountain range in full, the forest rising up the mountainside. The hill to her right and the woods to her left framed her visual of the wreckage mound from the landslide, dead center under the mountain. She thought that the mound of broken trees and dead bodies bode an ominous omen towards the mountain.

Zombies lay like mortar between the rocks, mud, and trees, piled high in a mound that resembled a Wedge Tomb—burial chambers found in Ireland. The left hand of the Fomorian stuck out, like a hand from the grave reaching to a stormy night sky, fingers twitching and half-rolled in a fist.

She thought—hoped—that the slight movements of the fingers were nothing more than death twitches. She was dismayed when the movements became more intentional and deliberate as they coiled into a fist. She sat up, her back resting against the trunk of the tree that had been her roll cage, and her head fell back. Her whole being throbbed and ached as she watched the fist tighten.

Using the tree to push herself up to her feet, she held her side, tender to each breath, climbing up to a wobbly stance; her knees were jelly, and her legs were like blades of grass, easily moved in the wind.

A soft drizzle rolled over her and the wreckage, like an unrolling carpet from the sky, washing away the mud and blood from her skin. All had become silent as the Fomorian's fist weakened, a final clench before the fingers released in a motionless curl.

The cries of hunger pangs and dry, raspy growls of the undead now pierced the silence. Muffled by the rain, she glared over at the monsters crawling from the mound. Deciding she had caught enough breath, she pushed off the tree and moved around the mound of monsters in a wide pass. The threats behind her, she opened her mouth to the rain, moistening her dried throat.

Autumn sighed and looked down at herself in Lossif's large coat, the chest rig. She hadn't packed any provisions, nor did she have anything with which to collect rainwater. Sudden realization came to her in a feeling of self inadequacy, Autumn felt as if she was in over her head.

She looked to the white summit of Pikes Peak. The Inca Society held a certain belief for such awe-striking features of nature, one she now felt applied to how the mountains made her feel. Apus, the Inca would call them, the personification of nature as deities. Then and there, she understood how people could feel inclined to such beliefs. It was awe-inspiring and epic in proportion, just like the mountains back home. It made her feel small and perhaps, worst of all, lost.

Fatigue gripped her, and all else faded into the background. She stole away her thoughts of the Apu and how it poisoned her self-image, correcting the wrongs she accused herself of when staring at the force of nature. Yes, she was lost, indeed, but not in a sense of her self-image. She was directionally challenged. The Apu itself was now like a lighthouse, guiding her to her objective and contradicting the poisoning it gave her.

Autumn continued down the long, dark road, cold and wet as the rain became heavier.

Chapter Four – The Woods

Whether by providence or perdition, she found herself staring at the visitor center of Garden of the Gods. The rain fell in a steady drizzle, the cold wind making her shiver, and she crept up to the side entrance of the building. How many nights ago had it been since Wolf Pack had hunkered down in the building? A week? More than that? It was the last place she had seen Lossif alive, when he ordered Demitri and Michail to take her back to the helicopter. Her hand fell over the embroidered name of the coat as the side entrance drew nearer.

The sky's dismal beige-green color stood over a veil of fog spanning far out, hiding everything except for the visitor center and the mountains beyond. Storm clouds rolled over the edge of the peaks in an avalanche of water and ice crystals. Pikes Peak gloomed through the thickening coverage, an Apu of storms, casting down its malice upon her: a lonely tugboat lost at sea.

She pressed open the side doors, the very same ones Demitri and Michail had taken her through. Her arms folded over her chest, holding herself tightly to prevent any body heat from escaping. Her weapon dangled down from its sling at her sides. Flat *thuds* from her boots landed on the dusty tile floor. All was still inside; gray light illuminated the wall of glass panels around a small food and café court that was straight ahead.

Her boots came to a *thunking* stop, standing where she had last seen Lossif. Her breath fell silent at the sight of something that had not been there before: crimson-brown splattered over the door had dried in a puddle on the floor. A trail of it stretched under and out the door.

In her mind, she saw Sergei drag the man's body out into the storm. She didn't cry, didn't speak, only confirmed her theory of the man's fate and simply mourned in silence.

Outside the glass panel of the door, the drizzle increased, and thunder rolled in the distance. The old structure creaked from the barrage of the storm, holding its ground. Her BR-Hostiles 101 course had taught her that the rain typically forced the monsters into shelter themselves. She reached out and closed the doors at sudden speed, alarmed by the idea that her shelter may just be one of them.

She turned around and looked back at the darkness of the first floor; there was only a bit of light offered from the front doors down a corner. From up the stairs, she came. Her fingers matched her breath in shakiness, and she found her weapon and raised it. Towards the end of the barrel, mounted on the side, was a flashlight, and she turned on the light. The weapon's stock was now snugged against her left shoulder, barrel raised with the light splashing a circle of bright white contrasting with the black dark; periphery light rippled off into the ambient lighting of the dark interior.

Phil jolted awake at a crackling score of thunder. Eyes opened wide from the bright flash of lightning that split open the darkness, the sensation of sitting up brought on a wave of disorientation, his belly waking with a gagging urge. He looked out the window and outside, and he saw the rain coming in sheets, lightning flickered in an endless bombardment across the sky, illuminating for quick milliseconds the devastation of Colorado Springs in the distance.

A flickering lightbulb over a corpse, came a thought he didn't recognize.

Thunder rumbled and rolled in the distance while clapping and crackling nearby. Lightning flickered in the night like bombardment from artillery shells. A dissociating spell swooned him, disconnecting him from himself, as if Phil Shurlan was but a thin layer of cotton laid over the shell of his body. He was a garment that was now being undressed and separated; he still had control over his motor functions. The commands over his body felt stretched, such as how he moved his hand to his forehead: the order took longer than usual to travel from his mind to his limb. When his hand finally contacted his forehead, he detected the still-present fever.

The dissociating spell he felt was the worst of the two; the fevers he could deal with, and he understand what brought them about. He didn't understand the dissociating spells, however, and they troubled him a great deal, being enigmatic to him. That feeling of disconnection was more than just a "thinning" or "stretchiness." Such feelings were common enough despite the surreal distractions they could be. Lately, the spells had worsened; he would wake up in the middle of the street outside their home in Alyeska or forget simple details of Phil Shurlan, such as his date of birth or the names of those he loved. It was like he was staring off into the vacuum of space, floating in a drift like a speck of dust in the air. All meaning, wants, needs, and desires became faint echoes of before, and sometimes he felt as if something deep inside that vacuum of nothingness was staring back at him.

Such spells were becoming more and more familiar, regular even. A dissonance in his head sounded like a chorus of baritones humming that echoed down a long tunnel. His right hand would go numb. Most of the time, when he was in such a state of mind, he was accompanied by a sensation of falling backwards into the coming blackout. These "dissonances" heralded the coming absence of consciousness.

Sometimes, he would be spared from blacking out, and now was one such moment. The spell passed, leaving his thoughts cold and empty. But the bodily sickness still ran its course. His stomach convulsed, sinking inwards as his head jerked forwards. Rolling off the bed in time to wretch on the floor, he fell on all fours and puked. The heaves continued, even when his stomach was completely vacant.

Only when his panic ceased and he could hold back the convulsions did he register his side flaring. His knuckles turned white upon clenching his fists. Tears made an involuntary presence, with a fresh layer of sweat that chilled his skin as the cold outside air ingressed through the cracks and holes in the wall. Every part of him shook, from fingers and arms to knees and insides. Climbing up to his feet, he leaned on the wall like a crutch and limped over to the teacher's desk.

"Autumn," he called out in a dry rasp ending in a cough. Working some spit into his mouth, he paused with an ensuing gagging spell that threatened to return. "Jade?"

Silence followed.

His maps were gone, and in their place was a sheet of paper addressed to him. He picked it up and felt nausea in his belly rumbling into a near eruption up his throat; he tasted bile at the back of his tongue, and his heart was in fifth gear, beating in his chest, primed and ready for the coming stress of discharge. He read the note: *Pushing the objective, as you'd say. Stay and rest. I'll be back.*

Ooxo – Autumn

The vomit shot out, and he fell over his knees, puke falling in a steamy mess over the mush of ceiling tiles. His breathing was deep and heavy as he craned his head sideways, over the sandbags and out the window; the Wastelands outside were now one great haystack spanning the horizon in the ruins of the Old World. His eyes followed the line of jagged silhouetted peak's that reminded him of the bottom mouthpiece to Sergei's mask. A shimmer traveled up his spine.

Somewhere out there, Autumn was by herself; the poor kid couldn't find her way around her school without help. Worse than that were the threats. He knew her schooling, more military school than anything, had taught her, by verbal means, how to deal with zombies. But she hadn't the exposure to such acts to season her instincts away from hesitation to the violence of action without pause.

The dissociating spell still lingered. From the person of Phil Shurlan, one aspect of his being remained while all else faded into echoes. In this "separateness," he felt that single remaining aspect floated in a sea of nothingness with him as he stared into the void, and it evolved from top priority to the single meaning of his life: the girl's well-being.

His radio was still on the desk. Taking it and limping over to the sandbags before the glass, he looked back out the window to the ruins of waste under an explosive storm. Favoring his right side, his thumb pushed the PTT button: "J... Jade."

The visitor center was empty of threats. The doors she had passed were barred down, and with the rain, she felt reasonably isolated from any threats. Save for the madman. The only other presence was the rodents scurrying about. But they didn't bother her; she honestly found them cute. Her uncle would say she was "weird like that, but a good weird."

Now she lay curled in a fetal position under a bench. No thought of Thor, Zeus, or any mythical association with the storm provoked a captive imagination as they'd used to. For now, she discovered that the storm had provoked other workings in her mind, things that weren't there before: new additions that reduced her to the pitiful state of sobbing and cradling herself.

Lightning flashed, and she recalled the night of Sergei's slaughter in rapid succession. She was back in the mud, under the weight of Demitri who was riddled with bullets and dying upon her. His blood seeped onto her skin and into the clothes she still wore. With the clapping thunder, she heard the bullets *CRACKING* over her through the rain.

Her hands departed from her vain efforts at comfort—clasping at her ears as if to shut out the sounds. But they were internal, loud as they had been the night of the slaughter. Lightning flashed again, brightening her vision behind closed eyelids. She saw Michail wrestling with the psycho, Demitri trying to get his pistol out, and choking in his own blood.

Tears soaked and pooled around her face, which was pressed to the floor. She wished it all would stop as she shivered in the cold; the nervous highs the thunder brought wouldn't lower but were held in place by the persistent hell storm—waiting to bring her to greater heights of sobbing with the next clap of thunder.

Every clap brought memories of that night in a scene-by-scene loop, ravishing her mind without room for rest or calm. She would find no peace or respite, and she fell into hysterics when the looping memories brought her right back to the two butchered pilots inside that blood-soaked helicopter. Uranus showered Gaea, the earth, not with rain, but blood; Thor gutted a Jotnar in the sky over them.

She whimpered for it all to end, and at the brink of her panic, she cried out in one exhausted plea, "Please, God." She supposed the storm drowned out her prayers to an entity she didn't believe in. Another clap of thunder ravished the old windows of the visitor center with a violent rattling that reverberated her memories.

No, please no.

The next thing to come, heralded by the very thought of his name, was Sergei. He grabbed her by her hair and neck, shushing her, mumbling his cryptic speech of scarecrows while holding that crooked scythe. Then Igor arrived, and in a fruitless effort of rescue, she was knocked out. With the ensuing thunderclap, the night replayed once more, looping her in an endless hell.

"Please," she cried, sniveling and sniffing with each choking sob. But the storm wouldn't listen, yielding her not a moment's respite.

Her hands remained over her ears to muffle out what she could. If God wouldn't listen, nor Uranus, perhaps her pleas could reach someone else.

"Please, Phil." But he wouldn't arrive; she was alone left to drown.

Whether by some act of providence, or just straight coincidence, like a hand reaching down to pull her up out of the waters, her radio cracked. The transmission was choppy, contesting with the static for dominance, but at the end of the brief struggle, her friend's vocals won out. The sound of his voice was an answer to her prayers, a lifeline she desperately latched onto. She freed her hands from her ears, opened her eyes, and looked across the floor to her chest rig; she had taken it off and left it on a table. Her radio spoke peace, shalom, to her.

"J… Jade."

"Pha, Phi, Phil. Phil," she replied, waiting for a response that didn't come. "Phil?" she uttered again.

She hadn't picked up the radio and keyed the PTT button. Instead, she spoke out to the device like it was a conduit for speaking with the dead. She crawled out from under the bench, leaving the safety of the shelter it offered her, and she raced for the radio. Sliding down onto a chair, bringing two legs off the floor, she teetered to fall. She used her leg opposite for a kickstand and brought it down to all fours. Her hands hadn't waited for balance. She took the radio and squeezed tight the PTT button.

"Phil!?" she cried out, tapping her feet in her wait.

"I'm here, kiddo," Phil's voice panted back. He was tired and in pain.

"I'm sorry," she exhaled, "I thought I could do it, make it there and back. I really did but… I'm scared."

"I know, I know. So am I." His voice cracked, actually cracked, which she never thought could happen. It cracked just once and would have been easy to miss, but she had caught it, and she heard his fear: "What's your sit-rep?" the calm collectiveness of his normal-self returned, weighed under the duress of his illness.

"What?"

"Situation report."

Her stomach growled and contracted in a painful reminder that she hadn't packed any food from Sergei's plunder. Tapping the radio on her head endlessly, she did not realize she had jammed the line by keeping the button down.

"I'm okay," she replied, "Umm…hurting... no food or water. But I'm okay."

"Anything requiring immediate aid? Head concussions, arterial bleeding, difficulty breathing?"

"No, just bruised, scrapped. Cold." She shrugged at that last one; she was freezing, really.

"What's your location?"

"You should know better by now; I don't know. I'm in a visitor center at Garden of the Gods, but I don't know where that's at."

"But I do. See? I know where to find you." There was praise in his voice, bringing back hints of the pride she felt before. "Listen, the storm doesn't look like it's letting up. Keep your head down and if night falls, for the love of God, do not go outside. Wait there until morning. At first light, I'm on my way."

"Can't you come now? Please?"

"Jade, listen to me. I want to, God knows I do. But I'm in no condition to fight, and if the storm lets up and the monsters leave their shelter then I'll have more than I can handle and won't be able to reach you. Do you understand?"

She leaned into her radio, a quick sob escaped her lips as she nodded, and with a whimper replied "yes."

She leaned her elbows on the table, wondering if she could wait that long. The silent darkness of the visitor center, the storm, her nightmares, all of it…she didn't want to be alone. It was odd to her that in his voice alone she found anchoring sanity from it all. She didn't want the sound of his voice to leave her.

"Will you stay on the radio with me?" she asked, knowing the answer. Her battery wouldn't last forever, and she didn't know the charge level. It was a luxury to have a powered radio, and she couldn't be excessive with it. Still she hoped to hear his "yes."

"I'll check in on the hour, but we'll have to conserve the batteries. I'm sorry."

"Thank you," she replied, looking out at the storm. A flash lit up the world outside through the windows. Two seconds later, thunder cracked, rattling the glass and scratching at her thoughts again. A tear escaped her right eye, and she flinched, looking away from the glass.

Phil clipped his radio to his belt, holding his side and wincing as he walked. Stopping every other step to catch his breath, he smiled when he came to the sight of a haphazard barricade the kid sat up at the door. Moving the obstructions one at a time and opening the door, he found another barricade on the outside of the door. The kid wasn't as helpless as she thought she was; she never gave herself enough credit, and neither did anyone else, including him.

The barricade didn't change anything; one secured room in a large building wasn't good enough. He would have loved to have several squads of soldiers with him, keeping sectors secured, holding down sections until the whole place was swept and made safe. But one-man clearing was the name of the game.

He had only his revolver now, and the last of his six rounds were loaded in. Before, he had 18; six had been emptied into Inimicus, but he recalled none of that. His memories were a garbled mess after leaving Garden of the Gods with Dakota unconscious and Tim behind the wheel. It was all blank, until waking up on that dank basement floor with Sergei standing over him. After that, it had been waking up in the sped room, with blurs here and there—fragmented memories of scavenging, hunting, and distilling water.

Taking in a deep breath and releasing it in a sigh, he couldn't think about the last several days. It was a rabbit hole of madness he'd sort through later. For now, they needed a safe place to come back to. Shut in from the storm, it was all he could do; the night also factored in.

Left hand reaching into his pocket, he retrieved a dusty old lighter. Unsure how it had gotten there, he flicked it several times before getting a warming glow that offered a three-foot visual around him.

God, thank you for small favors, he prayed, grateful for something, and he started down the long dark of the hall.

Moving along with the warm flame to keep him in the light, he felt consumed by a different dimension. Being consumed in darkness and prowling around in silence remained a guilty pleasure. The black darkness invigorated him with new strength. *An odd trick of the mind?* He didn't know, but the added pleasure of it helped to shoulder the fatigue and sickness that chipped at him.

He hated how much he loved the high of it, of creeping and moving about like a phantom in the decrepit halls of a decayed building. Moving about the shadows and darkness was akin to feeding table scraps to the things he kept repressed. Demons rattled in their cages; dogs could only be content with scraps for so long.

He mumbled "Cluj-Napoca," hoping guilt would keep him level, but every time he tried to shame himself, he only felt his clenched fists shake his right hand numb, with bare signals of a crippling pain deep in the bones of his forehand. A heat came over him—not the heat of the sickness he was plagued with. It was the sickness of his soul: hatred, a seething loathing that, unlike the table scraps, fed the caged demons now rattling recklessly within.

One of his fragmented memories since—well, he didn't know how long it had been since—the GFOABs wrecked his memory, waking from a state of sleepwalking. Scavenging around the ruins of Colorado Springs, for what he didn't know, he came to the sight of a Mil-Mi, that Russian helicopter, landing in the GFOABs crater. He was lying on his belly over the crest of the crater's edge and looking through his binos, seeing the men of Wolf Pack and Autumn disembark the bird.

Now, remembering the events that transpired in Romania didn't burden him with guilt after seeing those men—those monsters. No, guilt wouldn't consume him and keep him grounded; it was hate that consumed him, a spiraling whip of flame that blinded all else. Neither Tim nor Dakota were there to keep him grounded when guilt failed to anchor him from the darkness that called to him; now he found the absence of guilt feeding it.

Room to room, bathroom to bathroom, every nook and cranny: he searched and cleared without a second's rest. By the time nightfall came, it seemed all but inevitable that the darkness would bleed through him to that within. It was as if the good man he had tried to be—the husband to his dear Sarah, the father to his baby boy, and the eventual God-fearing man—was now but a piece of cotton, and black blood bled through the fabric, outside and in.

The building was empty, and, along the way, he found the woodshop. From the plunder of Wolf Pack, he took up Igor's AK-12. It came equipped with a fore-grip and tactical LED mounted on the side rail and a red dot laser on the other. With the new weapon came a sense of comfort, and by the end of scouring the entire school, he found the points of egress and ingress secured.

On his way back to the sped room, he passed through the courtyard. The trees made a canopy over the cracked path, shielding him from the rain. Midway through, he stopped and looked around. There came to his nostrils a familiar scent, one he first encountered recently, and it gave him pause. The ground was veiled by a vaporous fog, lingering just below his knees, transparent and thickening as if just recently bellowing up. There was so much that he could see points where the fog was thickening.

The veil rose upwards from certain weeds in the tall grass, nearer to the cracked cement walkway leading across the courtyard to the building's western half. He thought it looked like bitter lettuce, or wild lettuce, as others called it, a weed with lance-shaped petals and long, very fine-toothed ridges traveling down each. But this was larger than the wild lettuce he was familiar with.

The scent came from the vapor, coming from the plant. A second passed, and he recalled the scent he recognized before. The first and last time he smelled it had been in the White River Forest, where he had first met Sergei. At the same time, the unpleasant aroma seemed to ease his labored breathing; there was a calming that came with it—one of the medicinal uses of wild lettuce.

With that ease, Phil felt the pull to the darkness stop as if it hadn't been there at all. No longer pulled between Phil the Butcher and Phil the Christian, he was solid of mind, like a train bursting through a tunnel and into the light of day; that distinct feeling came with only one other he had recently experienced.

Phil leaned into Igor's rifle, not using the LED light lest he give himself away, and he listened to the silence: wind, grass rustling, his breath, the soles of his boots moving over the crumbling path. There was no other disturbance in the lulling melody he heard.

He thought of Sergei and the night they met: how when he had first met the madman, he faded back into the darkness of the forest. Those two silvery eyes pierced through the dark black holes between two trees and the mask was no longer visible. He often felt like fading into his darkness, like an animal caught in a bog and unable to escape.

Moonlight cleared the clouds above, and just for a second, illuminated more of the courtyard, creating a glimmer when it touched the wedding band on his finger. Memories of Sarah wrestled with his focus.

He remembered coming back home from his six months in Romania, not as Special Forces 10th Group, Engineer Sergeant Phil Shurlan, but as CIA SOG Operative Gabriel Albescu. Sarah found him at a grocery store with the bulge of her pregnant belly. Six months before that, he had set off for Romania for the second time in his life. They went out for coffee later that day, where Sarah had promised it was his, and she said she had been on the lookout for him ever since she found out. She sat across from him, teacup in clenched hands, her bright blue eyes that were nearly gray, stressed. They were so beautiful he could get lost in them, and he felt genuine joy overtake him.

One DNA test and three months of courting later, and the two were due to be wed. The night before their wedding, lying in each other's naked warmth, he had confided everything to Sarah: the shattered mess he had become in Romania, broken glass barely held together. His head was cradled in her bare chest as she held him to keep him from falling apart. She had accepted the monster inside him, the monster he came home as. But from that night on, for the sake of his newfound family and his little Benjamin, he vowed, "I promise," to Sarah: he would never go back to being that monster again.

The memories wouldn't stop there, and they overtook him. He cupped his hand over his mouth, slowly lowering to his knees, and the warm air of his nostrils blew against his index finger and over the knuckles of his hand. Tears were building that he refused to let loose lest he became completely compromised.

"I'm sorry." he sighed, collecting his pieces. There was no more Sarah, Benjamin, Tim, or Dakota to hold him together; he was now a shattered mosaic of glass art held together by scotch tape.

His words reached out in the fogged air, reaching out to Sarah and to Ben in the unseen beyond. His thoughts moved to Autumn, out there by herself with monsters, and Igor, unaccounted for. He had made a promise to the kid as well, words he now felt forming a new divide within him: *I'll get you home. Whatever the cost.*

"I'm sorry," he said again, his breath now calmed, his old promises fading into silence. The old him sunk further into that bog.

He stood up, not noticing the two silvery eyes piercing the brush and tall grass before him. Instantly, he raised his rifle to the high ready, finger on the trigger, until the godforsaken mask emerged from the wild; Phil's feet moved to a stable shooting position over the concrete path. Sergei came forth from the woods.

Phil didn't shoot; it brought no good the first time they met before. Instead, he waited as Sergei stepped out of the thickness, this time dressed in a red and black checkered flannel like his, under a pair of coveralls. The noose still hung around his neck. Sergei's demeanor had a lack of animosity this time.

"What do you want?" Phil demanded.

Sergei remained still, facing him. The man's labored breathing was his only movement. Phil's finger now itched to pull the trigger: if not for effect on the target, then just for the sensation of shooting at the man.

"No scythe?" Phil mocked, but he was met with only silence between the madman's labored breaths. "Why am I still here when you promised to kill me? Why did you drag that kid into this mess?"

Sergei took in a deeper breath this time, and, as it deflated into a vapor out of the jagged line of his mouthpiece, an odd thought came as fast as it went: the slopes of the mouthpiece resembled a mountain range between the sinews that held the bottom to the top.

Then a response issued forth in that bloodied, hoarsened voice, through the mouthpiece. Sergei broke his silence: "Te Rog Philip." Those silver pupils were cold as the night and lifeless as the undead, stabbing Phil's. "I may not kill you. But you, you will kill me, and once you have, Phil, then you will kill yourself."

Great, I got a fuckin' poet on my hands. Phil shook his head, "Why don't you just go ahead and die then, fucker, and leave that girl be."

"There's no outrunning this, Philip." Sergei shook his head slowly from right to left, the way people shook their heads in Romania. Typically, in America, Phil noted that most people went from the left to the right at the start; the inverse was the norm in Romania, adding to his suspicions of Sergei's nationality and, by proxy, why the man was hostile.

The hourly checkup on Autumn was coming, but Phil was stuck between a rock and a hard place, unable to take his gaze away from the madman. He kept his eyes trained on Sergei, watching as the man stepped back into the underbrush, into the thickness of nature, wild and uncouth. The dissonance in his head was fading, but the splitting returned. Those baritones faded out as the prowling sensations came back in full.

With a parting word, Sergei replied in a low whisper, like a puff of wind escaping out through the trees, "Break the Silence, Philip. Or it will come to break you."

Chapter Five – Capture and Release

-October 23rd, 2030-

Lossif's coat covered her like a blanket, from shoulder to thigh. The world was quiet in the sound of her breathing and the calm force of the wind—the lingering breath of the storm. She crawled out from under the bench, the floor like a sheet of ice under her palms. Her inhales were chomped by jittering teeth, and her exhales wisped into the air like smoke. In all haste, she slipped her arms through the coat sleeves and zipped it up where she could feel the metal zipper pinch at her neck.

The wall of glass panels was coated with frost, and with a rolled-up portion of the coat sleeve clenched in her hand, she cleared a peephole. It wasn't sunrise yet but the beginning hours of morning twilight. The sky was thick with layers of clouds, varying shades of gray contesting with one another and completely blotching out the sun's warmth. Trees stretched westward in deep green. It was as if gray and green were the only colors in the world, contrasting with one another with the gloom of the mountains as mediator.

She rubbed some warmth back into her arms, suddenly realizing all the missed checks-ins from Phil. Rushing back to the bench, she found the device next to where she had previously laid it. She snatched the device and pressed the PTT button, holding it to her face.

"Phil? Hello?"

Seconds passed in agonizing ticks of mental clocks that felt like minutes. The line cracked and static vibrated forth; Phil came back with the warm comfort of his voice calming her nerves.

"Kid." The line went dead, and she pictured him holding his radio to his forehead. "You gave me a scare. Is everything alright?"

"Sorry, I just dozed off."

"I figured as much. I'm prepping right now; sit tight, okay. I'm on my way right now."

Just like the tree stump. She smiled faintly, looking around at the visitor center while stepping over to her gear, sliding her arms through the holes of the chest rig and zipping it up, then into the sling for her weapon. Turning away as she patted her Leatherman, she made for the glass panel set in the frame of a door, rubbing another peephole through the frost. Over Garden of the Gods, she saw a trailhead down below, and the white crest of Pikes Peak, still an ominous finish line.

Autumn raised the radio back to her lips: "Do you know how long you'll be?"

"I don't know, a few hours. From there, we should make it to the peak by sundown if all goes well."

But there was a rule she had been taught, one that Phil, or Thomas at the time, had shared with her long ago. He had shared the story of him, his brother, and his sister's encounter with a monster called Jackle a decade prior. Every collision with the monstrous brute was a gamble of survival, evasion, resistance, and escape. He had come to a lifesaving conclusion, "the rule of life in the Wastelands" he had called it: "Pray for the best and always assume the worst-case scenario."

The question she had, one she knew he'd have the answer to, came to her lips: "What is the worst-case scenario now?" Her finger touched the PTT button but didn't get the chance to press it. Through the peephole in the frost, she was given her answer.

She felt the tremors heralding the arrival of the Fomorian, and the shakes from his steps reverberated across the floor. The wind carried his low growl through the cracks of the glass and frames, sounding like the rattling of chains. She might have frozen in place, paralyzed at the sight of the one-armed Behemoth, yet she didn't; instinct took over, and she fell from the sight of the monster, the expanse of the balcony concealing her.

"Phil! He's back." A tear escaped her eye, her voice shook, and her body tremored from the cold and fear.

"Sergei?" His transmission was an immediate response. "Are you still in the visitor center?"

"No and yes." She dared to look up, peering up the glass until the faded edge of the balcony's railing gave way to a blurry mass of black malice. "He's bigger."

"Does he have skin?"

She thought about the stories she heard of the Jackle, the picture her mind gave of such a monster without skin. Phil's question hammered her hard. *No, why would he ask that... Oh God, that one's here, too?* The dots connected, and her bottom lip quivered. She shook her head as if Phil was right there to see it. "No, the one with one arm."

"Listen to me, and listen good. The bigger ones have incredible sensory systems. The one-armed bugger is faster and more intellectual. The skinless one is stronger, with a superior sensory system. Either way, the storm would've washed away any scent for them to locate you. He's probably tracked you that far. Stay hidden and wait for him to pass."

And if he doesn't? she wanted to ask, but she bit her tongue and followed his instructions. "Phil. Please tell me you're close."

"I'm working on it. Just lay low."

She found a corner, giving a good enough view northwest by keeping the Garden, Pikes Peak, and the Fomorian all in her field of view. She could see the thick brush and spotted trees shaking and swaying in the wind. The corner was in the shadows, covering her. The black attire acted now like camouflage, and she waited and watched.

The cawing of crows could be heard, and a raven landed on the balcony's edge. It was a carrion bird of intellect among the myths she so loved. Now, the bird was like a slap to the face from some unseen force: Heraldry of the Fomorian, a monster of death and intellect.

She waited, holding her breath for as long as she could manage, and vented in slow, measured disturbances of the silence. Pressing her radio to her chest, she muffled any future transmissions from her friend. She dared not cut off the comfort of her friend's voice, and she did not want to create too much movement by turning down the volume. She waited and watched the fiend cross the furthest edge of the parking lot. Stopping at an old Ram, he fell to a knee as if to catch his breath. His crude Nordic hammer was now like a cane he leaned on to keep upright, and light pulsed through his body.

She looked, enraptured by the sudden glow of light traversing under his skin. Then, interrupted by the shattering of glass that stabbed all through the air and echoed all inside the building, her hard-fought silence was broken in a cry. There was only enough time for her to slip her radio into a pouch when the intruder's footfalls came in violent clashes up the stairs. Her hands searched without the support of her eyes to guide them. Her sight was glued to the top of the stairs where a figure emerged, a zombie unlike the wraiths and draugrs from before. His skin was like black granite, not black from melanin.

From school, she knew the zombie to be the worst of the known breeds—a satyr. The dark exterior was a shell of dead skin that had long since molded over and calloused into a thick exterior. Bony claws for fingers were snipping like razors when the satyr's eyes locked with hers. The zombie was once a woman, whose dead, silvery pupils pierced the deathly cloud over her corneas. Like headlights lancing through dense fog, the UF-Radiation kept her pupils active and alert.

Autumn broke into a run, reaching the north, or west, exit, bursting out the door into the parking lot. The satyr's violent clashes followed her in feral pursuit; it was in all cases akin to a wild beast, uncouth and savage. Autumn had the advantage of a head start, but as with most cases, the monster was faster. By the time she reached the door and slammed it shut, the satyr rammed into it, throwing her face forwards down a handicapped ramp.

The instinct to flee took over, and, following the momentum, she rolled back to her feet. The ramp had a waist-high red wall lining it, giving her a gradually descending overview of the Fomorian now staring at her. The fiend's charred gingival tissue, exposed from a missing upper lip and salivating bottom lip, grinned at her. His tongue licked at his bottom lip, then over the gums of his upper teeth.

The satyr was making leaps behind her, closing the distance fast. The Fomorian thrashed his way through the old rotting cars as though wading against a river current to intersect her.

Autumn reached the parking lot in time, hearing the zombie's footfalls change in rhythm, a predator about to pounce. She dived over the nearest car, a sedan's hood that was just low enough for her dive. She heard the satyrs leap and leapt over the hood, it was still wet and slick allowing her to slid over and across. Without looking, Autumn heard the Satyrs subsequent ramming into the car bumper.

The trailhead to the Garden was dead ahead, and only one car, a two-seater convertible, now separated her from the trail. She dared a leap over the hood, her left boot catching, while somewhere along the way she felt a snip at the back of her right boot. She suddenly feared her Achilles tendon being lashed open. Her right leg missed its mark, her left slipped, and her chest pummeled the hood. Within seconds, the satyr was pulling at her right leg, teeth cutting through her pant leg and digging into her flesh. Her fingers found nothing but the smooth surface of rusted metal to latch onto, fingernails dragging fresh imprints through the decaying metal hood as the satyr continued to pull her off the car.

She screamed as she felt teeth like dozens of serrated razors dig into her lower calf where she had scraped it over the drain the day before. She kicked with her leg, the satyr's breath puffing against her pant leg before it pulled at her flesh, which was caught between its jaws. Giving up her fruitless efforts, her hands went from the hood to her primary; she aimed her gun at the monster and fired. The bullets just bounced off its skin, ricocheting elsewhere.

The car disappeared under her, and she fell in a hard thud on the pavement below. Her head struck the ground, leaving her in a dazed state that blocked out the pain—until the monster's bite dug in deeper and pulled harder. She could feel a chunk of her flesh begin to tear, and she cried out at the inevitable. The ground quaked in jealous tremors.

The satyr released her leg. She was filled with relief as her calf burned and blood soaked through her pant leg. The monster reeled back like a cat about to pounce. Its teeth were poised, fresh blood dripping off them in a twisted sneer. Then, just as the monster leapt forward, it fell. It was as if a hole had opened and the earth swallowed it. The giant mass of the Fomorian's hammer came crashing down in a thunderbolt of fury. The Satyr was flattened under the strike in an instant kill that puffed dust in all directions, contaminating the air Autumn breathed.

She coughed as the dust scratched her throat; she used her sleeve to filter the air, her eyes locked with the Fomorian's.

"PHEL." His voice shook the air between them, his breath smelling of putrefaction and rot. "WANT PHEL."

It speaks. It freakin' speaks!

She got up, and the added pressure on her leg almost made her topple. Unable to run at her fullest, she limped instead as she dove back onto the hood, where her fingernails left lasting trails through the rusted surface. Clambering and flailing her limbs, she crossed it before the hammer came down again over the old engine block. She landed in a hard bounce, whimpering a single cry as she bounced and rolled.

Forty percent, she drilled herself, gasping for air. *Forty percent.* Tears streamed down her face as she fled straight to the trailhead and into the Garden.

Running with a limp, her pace was more like a fast jog now. Looking behind her now and again, she saw the brute following at a seemingly leisurely pace—a cat playing with the mouse before eating it. She couldn't cry anymore; her nerves were shot to hell and back. All that was left was the will to survive, and she feared her only ability—endurance—wouldn't see her through. Not when the monster's limping pursuit was faster than hers.

Sweat fell down her cheeks, forehead, and neck like rain, salt stinging her eyes and parching her mouth. Her throat ached.

She came to a site along the trail with a sign that read, 'Siamese Twins,' but all she saw were two vacant scarecrow posts with dried blood staining the wood. A mass of shattered stone and rubble and bullet casings covered the area. Here, her left leg finally gave out, bringing Autumn to an instant stop. She dropped mid-sprint to her hands and knees over a large stone, Panting as she felt the steady quakes of the Fomorian's approach—it was closing the distance and stopped not ten feet away. She rolled over onto her back, staring at the fiend, perched on her elbows as he stared back.

The Fomorian's look of pleasure transitioned to a scowl, a look that to her said he was disappointed. He took in a heavy intake of air, with no signs of fatigue, releasing his displeasure in a large smoke plume of CO_2 that dissipated above him.

Autumn was met again with the same feeling of helplessness as when Sergei slaughtered Wolf Pack. She hadn't given up, but her legs wouldn't obey her decree. So, it was no different to her, not any different from when she had failed to escape Sergei. At every turn, she felt her efforts would always fail; she would never measure up, even when Phil needed her the most. She shook her head to rid her eyes of the tears, but she couldn't stop her bottom lip from quivering.

The one-armed fiend took a step closer, and she picked up her radio. "Phil!" her cry screeched, passing through the radio and up to the heavens.

"Hang in there; I'm coming." Phil's voice returned, mid-breath, as if running. A gush of wind followed from his line, drowning out his voice.

"I'm sorry, Phil." she cried, "I tried."

"No. No, don't talk like that." There was recognition in his tone, an understanding giving a shaken desperation to his stern tone.

The Fomorian closed in and dropped his hammer with a quaking thud; the shaft stood taller than her height. Everything would always be greater than she was, too much for her to handle. She cried, hating herself, and thought maybe it was for the best. Phil could get further without having to look out for her; certainly, it would be easier to keep oneself alive than the self and a liability.

His left hand reached down and gently pushed against her chest. Her elbows instantly gave out under the force of the monster, and her back flattened against the stone. She rolled to her right, attempting to run again, but his hand grabbed her and rolled her back into place. His fingers latched over her chest, shoulders, and sides like a harness, keeping her still. Panting and wheezing, she watched as the fiend stood back straight, his one arm latching around his hammer. He hefted it towards the heavens.

"DIE NUW." His voice was deep like distant thunder that made her spine shake. The heavy weight of his foot kept her still, too much for her to resist.

Then, in the distance, easy enough to miss if not telegraphed by the wind, there was a loud *POP* that brought pause to the fiend. Even the wind itself seemed to stall to a still. The monster lowered his hammer and turned his left side was facing her, and she could see what had Stilled time. The world gave pause, even evil, to the self-sacrificial rise of a single bright red flare that reached the heavens. The red flaming dot sailed vertically to its limits before beginning a slow descent, floating in pulses of red, transparent light over a school building barely visible over the trees.

Inimicus stood there, torn between his options. That red flare, he was positive, came from his prized prey's location. He wanted that high of a hunt made complete, the trophy of his prey. It was his, and yet as he looked at the flare, he could only assume the other one, skinless with a hook for a hand, would see it, too—would beat him to his prey and take what was his.

The "Little One" at his feet offered some amusement, but at the end of the day she was much like fowl game—distant memories from his old life, long since gone in a mangled mush. He recalled what pleasure small game hunts offered and what satisfaction came with hunting bigger game. She wasn't a predator; she was prey. What he needed was to hunt for another predator. After all, when it came to eating, what was an appetizer to the main dish?

Looking down at the Little One, a new idea came to him, instilling the seeds of anticipation. Let her live and let her have one hell of a head start. Then, after collecting his prized prey, he could enjoy the dessert of a leisure hunt to celebrate. Why not get more out of her than one simple high of slaughter? She was already done; finding her again would be easy and fun. Her suffering, by then, would be prolonged. There was something about pain and fear in prey's blood that made it more delectable. He found meaning in that, longing anticipation as his mouth salivated. He wanted her now; he was hungry, and those hordes of monstrous doubles that looked like the easy prey—only they too ate the easy prey—weren't tasty, to say the least. Against the needs of his stomach, Inimicus took another step away from her.

He dropped his hammer, the giant cluster of debris and metal pummeling the ground between her legs. She jumped back, a shaken cat, as he reached down and picked her up by the leg that was bleeding. She cried and struggled as he lifted her until her upside-down head, framed by her dangling hair, was now facing him. He was inches from her face and she looked away, wincing and shielding her head with her arms. He could feel the blood from her calf travel down his wrist and arm. His eyes rolled up and he grinned in pleasure as her blood rolled down into his left armpit.

Soon, he'd be soaking in the blood of all his game. Patience would marinate the whole experience in true ecstasy.

"SOON."

Anticipation was already building up into a moan of excitement as he licked the space between them. Her fear and pain added flavor to the cold air, and he could smell the pheromones of it all; he opened his mouth, ready to bite out her jugular then and there, but refrained.

He dropped her like a rock, and she landed in a pitiful thud, a defeated and whimpering puppy. Even better than a successful hunt was truly defeating and dominating the game; sometimes, such as now, he had the notion that she wasn't even worth his time. His left hand grabbed the handle of his hammer and used it as a cane once more.

Primed by the victory of one hunt, heart dancing in his chest, he looked forwards to the true hunt. Inimicus turned his back and limped towards the flare.

She had promised herself no more tears. No more panic attacks, no more being helpless. And yet, as she lay there holding her hurt leg and sobbing, any progress she thought she had made came undone. Worse than feeling alone like she did before, she now felt worthless. How did a carpenter feel when building a house if it fell apart before completion?

She grabbed her radio in a snivel: "Phil." Her breath trembled through clenched teeth.

"Did he take the bait?" came the staticky reply. That same sense of 'knowing' was in his voice, the desperation replaced now with a warming acceptance.

"What are you doing? He's coming for you."

"Giving you a chance. I'll keep him busy; you push the objective."

"I can't. I thought I could, but I can't"

"You can do this, Jade. I know you can."

She pressed the radio to her head, clenching her eyes. Her thoughts pulled and pushed at her, like a group of school kids picking on the runt of the class. They were surrounding her in a circle, harassing her with volleys of verbal abuse:

"It's too far, and you'll get lost."

"You'll just screw it up," said another.

"You always need saving."

"All you do is freeze up or run; you're no fighter."

"Not even the monsters want anything to do with you. How pathetic."

"Your parents wasted their lives making sure you lived. Your uncle would be disgusted if he saw you now."

"Maybe you should've died and your folks lived."

Phil's voice spoke through the assembly of bullies, the teacher to the rescue as if he possessed long-distance psychic hearing of her self-slandering. His words were a gentle echo, pushing through the loudness of the abuse: *You can do this Jade.*

The line died, the battery charge now spent. The echo lingered. The last time he gave her such encouragement was two years ago when they had spoken and hung out at the same hollow tree. She was but thirteen at the time, and she confided in him what she couldn't to her uncle. She talked about doubt, a lack of confidence in her school courses that prepared young adults for their required military service (SOP 100, MOS 100, Basic Firearms Safety & Handling, PT, a lecture course over SERE's, BR-Hostile 101), and so on. She wasn't a fighter, didn't want to be a fighter, and wanted none of what society demanded of her. She just wanted the safety of Uncle Richard and the humble little nest they had together.

She had been scared then as she was now, the fear coinciding with that same feeling of worthlessness. Other kids had tried to make friends with her, but she didn't try to make friends with them. They didn't understand, not like Phil did. She'd just screw things up, push people away, and in the end, she'd add up to nothing.

But Phil—Thomas back then—hadn't thought so. Encouraging her when she finished expressing her worries, he listened, patiently silent. At the end of it, when she gave him a tight hug, he gave her head a gentle pat, and the very same words echoed then as they did now: "You can do this, Jade."

He knew how important the name her late parents gave her was to her. He kept sacred the confidence and trust she gave him and now he believed she could do it, not because she wanted to, but because she had to.

He returned to her the same trust and confidence she first gave him. Something sparked in her, and she shoved the doubts and worries aside. An empty closet in her mind was now filled with her nagging worries and insecurities. Those bullying voices in her head were dispatched into the dark and sealed away, reduced to a present nagging in the back of her head. She reminded herself that she still had sixty percent left to give. Phil was giving his all; she had no reason to give any less.

Sitting upright, she brushed her hair behind her ears. Her stomach growled at her with indignation, a hungry dog waiting to be fed. Her throat was parched and her dry mouth longed for water. She had not brought any; what she did bring was a pouch with a red cross on it, attached to her chest rig. Sitting in a half-split, her right leg to the side and her pant leg rolled up, the nasty bite the satyr had left was exposed. Blood wasn't pulsing out of the wounds, and from the SERE lecture class, she knew that was a good sign.

There were simple wound dressing items in the pouch: gauze and medical wrap would have to be good enough to keep the deep bite covered. Better than nothing. There were painkillers, in the form of pills. Taking a packet out, she swallowed them dry, leaving behind a feeling of pills stuck in the back of her throat.

She zipped up the pouch and brought the sleeves of Lossif's coat over her hands, and dried her tears.

No more crying. No more, she willed herself.

Wincing and leaning on the slab of rock near her, she used it to help her stand. Easing her weight on her leg, wearing it in with the pain and weight together, she looked up at Pikes Peak, the Apu Mountain. It was casting all it could at her, all its principalities and forces of malice, but she had Phil helping her, and that would be enough.

"You'll just screw up." The abuses muffled through that closed closet in her mind, quickly replaced by Phil's confidence.

"I won't let you down." She mouthed without speaking, taking her next limp to the peak.

Chapter Six – Vita et Mors

Gasoline, no matter how old it was, left a strong impression in Phil's nostrils; his sleeves were soaked in it. Coming to a stop at a rusted GMC, faintness clawed at him, and fatigue pulled at his eyes. Taking in a deep breath, he got down on one knee, then the other. Falling flat on his back, he crawled underneath a truck, the chassis being high enough to permit him under even as it sat on flat tires.

With his survival knife, he punctured a hole into the old gas tank and yanked it out. More of the liquid dripped down on his shirt, beads of the fuel traveling to his armpit. The strong odor forced out a cough. Sheathing his knife and grabbing onto the framework of the chassis, he pulled himself under the engine block in a drag. The bolts and support holding the old 5.3 liter V8 block were questionable as he stared up at the mass of metal.

"It's gonna be okay, ol' girl," Phil lulled to the engine. "I'm just gonna drain your oil, so please don't fucking fall on my face."

The oil pan wasn't brittle enough to puncture, and the plug wouldn't unscrew. So, he crawled further underneath the engine block, the ground already tremoring under him. Pebbles shook next to his head and puddles rippled, heralding the fiend's arrival.

Phil steadied himself with quick but calm breaths as he stole away his mind and studied the oil pain. In the many workings between the pan and block, he found a line of tubing and reached up. Snapping his fingers around the tube like it was a snake about to strike, he broke it off with ease. Oil spewed and dripped over his sleeve and the weed-infested pavement. A good splotch of it fell over his chest before he fully moved out of the way and out from under the engine block. Strong odors of the old, thick oil stabbed at his nostrils, yet it was a welcoming scent of familiarity, reminding him of the many times he and Tim worked on their vehicles in Atlanta.

The ground was now thudding with the limping rhythm of Inimicus's approach. A grimace clenched up his face in response to the sharp pain he felt in his side. Phil had made it only halfway across the parking lot draining oil and gas. The wind was not ceasing blowing cold air, the labored breathing of the monster, and the crude sound of something being dragged.

His advantage was the odor masking his scent. Phil remained under the GMC, watching from an angle past the tires and other vehicles. Inimicus shuffled down a steep slope of the parking lot's northern entrance. The tyrant hadn't noticed him but was searching, knocking the first vehicle next to him on its side.

Phil envisioned a mouse in a maze looking for a block of cheddar. He froze still, adding no movement to attract the monster's line of sight. Any movement of his would have been horizontal, easier for human eyes, and he expected the monsters as well, to pick up than lateral movements. Waiting, still as a corpse, he watched until the fiend was fully out of sight of the cars. He crawled out from under the GMC and hurried over to the next: a sedan whose dry, rotted tires blocked him from reaching underneath. However, the wheel well had enough space to reach behind the gas tank and free the hose; adding at least a little more fuel for his plan.

He had hoped to get to more of the vehicles, and as he heard the gas drain onto the cracked pavement he rolled over, he looked back at his way out. On the southern edge of the parking lot was a sidewalk and a service lid to a storm drain; the lid was already removed and staged for his exit.

The sedan's driver-side mirror was above him, which gave the view of a skull staring back at him through the glass window. Climbing back up onto his knees, he looked around, he heard and felt the presence of the monster but could not see him. His search brought him to the sight of a person's remains inside a metal tomb. He had been a young man, judging by his backpack, small stature, and clothes, a former student of the former school.

Ignoring the tragic end of the young man, Phil moved from the car in a hunched dash to another truck. No more than fifteen meters away, Inimicus's growls shook the air, and his shuffled movements and metal scraped over the pavement. The ground shook from every other vehicle the fiend tossed on its side.

Phil dared a peep over the hood of the truck. He exhaled frustration when seeing Inimicus between him and the storm drain. A sudden heave brought him back down to his knees. His face flushed and stars blurred his vision as he held back with all his might. The cost of silence nearly forced him to pass out, but the heaves ceded to his will. He took slow, silent breaths while resting his back against the side of the truck. Feeling the tremors of the monster's footfalls, he was somehow able to discern the direction and turns of its steps from the intensity of each one. Realizing Inimicus was closing in on his location, he took another look over the hood. Inimicus was now about to cross down the column of cars he was seated in.

To his belly he went, and rolled under the truck. Pebbles and stems of old weeds pricked at his arms and back. Looking down his chest and boots, he saw his enemy's feet crossing into the column of cars, limping his way. The giant, elephant-like foot came crashing down next to the truck, a few feet away from his head. The foul, acidic taste at the back of his throat contested for his silence as he prayed that the truck wouldn't be another victim of the monster's search.

Like a bloodhound on the scent, Phil could hear that rattling *sniff sniff* of Inimicus. He recalled when the skin of the monster was more like leather than the raggedy, linen-looking texture it now was. A thought came to him that the fiend was like the faded and torn seats of an old Mopar leather interior, decaying and falling apart from use. The crude instrument Inimicus dragged behind him came into full focus like a giant meat tenderizer.

Something grabbed Phil's right arm. As silently as possible, he took out his knife and looked over to a wraith crawling at him. Teeth chomped at him in hungry rage; nothing could be louder at that moment, not even a blow horn, to give his position away. The zombie's lower half was pinned to the ground, crushed under the car next to the truck. The monster scraped at the pavement and growled in dry rasps. No sooner had it started to disrupt the silence than Phil's blade came down like a guillotine, executing the transgressor. The hilt came to a crashing stop, indenting into the top of the skull.

Lying still as could be, he kept the zombie's corpse gripped in a hug daring to not risk noise by releasing the carcass onto the pavement.

Looking back to his left, he saw the brute's hammer come crashing down on the pavement. Standing erect, Inimicus's left leg folded, and he fell to his knees. His body lowered, and the thinned area of his lower belly came into view, the scars from when they had blown a projectile through his guts still there, threw off his balance. It was a tipping point, the center of gravity easy to trip. The monster's upper chest came into view, and his lower jaw dripped in fresh blood and saliva. Finally, his left hand fell to the ground, indenting the old pavement and cracking it. A shaking traveled from shoulder to palm as the monster started to wretch.

Radiant pulses shone through the layers of flesh. From his heart, traversing all around his body, brass-yellow pulses of light illuminated his veins. They brightened and dimmed with each pulse from his heart. Phil was enraptured by it, furrowing his brows at the sight of plasma-like vomit ejecting from the fiend's mouth. The plasmatic substance irradiated the air around it with waves of heat, spewing onto the ground in a spreading puddle.

Inimicus licked the substance off his mouth and chin and swallowed it. Phil fought back his heaves, his gags now resurrected. Willing nothing but still silence from under his concealment, his retching urges pulled at him.

The monster's gagging came to an end, and Inimicus spent a few seconds catching his breath as he climbed back to his feet. The hammer was an improvised crutch as the fiend continued the hunt. Slow, shaky breaths venting in and out through Phil's lips, and his head felt weightless as he inhaled, bringing fresh oxygen back to his head. He wedged his knife back and forth, freeing it from the skull.

The sound of Inimicus's frustration came loud and reckless, bellowing out a challenge from his bloodied, congested throat "PHEL! WHUR AR YU?" followed by the thunderous quake of his giant hammer down on a mass of metal.

"Ah, shit," Phil grumbled, and he crawled out from under the truck. Holding onto the side of the back bed as he stabilized his stance, his right side flared in discomfort. The area the fiend was in already spewed forth flammable substances. Phil hoped there wouldn't be enough, or any sparks from metal-on-metal contact, to ignite the gas or oil. But upon a sudden bark of surprise and fuming growls, he looked back up to see his worries already come to fruition and his plan prematurely executed. Flames consumed the ground around Inimicus. The fiend wailed and barked as the flames made a slow climb up his legs and licked at his arms.

Phil didn't expect it to hurt or harm Inimicus. If the thing could survive falling into a lava pit, he felt pretty sure of his theory.

Sometimes, though, winning didn't mean defeating the enemy; he just needed more time. Like with the Jackle avoiding poison ivy, he figured fire would be a similar natural repellent.

The flames spread across the inflicted areas of leaking gas and oil. Paths of fire blazed from where gravity had pulled at the substances traveling down the sloped edges of the lot. Phil hobbled to both feet and started running as best he could. An enraged Inimicus fumed out a roaring cry at him.

Phil spared a cautionary look behind him to see the tyrant fleeing the parking lot in the other direction. A flaming mass disappeared into the nearby neighborhood and wild thickets.

Tim's voice, from a day when he made a similar gamble with the poison ivy and the Jackle brought out an inner laugh. *You figured?*

Only for a second did Phil smile at the memory, huffing each limp after the other. Fire pounced at his heels, his attire practically covered in the old, flammable fluids. There had been no time to think two or three steps ahead. He made it to the service lid, grimacing, as he jumped down through the hole in the absence of time to properly descend. His hand found purchase on the old rusted ladder, but a nasty gash slit at his throat from a stray piece of metal when his fingers latched on the bars, and he came to a jerking stop.

A wooden *POP* noise came out from his right arm, and, instantly, he could feel the ball of his upper arm bone dislodging from its socket.

He yelled out a cry as his left hand grabbed the ladder, relieving his right hand that now dangled at his side. The initial flares of pain subsided in residual pulses of discomfort; the stress of it fumed through the sputtering of curses and mutters. He saw the loose piece of old, rusted metal sticking out from the wall—some kind of anchor for heaven only knew what—wet with his blood.

The light of fire shone down into the storm drain, and waves of yellow and orange danced around the blackened darkness underneath as he made it down to the bottom. His back fell against the wall, and, feeling his neck with his left hand, he took the little tidbit of good news when he found no blood was pulsing out. His back slid down the cement wall, and he landed on his rear, looking at his motionless arm.

There, in the beckoning darkness, he felt it again. The calling, the persuading seduction of malevolent desires. The kind of desire that brought pleasure upon suffering. That need to prowl, stock, hunt, and eventually slaughter. It came at him in full force, the dissonance of thought dissociating from reality. The chorus of baritones sounded as real as if it was humming from a stage concert somewhere in the deep of the drain network. It echoed out to him, an incantation of a single note spell, a ritual of summoning, instilling in him sudden dread and fear.

I promise. He had spoken these words to Sarah, but to Autumn he had promised as well: *whatever the cost.* No time was allotted to stop, steady his thoughts, and center himself. Sergei's words came at him in full force: *or the silence will come to break you.*

Not knowing what came next, not knowing where he'd end up—these thoughts held his mind hostage. Would he wake up in the middle of a horde swarming him? Or perhaps right before Inimicus's foot or hammer came crashing down over his face, flatting his head like a grape? Maybe he'd wake up safe and sound, while Autumn was left alone pushing to the objective and in desperate need of his help. Or worst of all, he would wake to him and Autumn tied down to chairs, naked and bruised, awaiting the execution from Igor or any potential survivor of the Wolf Pack.

"Fuck it." He wheezed, leaning in with the tide, allowing the pull of the current to take him to whatever end, if only for the hope that his last lucid thought might resonate with his unconscious self. *Just help me save Autumn.*

His breathing slowed and calmed, and the last thing he registered before passing out was the sound of a helicopter's blades in their rapid rotations. One noteworthy thing he could discern, though, was that there were two helicopters instead of one. Igor and his team of bandits had come in on only one bird, and now there were two. His thoughts went out to the kid in a quick prayer for her deliverance.

He couldn't pull away from the currents now. The tide was taking him, and the inevitable became too much to resist. He faded to black.

Chapter Seven – Nine-Line MEDEVAC

Holding the sleeve of her coat as a wad in her fist, Autumn wiped the street sign above her head. A truck had crashed into a tree long ago, permanently resting in its rot; its bed was right under the sign, giving her enough of a boost to wipe clear the dust from the sign. The further away from the city she went, the signs became less scorched, twisted metal and were just old slivers under a thick coating. With Phil's maps in hand, she stopped at each intersection. Relying on the gloomy presence of the mountain for a guiding landmark, relief bereft her lungs as she read "Barr T i" in white letters painted over red with a white tent symbol next to it. The paint was fading, the rust and dull red paint blending.

The street she was on was Ruxton Ave, and behind her many of the structures had collapsed as if a great wave of force had rolled them over—the shockwave of the explosion preceding the hell fire before it. She imagined the tall grass and vegetation that once stuffed the old structures and housing, now the charred, ashen landscape around her.

She could hear the slow moans of the structures creaking and swaying from the slightest movement like the wind. Every building was due for an inevitable collapse. Along this street of desolation, the Barr Trailhead remained. Sitting behind a hydro plant, a surviving sign on the street pointed her to a parking lot behind the plant.

She limped up the driveway, favoring her leg the best she could, and she came to a stop inside the parking lot; the trailhead was now before her and the peak's summit in her upper periphery. Had there not been signs, or a wooden fence, she wouldn't have guessed there had been a trail there to begin with. The overgrown vegetation, now burnt and swept away, covered the whole base in ash and trunks were reduced to coal. There was no sign of the dirt trail that had once existed.

Autumn got down on her good leg's knee and rolled up the pant leg on her bad leg. Deep red blood was bleeding through the dressing. Her head dropped and a tired sigh escaped her lungs; she limped over to a bench next to the wooden fencing and sat with her leg stretched down beside her.

She removed the dressing, looking at the coagulating blood drying up and down from the bite marks on her calf, still wet near the punctures. A leaf scuttled over the pavement, and her eyes shot up, looking around and over her shoulder. She listened in a death-like stillness, but it was just the wind carrying more leaves across the ground.

Her attention went back to her leg, and she opened her first aid pouch, knowing there was a name for it that she couldn't recall. It didn't matter to her; she just hoped there was enough bandaging left to redress the injury. The scraping she suffered from the storm drain cover traveled through the punctures and merged with a couple, looking like a 'No' symbol with a dotted oval.

Her face and arms tightened as she redressed the wound, discarding the bloodied rag and rolling her pant leg down.

The world remained silent around her, save for the leaves gliding over the ground. The dying pains of unstable structures moaned with the wind. She hobbled back to her feet and turned to look up at the peak. The mountains were engulfing her the closer she got. Pikes Peak, the Apu, with peaks to its northern and southern flanks looked like a hungry, gaping maw ready to devour. The scorched vegetation ended not far up the base of the peak, where green had survived the explosion.

Her first step into the ashen forest was met with prickles of twigs that broke apart into dust after poking at her arms and legs. Keeping her face and neck protected from the brittle lances of the forest, she paved a new way through and up the Apu.

The guidance of the mountain's summit became hidden behind the trees, the lighthouse veiled in a thick fog of ashen gray and charred black. A slow transition was at play, from the cinders of the forest to green pines, marking where the fire of the explosion had burned itself out.

The bare light still shone through now and again through the openings in the canopy. The ground was a bed of weeds, grass, and dirt, where no hope of following the old trail would offer aid. The only clue that she was on the right path was the grueling uphill battle and wooden posts along the way where at one point wooden rails connected them.

The climb was a constant trial; she refused to stop and rest, for every second felt critical and crucial to Phil's fate. Every second she thought about taking for herself, she thought it would rob her friend of time he didn't have. Even if it took her longer to make the next step, she continued to press on, refusing to stop.

Good job Nector. Keep going, girl. Keep going. Petty Officer Grant's voice cheered her on in her thoughts.

The grass and weeds on the mountainside were in another transition, this time into a bed of rocks; one rolled under her boot, stopping at the arch and jabbing upwards through the sole. Her knee buckled, and she fell, releasing a cry of surprise. She caught her fall before her face kissed a half-buried slab of stone.

She was down, panting and sweating. She couldn't stop her face from wringing, eyes watering. The smallest momentum gained traction into a full tumble as she cried. An opening in the pines above offered a glimpse out to the dead world behind her. She thought the Hebrew word Sheol was fitting: the Abode of the Dead.

Wiping the tears and snot from her face, she hobbled back to her feet; the bite at her right calf flared up again. Gently, little by little, she worked the pain to numbness and took back up the climb. Tree by tree, stone by stone, she paced herself, coming to a stop when the wind telegraphed a new sound to the silence. It was one that weighed over the noises of undead moaning, howling wind, the yelps of coyotes, and the dying breaths of the world of men. It came in a low, guttural voice, rumbling like the chains on an anchor sliding down a ship; it gave the Apu a malicious voice, punishment coming for her trespassing on its sacred slopes.

The trees came to a full transition from a pine slope to a rocky slope further up. The mountain appeared more vertical, and the air thinned. Rocks lined the mountainside, and what she had thought was snow was the illusion of white stone. Like a lizard on all fours, she climbed up in a crawl. Her arms flailed for purchase as the mountain's growl followed her. Her sweat froze at her skin with each gust of wind no longer held back by the trees; the chill of the higher altitude penetrated her clothes, flesh, and muscles to her bones and deeper into her soul.

All she saw was the summit; everything faded past her periphery into nothingness. She felt as if she could just get to the peak, and then all the evil and cold would disappear. Or at the very least, she could figure out what to do next.

Forty percent, don't freeze. Forty percent, don't freeze. Her thoughts chanted behind her focus, but more than that, she felt as if a choir of angels was behind her, cheering, as the growls at her six were closing the distance. She dared not turn around and look.

Reaching the peak didn't bring an end to her troubles; it only added to her roster of them. Her arms reached the top of the peak from her crawl, and she rolled over onto the gravel summit. Dozens of frozen rocks poked at her backside, and her chest rose and fell in quick succession, gasping at the thin air. Parched and thirsty, her body demanded water. Her mouth couldn't produce any saliva, and her body had stopped sweating long ago.

The gray clouds were above her, closer, and they seemed like a fog over the sea that shrouded her. She had entered a whole new dimension of existence, the abode of the gods upon Olympus far removed from the world of the mortals but not the toils. It wasn't a warm and blissful abode to contrast the ills below; it was just more of the dismal echoes of a Dead World, cold in rigor mortis.

I made it. She chuckled weakly, motionless in place, the laugh fading and leaving only a small smile. Phil had been right. She made the climb, and in her revelation, hope seemed more like something she could afford. The motivation it gave her was small but went a long way. Rolling over, she pushed herself back up to her shaky legs as her eyes fell on the Humvee.

It sat there just as Phil had promised, vacant and abandoned. A shadow figure in the fog, sitting still and motionless like a headstone. It was odd, but just like with the mountain from a distance, the vehicle had an ambiance of foreboding. It was as if it were a small Apu itself, and she walked widely around it, inspecting for threats that weren't present.

Tired legs permitted her to reach the HMMWV when she deemed it clear. To the fastback she went, popping the release lever and lifting its rusted joints that squeaked in displeasure.

Sorry, she mouthed to the vehicle.

Inside the vehicle was the viasat dish, just as Phil had said. *Three for three.* She smiled but tilted her head as she looked at the contents. They weren't packed up or neatly set aside but looked as if they had been shoved in; the previous owners had left in a hurry.

She pulled the dish towards her, looking at the connection ports. There was a line to connect to Phil's sat phone, which she freed from a pouch in her vest. Holding the phone in one hand and finding the cable to connect it to the dish, she set the phone down, keeping it steady, and looked at the dish. *What now?*

Two wires traveled out from the dish's backside, and a black wire was connected to a steel bolt head on the interior frame of the vehicle. The other, a red wire, traveled deeper inside the Humvee. Another bellow of a howl traveled up the mountainside, the Apu's reminder not to lower her guard.

Like a pup in a sudden leap, she jumped into the back of the Humvee and followed the wire past the back seats, up the front, and through a hole drilled in the dashboard. Sitting in the driver's seat, she found the release lever and pulled it. The hood *popped* and she saw it bounce upwards, out the windshield. Out and around to the front, she lifted the heavy chunk of metal, grunting, with her breath held. She was too short to raise the hood all the way and set the strut.

She could feel the reddening of her face, and stars filled her vision as Autumn looked inside to see the red wire left next to the battery, one of the terminals red. Her held breath was forced out her lips as she freed a hand, the hood dipping lower like a snapping turtle. She used her freed hand to connect the wire to the terminal.

Leaping back as fast as she could, she released the hood, snapping it shut fast and hard. Pacing her breaths, she went back to the driver's seat, feeling the beginning of tremors under her feet, the growl never leaving her side.

The Humvee had no keyhole for ignition, just a simple red button labeled "push to start."

"Simple enough." She shrugged in a deep inhale, holding her breath as she pressed the red button, and the engine rolled but didn't start.

"C'mon," she grumbled, pressing it again. Nothing.

The tremors now became audible, ripples traversing the puddles next to her outside the open door. She jammed the button in fast repetitions, hoping for results, but she was rewarded with nothing. She heard the coyotes' howls and cries, now closer than before, and amid them came that rattling growl—a drone, like in old Gregorian Chants, from which the higher notes of the coyotes built on in a chorus of impending doom. That droning note of a growl then rose in a high crescendo, a deeper but louder bass over the coyotes, silencing them into fading notes of whimpers and whines.

Rapidly, she jabbed at the button, her sudden newfound hope now fleeting—spent almost as soon as it was received. On and on until the metal beast finally woke from its slumber, metal racketed and clanked, sputtering from the exhaust as cold engines did so when they needed to warm up. Uncle Richie's tow boat was very much the same, needing urgent maintenance but coming to life all the same.

"Thank you." She gave the dash a gentle pat.

Back to the viasat, Autumn let out a cry of joy when she saw the sat phone now had a charging indicator. Pressing the power button, she saw the screen come to life. The peak was now shaking, distinguishable in the rhythm of steps. The Apu's champion, or guardian, was coming to remove her, the transgressor.

An impatient index finger tapped at the phone when at last the device fully booted to life with a whopping five percent battery life. Alyeskan sat phones were never reliable with battery life; she knew this from helping her uncle on his tugboat. It varied per phone, but Richie's sat phone spent ten percent battery life on just a two-minute call.

The phone's contact list had just two numbers listed: SRT-Bravo and Oscar Charlie Romeo. She hit the latter, sounding more formal and direct. Hearing the dial tone, she held the phone to her ear with her shoulder, her hands unfolding Phil's map, and laying them flat on the fatback's gate. She set stones over the map's edges to hold it down. The ringing stopped, but only for five seconds before an "Oscar Charlie Romeo to…" came over the line.

"Hello," Autumn started, but she stopped after hearing the voice on the other line.

"SRT-Alpha, this is Oscar Charlie,"

"Oh, hi, sorry. We need…"

"Go ahead…"

"What?"

"Miss, there is a few-second delay. Calm down and listen clearly before you speak."

We don't have seconds to spare. She bit her tongue, waiting another few seconds, fingers tapping relentlessly against the metal gate.

"My name is Autumn, and my friend and I are sick and hurt and need you to send help, please."

Five seconds passed.

"Oscar Charlie copies Alpha; do you know your medevac request?"

A spark came to her thoughts, the word familiar, and she looked down at the map. Counting five seconds as she read the map, Phil's notes were clear, almost as if he had considered it would be her to phone home. He had underlined "9-Line MEDEVAC."

You really do think of everything. She rejoiced again, and read after the fifth second: "Okay, I have it here; it's written down. Uh. Okay, it is, Line One: One-Tree-Sierra-Delta-Charlie-Niner-Six-Zero-Niner-Niner-Niner-One-Zero. Line Two: GEO-Viasat sat Phone, Tree-Four-Dot-Five-Four-Six, SRT-Alpha. Line Three: Two Charlie. Line Four: Alpha. Line Five: Two Alpha. Line Six: X-Ray. Line Seven: Charlie, Green Smoke. Line Eight: One Alpha, Break, One Bravo. Line Nine: None, Mountainous Region. Did you get it?" she asked.

Five seconds later, ladies' voice stammered over the radio for a second as if scribbling. "Standby. Your nine-line request is as follows. Line One: One-Tree-Sierra-Delta-Charlie-Niner-Six-Zero-Niner-Niner-Niner-One-Zero. Line Two: GEO-Viasat sat Phone, Tree-Four-Dot-Five-Four-Six, SRT-Alpha. Line Three: Two Charlie. Line Four: Alpha. Line Five: Two Alpha. Line Six: X-Ray. Line Seven: Charlie, Green Smoke. Line Eight: One Alpha, Break, One Bravo. Line Nine: None, Mountainous Region?"

Autumn followed her word for word with her finger on Phil's writing, confirming each word as it was repeated back to her. It all matched up according to Phil's writing, despite being gibberish to her.

Five seconds later, she confirmed with a "Yes Ma'am," and waited for a response.

"Alpha, your MEDEVAC has been approved. Standby for ETA. Over."

Autumn didn't have that much time; in that same second, the force of the tremors became like a bombardment of earthquakes under her. The sat phone vibrated over the fastback's gate, and she steadied it with her hand.

"Alpha, is everything okay?" the lady on the other line asked. She was focused and firm with an underlying tone of worry.

Autumn had frozen up, shaking, as her joints trembled. All hope and confidence seemed to wither and falter, hanging only by a thread, as she looked over at the Barr Trail where she had come from. As if climbing up from a ladder, a gnarly, jagged hook of bone where a hand should have been reached up and hooked into the summit of the peak. Another hand pulled into view—it was skinless with charred muscle tissue, tendons, and exposed beige bones. It started with the skinless hand, arms, and head, down to the shoulders, until the monster's giant form lifted onto the mountain's summit. His eyes were matted mush, and his nostrils flared in congested sniffs, searching the air. His face was broken and contorted like a flattened snout; nothing about it was natural.

Autumn lowered the sat phone as she stared at the skinless mass. She was stripped of any scrap of hope she had upon the sight of the Behemoth. She had the feeling that everything she would do would end in utter failure. Nothing in Sheol came without a price; she just couldn't take two steps forwards without at least one step back. Now it seemed as if she had taken three steps back, and the cost for contacting home would be her death. Those voices in her head broke out from the confining room she had locked them in; they were like so many girls in school who returned to their exes who had treated them like garbage. Likewise, Autumn regressed into herself, feeling inadequate, worthless, and helpless.

Not enough. In need of rescuing. How are you going find your way back to Phil? You won't even survive this. All you do is fail. Your parents would be disappointed in you. Just give up.

The monster's head moved as he sniffed in every direction, not yet fully pinpointing her location. She thought of Phil's warnings about the brute. She understood that the Behemoth had greater senses and strength than the Fomorian. Words escaped her lips, and there was a trembling cry for help to the woman on the other line: "Oh, God."

The battery now spent, the phone died in her hands. The skinless Behemoth perked at the sound of her voice. Phil was now four for four, the monster's head turning and stopping in a shake like an irritated dog with perked ears. The Jackle leaned back, sucking in air like a vacuum in space before discharging it in a bellowing rage that thrashed Autumn in a gust of putrid breath.

Chapter Eight – Race from the Clouds

In one great push, Autumn shoved everything back into the vehicle and jumped up to reach the fastback and pull its top down, latching it with the tailgate. Not a second after the mass of the skinless Behemoth rammed into the rear driver-side corner of the Humvee, the bodies of metal and flesh missed her by a hair as the monster fell and rolled past her while the rear of the vehicle skidded in a quarter turn. She fell on her back in a hard expel of air as the driver-side door came to face her, the tires grinding into the summit's dirt.

Over her shoulder, she saw the beast roll onto his belly, hook, and fist-push himself back up to his knees and feet. His head craned left and right again, neck popping as he sniffed the thin air. Rocks crumbled under her as she climbed back to her feet, the monster's nostrils flaring in a huge intake. His smashed face turned to her. Her left hand grabbed the driver's side mirror, and her right hand yanked the handle. She hopped inside.

The mirrors vibrated, the vehicle shook, and out her rearview she saw the beast limping now, sniffing in fast repetitions, closing in on the source of the noises. She removed the parking brake and let the vehicle idle forwards; then silence fell, and the engine died.

The congested snorting, as if an asthmatic was in desperate need of an inhaler, drew nearer. In the mirror, she could make out a malicious grin on his lips. Broken and serrated teeth twisted in upwards turns at the corners of its mouth. The absence of cheeks allowed her to see into a salivating mouth through strands of sinews as if a thick spiderweb connected its bottom jaw to the top. For a second, she thought it might be Sergei's mask now covered with muscle tissue.

Her index and middle fingers jabbed the push-to-start button several times. She rammed it so much that her fingertip became numb and red. The engine's rolling continued, but without a start, and she looked out the windshield to see where the momentum of the rolling tires was taking her. She froze when the hood blocked out most of her view, offering only a sliver of a visual between the window frame and hood as the edge of the summit disappeared from view under the dash. *Oh, not good!* She hit the brake, but it was stiff and unyielding. She arched her back to get both feet and her whole weight onto the pedal to bring it to a stop.

The monster collided again with the vehicle, from the rear this time, ripping and gnashing through the metal. The force of the impact sent her jerking forwards, her head thumping into the steering wheel, leaving her dazed. The tail end of the vehicle's destruction came without rest. In intervals of violent grating, bit by bit, the Humvee was a block of cheese, and the Behemoth the grater.

The fastback ripped open, allotting gusts of cold that blasted in through the back, pushing the foul body odor and breath of the monster to the front. That jagged bone of a hook came gashing down through the roof, peeling and cutting through the metal as it pulled back.

She looked at the edge of the summit, the Apu in its endless malevolence towards her, leaving her with a dilemma. Autumn cried out, buckled the seat belt, and braced both hands on the steering wheel; it too was stiff and unwieldy. Her left foot pressed hard against the floorboard, pushing her back more firmly against the seat as she pulled her other foot off the brake pedal.

The tires gained momentum, speed increasing, and the passenger door hung and swung on its hinges, a limp limb flapping as the Humvee rolled. The front tires crested over the edge, and then there was no turning back. Her stomach twisted and her heart jumped upwards to her throat as the edge of the summit passed under the hood, and the horizon beyond rose upwards and vanished, replaced by the mountainside. She left the Behemoth behind as she gripped the steering wheel until her knuckles turned white.

Autumn tried to steer the metal steed; she knew Uncle Richie or Phil would have been able to force the wheel into submission. But her thoughts betrayed her, and the difficulty of turning the wheel gave proof of to the internal lies with which her thoughts abused her. Fruitless effort transitioned to a desperate hold on the wheel; she was like a safety bar bracing herself for the ride down. The hood bent and twisted at its joints, ripping off and traveling with the wind behind her.

The Humvee jerked, bounced, and shook down the rocky tip of the peak, and her whole body thrashed around in sync with the movement. Saved only by the seat belt and wheel, the steering became easier the faster she went, and it didn't take much turning of the wheel to swerve around the first of the trees. The Apu's rocky tip transitioned into the forested base around it, the trees passing left and right breaking off the rearview mirrors. Wooden trunks hammered against the steel body, and branches smacked the windshield in an endless barrage, cracking it to a point that a giant spider web formed, making it hard to see through.

She heard the monster behind her. The force of his cries was like a thunderclap of bloodlust that shot after her in a force of maddening rage, pushing against the wind. Worse than the Fomorian, she felt the Behemoth's cries piercing through air, metal, and flesh. The thundering force of the sound pierced her thoughts and reached her soul. She no longer saw the thick spiderweb crack of the windshield, but the fruits of Sergei's labor. The mutilated and flayed remains of two pilots silently screaming permeating the air, and the two butchered men's corpses froze her.

The thunderclap cry of the monster had past, taking with it the spell that had enchanted her. The memories pressed down under, forced into some hole that hadn't been there before. She realized upon her release from the spell that there was a tight pain at her biceps, elbows, and forearms, and soon, her arms just gave out. She was unfit and ill-conditioned to keep such taxing demands going. The Humvee's present trajectory passed the next tree but couldn't avoid the next.

The thick trunk of pine missed the passenger side door and battered into the rear passenger side. The front veered rightwards, and the driver's side ground against another tree; then it all stopped. The seat belt kept her head from ramming through the windshield—but not the steering wheel that came upon her like Sergei's boot to her face, leaving her in a daze. Sitting there, with the shaking of the ground, the windshield mirror vibrated from the stampeding force of the Behemoth; the force of his footfalls reverberated up the metal steed.

Coming back from her daze, she looked to her left, out the passenger side window, and saw a teetering view down the edge of a sheer drop. Her right hand held her head while her left fumbled for the door latch. The berserking Behemoth was but a blurry image, distorted through the cracked window to her left, which showed the monster ramming through tree and rock, blasting through creation after her.

Before she could comprehend everything, the brute rammed into the driver's side, and both Autumn, metal steed, and skinless mass went over the edge.

There was a splash; it cushioned her, and the seat belt kept her head from striking the roof of the vehicle. The sudden influx of cold water wakened her from her stupor, and the water quickly filled the car, touching her forehead. Her fingers found the release for the seatbelt, and, unstrapping herself, she fell onto the roof. A gash of metal bent inwards landed between her knees, nearly carving into her calves.

The broken window and a hole for the mounted gun gave her options; she chose the latter. Quickly, she climbed over the driver and passenger seats. She noticed the defining smell of men, the kind of smell that went hand-in-hand with the age-old saying "boys will be boys."

In a moment, she paused, looking behind the driver's seat. Tucked under the seat and floorboard was a container. Remembering her other objective, she reached up and grabbed it, a soft but firm case sealed with a zipper. She read the front and her heart leapt in joy before the feeling disappearing just as fast as it had arrived. 'Broad-Spectrum Field Injection Kit' the front read, in letters of bright red over a white background.

She held it close to her chest. *I'm not letting go, Phil. I'm almost there.* She stuffed the BSFIK inside a compartment of her chest rig, an interior mesh pocket, and zipped it into safety. *I'm not giving up.*

She wormed her way over into the weapon mount, pulling herself out of the hole, her shoulders scraping at the sides, her legs caught at odd angles within the gears, levers, and other metal objects that rubbed and felt like they were a rolling press over her legs as she entered the depths of the waters. Holding onto the vehicle as she climbed over and onto the undercarriage, she used it for a push-off against the weight of the water. The only issue was she couldn't swim.

Some internal guidance was there, guiding her arms and legs to move in her panic, sink or swim. With her push-off and stroking limbs, she broke the water's surface, gasping for air. Yet, she could not float, either, and she barely kept her head above the water. Further down the current, she saw the skinless brute, flailing and going mad. His body steamed when the water touched him, and soon, he disappeared, falling from a sudden drop in the current.

"Not good!" she cried out, holding onto the branch as if it were a rope tethered to a tree, kicking her feet against the current. Soon, she joined the brute, crying out as gravity hurled her over the waterfall and into a large body of water below. She splashed into the bottom, and the force of the splash felt like running into a cement wall before sinking into the depths.

The first thing Phil registered upon waking up was heavy throbs at his temples; his right hand was still numb and now shook. The dissociating spell that preceded the blackouts faded as his thoughts spun in a whirlpool of dizziness and fatigue.

He fell to his hands and knees, landing on a cracked and weed-infested street between two trucks that took up most of his vision. Both his arms were ready to give, threatening him with a face plant upon the old road. He almost did, but instead he landed on his left side. Tired breaths puffed out in wisps of visible warmth in the cold air, sleep dragging his eyelids down.

The nearby buzzing of helicopters pulled some focus into his thoughts—all other thoughts and implications gathered from the revelation. Help had come to Igor, and that gave him enough strength to climb up to his feet.

Find the kid.

Something crumpled in his hands, and he looked down at his wrist to see a piece of paper tucked under the strap of his watch. Leaning against the rotted-out wheel of the truck to his left, he took out the paper and unfolded it. He read the note left behind by his unconscious self: *Current route, 24 Northbound, Pikes Peak Highway close.*

"Thanks, I guess." He crumbled up the paper and let it float with the tunneling breeze gusting through the column of Dead Traffic he was in between.

The truck behind him was an old Ram 1500, there to help him climb back to his feet, and as he passed the carcass of the rusted truck, he gave the hood a soft pat, limping down the highway.

Four times his belly brought him to a stop, and he leaned on the nearest vehicle and heaved in a puking spell. His sense of time was non-existent; it only mattered that it was daylight. The sun was blocked by the clouds but brightened up a spot in the sky, a circular blur of light gray engulfed by the dark gray of the overcast. By the placement of the sun, he guessed it was late evening.

At his fifth stop, his gagging resulted in dry heaves with nothing to offer but putrid-tasting spit. The heaving fits lasted several minutes and blurred his peripheries; stars filled his vision. The pressure letting up, the warmth at his head cooled him, and while he calmed himself, he took stock of his surroundings. At his twelve, he was closing in on the road leading to 'Pikes Peak Hwy', a direct path to the mountain, and, at his six, smoke rose in the distance, several miles back.

He now regretted his idea of burning the parking lot: Indian smoke signals, calling out to all evil where they could find him and Autumn. There was no other relatively safe area they could fall back to, nor did they have the time it would take to fortify a new safe house before night fell. Options were limited, and desperation would bring them back to the school; his only prayer was that the place of refuge would last another night.

Inimicus was Lord knew where, and zombies idled about. There were no draugrs, for which he thanked the Lord, just simple wraiths, easy enough to move through and around without using a weapon's discharge. He leaned on the buildings, trees and cars in between as he walked. The corners gave his heart hefty doses of adrenaline as he pied each one with his AK-12.

When an old brick building's corner sent fresh doses of adrenaline coursing through his veins as he pied the edge, he caught sight of where the road intersected with Pikes Peak Hwy and traveled up to the mountain. The other, lesser peaks surrounded him, and there were dangers of rockslides and old netting long past its use. This was the Wasteland's No Man's Land, complete with the landmines of falling rocks, and only two possible routes.

A fainting spell came upon him; he stumbled, catching himself on the side of an old Buick. The vehicle's last usage had caused it to mount the curb and bottleneck a building's corner. Holding onto the rusted side, his stomach-churning threatened another upheaval. The air between the mountains seemed heavier, and any disturbance in the buoyancy was tenfold. The *thwapping* of helicopters came to him as if they were near.

One of the birds came over the trees south of Pikes Peak. The bird came to a hover over the base of the mountain. Gunners manning the mounted machine guns fired down. *NO, God, please, no.* Phil's soul cried out, and he fell into the fastest sprint his body could muster. Every step, every sweating huff of breath was a silent prayer: *Please, God.*

The dissociating spell felt heavier, like a bog in his head. It threatened to make him fade into black, he could feel his unconscious self wanting to take over. But not this time, no. He managed to stop it, if only this one time, pushing aside the ensuing blackout. He was immediately responded to by the same voice he heard now and again.

Everything in her wanted to open her mouth to gasp for air, but instinct kept her from doing so. She could feel the pressure building in her head; every flail of her arms and legs was an exhausting effort to swim, wasting air and energy. The pressure turned to pain and agony as she felt a whole new kind of panic: chaos. In her imagination, she saw her parents hand off their baby girl to Uncle Richie, their hopes and dreams for her suddenly drowned in the waters with her. She saw Phil slowly dying of pestilence at the school. Uncle Richie, in drunken grief, tasted the metal of his .38's barrel. She cried out for help, for anything.

Then came a moment when the panic and pressure turned to peace. When her efforts to swim back up to the surface failed, the simple thought of opening her mouth and letting the waters in came to her. She could rest and be free from the grievances of life. If heaven, earth, or hell should reach out a lending hand to her, she would accept. And so it was.

A skinless hand blasted down through the waters, his fingers clenched around the left side of her face, the other fingers on the back of her head as his thumb latched down under her jaw to her right. She grabbed onto his fingers, feeling herself being pulled out of the water, but the grip over her head was tightening, squeezing her head like a grape. The meager remains of her held breath transitioned to screams as she was lifted out of the water.

Autumn pulled and pried at his fingers, the muscled flesh of the ball of his palm pressed to her mouth. She screamed as she could taste his flesh, a rancid flavor of rawhide and burnt coffee. She couldn't see from behind the mass of the hand that now dragged her through the water. Her legs kicked, her body squirmed, and her arms flailed, splashing in the water with the brute.

They reached the shallows, and rocks scraped at her legs and lower back, digging under her shirt and pants as sticks poked and stabbed. Finally, she was jolted out of the water by the beast, and there was the unmistakable sound of steam rising off his body with a guttural breath. In one great heave, he lifted her up, and, suddenly, she was falling backwards. Her eyes were freed from the darkness of his palm before she made a splashing impact into the shallow end of the water that now swallowed her whole.

There wasn't enough time to catch her breath; she took in some water with her gasps as she looked up through the waters and the menacing face bared down at her. Her struggling waned, and her efforts grew lax. By either act of instinct or memory, perhaps a bit of both, her left hand found the knife in her vest. Fingers fumbled to release the safety strap, then to even find purchase over the handle. She wasn't herself now; something else took over. Wild panic that exploded in thoughtless efforts as she ripped out her knife and began shanking as fast as she could. She jabbed several strikes into the hand of the monster in hopes of release.

But in return, she caught a glimpse above the water: the Behemoth raised his bone hook and brought it down in a hard jab. The blow slowed upon breaching the shallow surface, but not enough to cushion the strike of the curved top. It struck her hard below her left eye, traveling up to the bridge of her brow. It disoriented her and brought her low as her fingers loosened around her knife. Soon, she felt its handle gone from her grip. It was just instinct now that kept her from breathing in the water, and even that was fading. She could barely make out the distorted sight of the monster raising his hook for a gutting strike.

She seemed to have two options: she could either let the waters of chaos inside, dulling her senses to the impending doom, or she could fight and be fully cognizant of the inevitable pain; either choice led to death's embrace.

Her choice came to her in rounds of bullets pummeling through the water's surface to her far left. Danger was close, but dead on target as red mist sprayed out from the Behemoth and bloodied the water over her. His hand, over her chest, was lifted, and she could raise her back from the shallow floor. Like a fish pulled out of the water, she thrashed and flailed, splashing all her limbs to orient herself to the forest floor and to get her hands and knees under her in a desperate scramble to get her head over the water. The moment she breached the surface, she gasped for air into the hellish sounds of bullets whizzing and splattering into flesh. Red mist sprayed over her. Helicopter blades spun, and the monster's roars crashed through the air at the bird.

She crawled to the edge of the water, dipping into it again to rinse off the blood. She crawled onto dry ground, her boots still in the gentle current as she rolled over onto her back. The shooting from the helicopter went from three-round bursts to hellfire and brimstone now that she was far removed from the target. The Jackle's body steamed in the crisp air, drying his skinless flesh. A round bounced off his skull, denting the bone. He fumed a low growl before picking up a boulder, the size of a golf cart, with his left hand and hurled it at the helicopter with a reflexive explosion of irritation.

The nose of Wolf Pack's helicopters rose, and the bird moved backward, avoiding the projectile. She could make out Igor Petrov operating in the co-pilot seat and looking down at her; Anton was in the pilot's seat. Petr manned the side gun, held his fire, and braced himself for the sudden evasive maneuver.

A look of relief dressed Igor's face when he saw her, and he leaned back, hollering something to Anton in the pilot seat; the bird's nose dipped. Moving on, Petr fired another volley of hellfire at the beast. The Behemoth, in his irritable rage, set off in chase, following the direction of the bullets as he toppled trees in his pursuit. And like that, they were gone.

Autumn's head fell against the ground as she gasped and panted. Slowly taking back control of her thoughts and situation. Cold wisps of air shriveled her lungs and chest, vision out her left eye was squinted in a swollen slit of sight with a burning discomfort that throbbed across her face and chest. Her nose was congested, and she was unable to breathe in; the fatigue was taking over. She remained there like a corpse, fighting back the urge to sleep. Before she thought she had more stamina than a normal person. She was never the fastest, never the strongest, but she was always the one who could outlast the others. But now, her failures with both titans made her realize that this wasn't the case at all. She escaped the Fomorian, only because Phil had taken her place on the chopping block; likewise the Behemoth left her alive due to some short attention span and a quick temper from being shot at.

After a while, she rolled over and pushed her hands against the grass and up to her knees. She placed one foot against the earth, then another, in a wobbly stance, using a tree to keep herself standing. She waited, getting used to the effort of it, before putting one foot forwards. Her depth perception was thrown off by her swollen eye. She craned her head all the way to the left to get to the next tree.

The trees were small goals, checkpoints to keep herself standing. Eventually, she found enough strength to walk on her own at a slow, almost bare, pace; she had pneumonia once, and it had rendered her in a constant dazed state, much like how she was feeling now. Her head was heavy, her thoughts bogged, and all her focus was spent on breathing in and out. What used to be second nature now had become her only rational thoughts: breathing and walking. Anything else was too tiresome to think about.

Chapter Nine – Respite

The ground traveled in a steady decline, offering ease to Autumn's progress. Her goal was reduced to just making that next step. She was oblivious to all else, until the beginnings of fencing and backyards forced her attention to her surroundings. A second wind invigorated her, giving her steps more ease as she stumbled to the nearest house with all the pump she could put into her steps. Reaching the rotted red vinyl siding of a single-story house, she used it like a crutch to help her to the front and came to the sight of a road branching off from a highway and disappearing up the mountain.

Her heart jumped inside her chest. A second wind came at the sight of Thomas wading around the remains of an overturned semi-truck clustered with sedans and trucks all around it. His eyes met hers, and she couldn't hold back her excitement. "Phil!" escaped her lips in a sniveling cry.

At that moment, the air was heavy and thick, and she fell to her knees. Her right hand held onto the corner trim of the red vinyl house as her friend raced to her with a stiff leg. The strength in her fingers gave out when Phil came into arm's reach, and she fell, the ground coming at her fast. She thought Phil wouldn't reach her in time, and she clenched her eyes before impact, but she did not feel dirt and rock smack her face. Rather, she felt the chill of Phil's coat sleeves and the warmth of his breath on her head. One hand held the back of her head, and his other crossed her shoulders.

"I did it." Her words were a bare whisper, escaping her lips with a tired exhale, proving the lies that were the false witnesses in her head. She had pulled through, and now she felt she could rest.

"You sure did." There was a warmth in Phil's voice. Aside from the accepting and friendly nature he held, there was something more behind it. A kind of warmth that Uncle Richie had in his voice.

Her eyes watered, and the first thought that came to her mind was of when she had caught the flu from one of her many exploits into the wilderness. Phil, Thomas back then, had found her and taken her to the hospital. Things seemed to be alright until the fourth day, when she could barely walk. Richie carried her from the living room to her bedroom, turned on her favorite anime, and tucked her into bed. She had been so scared, and his voice had gently lulled her as he comforted her, sitting next to her bedside. He may have been her uncle on her mother's side, but to her, uncle was synonymous with father. A passing thought came to her that, based on the same intimate nature of Phil's voice, friend could be synonymous with uncle.

"I'm proud of you. Was worried as hell, but you did good, kiddo."

There was something else to him that worried her, though: his stiff leg, the favoring of his side, the way his voice sounded, and the wild look in his eyes. It kept that internal switch from turning off, keeping her awake as she pulled back and looked up at him. Her hand shot up to her mouth, speechless, at the blood drying around the gash in his throat and staining his shirt. His arm dangled limply despite the comfort it offered around her shoulder.

"What's wrong?" she asked.

"Nothing that can't wait." He gave her shoulder a gentle squeeze; it was time to go. He stood up, and she stood next to him as his arm stayed around her, a safety blanket from the evils of the wasteland. She was ready to catch him should he fall.

They arrived at a gas station not fully cluttered with Dead Traffic. The school's football field was on the other side of the street. The sky was darkening with a pallet of orange light through the cracks that otherwise would've been a beautiful sight, back home. A gentle breeze smelling of rain soothed over her swollen skin as Phil came to a stop. He took a knee behind an SUV, studying the school. His eyes were steady, open, and focused, but she felt burdened with fatigue, longing for rest. His conviction seemed to shine on her as she awed at his discipline, syphoning his resolve and keeping herself going. Had she been alone, without anyone to inspire her, she might have fainted along the way.

Each of his breaths was slow and calm—in through his nostrils and out the narrow gap between his lips. He was a stone. Her breaths were more akin to ones taken when you laid your head down on a pillow to retire for the day.

To the right, past the football field and over the twisted tops of the trees and dilapidated roofing of the neighborhood, Sergei's scarecrows remained, an eternal torment of observant sentries. She looked away from the tragic doom Wolf Pack had suffered.

"Anything?" she asked.

"From this angle, no." Phil shook his head, then moved in a crouched stance to the street. "Follow me."

The student parking lot was a scorched heap of cinders through which they navigated around the building's right flank to the back parking lot. The zombies that once occupied the area were now gone, and they came to a door where plyboard was bolted over the bottom glass panel. For a second, she wondered if this was the same door that she passed out on the other side of—the place where she had given up at Sergei's feet. With Phil here, she thought, *let the psycho come.*

"How did you get out?" she asked.

"I jumped out a fucking window." There was a hint of humor to his voice; the rest rang with the kind of irritation that came with unpleasant memories. Again, he read her like a book, saying, "I don't think I have the strength to climb up through it though."

Phil released himself from her, using the door to ease himself down next to the bolt as he tried fiddling with it, but it was rusted and stiff. She lowered to her knees and searched her chest rig while he used his knife on the bolt. She found her Leatherman and offered it to him.

His brow raised. "Your uncle?"

"He said to never leave home without it." She shrugged.

"Richie is a wise man." Phil took the tool and waved it up and down as if it, too, nodded in agreement. "Keep an eye on our six; I'll get this sucker loose."

With the pliers feature and a good amount of tapping—hammering, with a rock—he worked the bolt, freeing it from its rust. Everything in the darkening world behind them was silent save the never-ending moans of the wind, the cawing of crows, and the rustling of leaves and debris fluttering over the ruins of the neighborhood.

It seemed to her that the fall of darkness was like a tsunami, and on the other side of that door was their refuge from it; the sound of Phil's quickening huffs and grunts added to the sense that they needed to get inside before night fell. Then she heard the plyboard collapse and a metallic *cling* from the other side of the door.

Hairs raised on the back of her neck, and she looked around for any potential threat the noise may have harkened. But the only response they were given was more crows cawing. She turned around to see Phil lay his coat over the hole in the door. Inside the square frame, a row of glass teeth sat, lining the frame's four sides. It was a gaping mouth with an endless abyss of darkness for a throat.

"I'll take point. If I say, run."

"I know." She nodded. "I run… But I won't."

He didn't respond, and a tender smile crossed his worn face, one she might translate as "fucking kids." She returned the gesture with a shrug, and he crawled through the hole. A second later he gave her the "clear," and she crawled in next, taking the coat and shaking off the glass before giving it to him.

"Mulţumesc." He took his coat and slipped back into it.

She had to think on it, snapping her fingers when the word came to her. "Cu Plăcere?"

He patted her back, giving her a proud smile and pointing his head at the door. "Help me block this."

Together, they pushed a filing cabinet in front of the security hazard, then lined the flanks with bricks they found in the nearby woodshop until the point of entry was relatively secured. It was too heavy, at least, for a zombie to get through. Even with Autumn's skepticism, Phil simply shrugged and responded, "Zombies follow the path of least resistance," as he leaned against the filing cabinet, catching his breath.

"But Igor and the others…"

"If a person wants to get inside this building—" He cut her off, "—they will."

"Why don't we just hunker down somewhere else?" she asked.

"Night's closing in too fast, and there's already food and water here. And the building's relatively secured." Phil lay a hand on her shoulder. "Come dawn, we'll break for a better location, closer to the base of the mountain, where our exfil will meet us."

"If you say so."

"And I'm always on point. You stay as my shadow, okay?"

"Okay."

Autumn clenched the back of Phil's shirt the whole way through the halls and up the stairs, looking through the gaps of his arms, holding up his rifle, and his sides. He was slow and methodical, and she noted the caution in every movement—the pitch of his feet, his pieing around every corner. In the ten-meter increments they moved, he would activate a LED light of his weapon, splashing a circle of bright white light ahead for a millisecond view, and just as quickly deactivated it. Then, consumed again in pitch blackness of the dark he moved, towing her with him as she held onto his coat and shirt. Come to a stop where he had shined his light, rinse and repeat.

The halls were like mine shaft tunnels leading into nothingness—haunted stairwells cluttered in junk and spiderwebs. By the time they arrived at the sped room, night had completely fallen and only the moaning wind and creaking of the old building kept the silence at bay. They restored the pseudo-barricade she had installed the day prior, and Phil transformed it into what she saw as an efficient barricade.

By then, his strength was completely spent, and he was holding onto the wall, wheezing, arms shaking. She helped him to the bed. A great relief came over him as he promptly collapsed onto the old mattress face-first. She felt his forehead; his skin was on fire, and she pulled back, figuring he had the flu, or heaven forbid, something worse.

"You're getting worse," she murmured, but he it off.

"It could always be worse, kiddo. Da, it could be worse." His voice fell faint, like an echo fading down a tunnel.

She grabbed a chair, and by the time she placed it next to the bed, he had already fallen under. His internal switch was now turning off before anything else could be said or done. She sighed, repositioning him in a more comfortable posture. Walking over to the window, she pulled down the drapes and sat next to Phil. An LED lamp, from Wolf Pack, was on the nightstand, and she set it to its dimmest setting

The BSFIK opened on her lap, and she studied the contents therein. Auto-injectors were held firmly in the sleeves of the sturdy container labeled: *Epinephrine, Penicillin, Morphine, IIV4 [Influenza Vaccine], and Tetanus Boosters.*

She recalled all four from her studies in her SOP 100 class, and she took out two shots of the IIV4.

There was a hole in Phil's pants, over the thigh, and it offered a good spot to give the injection. First, she wiped it with a wet wipe from her first aid kit; then, she gave him the shot. She started to clean off the dried blood from his neck, getting her own hands bloodied as she wiped it down the untreated gash, receiving grimacing snarls from a passed-out Phil along the way.

The cut hadn't been deep enough to kill him, but the lips of the cut looked nasty and curved upwards like the rim of an impact crater. There was a fleshly gorge of red between the lips of the gash. Then she held a gauze over it; she wasn't confident enough to use a needle and thread, let alone at the neck. So, she taped the gauze in place, took the tetanus booster out, and stuck it in his thigh as well. Then she gave herself the same injections.

She tapped her fingers over her knee, wondering if that was all she could do. She tried to recall more from SOP 100. But nothing else came to mind, save for the fever Phil had and the deepening cold of the night in this Sheol. She imagined the land outside frosting over and the cold reaching inwards to them. So, she covered him with the blankets on the bed and tucked him in.

God, if you are there... She thought about repeating her prayer, almost diving into the rabbit hole of theological discussions she and Phil would have from time to time. Had her prayer from before been answered? If God was all-powerful and benign, why not just restore them both to good health and get them home in that instant? Or was he answering her prayers yet somehow unable to deliver them instantly? Wouldn't that contradict the belief in God's omnipotence held by many faith followers?

Sometimes she would come at Phil with her questions, and every time he took each one with careful and patient consideration. Many times, he'd chuckle and tell her, "I don't think I'm wise enough to offer an answer yet." But he always reaffirmed that "not knowing" wasn't the same as a lacking of faith. He just didn't know the answer, and he was straight about it.

It was the opposite answer she had received from other believers. Phil was okay with doubt, and his faith remained. She guessed that's why they called it faith—believing, even blindly so, in the face of everything else. Maybe that was why she could talk to him freely about it.

She didn't know the answers either; she was only sure of her skepticism. Yet she had prayed before, and she wondered if her pleas were answered. She had reached the mountain, she had gotten word home, and they were safe. Worse for wear, sure, but with medicine now in their systems, they were better, *right?* Was it the providence of a limited divinity? Or not? She didn't know.

"Don't worry," she mumbled, feeling his forehead, in an impatient fervor of confidence for the medicine to work its magic. She frowned when she felt the still present fever. "We're gonna be fine now."

Phil woke to strobing lights, and he could hear rolling thunder in the distance. He craned his head to the window to see lightning flickering far off in the night sky. Thunder seeped out in a wave over them like an unfurling carpet. Sweat drenched his body, either from the illness or the sweat of being under so many layers of blankets—but with his waking came the alleviation of the fog clouding his thoughts. The disorientation of illness was no longer as thick within, offering more vacancy for thought and focus. But it was only for a moment, like the waves pulling back before making another push, only weaker, and the fog returned. He felt it take over again, but now, with a broken fever, he was more himself. His body was trembling, his teeth glittering with each breath, and the cold of the room contrasted with his sweating skin, providing an Arctic freeze.

Sitting up, he found himself torn between two realities: one in the present, in the desolation of Colorado Springs, and the other back in Atlanta. The thought that Dakota would never return home came to him as an all-consuming fear. He looked around the room, his heart hammering harder in his chest. He saw a couch in the room, but no Tim sleeping on it. Dread came to him at the sight of Autumn lying in a fetal position at the foot of the bed, in need of his protection. However, his sister just was just as much in need of rescue in Kansas City. Which one would he choose? Would he go look for Dakota, or remain, and keep the kid safe?

His breathing escalated, and a minute or two passed as the present washed away the past. He realized he wasn't in Atlanta; he and Tim had gone and rescued Dakota, and now his brother and sister were back home. Only, that fear had never truly left him, had it?

He rubbed warmth back into his chest, looking at the young woman at his feet. She lay with just one blanket, trembling as much as him, and Phil felt his heart calm, his breathing slowing, as the kid stirred. Just once, in the light of the dimmed LED lamp, he saw not in a state of panic or fright but in a restful calm. Her bruised right eye was now almost fully healed, but her left had a new shiner spanning down to a swollen left nostril and a bruised cheekbone. Her breath was visible in the dark air.

The sight harkened in his memories his little buddy, his baby boy, Benjamin, and with those memories cascaded an avalanche of emotions. As Phil felt the dressing over his neck, he recalled the times when he would go to sleep early for work. Back in those days, after retiring from the Army Special Forces and the CIA Special Activities Division, he was a freelance advisor for the Special Forces SERE training in Fort Rucker, Alabama. First to bed, first to rise, it had been.

Going to bed early had meant not tucking in his little boy, Ben, to sleep; getting up early, he never had enough time to make lunch although he didn't relish dining on base or eating MREs. He would just wake up, get ready, and kiss his wife and boy goodbye. But one morning, after waking up and kissing his sleeping Sarah goodbye, he found a note in his wallet: "Look iN duh FRigerator Dahdy." And he did, finding a sandwich, a box of raisins, Pringles, and a Sunny D, all in a shopping bag, ready to go.

Every morning, he'd quietly enter his boy's room to kiss him goodbye and check on his buddy, consumed in a wave of loving motion. He would give Ben's face a gentle rub. *My baby boy.* The thoughts would echo in silent murmurs and never leave, even in the present when he thought about his son. Phil couldn't explain how much he loved his son; there were no words. Only those who shared such a passion could understand. After a while, the notes stopped, but his little boy still made him lunch at night, and Phil would always take it to work the next day. Stopping at the kitchen on his way to the garage, he'd remember, *look iN duh FRigerator Dahdy.*

Family had always been the anchor that kept him grounded. It started with his mom and dad, then Sarah and his baby boy, and then Tim and Dakota. Now the words threatened to come unannounced from his heart, and without prompt, in a consuming wave of affection as he looked at Autumn, restful but cold. But he couldn't, wouldn't entertain those words. No matter what the heat of the moment brought out of him, she wasn't his kid. So he bit down that affection, pulled it back, and shoveled it back down that dark hole inside. For with it, he felt the same pain that never went away—thinking of his little boy, the hurt was still too fresh.

He took all but one of his blankets and added the layers over her. Then he lowered to his knees and tucked her in, inspecting the bruising on her face and eyes as he did. The contusions were many, not just on her head but dressing her arms, legs, neck, and face as well. He thought she looked spotted, like a Dalmatian, and while he didn't like comparing people to dogs, there was a quality so admirable in the latter: loyalty, unwavering loyalty.

In the intermissions between every chapter of life and every new family he'd come to know, the darkest recesses of his being came into the fold. In the absence of his parents, then of his wife and son, and now of Tim and Dakota, he seemed lost and uncouth. He was already in such a state when Igor and his Wolf Pack arrived in Colorado Springs with Autumn. Instincts of a predatory nature were always readily available, driving him to a desire to hunt, torture, and kill; there was a pleasure that was deeply satisfying in it. These longings and desires were always intensified during each of these "intermissions," when he was without an anchor to keep him centered. Without Tim and Dakota there, he felt feral.

This new intermission started months ago when he was infiltrating a politician's office. He had obtained information needed by Colonel Winston and planted incriminating evidence in its place. In addition, he took photographic proof, for what "incriminating evidence" would be complete without proof to use as blackmail?

Inadvertently, he stumbled upon the name Igor Petrov, and from there the voices, amnesia, blackouts, and so on started. The turbulence in him instantly gave way to violence, like a high-category hurricane, upon the sight of Wolf Pack landing in that crater. It intensified when he saw they had brought Autumn into the fold.

Then he had blacked out, and yes, he was scared. He didn't remember everything and losing periods of time felt like losing pieces of himself. But that familiarity of an anchor seemed to return as he considered all that Autumn had done on her own accord. The issues of the mind suddenly took a backseat as he tucked Jade in under the extra layers of blankets she had so selflessly given him. He knew her, and a weight seemed lifted now that she knew just a bit more of the truth; she knew him not as Thomas, but as Phil.

The weight of his promise to Sarah, which he had reinforced for Tim and Dakota's comfort, felt more like a hindrance. What could you do when one promise collided with another? Which one did you pick? In the absence of his anchor, he felt there was only one option. The cage inside rattled, the hounds of hell barking and clawing to be let loose upon Igor, Anton, and Petr. For this little girl's sake, he knew which promise to break.

Yes, it was all made simple at that moment as he held her swollen cheek with tinder care.

I promise, whatever the cost.

Chapter Ten – Narrow Corridors

-October 24th, 2030-

The smell of meat was the first thing she noticed, then the sound of sizzling mixed with dancing flames and cracking before her eyes opened. She felt the warmth radiating from the nearby kitchen in the sped room. She sat up, though the extra compression of covers over her made her want to fall back asleep. She had been in such a comfortable position that had it not been her stomach demanding substance, she probably would have lain back down. Her hands held a blanket around her like a cloak; she turned around to see Phil standing up straight in the sped room kitchen.

He had a small, open fire set on the old stove with a skillet on which meat sizzled. It smelled like bacon, but the squirrel furs hanging over the sink said otherwise. His red and black flannel was draped over a chair, the floor wet underneath. He looked cold in his simple black undershirt.

"How are you feeling?" she asked.

"Mending." He nodded a tired smile. "Thanks to you. Mulţumesc. How are you holding up?"

"Honestly, I'm starving."

A smirk sparked on Phil's face, and he gave a turn of the wrist holding the survival knife that he used to cook the meat and looked at his watch. "I found some critters in the courtyard earlier."

"You weren't worried about Sergei ambushing you or me while you left?" she asked.

There was a pause in his voice, cutting off right as he spoke. His whole being just seemed to freeze. The lights were on, and nobody was home—he went distant and blank—and then a second later he was back, speaking, as if nothing had happened. "We're not out of the woods just yet," he said, dumping the meat on a plate and walking over to her as if he hadn't heard her.

Her eyes didn't leave the plate of steaming meat as he approached. Her belly growled in hunger pains. Instinct took over and her mouth salivated at the promise of food.

"We have a few minutes before first light. Get some grub in you, and we'll head out," he said, offering her the plate.

She took it without pause. The heat of the meat mattered not as she shoved a strip of squirrel into her mouth. Chewing, his words about heading out sparked worry in her as she looked over her shoulder, fearing they had slept past dawn. The drapes had been pulled back, the windows revealing a sky whose horizon was still dark as night, dimming to brighter shades of blue passing over them. There was still a little bit of time, and she looked back to Phil, offering him the plate as he took a seat on a chair before her.

"You're not gonna eat?" she asked as he returned with a simple shake of his head.

"I already did." He offered a smile; it felt forced, something she'd hadn't seen before.

There was a subtle shift in his tone, easy enough to miss for those who didn't know him. But they had been friends for the last two years, and Autumn raised a skeptical brow. He was always honest with her, but right then and there, she saw the lie. She could sense it, and she frowned, looking at the plate in selfless refusal while her stomach growled greedily.

So, she took half the squirrel strips in her hand to nibble on, saying, "I don't think my stomach can handle all of it." She motioned for him to take the rest.

"For later, then." He set the plate down next to her.

Autumn deflated, biting off a piece of squirrel and casting a glare at him.

For God's sake.

She couldn't argue and just let it go. She intended to bite off a small piece, but that greedy stomach prompted a scarfing of the strip of meat instead, and with a full mouth, she asked, absent of embarrassment, "Do you have any idea of where to go?"

Phil walked over to his flannel, picked it up, and rolled it, ringing out just a little bit of moisture; the water was gray and dirty. Then he slipped into it and nodded. "You haven't been paying attention in your SOP Prep class, have you?"

"It's boring." She shrugged. "They just tell us abbreviations and lines of dialogue…"

"For good reason," he replied. "From the Nine-Line MEDEVAC you sent out, recall Line Seven? It's our method of marking the PZ." He took a chest rig, one of the many from Sergei's Wolf Pack plunder, and slipped his arms into it.

She thought about it, standing up as she found her boots and slipped into them. Phil's hurried readiness was contagious as she suddenly understood they were short on time. "Oh, um, that's the Pickup Zone. You had said Green Smoke." She snapped her fingers, receiving a nod from Phil complete with a soft smile; he looked proud.

"And the First Line is our MGRS coordinates, which I marked for Pikes Peak. I don't know if the summit is a good place to wait, but nearby will work." He held up a smoke canister. "All they'll have to do is look for the green smoke."

"You do think of everything." She was amazed and inspired by his ability to think and plan in such distress. It was inspiring to her, fueling her motivation. She scarfed down the rest of the squirrel like in her lunch breaks at school where only a little time was given to eat, and she hurried to get ready alongside him.

Together, they were both armed with weapons. Phil explained that an SMG fit for her stature and height was called Vityaz SN. He made sure it was on single-fire before giving it to her. He took up the same AK-12 he had from before. The bags on their backs were already packed with supplies and provisions.

THWOOPING came in relentless rotation outside, and the windows shook from the force of the helicopters. Phil ran to the window. Standing off to the side, inside a line of shadows, she mirrored his posture on the other side. First, she looked at him. The tender and gentle man was gone, quick as a flash. The man now in her company was someone else, with hard-focused eyes of onyx set in the stony features of his face. Her gaze shifted to the window, looking outside at the front parking lot, and she saw nothing. She looked up, hearing the helicopter but not seeing it.

At first, she thought maybe it was the rescue from the MEDEVAC, until she realized they were not close to the MGRS coordinates, nor was there green smoke marking their location. Wolf Pack had found them.

"To the roof," Phil said.

He led the way, walking with a brisk limp down the hall to the custodial closet, Autumn as his six. The door was left open long ago, and inside he found a ladder climbing up to a roof access point. Instructing her to wait there while he ascended, he scaled the ladder and cracked open the hatch just enough to see outside. The bright, sunny morning was now in full dawn to the east. He thought it was a ruse, a trap that set hopes far too high. In light of recent activities, he had fallen hard for the hope.

Sure enough, he saw what he expected—a Mil-Mi patrolling the air. He ridiculed himself for the giant smoke signal he had created the day before. Yet something wasn't right; yesterday he had seen two of the birds, and only one patrolled the sky here.

In less than a second, the dots connected, and he understood. You send in the hounds to flush out the game. Reality crept on him understanding the distraction for what it was. The other bird had already landed nearby, and the men were infiltrating the building that very moment. They had sent in the dogs to flush out the game.

He descended as fast as he had climbed up, fearing the kid was already subdued with a gun to her head or a knife to her throat. Every step down couldn't have gone by slower as his stiff leg made it difficult. Reaching the bottom, he turned to a wide-eyed Autumn; she was already alert to his visible change in demeanor.

He grabbed her by the arm and walked in as brisk a pace, freeing her when she got the message. She asked him several beats along the way the same question: "What is it?"

But he didn't respond; he just stopped every fifteen meters or so for a "Stop, Look, and Listen," and then pressed forwards. His rifle was at a high ready, and light from the morning dawn reflected and bounced through the interior, providing enough ambient light to see. He saw only silhouettes of barricaded doors and furnishings expected to be found in classrooms, push carts, and custodian's cleaning carts. Nothing detailed the shape of a human. At the first intersection they came to, he came to a full stop.

Something caught his ears, a sound in the distance. He stopped, looked around, and listened, seeing nothing but hearing it. Autumn, continuously pounding the silence in her persistence, bit her tongue and listened as well. It was faint: echoes in the deep, rhythmic and steady—the pacing of a squad of men moving with ghost-like stealth.

"We stayed here for too long," he whispered, "No more talking from here on out. Understand?"

She understood, and he went back to his twelve, rifle at the ready, and pied the corner. The iron sights of the weapon kept a hair at his lower periphery, so the moment he saw a threat, it would take less than a second to aim and engage. He longed for night vision, something to help him see into the shadows of the nook and crannies—perfect places for threats to lie in wait for an ambush. But the intersection was clear and the halls vacant. The presence of the rhythmic *thunk* of boots was still audible; Phil counted at least seven of them in steady strides. Their echoes were a constant audible presence.

They reached the first stairwell and went down the first floor. They were filled and blocked with desks, chairs, tables, filing cabinets, and other assorted furnishings.

"Here, this way." Autumn pulled at his arm to stop him, and she lowered her weapon, letting it dangle at her side from the sling around her shoulder. Before he could stop her, she took the lead to the corked stairwell, almost as if with practiced ease. The kid got down and crawled through a gap in the barricade. Like a mole burrowing underground, she disappeared.

Fuck. He grimaced, lowering down onto his left leg, his good one. His right leg was stiff, with an unwieldy, straight posture. A jolt of pain shot up from his knee and across his back. He followed her through the gap. The soles of her boots were near his face as she maneuvered through the tight space, wiggling and squirming without much resistance. While she had no trouble navigating her small form through, his larger build pressed at every angle. He was a giant, worming through a narrow tunnel, and every odd turn and step down made him glad he wasn't claustrophobic.

Autumn waited for him in a little expansion of space, underneath a teacher's desk on the first landing. Her hand reached out to stop him, and the silhouette of her face contrasted with a splash of light, bleeding through the clutter and over her eyes, giving a view to their greenish-gray irises. Her eyes looked down from him, and he followed her gaze to where her hand landed, warning him of a rusty piece of metal from a filing cabinet that nearly gashed his bicep.

Phil nodded his thanks, and she smiled in return before turning around and continuing. They disappeared down the next flight of stairs in a bend made by several cabinets and push carts. By the time he got around the little turns, Autumn vanished out of view.

His own pace quickened, and the same fear of a hostile holding a gun or knife to her consumed him again. He breathed in dust and dirt as he reached the first floor. She was in a kneeling position with her gun at the low, ready. He had to give her praise for holding point, and at the same time he doubted if she would really kill someone. He hoped she'd never have to find out.

His stiff leg made climbing back to his feet a challenge. He held onto a desk as he did so, and he gave her arm a nudge with his elbow. She smiled at him, and he took point. Autumn seemed far more mature for her age at that moment. She returned to his six as they pushed on.

Phil considered heading out the way they had come the night before. But the noise and ruckus of moving the barricade made him rethink it. His internal GPS connected floor plans and pre-explored routes to the courtyard, other side entrances, and front door. The cafeteria's barricades would make any attempts at egressing too loud.

Autumn pulled at his sleeve. "The courtyard doors," she mumbled. "There's a tunnel system. It leads to a garage, and the garage to the outside."

Phil rested his hand on her shoulder. "You may have a horrible sense of direction, kiddo. But right now, you're the one saving our asses, again."

She beamed at him, and he took point, mentally mapping out how to get to the courtyard. At one point, the other presence in the building with them was so close, right above them. Phil stopped, Autumn behind him, both looking up and listening. He counted each step, doing math in his head, and his tentative count of seven men then became ten. The mush of old ceiling tile muffled their boots as they moved in that near-death-like silence, but they couldn't keep the floorwork under their boots from creaking and moaning. Dust peppered down upon him and Autumn.

The back of his head started to echo that dissonance, the baritones arriving on cue in her distorted humming. But the blackout didn't follow, it only remained a presence, too far removed to cloud his thoughts. It was a presence in the passenger seat while he remained the driver. Adrenaline gave more pep to him, and his energy was renewed by the thought of more men in league with Igor hunting them down. Hunting Autumn down.

Heaven will burn first... A thought that wasn't his crept into his mind from the passenger.

The courtyard doors remained undisturbed. There were no extra footprints in the mush covering the ceiling tile. One sector unexplored by the hunters meant that they would be there soon enough. Phil eyed the path leading across with a skeptical sneer. Opening the doors and stepping outside, he scanned the roof. The other bird's rotating blades and engine no longer gave an indicator of its whereabouts.

The roof was clear, and he turned counterclockwise, scanning the edges around and behind him as they came into view. No threat came into view; it felt more like a hiatus, a pause in reality in which precious seconds gave them a narrow window to cross the courtyard before time resumed.

He took to the thick underbrush of the courtyard, Autumn close behind him, concealing their travel across and reaching the other doors. Again, Autumn had taken the initiative; once through the doors, she pulled at his sleeve, pointing to an open service hatch. She didn't wait for his approval, instead going ahead of him and sitting over the ledge before hopping down. He followed her down into the maintenance tunnel. He looked to his twelve, then six, finding it clear.

Phil reached up, grabbed the release lever, and pulled it and the hatch shut.

It was a slow crawl through the cramped confines, and the path turned to a slope that spanned dozens of meters until the roof and pipes lifted to a small maintenance room. Through a door where a shattered broomstick rested, Phil found a crowbar sitting on a top shelf of a storage rack. He rammed it through the door handle and cement wall.

Autumn was already at the garage door, on her tiptoes and looking outs a window just a foot taller than she.

He stood beside her, looking outside at the back parking lot, Sergei's scarecrows poking up above the houses and trees beyond. They were ill omens, spelling ultimate doom—the edge of an old, medieval map, warning the traveler of the end of the known world. Should you choose to go further, then *here there be monsters. Here there be scarecrows.*

Sergei's cryptic words resurfaced in his mind: *Scarecrows don't get to pick their faces... Not my face.*

"Last time, there were zombies all over the place." Autumn interrupted his thoughts; she could just barely look over the bottom edge of the glass panel.

"All clear now." He grabbed the old, rusted locking lever, and gently worked it. A metal screech sent waves of erect hair down his neck and spine. The lever slid with resistance, and the old springs and wires of the door resisted his attempts but failed and gave in as he lifted the door open. He stopped just enough for Autumn to get down and crawl through.

"Alright," she huffed, the tip of her fingers poking out from under the door, latching onto it. "I got it."

Phil released his hold, and the door dipped but steadied with an "umph" from the kid. "I still got it, for a second!"

He dropped down to crawl through, Autumn's black jeans to his periphery, and then, coming from behind her, another pair of legs charged in. In the blink of an eye, she was swept away, her hands no longer holding the garage door up.

Phil hadn't cleared the door yet, and it fell on his right foot. A hoarse cry shot out his lips as he pulled it the rest of the way out. His first order of business had been to get his rifle at the ready, only he was prone. He got the weapon aimed at his twelve and lined up his sights at the man holding Autumn back; he was no other than Petr Popov.

But there was no pistol or blade held to the kid's head as he feared. Nor did the man hold Autumn as a shield. Rather, he was dragging her away, holding her back like a dog on a lead. Petr's head was fully exposed, and the time it would take for a bullet to snap through the air and his skull was too fast for him to move Jade in between.

Phil's finger moved to the trigger until one hand fell over the rail system of the rifle and another to the butt. The weapon was jerked away by Anton Federov, and Phil with it. The other man stood over him and his foot crashed down on Phil's face.

Phil tasted iron in his mouth, and he cast a loathsome grin at Anton, getting his legs between him and the man and pushing back. He freed his rifle from Anton, who now tumbled back. Somewhere during the scuffle, Anton had ejected the magazine, but Phil still had a round hot in the chamber.

With lightning-like movement, Phil shot up to his knees, the stiffness in his leg now absent, aiming at Petr once more. He realigned the iron sights at the man's face, finger to the trigger, then he stopped. Someone else, a third person, was now behind him; he could sense the barrel of a gun aimed at him.

Then he heard it—Igor Petrov's voice, demanding Phil to yield. Petr came to a stop, far from the radius of the scuffle. Anton was back to his feet, raising his rifle at Phil. "Lower gun," Igor demanded.

Phil's eyes hardened at Petr, who still held Autumn back. A sigh flared his nostrils as he lowered his rifle. Feeling his Colt being yanked out from his holster, Phil turned around to see Igor now holding his revolver and aiming it at him.

"You," Phil hissed, feeling his knee close to giving in.

He could hear Igor's breathing, and the man stepped back and out of arm's reach. Anton picked himself up off the ground. That dissonance of baritones at the back of his head was building pressure, an unrelenting wave flooding his thoughts as he looked at his old enemy. Memories long haunting him, repressed, set loose the ravenous hounds of hell at his sanity. Grief and hatred consumed Phil as he glared at Igor, and Autumn's cries for them to make peace filled his ears. But Phil found only hatred in his heart.

He could hear Anton step up behind him, and he waited for the hard strike that knocked him unconscious.

Chapter Eleven – Perdition

Phil could feel his boots dragging along each bump of every weed-filled crack, hole, and chipped edge of pavement. His head was lowered as his arms were pulled against the cold air, breeze slithering over his neck and down through his shirt over his back. There was a metallic taste wet in his mouth. In his near unconscious state, the chorus of distorted waves of humming baritones was loud, their hums in high crescendo—satanic chanting's conjuring an evil one, building up to what sounded like chanting that was incomprehensible. It was a gathering of demonic worshipers seeking to conjure their dark idol from hell.

He faded out and felt the pavement transition to dirt and grass under his feet.

Now Phil was sitting, his hands bound to the arms of a chair. Bludgeoned and tired, he hunched forward, head falling with blood dripping from his lips. The other eleven members of his A-Team were wheezing and sputtering curses following their recent interrogations. Phil had been the last of them to receive the tortures of Amur Tigr.

Some of the men, primarily Weapon Sergeant Hammons, offered words of comfort to him. He looked up, feeling cold air coming over his face, and met his long-time friend's gaze. Phil moved the muscles that would produce a grin; they were heavy and taxed, and beads of blood spilled over his bottom lip as he did so.

"Atta boy," Hammons praised.

The door at the front end of the basement opened, and the two men of Amur Tigr standing guard joined with the rest of Igor's Spetsnaz team. They didn't speak a word; their weapons were no longer in a position aimed at the ground but up and ready to be used. The sight of their approach came like the footsteps of a hangman to the lever of the gallows. Phil's heart pounded like a hammer-forging machine. The ten members of Igor's team each took a position behind each of Phil's brothers—all but himself. Igor stood behind Operations Sergeant Warburton; it was only proper for a leader of warriors to be executed by an equal.

Somewhere in the shadows, he saw Sergei's silver-moon pupils pierce the black darkness of the musty basement. Not in full form, just the crescent glow of his eyes, watching, waiting. Phil heard his voice harken in his deep thoughts: "Break the Silence."

Autumn's whimpering brought his eyes to flutter open, seeing the charred side-lawn of the school pass under him. Dirt and ash puffed up to his mouth as he coughed. His right hand was numb, and he heard Igor's voice: "You do understand?"

Yes, Phil understood, just as he did a long time ago and as he did now. Revelation dawned on him, Sergei's cryptic conundrum like a warm sunrise illuminating the night.

Hammons had been first, and one by one, his brothers' executions followed. On the outside, Phil remained jaded, still as a stone that twitched at each pull of the trigger. All ten clicks of the hammer carved a permanent echo in his memories, along with the BANG of the pistol. The executions came to an end with Warburton to Phil's left as Igor raised his AK-12 and murdered his leader. As his last remaining brother's head fell forwards, Phil looked up at Igor, his vision blurred by the tears he held back as the Russian spoke.

"Living with the reality, the memory, of the ones who conquered you. That is the true way to conquer one's enemies." Igor had spoken in a clear, thick, Russian accent. "You do understand."

Yet before, there had only been twelve chairs, including his. Now a thirteenth chair manifested from the murky air. Autumn, bound and gagged, sat in it. She had wide, reddened eyes, facial bruises, and cuts up and down her exposed body up as she wept and begged. Sergei came forth from the shadows, arms folded across his waist with Phil's Colt resting in a comfortable place over his other wrist. The masked man took a stance behind Autumn, the antique revolver now lifted behind the kid's head.

Next in line.

"Break the silence."

Phil shed a tear, finally, and he heard dear Sarah's voice on the night they had consummated their marriage. Benjamin hadn't come into the world, but he could hear his baby boy's laughter and feel their unborn child's kicks at the belly, and Phil's promise echoed back from the years ahead. That night, he spilled everything to his wife: his brothers' deaths, his return to that country, and the butchering he vindicated.

"I'll never be that man again," he promised her, a promise that now bound his hands to the chair, preventing him from fulfilling his vow to Autumn. "Whatever the cost."

When he woke up, the distorted baritones hadn't ceased; their humming remained in crescendo. He could feel the rising headache splitting his thoughts. Igor stood with Autumn next to him, Anton and Petr at his flanks. Autumn wasn't bound to a chair, nor abused, at least not yet. Her arms were held back by the two men as she begged for Phil's life. She pleaded his case before the judge as a look of indifference frowned across the man's face. They were in the circle drive of the school's front; he was on his knees, his hands dangling down his sides. Igor stood closest to him, admiring his revolver with a scornful expression, and everyone else was well out of arm's reach.

The reinforcements that had arrived, a squad of five men, formed a perimeter around them. On the school's roof, Phil spotted another five on overwatch. Around him, the five holding the perimeter faced outwards.

"You do understand?" Igor asked, finally looking from the gun to him, his eyes then looking at the nearby flagpole.

Phil tried to breathe through his nostrils, but there was a clog, and he sniffed to clear it. The phlegm fell in the back of his throat as he spat it out on Igor's boots. Igor didn't seem to care. He looked up at the flagpole as well, with just bare rags of what used to be an American flag still tethered to the cord, and he understood. He remembered the double agent who caused his A-Team's deaths, and later her skin hanging in the place of the flag at the Romanian capitol.

"Please. He's the one we came here for," Autumn cried out. "Igor, tell them. That's Thomas. Why are you—"

"Enough, child!" It was not Phil's voice, nor even his own words, that came out in a shout at her. There was no stopping this storm.

Autumn recoiled, her bottom lip quivering as she fell silent.

“I know who he is.” Igor’s voice was low and leveled as he stepped before Phil, their eyes never parting.

The team leader of Igor’s reinforcements stepped up to the lieutenant. “Sir. Zey got SOS out before apprehension. Major General Petrov has dispatch Colonel Reznov from Sahtu. Dey’re here in few days.”

“By zen, ve’ll be long gone before any search and rescue arrives,” Igor replied, nodding at Autumn. “Take her to rendezvous, ve’ll finish up here.”

Autumn cried out again, and Phil’s eyes leveled with hers. She fell back into a comforted silence. “Be strong, okay.” Phil couldn’t hold back the cracking of his voice as she wept.

Two of the Siberians pulled her away, and the group of ten departed, leaving Phil alone with the remains of Amur Tigr. He saw Autumn struggle against their orders, looking over her shoulder to not lose sight of him.

They held sight of one another for as long as possible, and the three men of Wolfpack waited. They gave him that mercy at the very least, until Autumn was forced into the helicopter and finally out of view. Phil saw his last bit of humanity, his anchor, vanish. The bird's doors closed, and the blades spun in a steady increase of RPMs as the metal beast lifted and the nose tipped. Before long, it was out of sight.

Phil didn’t look away, listening to the sound of Igor’s feet shifting. The man’s breathing was now labored, his injuries demanding rest.

“Just promise me you’ll get her back home. Safe and sound,” Phil uttered, looking back to his old enemy. His voice broke under the weight of his failure. “Don’t hurt her. Don't kill her.”

Igor squatted down, his eyes hardened, yet Phil swore he sensed understanding in them. “She was never in danger.” A sadness came over his eyes, still bearing that ever-present jaded remorse.

Anton and Petr walked behind Phil, a pained strain crossing Igor’s face as one hand held his side and he adjusted a wounded foot, resting on his knee instead. Igor’s lips fidgeted, searching for words that he didn’t know how to say.

“Had things go different…” He sighed, and there was almost a disappointment—a longing for something else other than this. “Ve would bring you home, but you, you're still very much the same man I remember."

Phil looked at the helicopter, disappearing in the distance. Home was already gone. *Break the silence, or the silence will break you.* His revelation of Sergei's words flashed in his thoughts like the flicker of lightning. He protested, *please, no. Anything but that.*

"I am sorry." Igor sighed, standing back up.

Without Tim and Dakota, reinforcements, or any source of aid, there was only one way he could save Autumn and get her home. Phil—Thomas Nilges, the God-fearing man—wasn't enough to get that done on his own. He could feel the Holy Spirit within him grieve, and a tear fell from his eyes. The suicide of all he strived to be came undone at that moment.

He broke the silence that bound him to that chair; Sergei holding that gun to Autumn's head lowered the weapon as Igor raised the revolver to his head. Phil shook his head right to left, feeling tears swell behind his eyes.

The world seemed to react to Phil's acceptance immediately, followed by his regression. Igor didn't trigger, he never got the chance; the air around them tensed. He could sense Anton and Petr shifting positions, feel the rumbling traversing the ground to his knees and up his thighs, pounding with the war drums of his beating heart. His breathing escalated as he saw ripples travel across the puddles of water around them. Heavy breathing, like the rattling of chains, labored across the parking lot; it was a familiar growl Phil never thought he'd be glad to hear.

Then, from the trees behind them, Phil looked over his shoulder and saw him. Sergei Cultivascú emerged forth from the woods, freed of the chains that bound him to the wild. Before the uncouth madman dared not leave the wild, and now he freely traversed over the remains of civilization, set loose upon the world, upon the foes of Philip Shurlan. The splitting inside his head receded, and his thoughts felt anchored in a new light, a new status quo upon the working tumblers of the cage's lock. Regression drowned out twelve years of adversity.

The masked madman was a harbinger of death, as behind him the Jackle followed, sniffing the air like a bloodhound. Anton and Petr raised their weapons, and Phil let lose a rueful grin, looking back to Igor.

Now, you're all going to die.

Darkness closed in around them, and a powder keg of increasing pressure was soon detonated by a single round that ignited the powder, sparking a bloody screech of wrathful hatred from the monster.

The silence was broken.

Chapter Twelve – O'Death

As with the first time he had been mounted on a post in Garden of the Gods, it felt like he was being crucified. His arms were pulled, outstretched to his sides, at unnatural lengths; he could feel the bulbs of his bones displaced from their sockets. No nails were hammered through his wrists, but barbed wires looped around into his bare skin. It was so tight, they felt like wire cutters sawing through his skin, and the rusted barbs dug deep.

He tried to move one arm, looking for slack under the rope, but his limbs were unwieldy. Even his legs felt the same, though he couldn't look down to see their state. The little he could move came to no fruition. Registering the iron taste in his mouth, he looked up and around; they were all here, his brothers, dead and tied up just as he was. Scarecrows lined the cul-de-sac, keeping the birds away, who cawed in the nearby distance.

The suspended body across from him was still moving. Petr harkened to his brother to see Anton's face looking up at him. They were at the end of the round, dead-end street, with only one scarecrow separating them from each other. The body was dressed in red and black checkered clothing, blue jeans, and brown hiking boots, and his head was covered with a burlap sack.

Anton's head dipped back down, and Petr could hear his comrade's hoarse breath.

Petr was too weak; it felt as if someone had used his whole abdomen for a drum and a hammer for the drumsticks. The fight with the big, skinless brute had been costly; the several broken ribs stabbing at his innards reminded him as such.

Petr sought the strength to speak, calling out as Anton raised his head once more, but he said nothing else when, in his periphery, from behind Phil's scarecrow, he saw movement. A masked figure emerged from the failing house behind Phil, dressed in all black.

Mumbling in a low voice, as if in counsel with himself, his words came to Petr's ears: "…and I saw a beast and it held a number. And this number wasn't that of my face, but of a lie. And let yourself understand, for its number was twenty-two." The masked figure came to a stop beside Anton's bound feet. His hands wielded a rusted-over tree cutter, its cutting edge and teeth beveled. It had a silver shine as if freshly sharpened, contrasting with the composite colors of the rust.

"Who are you?" Petr asked.

After the skinless brute had attacked, Phil had gone missing, and only now Petr saw his fate, strung up as they were. Igor, Anton, and he understood the monster's blindness and retreated into the school. But the labyrinth of its many corridors and classrooms had them running in circles. They were stuck, fish in a barrel, a blocked exit behind them, and that giant skinless *suko* in front of them.

Igor had found an alternate route of escape, racing against the monster, which beat him to an intersection. They continued in their flight as Petr followed with Anton behind him. They lost the monster by the cafeteria, tossing a grenade down another hall to lure the monster away.

They hadn't realized they had stepped into a game of cat and mouse. One by one, they were picked off, unseen and unheard. It started with Anton. One minute he was behind Igor, and the next he was gone. They followed a blood trail to a service hatch, and that skinless *suko's* rampage vibrated like an earthquake across the whole building. All was blank after that; he only remembered the mask of this enigmatic figure standing by Anton's feet.

"Sergei." Petr understood. He had read the report—they all had—of SRT-Alphas encounter with a man in a mask.

Again, and as if rebounding from a spell, the figure twitched and looked around, picking back up his mumblings: "And with all the miracles he was allowed to perform on behalf of the first beast, he deceived all the people whom he ordered to make a great statue of the first beast who was fatally wounded and came back to life."

"No, vat are you…"

The masked figure looked up at Petr and pointed a finger at him. "For it was the first beast, that one who came from the sea, who erected the young as scarecrows and killed the innocent." His voice clawed out through the gaping mouthpiece of the crooked mask, and then he hitched his thumb at himself. "And it is I who am that statue of the first beast that was wounded, commanding all, who refuse to protect the young or innocent, to die."

Without warning, the man swung hard and fierce, ramming the rusted blade into Anton's chest. Petr's heart cried out, enraged, eyes widening, as a wild rebuke barked out at the madman as he could only watch and wait. The masked man left the blade in Anton's chest, the black clothing now deeply wet where the old tool hung. Crimson trails followed down the rusted weapon's teeth, dripping down each one and traveling down the shaft.

"Blood is in the water," the man said, not to Petr but to himself, in such a manner that Petr expected him to check his wrist for the time.

Anton lowered his head, and weak, faint grunts and repressed cries escaped his mouth. The madman pulled out a hammer from a loop in his vest, and before Petr could offer a plea for him to stay his hand, the hammer came down in violent and hard *thwack* at Anton's knees, joined by the *cracking* of bones. A cold chill shot up Petr's back as Anton's eyes woke with a frenzied breath.

"Stay the fuck awake for this," spat the madman at Anton.

"Look to me," Petr called to Anton, receiving a weak but steady stare from Anton, who could look only from under his eyes.

The man now was walking over to Petr, hitching a casual thumb over his shoulder and pointing at Anton. "He'll die soon, but it'll drag." He mumbled. His tone was indifferent, save for a hint of pleasure. "In a way, you should know this was long overdue." He asked, "You do understand?"

Petr looked over at Phil. "I understand." He panted, but the dots weren't connecting; there Phil hung, and here this madman, this Sergei Cultivascú, was both punishing and avenging Phil? It made no sense. More confounding was that the madman was now dressed in Igor's uniform.

"Vere is Igor?"

"Scarecrows don't pick their faces. Statues don't choose to be created." Sergei shook his head, walked back over to Anton, and turned around to face Petr. "He can have a quick ending or a slow one."

Petr studied his dying friend; his chest failed to rise and fall to supply itself with enough air. His heart was pumping blood that was just pulsing out around the blade in his chest. The chest falls became increasingly shallow with each attempted breath.

"There is a lot more I can do until he fades," Sergei said, picking up a pitchfork and poking the tip of the center prong into Anton's armpit, whose breathing rattled with a wheeze and shaking anxiety.

"Don't give him anything." A raspy wheeze passed through Anton's snarling upper lip.

Sergei plunged the blade into Anton's armpit, the upwards jerk coming to a sudden stop as rusted metal scraped and rammed into bone. This time Anton did cry out, loud and riddled with panic.

"I need you awake!" Sergei growled at the dying Anton.

"VAT IS YOUR DEMAND?!" Petr shouted, glaring at the man.

Sergei looked back at him. A twisted look of infuriated anger and sadistic glee sparkled in his brown eyes behind the mask's horrid eye holes. He retracted the pitchfork and rammed it into Anton's right shin, leaving it there.

"Ty Pizda Sergei!" Petr screamed, the dryness in his voice ending in a coughing fit. Those many knives stabbing at his sides were digging deeper.

"Where did they take the girl?" Sergei's voice came straight and stern without any hesitation, and he walked back over to him.

Hesitancy came with the crossing of a line as Petr closed his eyes. He knew the game he was in now, and he knew it well. Phil had suffered through the same setup in Romania, right before his whole team was executed. It was a "no win" interrogation, which to Petr meant Sergei knew exactly where his thoughts would go. Petr did understand; this was a long time coming. He deserved this, he thought, looking back over to Phil.

He recalled the night perfectly, for it haunted him, too, just like it did Anton, Lossif, Michail, Demetri, Yuri, and all the others. There was the greater good and the immediate good to consider. Endure the pain for the greater good or give in to the pain and doom everyone else. They had paved Phil's path while torturing him—not with his well-being but with the immediate well-being of his comrades. It all led to just one inevitable ending.

The greater good was simple: the location of the girl, which was the same rendezvous point with Colonel Reznov. How many others would be killed before the colonel's men put the man down? However, the immediate good, bringing Anton's suffering to a faster end, blurred the line between the two, clouding his judgment. The paved path would eventually break him as it had once broken Phil.

Suddenly, he wished he had a gun; he would just put the barrel into his mouth and bring everything to a quicker end. It would all be over soon enough, and, he thought, if there was a God, perhaps this was a *wergild* of sorts. He had tried to repent, all of them had, after what they had done to Phil and his comrades. In the end, he guessed, an eye must be given for an eye taken.

Petr bit his tongue, remorseful and ashamed of the past, present, and future. He couldn't, no matter how much he loved his suffering comrade. He wouldn't. But Sergei remained patient, releasing a long-held exhale. He walked back to Anton, set a ladder against his chest, and climbed up. The madman removed a large bowie knife and proceeded to carve into Anton's forehead. The ladder pressed against the tree cutter pushed the rusted blade deeper into Anton's chest, making him too weak to vent his pain with cries and yells.

Bloodied grunts and congested slurs came from his dying comrade, too weak to scream or shout. Petr could feel his seams breaking. Looking at Phil's suspended body offered no reinforcing of that line between the greater good and the immediate good. His hatred for Phil was gone, and a kindred suffering now softened his heart towards the man he had so terribly wronged. To his old nemesis, his soul cried out, bearing shame and regret: *Tysyacha Izvineniy, Tysyacha Izvineniy.*

Not even a thousand apologies could deliver him or Anton from their strife. That line was now fully erased with the garbles of Anton's bloodied grunts. The bite on his tongue loosened, and he knew he couldn't take it. Much to his shame, he caved and barked at Sergei: "I will tell you."

"Then tell me. Now." Sergei thundered, not ceasing his engravings on Anton's skin.

Petr felt faint, thinking of the words to form in English. "Zey take her to rendezvous point," he cried out, hoping it would be enough.

Sergei continued until he was finished as bloodied lines traveled down Anton's face like beads of sweat: vertical, crimson rivers traversing over, up, and around the structure of his face. Once finished, he climbed down the ladder, revealing his work. Carvings of words in Romanian read, 'Not my face' upon Anton's forehead.

"Where is your rendezvous?" Sergei demanded.

"Please," Petr pleaded. Suddenly, Anton's agony became all that existed; Petr needed it to end.

"Where?"

"Air Force Academy, Northwest here," Petr finally let out, "It's to be FOB when reinforcements arrive." He panted as he looked at Anton. Streaks of blood ran down from the carvings in his forehead, some curved around his features and into his eyes. Anton clenched his eyes shut against the invasive liquid that was diluted by the well of tears forced out by stress and pain and mixing with the crimson. Streaks of transparent red ran down his face.

Sergei whipped his bowie knife dry on Anton's pants leg. Sheathing the blade as he turned and came back over to Petr in a casual stride, his eyes never parted from Petr's.

"Thank you," Sergei said, his voice now polar opposite of what it had been; it was soft, almost assuring as to the keeping of his end of the bargain. Some sinister sense of pleasure gleamed in the brown of his eyes as he started away from the cul-de-sac. "For being so weak." He passed Petr, his back now to them.

Petr gritted his teeth, muffled cries seething to a now satisfied Sergei.

"Do it!" Petr hollered. "You said you'd make it quick!"

"He deceived all the people who belong to this world," Sergei said, keeping his back to Petr and Anton. There, in his shame, Sergei left Petr, who watched Anton's dying breath come nearer and nearer.

The sky deepened in the twilight hours, reddening around them as Petr dropped his head. The world felt like a vacuum closing in, and Petr's breath was stifled as if he was being suffocated. He looked back to Anton, still hanging in there in a fruitless fight for life. More than anyone else in Wolf Pack, he had been the closest to Anton. It had been Anton to help Petr recover from their sins in Romania, Anton who had rescued him from a drunken downward spiral of self-destruction when the Old World died, and Anton who had brought him back into the fold of a reinstated Wolf Pack. Anton had become his brother, and now Petr could offer him nothing but words.

"Broter," Petr beckoned. "Luk at me." Anton raised his head to look at him, and Petr gave him a nod. "It's okay. It's okay. Just let go."

"Zis. Is." Anton uttered with labored effort, "Judgment." The words slurred into a slow silence, and before long, Petr understood Anton had passed. He was left alone, immobile, and bleeding out as the world closed in around him.

He felt himself start to go numb and as he hung there, dropping his head. He tried one last prayer to whomever might be listening. Tilting his head over Phil's motionless body, the crow's cawing came near; the time for feasting would come as the tolling of their bells.

"Ya Nadeyus', shto ty smezhesh," Petr begged. "I hoped you could forgive me."

Part III – Tim

Chapter One – ACE

-October 22nd, 2030-

Captain Shillings brought Tim and Olivia to an abandoned gas station off Highway 7, northwest of Juneau. Shifting the vehicle in park, out the window Tim saw the small convoy of five SUVs waiting for them. *Sore thumb*, he thought.

The captain's finger entered his periphery, index finger aimed at the glovebox: "I almost forgot, the envelope in there is for you."

Tim opened the glove box and saw the letter, wondering why it didn't just come in the mail. He inspected it and instantly recognized his mother's handwriting, two and two connected, and he understood; his parents were newcomers to Alyeska, "outsiders," per Puristan views.

He sighed as he folded it and shoved it into his pocket. If littering wasn't such a serious crime, he'd have thrown it out the window that very moment. The captain took note of his frustration but said nothing. Tim looked out again to the security force waiting for him. It was half the size it had been before he left for Colorado and waiting at the head of the convoy was Second Lieutenant Bracket, standing with folded arms. There had been ten units before. Now there were only five; the others had been delegated elsewhere to protect "outsiders."

Behind him, he heard the rear passenger door fling open and Olivia leapt out, making a dash for Bracket and hugging him. Tim sighed, rubbing his forehead, the next migraine already setting in. He could feel the captain looking at him, and he met her gaze. The middle-aged woman looked with raised brows as her blue eyes studied his discomfort: assessing, analyzing. He could feel the calculations behind those eyes.

"Yes?" Tim asked.

Her eyes dipped to his arm and leg, then back up to his eyes "Nothing," she said. "I'll be up in Fairbanks if you need anything."

"Thanks, Captain." Tim's hand found the release lever, and he opened the door and stepped out.

One of the men, a fellow Marine—one Staff Sergeant Hendricks—helped Tim get his crutches under him. He had spent a great deal of time "expressing operational concerns," or, professional bickering, as Dakota had put it, to the captain. After losing half his security force, Hendricks was added on. It wouldn't be fair to say that Tim thought that the new generation of soldiers, the ones formed out of necessity for survival, or in service of the new state, were incompetent. Yet, Tim found himself more at ease with the former generation; especially if they were of the same breed as him.

Captain Shillings took off after Tim closed both passenger doors, leaving a dust trail in the gravel parking lot of the old gas station. Tim crutched over to where Bracket and the diva stood. He nodded at Hendricks, who got the message and branched off back to Unit Five's vehicle. The closer he got to the lead, the more he could hear Olivia cry out as if she was just being freed from torture.

"You can't leave me with him," she fumed in jest, burying her head in Bracket's chest. "It's like watching paint dry. Oh golly, it's so miserable!"

"Second Lieutenant." Tim offered his hand to Bracket, ignoring the kid's "misery".

Bracket pulled Olivia off, thumping her nose like a puppy, and clasped Tim's hand. "First Lieutenant."

"Oh no," she cried. "You both are gonna be boring." A devastating look plastered her face, shoulders slumped.

"You're not going to behave like this the entire time, are ya?" Bracket asked her.

A raised hand pointed at the second lieutenant as she took a step back. "He's gotten to you!"

"That's it." Tim shook his head, the migraine setting in place like dried cement. It soured his mood and flattened his voice, tensing the air around them. He pointed back at the girl. "You. You're stuck with me now, Felicia. Get yo' ass in the car, now." He looked to Bracket with a quick, "You're welcome."

Bracket smirked, patting Tim "good luck" before backpedaling to the convoy's lead SUV and shrugging to Olivia. "Sorry, kiddo. Boss's orders."

"Wow," Olivia mumbled, wide-eyed. "You sure do know how to kill the mood. Don't ya?"

"Get. In. The. Car," Tim ordered, crutching over to the center vehicle. Opening the back driver door, he waited.

"Alright, alright." Olivia's eyes rolled up to the sky, her voice fading into a sigh as she jumped inside. Tim forced her to scoot behind the back passenger seat, getting his right crutch in, followed by his right leg. His rear fell onto the old leather seat, and the driver scooted his seat up, providing extra room for Tim to get his leg in and remain in a straight position. He grunted out "Thanks, brotha," before slamming the door shut.

Less than a minute later, the lead SUV took off, followed by the second, and then theirs. Heading northwest to Anchorage, the whole lot of SUVs sent puffs of gravelly dust airborne.

The outer districts of Anchorage could be described as decaying slums of the Old World: slums that were well-kept enough to be livable but run down and in desperate need of repair. The closer to the city they came, the more maintained and orderly the slums became, transitioning to worn-down neighborhoods with grassy lawns, rubble streets, and driveways. The windows of homes were fogged over and dirty. It was almost a cookie cutter version of how the world looked outside the state, save that elsewhere, the buildings were structurally sound, infrastructure and electricity were supplied, and an abundance of people, instead of zombies, populated the area.

The closer to the inner city limits they went, the more well-maintained the scenery became: trimmed lawns and hedges, construction workers repairing houses and repaving roads and driveways. The houses looked refurbished or new, and the streets were better maintained, not cracked with weeds sprouting outwards.

Restoration wasn't just needed in the newly annexed lands of British Columbia, however; all over Alyeska, such efforts were queued. Another reason why Anchorage didn't enjoy the same maintained appearance as Juneau was that Anchorage was a capital of sorts for the Puristan Party. The outer city districts were a clear indicator of where the party leader, and city mayor, Maximus McArthur focused his attention.

It sickened Tim; people could think would they wanted, but he did feel indignant about the party's priorities. The closer into the inner city they traveled, each checkpoint passed, Tim's paranoia, mixed with his sour disposition to the party, brought his headache closer and closer to a migraine. Every person not with his company was a potential wolf in sheep's clothing, including the men and woman frisking him, Olivia, and his team down separately at each stop. Every passing minute felt like an ambush just begging to be executed.

He kept his focus outside the window, looking for Persons of Interest. His eyes scanned, observing, playing at halfhearted verbal pop quizzes with Olivia. He found out long ago that when she was forced to concentrate it made her tamer and like less of an energizer bunny. The mundane quizzing of the Standard Operation Procedures bored her to death, but she sat still, her eyes set on the city passing out the window.

"If you're captured, what is your first priority?"

"My goodness, it's every day with you. I think I could ace a test with a hundred percent by now."

"Until you're able to respond to threats with 'one hundred percent' efficiency, we'll keep doing so."

Typically, it would have been a point of frustration for him; it was his duty, after all, to make sure she was safe. But ever since coming back from Colorado, he found his frustrations not tempered by her resistance. Usually, he'd pull her attention back to him, make her recite the correct answer, and then silence would fall between the two until they arrived at the safe house.

But now, it was different. He didn't want the silence to fall between them; he wanted her prepared and ready. His paranoia festered into anxiety as the driver spoke up from in front:

"We're coming to the next checkpoint."

"Copy," Tim remarked, looking back to Olivia as they came to a stop.

"It doesn't matter because once the Puristans are rooted out, I'll be forced into the required military service. I won't need to worry about being captured." Olivia raised her voice before he had a chance to speak. She leaned her head back against the headrest. "Keep calm and look for a way to escape. Yell and scream if near a public presence." She gave him the answer as if to prove her point.

A sigh escaped his lips. "Because?" he asked, the car coming to a slow.

"We've been through this, like, ten minutes ago!" she cried out. "Can't we just do something else? Like 'I Spy'? Oh look, I spy an anal soldier boy who should let me sign his other cast."

That did register a chuckle from Tim. *You motherfucker.*

Out the window, he observed the ration center, kept near checkpoints. People lined up at the door, receiving their daily bread and butter; those with families obtained more rations. The entire blue-collar, middle class population typically filled such lines: construction workers, maintenance men, custodians, you name it.

"Olivia." Tim leveled his voice. "Because why?"

She sighed. "The first moments are the most crucial after capture, and I'll continue to take every chance to escape."

"And aid others in escaping, if applicable," Tim added. "It's my job to protect you. But if I'm unable to prevent your capture, you need to be ready. It's as you said. You'll eventually enter military service. I won't be there for you after that; it all falls on yourself and your platoon to keep each other safe."

The vehicle slowed and stopped, the first car in their convoy coming to the next checkpoint. The people outside in the ration line looked over at them, some curious and some with features that made him feel a bit uneasy. It was as if they knew just who he was inside; he could be looking at enemies and not even know it. Bringing a question from the back of his head to the front, his curiosity now brought the change in topic that Olivia so desperately wanted.

"By the way," he said. The shift in his tone from stern to soft pulled the kid's interest away from the window. "Why do these people want you so badly?"

There was a change like the flip of a switch. Her dejected boredom was now displaced by a dispassionate frown. Her eyes fell away from the window, hands folded on her lap, fingers fidgeting with one another. She shrugged, "I dunno."

"That's a flat lie."

"I'd rather not get into it." She shook her head, looking back to the people outside. "Go on with your pop quiz or whatever it is."

Their vehicle moved forwards, next in line before the one in front came to a stop for inspection. He didn't press the issue further; feeling her silence more as a plea, he ceded to her request. From his ruck resting at his side, he removed a folder, reviewing the contents therein. It was a dossier reviewing the entire operation: the concerts and security detail all dubbed as Operation Lure and Hair. Along with it was a nearly full description of Olivia's physical status.

He knew every detail inside the dossier. In case Olivia needed a blood transfusion, he knew she would need an A- blood transfusion. All her meals were personally inspected for nuts because of a severe allergy; therefore, Tim and every security officer had on them auto-injectors of epinephrine. The vision of her bright blue eyes was 20/15, and therefore, he made sure that emergency exit signs were never more than fifteen feet away from one another at every location she would be present.

The list went on and on, some to more personal details she had blacked out such as her clothing size and, more personally, her undergarment sizes. Tim or Bracket would go and retrieve her new clothes and garments when needed, not wanting to risk taking her, the Lure, into a public place. They would keep her at the safe houses, protected, while her necessities were gathered. At one point, she had gotten ahold of the dossier and added her own annotations in blue ink: *"That's a little pervy!"* At the very end of the Physical Status list, she scribbled: "*Favorite Band: Def Leppard.*"

Still, the question lingered, and it wouldn't recede to the back of his thoughts. It had been well established over the last two years that Olivia was a priority target to the Puristans, but not *why*.

Their SUV was next in line, and Tim stuffed the dossier into a hidden compartment in the middle seat. The SUV stopped. There was a knock at his window, and Tim opened his door as a guard stood at the ready to help him out. Swallowing a bit of his pride, he accepted the help, easing his busted left leg out with ease. There was some pain as he put pressure on his left side, and the guard leveraged his weight to relieve his leg as he got his right one out, his crutches underneath his arms.

The whole SUV was searched, and everyone was frisked. In five minutes, they were cleared and on their way through, waiting on the other side of the barricade for the rest of their little convoy. They listened to Olivia sing in a mumble, "Cause we got a little ol' convoy, rockin through the night…" Tim thought that, minus the loud, reckless noise of her genre, she did have a lovely voice.

Each vehicle took five minutes, and that meant twenty-five minutes per checkpoint. After the next ten minutes, they were back to making progress deeper into Anchorage. At a junkyard, they made a stop and traded off their SUVs to a contact of Captain Shillings' for beat-up sedans and a Bronco that would blend in with the rest of the traffic.

ACE was settled on the northeast edges of Anchorage, nestled in a dense thicket close to Highway 1. The place was easy to miss and hard to find. The roads to the safe house were eroded and taken over by weeds and vegetation. The trees framed the sides, concealing the path. Once they had turned off the highway, they turned off their headlights and the drivers navigated with NODDs.

What Tim liked the most about the placement of the safe house was its proximity to Anchorage's northern city limits. They could be outside the city's jurisdiction in no time at all should the operation become compromised.

ACE was the callsign for their designated safe house, which was a retired fire station from the Old World, left to rot and decay—one of the many misplaced priorities of Mayor McArthur and his party. Now the building was for their gain. The exterior appeared rotted and decayed, serving as a ruse. Long ago, the foundation and interior had been restored and renovated to housing standards for military use as a safe house.

Before the vehicle was put into park, Olivia jumped out. "You think they have a pole to slide down?" She skipped backwards as she pointed to the old structure. She ran the rest of the way to the front, and Tim watched her ram into the door when the locked handles didn't yield to her entry. Tim rolled his eyes in a short sigh as a couple of security officers from Unit One caught up to her.

Bracket met Tim, helping him to his feet, and he got his crutches under him. Together, they met Olivia and the men at the entrance, the kid rubbing her forehead.

"Did you find your pole?" Tim asked, receiving a finger, but not the middle. She preferred to flip people off with her pinky, as she had told him it was, "A more polite manner of telling you to eff-off."

"Bring back memories?" Tim asked Bracket, the former fireman watching the structure, resisting waves of nostalgia from his old life.

"Too many to count." Bracket smirked.

Tim smirked, empathizing to an extent as he gave Bracket a pat and crutched onwards to the front door, yanking Olivia back as Unit Five arrived and formed a perimeter around her.

Tim waited at the front, and Unit One arrived, unlocked the door, and entered with Unit Two following behind them. Tim and the other three units remained on guard with Olivia until Unit One's team leader came back with an "All clear."

Like a dog yanking free from its collar, Olivia darted inside without a moment's hesitation, in search of a sliding pole from the second floor down.

Olivia collapsed into her office chair, her fingers feeling the layers of duct tape wrapped around the tears in the old leather seat's armrests. The chair's hydraulic mechanism was past its prime and the seat sunk straight down to its lowest setting almost as if it were calling her "fat" in protest. She blew a raspberry at the chair. *I'm not even a buck-thirty.* An adjustment knob under the seat lowered between two of the chair legs prevented her from spinning in place. The urge to spin endlessly was like an itch she couldn't scratch. She wanted to look around at her handiwork, but instead she just glanced over her shoulders and behind her.

Posters of *Def Leppard, Iron Maiden, Icon for Hire*, and other bands were stuck to the wall with tacks. A chargeable CD player sat on the desk before her, with a small stack of scavenged CDs next to it. The neck of her guitar rested against the edge of the table. There was a music stand with sheets of musical notes in front of her. The room didn't come with a dresser, so she left her clothes in her suitcase, resting on a table next to a TV and a couch. On a nightstand was a pumpkin that she took from the market in Juneau. A pumpkin carving kit sat next to it, along with other odds and ends. She had brought some life to the plain old room.

For all her hard work and busyness, Tyrese's persistent inquiries hadn't left her. His question nagged at her thoughts. Speak of the devil, and he shall appear; only, they never told her he wouldn't leave. *Why do these people want you so badly?* The question hadn't left her alone, and with it came unpleasant memories she tried hard to shake off.

Two years ago, in the middle of the night, the door to her school barracks had been kicked in as a group of twenty men stormed in. The leader of the intruders ordered all the girls in the barracks to stand in a line, and those whose names were called were to step forwards.

At first, she thought it was the head of the school, Captain Bernard, making one of his surprise drills in the middle of the night. But it wasn't, and they weren't Puristans either. These men were dressed in all-black clothing and spoke in Russian among themselves and in broken English with her and her fellow students.

Even now, she could feel her heart hammering in her chest when recalling that night. Her arms and legs trembled when her name had been called to step forwards. Tears formed in her eyes when that same feeling of isolation swept over her—the moment her peers outed her when she didn't step forwards.

The whole line of students took a step back, save for herself. The boots stomped across the tile, the ogre's giant hands gripping the back of her neck as she was hurled face-down to the floor. She squirmed and fought back, the taste of the old tile and blood in her mouth. She feared what might come, with one hand twisting her arm behind her and the other hand pressing down on the back of her head. She was subdued and at their mercy, but they didn't rape her.

All they did was roll her left sleeve over her bicep and send a needle into her arm. The long needle subdued her squirming for fear of breaking the probing device off in her arm. She waited and watched, feeling no drug being injected. Rather, hefty amounts of blood were removed, and they didn't stop stealing her blood until she was dazed and dizzied along with ten other outed peers.

She barely recalled the men leaving; her next lucid memory of that night was waking in the medical ward. A blood transfusion brought her out of a Class 1 Hemorrhage. The following afternoon, Captain

Shillings stopped by to visit her, with a proposition. After such unpleasantness, how could she refuse? That fear, vulnerability, and isolation—she never wanted to feel that again; she wanted Alyeska, the last hope of safety in a Dead World.

A house divided can't stand, right? Good Abe Lincoln I think it was.

But things had changed since then since the Lure and Hair operation began. She didn't go to Basic Training at sixteen; she graduated school early at fourteen and the concerts began. Concerts that showed her the many people still suffering and hurting as she did. Eventually, she stopped doing covers of songs and wrote her own, addressing her own pains in empathy with those who would listen. She prayed they would take something away from them.

Just go away, she mouthed at the memories, wiping her eyes dry and taking a couple of hard sniffs of the snot about to drip out her nose. She picked up a dishrag that served as a handkerchief and blew her nose.

Leaning over the table, she fitted headphones over her ears, turned on the CD player, and played a song from *Icon for Hire*. It was her favorite band, among many, and instantly she was nodding along with the music. A creative flow picked up in a current of musical inspiration, sliding the right headphone off her ears. Her guitar rested on her right thigh, and she started picking away.

With a pencil tucked behind her ear, she'd scribbled musical notes, mumbling to herself, and experimenting along the way. The Muse was upon her, and inspiration was effortlessly finding her. She was composing a cover of an old folk song, "Wayfaring Stranger." With her acoustic guitar, she planned to play the song during her next concert.

She was doing her part, baiting out these human traffickers, but after the first concert and zero kidnapping attempts from the Puristans, she found the concerts doubled in purpose. There was power in music, there was empathy and comfort, and it was there she saw some measure of hope and comfort it gave others. Kids, and young adults just like herself, stuck in their own personal hells. That made her love the operation. She could reach out to others. Lure and Hair wasn't just to make Alyeska a safer place, but a healthier place.

The sleeve of her right hand pulled back as she scribbled her notes; with the bracelets removed, the scars on her wrists served as reminders of her passion. She felt like she could reach out to others because she too had been where so many were. She had survived not just the Great Calamity, but her own demons as well. At times, she'd find herself regressing into her personal hell when looking at the dozens of horizontal scars across her wrists. It was only after surviving the lacerations that she clung to the comfort and hope she found in music.

Thoughts of the invasion at the school barracks, the millions of survivors still suffering, and her brother Al would bring her to that point of regression once more. Had the music not been pounding in her ears, lifting her spirits? She smiled, thinking of Al, and a tear lapsed down her cheek. She rubbed her wrists as if to comfort them and calm the stirred demons. She wasn't the only one to lose her family, her brother.

Tyrese was no different, and while he could hear her music, he never listened to it. *I'm just not into that kind of stuff,* she recalled him telling her. She didn't think he ever listened to the lyrics, just the beat. He judged a book by its cover, so to speak. That was fine; she'd find a way to make him listen, to reach out to him.

So she hoped, while looking at her scars. Maybe the acoustic might get his attention this time, and if not, then maybe she'd investigate other genres, maybe genre blend her concerts? Whatever it took, she wanted to reach out to him in his own hell, his own grief, that was still too fresh—a deep laceration that hadn't scarred over yet.

My friends call me Olive. Well, I don't have any friends, but if I did, I'd want them to call me that. She had told him once before, and immediately he had replied with a "Miss Blundell."

"Wayfaring Stranger" lyrics were memorized in her thoughts, and some places she had paraphrased. She just needed to get the right rhythm and the right riffs with the instrument. She pulled her sleeve over her wrist, laying her demons to rest for the night, and picked some more at the guitar, finding another chord that she needed.

She about jumped with excitement and almost screamed when the flow of inspiration increased tenfold. Her hand yanked the pencil off her ear as she wrote down the note. It was detailing a map of hidden treasure. A smile broadened her face, excitement fueling her endeavor. If direct communication wouldn't get through to him, or checking in when she learned he had lost his brother, or any other efforts, than just maybe this would.

You are not alone.

Chapter Two – Log and Specks

-October 23rd, 2030-

The day started with bad news. Night sentries reported several persons of interest lingering around the area surrounding the amphitheater; the area itself was of low pedestrian and residency traffic. That itself wasn't definitive enough to judge someone a Puristan, nor was it enough to apprehend them, but the news didn't sit well. The sunny morning had a certain gloom to it. If this concert was going to be the one where they captured a 'hair,' only Tim worried about the cost.

Anxiety made him unable to sit still; his right foot tapped in an unending repetition of a beat without melody. His eyes were glued to the analog clock as he waited with a migraine pounding without end behind his forehead. It was 1730. The cold metal bell of Laura's stethoscope moved from the left side of his upper back to the center.

"Breathe in," Laura instructed in a low voice, her tone soft like someone who just woke up.

Tim breathed in, noting the heavy bags under focused eyes, her features still as she listened to his breathing. She came to an eventual satisfied nod.

"Breathe out." Her instructions continued.

He breathed out, and a final satisfactory look crossed the doctor's face as she removed the cold bell from his back and withdrew her hand from under his shirt, removing the earpieces. Staring off at nothing in particular, her lips moved, mouthing something to herself. Tim noted the reddening of the whites of her eyes and the loose and out-of-place strands of hair from her ponytail. Even more concerning were the several brief moments of unintentional respite, moments where she just paused and checked out, removed from reality. Typically, she smelled of sanitizer and cleaner, but now that duality was a triality, with the smell of her body odor.

"You doing okay, Doc?" Tim asked.

There came a quick, easy-to-miss, shake traversing down her head to her shoulders, eyes blinking rapidly as she connected back to the present. Her hazel gray irises met his. It was the first time she really looked at him eye to eye since arriving for his routine checkup. She stayed there for a moment, in that space of dissociation; the demeanor of the good, friendly doctor was replaced with a fatigued doctor who moved slower than she did before. She finally spoke after a several-second delay: "Huh?"

"Are you okay?" Tim repeated.

Laura chuffed briefly and softly in a laugh, brushing those loose strands of hair behind her ears as she shook her head. Taking off her stethoscope and setting it in her bag, she patted her knee.

"Several of your fellow SRT units returned from the Northwestern States not long after you, Dakota, and Bravo did," she mumbled, "Many extra wounded to care for. Not enough doctors to render aid to Special Operations Operators." Then she scoffed, biting her tongue before more could escape her lips.

"What?" Tim asked, grunting as he lifted his leg. Her hands met his leg midway, gently cradling the bottom end of the air cast, and he raised his leg with great care on her thigh.

"There are not enough doctors for everyone, it seems. We're stretched thin, from physicians for military servicemen to civilians. The attention to the Northwestern USA is increasing, which means more people in danger, more wounded, and more medical attention needed."

Silence fell for a few moments as she removed the cast. Fresh air cooled his liberated leg, a stark contrast of relief from the migraine still pounding. He looked at the stitchwork holding his skin together where bones had snapped and torn through the muscle and skin.

"Well, girl, I just have to say this. I think my SRT buddies are in good hands," he offered.

The compliment seemed to pass by as she took a disinfectant wipe over the stitchwork. Spikes of tingling burns stabbed through the swollen breach in his flesh down to his broken bones. It was an instant reminder that his nerves were still functional and a lesser pain than the one drumming in his head.

"You need to take care of yourself as well." He exhaled through clenched teeth.

"Has it been irritating you?" she asked.

"Uh, yeah," Tim mumbled, wide-eyed as she looked at him, holding her breath. "I can't walk or do shit else."

She frowned, his jest ill-received. "Have you been applying the antibiotic gel to it and keeping it clean?"

"When I can think of it." Tim leaned on the arm of his chair. His right hand pinched at his temple and forehead. A passing thought crossed his mind and lingered; he wondered if Phil had headaches before he blacked out. The sudden thought settled and stayed. "You know how it goes. The list just gets bigger, not shorter."

"I'm assuming you're still not taking any of the medicine I prescribed you?"

"Two for two, Doc," Tim replied.

His thoughts drifted, curious about what Laura would have deduced about Phil from a psychiatric standpoint. If he had come back home, what would her conclusion have been?

Another sigh escaped Laura as she set his leg back in the cast, strapped the Velcro in place, and lowered his leg to the floor. Her hands cradled his leg until the foot came to a gentle rest on the old floor. She scooted closer, gesturing to his arm. He moved it as far as he could for her to inspect it.

"I know you're not gonna do it. But I prescribed you those pills for a reason, Tim. A lot of other soldiers who need them would love to have that option." There was a pinch of scorn in her voice, with added cinnamon. It was easily distinguished but not overpowering.

With care, and taking a great deal of time, she freed his casted arm from the sling. Undoing the Velcro straps to the air cast and liberating his arm brought on that same sensational feeling of cooling relief, contrasting with his migraine.

"They're glorified aspirin, and I don't need to take pills every time I feel discomfort. I'll take the antibiotics, but painkillers, I just don't agree with."

It had always been the same exchange: her wanting him to take medicine for his benefit, and him being too stubborn to do it. Sometimes it was playful banter during social visits, but as his primary doctor, that banter transitioned into scornful reproach. As always, she held her ground and remained persistent. The tired frustration departed her face, and she looked satisfied when she inspected his arm and cleaned it with more disinfectant wipes.

"Can I ask you something?" Tim pressed, a change in subject to which Laura gently nodded. Her eyes stayed focused on securing his arm back into its air cast. "What would make someone suddenly have blackouts? Like a full-grown man?"

"You mean a full-grown man in his late fifties, whose name was Phil, and who actually took his medicine?" she asked, raising a brow, gently securing his arm back into the cast and sling.

"You knew?" he asked, his posture instantly straightening. "About the blackouts?"

"Mmhmm," Laura mumbled, with pressed lips. That spice of cinnamon fading, she now held the look of a bashful, apologetic child. She leaned back in her chair, tired eyes warranting Tim to take it easy on her. But she continued, "Phil confided in me, several weeks ago during a routine appointment. He…" she stammered. "He expressed concerns and worry, explaining that he had been zoning out. Losing moments of time and experiencing memory loss. Going to bed before twilight and waking up in the middle of the field outside your home for example. Tuh—" she chuckled, shaking her head, closing her eyes as she did so; she seemingly dozed off for a minute.

Tim gave her hand a gentle pat, and she seemed to come back, slower than she had left. It pained him to think how she'd be driving in such a state.

"Then we talked more in-depth during your appointment after you three had finished reconnaissance over Lethbridge."

"Lethbridge was a damn mess." Tim cut through her words, shaking his head.

"I remember." She gave a moment of silence, and her eyes deepened, growing beady. "But I could only go as in-depth as I am allowed without permission to interview him as a psychologist." She bit her bottom lip, head shaking, as her eyes drifted off to somewhere away from Tim. "During that appointment, I had to leave the room to retrieve Phil's x-rays. He was fine, himself, when I left the room. But when I came back with the results, he wasn't," she sighed. She rubbed her forehead and brushed her bangs back as her hand traveled over her head and down the back of her neck. "I dunno; he wasn't himself. He couldn't remember his age, nationality, where he was born, not even his late wife and son's name."

"Seriously?" Tim nearly choked, holding himself back, but he couldn't keep the stress out of his voice. It felt as if he had just fallen into a lake, sinking with the weight of the water pressing him deeper. He deflated in his chair, the migraine irritating him. In a raised voice, he demanded, "Wha—why in the fuck. Lethbridge was months ago, not weeks, and you're telling me he's been like this for..."

Laura held a hand up, slow and calm, her nostrils flaring from an exhale. Closing her tired eyes, zoning out once more, she opened them back into the present from her micro-napping.

"He didn't want you or Dakota to know, and as the primary physician for you three, patient confidentiality must be respected," she replied, lowering her hand. "Even if it's confidential between friends. He explicitly told me not to tell either of you, and I couldn't pursue it any further."

"Why? At least gimme that much."

"Phil," she paused. "He said he had never seen you and your sister so happy before." Her heavy eyes teared up. She took a moment, and dried them with the sleeve of her coat, before looking down at her lap, and she sniffed hard. When she was ready, her face lifted back to his, and her discharge of breath before speaking caught short and stopped as soon as it started.

"What? What else?"

"There was more bothering him that he wouldn't tell me. I tried to pry, but he wouldn't open up. At least not until that night we spent together." A smirk sparked across her face in a frown, and she wiped her eyes again as she looked off to the side.

"Doc, tell me," Tim said, it was more of a plea.

"Who is Igor Petrov?"

The name took him back to a time twelve years ago when the rising dead put the final nail in the coffin of a world on life support. When the three of them were being hunted by the remnants of the federal government. The final breath of Langley silenced any loose ends with the detonation of the Exhaust Bomb P-1 that caused The Calamity in the first place—silencing anyone with knowledge of the P-1, anyone who could bear witness should the world ever recover.

It was in southern Missouri that the three of them had neutralized the team sent after them and raided the safe house. Taking up shelter as rain fell that night, they were still adjusting to a world riddled with monsters. An endless onslaught of darkness deepened the shadows and gloom the undead brought with them. But that was it. He didn't know why *Igor Petrov* lit a light in his head, dimly lit at best.

"I don't remember… Why do you ask?" Tim was lost in thought, his migraine suddenly tolerable.

"Well." Laura dried her eyes the rest of the way. "He said all of the blackouts, voices, amnesia, dissociative spells… everything started when he learned that 'Igor Petrov' was alive and active in Alyeska." She sighed. "In the two years I've known you guys, I had never seen him so distressed before... He was scared."

"And we had no idea."

He held the single tear trying to escape his eye. He was unaware his right hand was clenched into a fist. He didn't know when, but his fingers and palms ached, and he released the pressure. There was a list of people who Tim was okay crying in front of, a list he kept to a minimum. Before, there had been only two names on it. But now, as that tear managed to escape, he figured a third could be added.

"Before Lethbridge," Tim mumbled, sniffing, and wiping his nose, "your uncle sent Phil on an espionage side gig while we were on leave. That's all I got." He shrugged.

"Well." Laura gave Tim's hand a gentle pat, pulling his eyes to hers. They were always supportive and friendly. The good ol' Doctor Ellis seemed to come back through the thick veil of fatigue. "I'll be back in a few days to check up on you. There are members of SRT-Juliet expecting me by midday tomorrow and I need…" She started to zone out, a shorter spell this time, and she was brought back when Tim grabbed her arm with the same kind of care she had given him.

He didn't know why, but he felt a duty to look after the doctor as well. She and Phil weren't an item, though the path was paved in that direction. It came to him that he had some duty to look after Phil's interests. She was almost like a sister, familial titles being something he didn't take lightly. He would call her his little sister if he knew she felt the same way.

"I won't be able to rest knowing that I let you go driving around in the state you're in," he said. "We have room here. Shack up for the night and catch up on sleep."

Laura paused, the offer floating around in her thoughts. Tim thought she'd be her stubborn self and leave to do more work. But as her mind worked the math over and moved logistics around, Tim felt some relief as she sat her bag back down.

"Only if someone can cover for me."

Tim led Laura down the short corridor, towards the old breakroom, now Olivia's room. Laura had made a call and her uncle, the colonel, acting more out of paternal instinct than like a superior officer, had given her leave for the night. A Doctor Saddler was willing to take a double shift to cover her and check up on SRT-Juliet the following morning. At the very least, it was enough time to get a full night's rest.

Only then, it seemed that the doc's mind could shut down, finally at ease. Suddenly, she couldn't walk straight, stumbling and wobbling behind Tim. The small, empty corridor from the sitting room to Olivia's room was now an arduous endeavor for them both as Tim helped her keep her balance and crutch along the way. The hall was illuminated by fluorescent bulbs behind old amber glass that offered a dim, warm glow around the old brick-and-mortar walls and wooden floor.

Being so deep in the lion's den of Anchorage, and now having the doctor, Tim worried he was casting all his eggs in one basket. But at the end of the day, she needed the rest, and he wouldn't let her drive until she got some. All the security teams, save for Team Three, were in for the night, until the next shift rotation. Everyone was where they needed to be, and all security needs were covered and scheduled to be covered; he had to trust in his fellow security officers.

Tim knocked when in arm's reach of the door. "You really should know your limits, Doc." He huffed and grunted as she leaned on him.

"I'm sorry, I dund't know wat's comin over…"

He pounded on the door some more, receiving an "I'm coming, alright!" from the other side.

Olivia opened the door, her hair in an updo to keep her neck and shoulders free. She wore pajamas detailing some old Tim Burton movie underneath an apron and cleaning gloves, the latter of which were covered in the guts of a pumpkin. One hand cradled a bowl of popcorn and on the TV in the background played the original Halloween film, *Phil's favorite.*

"She finally passed out, huh?" Olivia asked, chewing on some of the popcorn, nodding at the doctor with a smirk. "That's what I get to look forward to becoming?"

"You have a loveseat and a cot; pick one, and the doc here needs the other," Tim said.

"Yeah, sure." Olivia shrugged. "Wasn't planning on sleeping much tonight, anyways. She can have the bed. Or stretcher as it should be called."

"Funny." Tim faked a laugh. "Help me get her there, will ya?"

Olivia set the bowl down, yanked off her gloves, and helped guide the doctor to the stretcher bed. It was a military-issue cot made of a metal frame with olive-green material stretched across, offering a place to lie down. Together, they tucked Laura in; she was already passed out and sound asleep. To her credit the doctor had some force of will Tim didn't see in many others; he didn't sleep much, and now, he was sure he slept more than his friend did.

Mad respect, lil' sis. He patted Laura's shoulder.

"She your gal?" asked Olivia.

Tim nearly choked, ending in a laugh as he shook his head. "Nah, she's my brother's gal… well, would've been, I like to think."

Silence fell, and it was odd enough that there was any to begin with. With Olivia not moving, humming, or making any kind of commotion, he looked up from the doc to the kid. Her eyes were transfixed on the doctor's arm. The sleeve was pulled up, showing single vertical scars down her forearms. Tim reached over, yanked the sleeves back down, and covered them with the blankets.

"I had no idea." Olivia's voice shook, and her hands moved to rub her arms under her pajama sleeves as if they itched.

"Neither did I," Tim mumbled, feeling himself softening, looking back to Olivia. "But it's not our business."

"Yeah," she sniffed, wiping her nose with the front of her hand. "You're right."

A scream ejected from the horror movie, loud and sudden enough to make Olivia flinch in a jolt of surprise. Tim's eyes snapped to the TV. He saw on screen a woman falling over a rail and straight down a flight of stairs. Like energy released, the tension was gone from the kid's face as she smirked, holding onto the surprise for a change in topic. "Been a while since a movie made me jump." She laughed, looking silly, and her giggling smile turned Tim's frown to a soft smirk.

"What are you doing in here, anyways?" Tim asked, looking around. A small, propane stove sat in front of the TV with an empty bag of corn kernels. A jack-o-lantern was next to the stove, and the room was furnished to look like a typical teenager's room. "Where do you find all this stuff?"

"You'd be amazed at how much stuff is forgotten about in storage units. Besides, it's October." Olivia shrugged. "Goodness gracious, do you not celebrate holidays, either?"

Tim rolled his eyes, sitting straight when he stretched out the stiffness of his back. It always amazed him how fast time could pass. "If I get a chance, yes." He nodded. "You should call it a night, diva; big day tomorrow."

"And the doctor?" asked Olivia.

"She'll be alright." Tim breathed out through his nostrils. "Just let her rest."

By some miracle, Tim had managed to get Olivia to retire for the night. The most that she was going to do was view a tape, *Nightmare on Elm Street*, she had thrown into the VHS player. Parting with an "I'll fall asleep to the movie," she snuggled in a ball on the loveseat.

"Yeah, okay." Tim left her, closing her door, and made his way to his room. His night watch shift rotation was the last one. And like Olivia, he didn't think he'd sleep. While the kid was excited, he felt nothing but dread and certain doom. He didn't approve of using people as bait and didn't like the risks the kid was taking. He thought about packing everything up, jumping straight on Highway 1, and making their way out of the city.

Like a thief in the night, he could sneak the girl away from these people. He could do that; he had the authority to remove Olivia from danger. The inevitability of him being replaced with someone who could follow orders and bring her right back to the lion's den stopped him. At least he could protect her, in this case; the kid was brave. He had to give her that. And he'd had to swallow that pill: the world didn't run the same way as it once did.

"Brave, or just plain ignorant," he muttered to himself.

He sat at a table next to his cot. The letter from his folks, still folded and unopened, sat on the table. He held a glass of bourbon in his hand as he stared at the paper, feeling a heat fill him from his belly. The very thing that kept him from throwing the cursed letter into the trash was Dakota's advice that lingered in his thoughts. It was what she believed Phil would have said, and if Tim was to be honest with himself, he thought Phil would say the same: *You can't forgive others until you forgive yourself.*

"You can't help your neighbor remove a speck from their eye when you got a log in your own," Tim chuckled in response.

He knew what Phil would have said. He would have quoted the seventh chapter of Mathew. Tim even had his Bible open to the exact verse that came to mind: "And why worry about a speck in your friend's eye when you have a log in your own..." he mouthed, reading along with the passage. He imagined Phil sitting down with him, asking him, "What's bothering you, buddy? C'mon, tell me."

Only you're not here, and it's not fucking fair.

Then, like a hammer to the chest, he thought it would be what Rufus would have wanted him to do as well. Tim didn't know if he could do that much. Forgiveness didn't mean he had to have a relationship with them, did it? It didn't mean he had to be their son again. Was it more for his own sake than theirs, so he could move on? Would it cure the pain and anger?

He didn't know, and it scared him, because, for the bigger part of his life, he didn't know what life would look like without it. It was a part of him, no matter how much he hated it. But he felt it in his heart, a soft whisper, a gentle voice, tenderly pushing him to that end. And yes, he wanted that, but at the same time, he didn't. He wanted the burden, the sudden weight of the boulder fallen over him to be lifted; yet, he couldn't let go of it.

He dumped the whole glass of bourbon down his throat, numbing his senses as his throat burned and a tingle rose up his spine. He refilled his glass and wiped the greasy sweat from his face. More than anything, at that moment he wanted to apologize to his sister, but she wasn't there.

"I'm sorry, sis." He said anyways. "I'm sorry."

He thought of all the random visits Olivia had paid him. All the snacks the kid shared, the attempts at starting conversations… on and on. Before, there had been nothing but tension between the two of them, but now it seemed it was coming only from him. Just like with Dakota, Olivia wanted to help him. Tim saw himself as a lonely island. While people were building a bridge to reach him, he was building a fence around his shore.

I just wanted to see how you were doing… Olivia's words had left an impression on him. It made him smile and frown at the same time.

Finally, he did something, taking out his knife and slitting open the adhesive layer of the envelope, liberating the trifold letter and unfolding it. Doing that much was like prying teeth.

"Hey, Baby," the letter started, and already Tim re-refilled his glass. "I know it's likely you won't read this…"

The writing was his mother's, he recognized this by the wide upper bubbles of her capital B's, the near-straight lines that made her S's sometimes mistaken for 5's, and the acute horizontal line of her L's. He knew her writing well; she had been the one to homeschool him, after all. Not to mention the fact that his father never spoke like this, and if Tim recalled the old dog writing anything, it was a signature on a receipt, or math when making measurements, or lines on wood for cutting.

His mother had been right; Tim didn't read further. Roughly folding the letter and stuffing it into his cargo pocket, he leaned over the table and rubbed his eyes dry as he looked out his room's window at the soft rain and lightning pelting the dense thicket between ACE and Highway 1. Everything was lined up perfectly for things to mend, to get better, but for some reason he still resisted.

"I'm sorry." He spoke again, his voice but a bare whisper, not wanting to hear himself.

He dumped his glass down his throat, setting it back on the table half empty.

Colonel Stacey was on her computer, sending an email to the President, informing him that the first ships bearing Siberian Reinforcements for the Canadian Confederacy had landed in Prince Rupert earlier that day when a notification popped up on her screen. She recognized it instantly: a black box with a green bell. She clicked on it, putting on pause her present inquiries, and opened the app. Her screen went black, and green words appeared.

It wasn't an email passed down from Colonel Winston to one of his fabled SRTs, or vice versa. The words appearing on the screen were voice-to-text from a satellite phone call being made to Winston's OCR. The name of the receiver was Second Lieutenant Cheyenne Willis, and the voice-to-text had already unraveled halfway through the conversation taking place:

"Standby for repeat. Your nine-line request is as follows. Line One: One-Tree-Sierra-Delta-Charlie-Niner-Six-Zero-Niner-Niner-Niner-One-Zero. Line Two: GEO-Viasat Phone, Tree-Four-Dot-Five-Four-Six, SRT-Alpha. Line Three: Two Charlie. Line Four: Alpha. Line Five: Two Alpha. Line Six: X-Ray. Line Seven: Charlie, Green Smoke. Line Eight: One Alpha, Break, One Bravo. Line Nine: None, Mountainous Region?"

"Yes Ma'am," came the unknown sender.

"Alpha, your MEDEVAC has been approved. Standby for ETA. Over… Alpha, is everything okay?" Second Lieutenant Willis replied.

"Oh, God."

The transmission ended and so did the updates from her cloning bug. Colonel Stacey's interest hooked, she closed the app and opened another that detailed the globe. A box at the top left labeled 'MGRS' was empty, and she typed in the first line from the 9-Line MEDEVAC into the box. The map zoned in on Pikes Peak, just west of Colorado Springs; a box appeared over the peak detailing the ID of SRT-Alpha's sat phone being used in the call.

The message did not read like it was from Sergeant Nilges. There was a timid nature she felt from reading the voice-to-text, a feeling she thought fitted more for Autumn Nector. She held hope that if Autumn was alive, then there might be hope for Wolf Packs survival, for Sergeant Nilges.

She meant it when she told Colonel Winston she never intended for SRT-Alpha or Bravo to be hurt because of her negligence. Although it had not been intentional, she had played a heavy hand in how recent events became as they now were.

Right away, she picked up the phone and dialed Major General Petrov's number. There were no units, regular or spec ops she could dispatch to the area. Not with the President breathing down her neck. But the major general wasn't under any such confines with his new missions: Project Dreadnought & Project Hydra. She simply added a new objective to his directive.

The line picked up. "Da, Colonel Stacey," Petrov greeted.

"Major General, I have some new intel concerning your forwarding forces to Colorado."

"Mission adjustment?"

"Mission adjustment," she affirmed.

Chapter Three – The Lure

-October 24th, 2030-

Tim's tastebuds were repulsed by the bitterness of the black coffee he downed, but it gave him what he needed; the hot beverage offered some relief to his throat, still recovering from when Inimicus had crushed his larynx. He felt like Laura looked, and he knew he'd need the help. Today was to be a double shift, and, as a new coffee drinker, the effects worked like a charm.

Tim carried a canteen cup with him everywhere that day, refilling it every chance he got. From ACE to the console trailer at the amphitheater, he had caffeine on standby for when he needed it. The morning he spent crutching around the place with Second Lieutenant Bracket and Unit Two; the latter keeping tabs over the place before the big show. There was no shortage of potential POI: people getting the audio equipment up and ready, electricians running checks on the lighting, and on and on.

In the middle of an apocalypse, Tim added, shaking his head.

Gates were checked and double-checked on an hourly basis, and two-man patrols kept tabs on the perimeter fencing. The previous day, while Bracket was on shift, he had a team ground a wire and connect the fence to the power grid to electrify it. On and on it went, turning over as many stones as they could. A chain was only as strong as its weakest link, and Tim was determined to find that weakest link and make it as strong as he could.

All the while, Olivia was kept with Unit Five at ACE, under constant watch. He didn't like leaving the kid so far behind but took solace in that Unit Five was looking after her. The men of that unit were all composed of soldiers from the US Military: three former Army men, an airman, and Staff Sergeant Hendricks as Team Leader.

Tim's anxiety was lessened knowing Unit Five was keeping an eye on the kid; Hendricks, perhaps, gave him the greatest comfort. He knew he was being prideful about the Marine Corps but having a Marine on board eased his anxiety a great deal. There was no such thing as an ex-Marine. Active duty or retired, it wasn't just a profession, but a lifestyle—a proper noun for anyone who crossed the Parade Deck at graduation.

By the time 1800 hours came around, Tim was sitting in the console trailer, more for his leg's sake than anything, and to spare him a berating from Laura. That's what he told Bracket anyways. In reality, he didn't want anyone to see him collapse on a chair from faintness.

Tim closed his eyes, straightened his posture, opened his mouth, and stuck his tongue out just past his bottom lip. He took quick breaths in his nose, and quicker exhales, as he practiced Laura's panting maneuvers. His breathing suddenly became difficult, and he was reduced to a state where all focus and attention was on breathing. His thoughts let loose, harkening to when his throat had been crushed, his feet dangling in the air, Inimicus's gleeful eyes glaring into his, the giant's thick fingers constricting his neck.

The stress of oxygen deprivation vented out in sweat and tears as that moment replayed in his thoughts on a loop. There, Tim remained, panting, beads of sweat streaking down from his forehead, waiting for his breathing to normalize. Stars clouded his vision, and he thought he might faint.

"Sir?" A woman's voice, riddled with concern, alarmed Tim. He hadn't even noticed anyone was inside. He looked over to where the voice came from, and one of the camera operators sat staring at him, her posture torn from a state of giving him space to being ready to assist him. "You okay, Sir?"

Being so close to that monster was burned into his memories; he could smell the foul breath and body odor of the monster. He still felt his neck being squeezed like a mouse caught in a snake's grip. Every moment his breathing fell faint was cursed: the fiend's face returned, his dead yet bloodshot eyes carving into Tim's soul. Inimicus had taken so much in less than an hour, and more tears escaped. Tim wondered who had really won.

"Yeah," Tim sighed, rubbing the sweat on his face dry with the sleeve of his shirt. Caught in the act, weakness exposed, he felt vulnerable and hated it. "This doesn't leave here," Tim waved his index finger around the trailer, and the operator nodded her understanding. He looked over, picking up the smell of coffee, and he saw a pot with a fresh drip in the corner.

Coffee beans should be the national plant. Tim repressed a chuckle and picked his canteen cup off the floor where it had fallen.

Hours passed, and the last of the security checks came in with a final "All clear" before the night's main event. That would have brought comfort to most. But to Tim, it was just a clear message; the Puristans had yet to play their hand. So, he stood next to the operator, who had seen his weakness earlier, his eyes glued to each screen, running a relay back and forth between the monitors, looking for red flags. The aluminum canteen cup was now half-emptied of the now-cold brown liquid, and his stomach protested the beverage with sickly threats bubbling up.

Banging came from the trailer door, like the cracking of thunder immediately after a bolt of lightning that had so often snapped him, Phil, and Dakota awake in Atlanta. The rhythm of *Rock of Ages* was unmistakable, and he laughed out his frustration, struggling up to his feet. He wedged his crutches under his arms and made his way down the short three steps to the door and opened it.

The last light of day was creeping down under the horizon of a rigid line of trees and rooftops. The horizon was just black shapes in front of the warm, receding light, whose rays warmed his forehead in an almost soothing and caressing touch by nature wanting to nurture, lulling Tim with a sudden desire to rest. The round, orange ball of light sat behind Olivia.

Her hair was now styled in an inverted bob, choppy and grungy, with blue highlights. She had one pant leg with holes cut in it, and the other pant leg was cut just above her knee, with a gray sock, decorated in pink skulls and bananas, rising just below the knee. She sported shoes that rose high above her ankles but tied below them and a pink skirt that had been cut short lowered down to mid-thigh. A pink shirt, under some odd vest, bore blue, black, and pink colors with odd designs zipped up the midriff. An old leather jacket, chopped down to short sleeves, hung just below her chest like a crop top with pink lining on the inside. She was also sporting fingertip-less gloves that rose to her elbows, decorated in her many bracelets.

"Huh?" she asked, twirling about, "New outfit. Looks good right?" Her spinning ended in a curtsy.

Sure, if you don't mind sweating your ass off; you're gonna get dehydrated fast. But instead, he couldn't help but wonder out loud, "I still don't get how you come by all this shit?"

"I already told you dummy, I'm a scrapper. Storage units and all," she shrugged in a gleeful manner, matching her happy-go-lucky prancing and dancing in place. "You know, some of it I sew. Others, I piece together from scrap and trash." She then took a single step up to the trailer, showcasing her skull and banana sock. There were fresh Band-Aids over her kneecap and a bit of red had bled through.

She gave a dramatic wave of her hands, chopping through the air and ending to point at them as if to present to an anticipating audience for the reveal. "I just love this, though. I found only one and not a pair.! I wish Alyeska made clothes that weren't just solid colors, like yours. This is just adorable!"

"Skulls and bananas? You're one odd scrapper, diva," Tim huffed, not hiding his ability to empathize with her blissful bubbliness. It bled through, her smile contagious, as Tim offered his fist.

Olivia stopped in place, reeling her fist back like a baseball pitcher charring up, and shot her knuckles at his, slowing before impact. It brought a smile to his face, and he supposed he could share that enthusiasm for her sake. Tim chuckled, motioning for her to back up. She took a step back, and he crutched down to meet her outside. Seeing the men of Unit Five standing, keeping watch around them he met Staff Sergeant Hendrick's gaze.

"How's it going Devil Dawg? Semper Fi." Tim gave Staff Sergeant Hendricks a greeting nod.

"Semper Fi." Hendricks greeted back, a smirk subtle and easy to miss hidden under a blank expression.

You can take the Marine out of the corps, but the corps never left the Marine. An older Marine had once told him long ago, before he had signed up himself. The words never left, just stayed glued in his memory, resurfacing from time to time.

"What are you doing here?" he asked, looking back to Olivia.

She seemed to deflate as if forcing on a face of frustration, but she still smiled as she rolled her eyes. "Geez, do you ever lighten up?"

Again, you should've met Phil, Tim thought. A chuckle found its way out, seemingly to please her, as she nodded.

"Well." She blew a raspberry. "I was hoping you'd wish me good luck?" She smirked, then shrugged. "Shame on me, I guess."

Tim gave her arm a gentle push with his good hand. "Hella shame," he mumbled. "Good luck diva, and be careful."

"Um, that last part is your job," Olivia remarked, looking at him. "Kinda what you're here for, remember?" She grinned with the rolling of her eyes, her lips falling into a soft smile.

Out of nowhere, she lunged at him, wrapping her arms around him in a tight hug and knocking him off balance. He caught himself on the trailer with his good arm, balancing on his crutch and repressing any cries of pain shooting up his body. The sudden embrace warmed him, and she gave him a soft smirk as he laid his broken arm around her in return.

Olivia uttered a quick "Thank you" before running off without a chance for him to respond.

Unit Five all sighed, and Hendricks caught Olivia by the back of her vest, like a puppy's scruff. Her legs nearly went airborne from the sudden stop in momentum as she was pulled back into the men's safety net. The men of Unit Five formed a perimeter to escort her, and she waved a thumbs-up to Tim before they departed.

For the first time in a while, his thoughts weren't a mixed bag of black-and-gray shades and emotions. The sun now was completely lowered over the horizon of trees and distant mountains, leaving behind a darkening blue sky. The twilight sky was "Phil's sky," he always said, where his brother would get lost in the evening. His thoughts clouded back to gray and black, lingering for a second longer on the evening twilight, an ill-received omen to which he turned his back and crutched his way back up into the trailer. He looked to the right at the operators manning the radio, then to the left at the two sitting before the monitors.

"Sir." One of the operators called as he looked at her.

The dim lighting from the old fluorescent bulb above them flickered on and off. He leaned over the operator's chair, looking at what she called him for. She didn't look at him, not showing any dread or anxiety; her eyes were glued to the camera feed, and he watched as the first of the audience showed up. The first potential Hair.

Okay, Lord. Here we go, he prayed.

Chapter Four – The Hair

The walls of the trailer vibrated with the pounding of the concert, the rhythm of punk rock and hip hop muffled and reduced to white noise as Tim stood in a vigilant watch at the monitors. The white noise spared his headaches from growing into migraines, and the soundproofing of the trailer made his frequent radio checks to all units audible.

In short, the console rooms and trailers at each event were a sort of silent haven for him. But somewhere along the roster of reckless music, it came to a sudden stillness, calm even. Tim looked at the monitor showing the stage, heart pounding. Something had caused the concert to stop, and he suspected some overt action from the Puristans.

Olivia was still on stage, not looking distressed, which brought him to a calm. His curiosity peaked when the band stood idle, and the drummer's arms were no longer waving the sticks. The diva took a seat on a stool, resting on her hip an acoustic guitar, and the arena was then filled with the soothing melody from the instrument. It was slow, pleasant, and didn't barrage Tim's headaches with threats of transforming into a migraine.

There was something off about the way she looked on camera. Her smile was gone, and though she was panting, probably sweating, and dehydrated, somberness shadowed her. She didn't look anywhere but at the acoustic sitting on her lap.

Tim picked up an extra headset, pressed it onto his ear, and came in mid-sentence of Olivia: "… a great many of our loved ones died from the Great Calamity. So, this for those of us who are still grieving." Olivia's voice was soft, panting as she spoke. "For those of us who never got to say goodbye to our mothers, our fathers, aunts, uncle, cousins, grandparents, sisters, or..." On the screen, Tim watched her wipe her eyes. "Or brothers. This is for you and me." Her face looked up. Not to the audience before her, but directly to the camera through the screen, and Tim felt, right to him.

The pleasant rhythm of the acoustic shifted tones, and melancholy music issued forth in notes Tim recognized. He didn't know squat about music; it wasn't the notes he knew, but the lyrics that would fit into those notes like a missing puzzle piece. The song lost in his memories harkened back to his time in England. Before the battle of Chiswick, two men in his platoon sang together for the last time, two men who'd be found KIA the next day and the song forever lost.

Tim paused, his grip on his mug tightening as he forced the thoughts of the war down before thoughts of that weeping mother and her deceased young in her arms could lure Tim into that rabbit hole of depression. He stayed focused on the cameras and busied himself with more radio checks, but when the lyrics poured into those melancholic notes, the missing pieces fell into place.

"We are but poor, wayfaring strangers.
Traveling through this world of woe.
There's no sickness, toil nor danger, in that bright world to which we'll go...
I'm going there to see my loved ones, I'm going there, no more to roam.
I'm only going over Jordan. I'm only going over home...
I know dark clouds will gather round me, I know my way is rough and steep.
Yet golden fields lie just before me, where God's redeemed their vigils keep.
I'm going there to see my brother. He said he'd meet me when I come. I'm only..."

In the entirety of the last two years he spent knowing the kid, never once had he broken. Not during the concerts, nor in any of her escorts. But now, like a wire strung too tight, he felt something snap. Tim blinked away from the cameras, setting down the headset. He turned away from the operators of the cameras and radios before anyone could see him. The feeling of their eyes on him weighed, and he didn't want to turn back around.

He stepped down to the door and took a deep breath. Steadying his thoughts and leveling his focus, he raised the radio back to his mouth. From outside, he could hear the song going on much longer than its original script. Inimicus no longer haunted his thoughts; it was Phil and Rufus's smiling faces breaking him down. Now wasn't the time for grieving, but caught like a deer in headlights, he took an unexpected fall down that rabbit hole.

"I know dark clouds will gather round me..."

The kid's voice continued, and Tim blinked away the moisture in his eyes.

"I know my way is rough and steep. Yet golden fields lie just before me..."

Wiping his nose, he didn't want to add another name to his list of friends. Knowing more people meant making yourself open to more pain, and he feared that. He didn't want to feel like he was replacing Phil. That hole left in his life could only be filled by one person, who, once gone, could never be replaced, and there were already too many holes in his life.

"Sir?" one of the operators called from behind him, her voice caught off-guard from her due diligence.

Like an anchor bringing a boat to a sudden stop, the shift in the atmosphere changed. A line was cast down into the rabbit hole to which Tim clung and climbed back out as fast as he had fallen. Turning around, blinking to clear his blurred vision, he hurried back to the monitors and met the operator, ignoring a little plastic jack-o-lantern sitting next to her.

He didn't need to ask her about the problem; it spoke for itself. The camera monitoring the front stage was now just a screen of static. His fingers went straight to his radio, jabbing the PTT button: "Big Hoss to Unit Four. Over."

"Unit Four here, Big Hoss, Send it."

"Have exfil prepped and ready for emergency evac. Stand by for updates. Over," Tim ordered, risking not even a second. Paranoia was the new "better safe than sorry."

"Copy that, Big Hoss. Standing by."

Tim leaned on his one good arm, looking at all the other camera feeds, but nothing of interest was being shown. The crowd had calmed and steadied during the slower melody of the kid's cover. None of the exits had been compromised, and all units were reporting no disturbances. Impatience gripped him as he adjusted his stance, the weight and pressure on his "good" leg that was now starting to make it ache.

"Big Hoss to Unit Five. Over."

"Unit Five here."

"Be ready to secure the Lure and get her mobile at any moment. Discretion for lethal use of force authorized. Keep me informed. Over."

Tim leaned on the operator's chairs for support, and they didn't seem to mind, ears registering but not listening to Unit Five's affirmation of his orders. They were glued to their tasks and waiting for orders. But that was just it—no further orders could be given until something else happened. Tim found it best to bet on the worst-case scenario; at least then he could be better prepared.

Five minutes later, Bracket's voice came over the radio, slightly elevated, sounding both excited and panting as he spoke softly. "Snare to Big Hoss. We might have something backstage. Standby."

"Big Hoss to Snare. Standing by," Tim replied.

A few minutes passed, and Second Lieutenant Bracket never reported in. Tim's headache drummed with the pulses at his temples. He didn't want to break the radio silence lest he risk giving away Bracket and his team. But every passing second felt like another nail in a coffin he wasn't ready to lower, a coffin far too small to be buried. Two more minutes passed when he took a gamble and keyed his radio, just one click. It was code for the last receiver and sender to break radio silence, if able.

Nothing came back from Bracket, and Tim sighed, staring at the air casts over his left arm and leg. They were residual signatures of Inimicus and the Jackle, lingering attacks to hinder him even when they were so far away. He hated them, hated the broken bones and haplessness they left him in.

"Big Hoss to Unit Five, do you have visual on Snare?" Tim asked.

Five seconds passed, and only silence returned. Tim waited for another ten and gave the once-click call for response over the radio to Unit Five as with Snare. Still, there was silence.

Two teams going silent was too much for comfort, and with all other units keeping the entry points secured, the crowd away from Olivia, and her exfil prepped, there was no reason for it. If only Captain Shillings had not taken away half of Tim's security force. That thought left a bad taste in his mouth, a correlation between the escalating Puristan activities and his halved security force.

Two dots connected, leaving him with an isolated feeling. He was alone among imposters, or, at the very least, a few. He looked at the monitor operators with newfound unease; the implications didn't stop with the operators in the console trailer but with the men under his command.

He sighed, unclipped the safety strap to his pistol, and crutched over to the door, giving a parting command in a firm bark to the operators at the radio and monitor stations: "Maintain surveillance and redirect authority to Unit Four. I'm en route to backstage." Then, he opened the door, crutching in all haste to the backstage.

A special route had been segregated from the console trailer to the backstage, more of a scenic route now. It took longer to go out and around the amphitheater, but with a now-packed amphitheater it was the quicker way. Rushing as fast as he could, he swung his broken leg through his crutches, landing on his "good" leg, before hurling his crutches forwards to catch him.

The route came to an end at a steel door leading backstage. Coming to a slow, he could catch his breath while departing with his right crutch so his hand could carry his pistol. He eased the door open, metallic squeals of rusted hinges telegraphing his arrival to unsuspecting threats.

The backstage was vacant, save for Second Lieutenant Bracket and the rest of Snare. The five men lay on the ground, fallen from their standard formation. Single stack, three meters apart from one another, fluffy ends of darts protruding out from each, all now resting unconscious.

Ambush. Tim understood, taking concealment behind a large metal box, storage of some kind. He was waiting, listening for movement, voices—anything his senses could detect.

Tim's pistol was loaded with hollow point rounds; when it came to protecting the kid, he didn't intend to take any prisoners. That was Bracket's concern. After fifteen seconds passed, Tim abandoned his place of concealment to a curtain masking his movements.

There was nothing but a thick curtain between him and Olivia, and subsequently between the Lure and the Hair. His priorities now altered: mission adjustment to get the Lure back to Unit Four and *the hell out of here*. First, he needed the backstage cleared, and so far, he had heard and seen nothing.

"Shit," Tim sighed, leaving the concealment of the storage container, going out and around the outer edge of the backstage. All the workers were gone, and when he came to the opposite side of the stage, the Lure's point of egress, he found Unit Five. Four of them lie unconscious with the same darts sticking. They had been moving in formation when ambushed, though about five meters apart from one another. Darts didn't have the same trajectory as a bullet; these men were good shots, hitting moving targets with the darts.

He moved to the front of the formation, around a corner where wiring ran up a cement wall. Staff Sergeant Hendricks was absent from the unconscious Unit Five. Tim's heart fell into his gut, his fears proving true.

Time slowed, and the entire stage now felt like a bear trap. Not one for Puristans, but for him and all who would protect the kid. Something smacked into his side; looking down he saw the red fuzzy feathers of a dart protruding from his shirt. The effects were instantaneous, flooding his veins and arteries, and feeding the invasive substance to his whole body; he thought it may have been anesthesia. But he still stood, leaning entirely on his crutch, eyes falling heavy as he held the pistol close to his chest, the barrel aimed at the now-darkening backstage.

His ears noticed the sound of a pair of feet rushing at him, though by the time the large mass of a man charged into him like a wrecking ball, he still heard the footfalls. The time delay in sound was disorienting. Tim lost his grip on his crutches and felt the sensation of falling backward; the same sensation kept him awake.

His body went numb, and he noticed he was now on his back. The fall had forced out his breath and he could feel the stretching wheeze. More sounds of footfalls encircled him. His fingers held a death grip on his pistol, and he aimed at the nearest man. "He's getting back up!" one cried out. Tim's sights were aimed at the hostile's center mass, but somehow, he fired over his targets head. A feeling of heat consumed him, and with the absence of feeling, he knelt on his bad leg and zeroed in his sights on a man reloading his dart gun.

Tim emptied four rounds, and three met their mark. There were two in the chest and one in the arm as the man fell in spasming pain. Another dart smacked into Tim's thigh, and two other men emerged from his darkening peripheries. The world started to blur while two men dropped their dart guns in exchange for their ARs. They stopped when they had their rifles raised as Tim charged at them.

Tim couldn't hear his voice but felt the vibrations of his roars—a savage and vicious bark that scratched his throat as he descended on them like a hound out of hell. His vision cleared, and he could see Staff Sergeant Hendricks standing with the Puristans. More of the dots connected, and the heat boiled up into rage.

His trajectory changed to the traitor, and before he could fire another round, one of the men intercepted him. Tim chopped the air in a bludgeoning blow to the man's throat, pressing his pistol against the enemy's chest, and he pulled the trigger five times, feeling the metallic recoil in five rapid successions. The gunshots muffled against the Puristan's clothing and kit, sequenced with the "oofs" that were gradually reduced with each bloodied impact. The dying sounds of the man expired in a quick death.

The whole exchange had been instantaneous, and Tim shoved the dead man out of his way and into Hendricks. His primary target caught the dead man in surprise; the others seemed dazed, in a state of surprise or shock—maybe both. Hendricks caught the body before shoving the man aside, and an open window was left. It lasted for only a few seconds before the other threats could recover from their shock, and all Hendricks had time for was to ready himself for Tim's collision.

Tim rammed his crippled body straight into his fellow Marine, driving his forehead with all the force he could manage into the bridge of Hendricks' nose. The two of them tumbled back in a tussle. The air cast on his left arm was now a club he used to smash against Hendricks' shielding arms. Another dart smacked at Tim's back, and the first two were diluting his blood, which the adrenaline was now wearing off.

They fought for control over Hendricks' M4 Carbine, Tim's window closing fast. His efforts faded in vain as he struggled to simply hold onto the weapon. It wasn't long before Hendricks got his feet back under him and pulled his rifle and Tim up with it. Tim got his good knee under him before feeling the weight of Hendricks bare down upon him.

Tim held onto the M4 like a lifeline, both his eyes and Hendricks' carving into one another's in the heat. Tim felt himself lowering, his leg bending under him, pushing back in futility. His vision continued to blur and darken until finally, he fell. Adrenaline spent, the anesthetic of the three darts overpowered him. His body smacked against the cold floor, the back of his head smashed in a dazing effect as Hendricks pulled away and stood over him. Tim's vision blurred down the barrel of the rifle.

He could taste iron in his mouth as he bared his gritting teeth at the traitor. Pushing against the floor with his right elbow, he unleashed a bloodied roar that sounded more like heated grunts. He swiped the barrel of the gun away. A round let loose to the side, and Tim reached for the staff sergeant's pistol.

Hendricks stepped back, keeping his pistol out of reach, and rammed the stock of his rifle into Tim's face. Tim fell for the last time. The fight was over; his strength was depleted. His body moved on autopilot, instinct harkening to muscle memory as his good hand searched for his KA-BAR somewhere on his side—one last-ditch effort.

But the patience of the Puristans had run out; three of them descended upon him in a hell storm of pummeling fists and rib-breaking kicks. They smote and struck his broken limbs and body with extreme prejudice. The tip of a steel-toed boot came straight to his eye; the only effect Tim could notice was the loss of sight. The only saving grace was the numbness of the three darts, shielding him from the pain.

He noticed the kicking and punching had stopped only when his body ceased to jerk or recoil from the impacts. He had no feeling in his body except that from head to toe he felt like one giant heart from the heavy throbs. His vision was just a blur of colors and shapes, and out his other eye, he saw the men take a step back. He could hear his breathing coming and going in short spurts of wheezing that sounded like whistling. Time passed in a slow concoction of tortuous inevitability; the storm had come, and he could only wait and watch.

Tim was unsure how much time passed; figures blurred, fading in with the shadows, and it felt like it was just him with wolves waiting in the darkness for the lamb to spring their trap. Prayer was his last offensive, and, for the kid's sake, he begged for some divine interception, some miracle.

A sudden drop in musical instruments and a rise in audience cheering foretold of the concert's conclusion. Tim watched as Olivia jumped backstage, her face bright and full of energized joy. That joy was all too soon replaced by dread, and her jumping came to a still, her face aimed at him. She cried out, running straight to him, crying for help.

Olivia dropped to her hands and knees beside him, coming to a short skid as she cradled his head. Tim's blurred vision came into focus, and she became his world, all he could see as her tears stung his swollen face. The trap had been sprung, and behind her, the wolves emerged, surrounding their prey.

The same giant who had rammed into him before handled Olivia like a rag doll, grabbing her, and the moment she fought back, he shoved her down to the ground. Her face smacked the floor and blood dripped from her lip. Tim watched as the man then climbed on top of her, spreading her legs as his hands worked at her pants. Olivia cried out, thrashing and crying as he pinned her arms against the floor. He sniffed along her neck and started speaking. Tim could only register, "We'll have some fun later on."

Hendricks' stomps came like a raging earthquake straight to the large man as he thrust the bottom of his boot hard into the giant's face. The big man toppled off Olivia and onto his back, meeting the end of Hendricks' barrel: "Do that, and I'll fucking kill ya," Hendricks barked, keeping Olivia behind him.

Tim watched the traitor remove a sat phone from his vest before pointing at one of the other men. "You keep tabs on her, and make sure that sick fuck doesn't touch her."

The giant stood back up, chest puffed, face flushed, before Hendricks could make his call. Tim watched, and even as Hendricks looked up at the man, he squared off with him. Chest not puffed, he stood in a readied and calm. "What?" he challenged.

The giant seemed to register how the fight would have gone and backed down. Hendricks returned between Tim and Olivia, dialing a number on the sat phone.

Sounds of gunfire *cracked* and *popped* nearby; Tim saw blurred outlines of what he thought looked like men from Unit Four. Hendricks covered his ally's retreat. One man collected Olivia, dragging her away, fleeing with the rest, abandoning their dead. He could hear Olivia screaming for help as her voice came to a sudden stop at the slamming of a metal door: "TYRE..."

Hendricks was backing towards the door, returning fire, until red mist blew out his leg and he fell to the floor, two men descending upon him. His eyelids started closing for good. He was passing out as a pair of hands lifted his head, and he noticed the pressing at his neck, the kind that came from a couple of fingers checking his pulse. The last thing he heard before passing out was: "Call in medevac, we'll need airlift ASA-Fucking-Now!"

Chapter Five – ULFBERT

Monika's heart was broken at the sight of Tim's broken body; what joy she had felt from their previous reunion was now repressed in a pain no mother should have to endure.

Do you even have a right to feel sorry for him? she wondered. She had wondered why this "Dr. Ellis" had allowed them into his ICU room. Over a phone call, the doctors simply said, "All will be explained soon."

There was nothing else they needed after that; she and Dereck walked half the distance from their safe house before the Marshal in charge of their protection picked them up, along with a severe berating that made even her husband sweat.

The only conclusion that Monika could infer was Tim's inevitable death, a slow passing in which the little time remained was given for them to be present. Standing there now with him, she wept inside, still not knowing what his situation was. Her eyes went from an intubation tube that fed down his throat to the mechanical ventilator the tube connected to. Without either, he wouldn't be able to breathe on his own. Her eyes went from the ventilator to the intubation tube, and back to the swollen features of his face, no longer recognizable. There were frequent *beeps* that followed every two seconds after an exchange of the mechanical intakes and outtakes of breaths. An IV fed essential minerals and aid to his body through the hinges of his elbow.

Tim's arm and leg were freed from their air casts, his leg resting in an incline position, where it was kept straight under a soft sling. His arm was set straight into a framework of plastic, resting on a cushion at his side. But for all the efforts of the staff, there was no restoring his broken limbs, bent in unnatural positions. They lacked any internal structure to keep them in their designed form. To Monika, it looked like how the fingers of a glove might bend and sink without the finger inside to keep them upright.

She looked over to her husband at her side. Dereck's eyes were latched onto his boy, still as a rock, the only movement being the calm rise and fall of his chest. There was no other movement, not even the occasional blinking. He shared the same fear as she, that these were Tim's final moments, and he'd spent every second he could with his boy in sight, bearing the same stoic expression of his. That look that was just part of his DNA, it seemed. There was no Dereck without the absent look of emotion. But for all that, that hardened outer shell hid, when cracked, the inside illuminated tenfold from within. He was a geode, and though others couldn't see it as his wife could, those cracks stood out plain as day. She could see the pain, worry, and dread inside an otherwise indifferent-looking father.

She wondered what demons he was now wrestling with. Repentance hadn't alleviated the guilt or remorse. But it made life bearable over the last twelve years. The humbled life was worth living, despite the parents they had once been. What better way to show repentance than action? Long nights in the hospital room, with their loved ones.

I was sick and you cared for me, I was in prison, and you visited me. Deep exhale. The words of Mathew 25:36 came to the fore of her thoughts. Monika had always been a believer, but a Christian, she didn't know. However, the verse came full circle when she had paid her nightly visits to her dying mother, Deshanna, in the hospital long ago.

No parents should have to see their child suffer.

Dereck's hand tightened over hers, always her rock, but sometimes even a rock may need extra support. She laid her other hand over his, brushing her thumb over his, and her husband's hand clenched hers.

"Was it too little, too late?" Dereck asked, his voice low but steady.

Rarely did the man, who was her compass after her mother passed, sound bereft of absolute certainty. He faintly choked in a dry husk of an inhale, ending in him coughing. He echoed her thoughts in such a way that riddled her with goosebumps. She recalled a hypothesis that when you held hands with the person you were the closest to in life, your hearts would beat synchronously, and a shared train of thought ensued. It was partly an old wives' tale, partly a proven phenomenon, she believed, feeling hers and his pulses fall in sync with one another.

She looked back to Tim and sighed.

Do you even have a right to feel sorry for him? she again asked herself, her eyes shifting from Timmy to the intubation tube and again to the ventilator. This time, they drifted upwards to the x-ray board on the wall. Her eyes now swelled as she recognized the Osteomyelitis infection that was setting into his radius, ulna, and tibia. Bones that before were simply broken now appeared as a shattered glass of white upon a black backdrop of sheets. Whatever fight he had been in, he had come out with a gamble of losing his arm and leg.

This much she knew and understood from her old life as a nurse. She saw the likelihood of Tim living without an arm and leg clearly, like writing on the wall. But this time, they wouldn't abandon him; they wouldn't forsake him. He wouldn't have to walk it alone. Even if he continued to push them away, this time they wouldn't stop loving him.

The sound of knuckles tapping on the door brought about a drying relief to her eyes. Answers at long last, the question of Tim's permanent handicap or death just a few seconds away. Like the sweep of an arm clearing a cluttered workbench, the door's inward swing brushed away all guilt and remorse. Guilt and shame were placed on hold as Doctor Ellis entered the room. Dereck was the first to stand, keeping his left arm bent so Monika could hold on as she stood.

Dr. Ellis offered a passing smile, slowing down as she reached Tim's bedside. Papers secured to a clipboard, she held up a patient index finger to them, pacing around Tim's bed to his vitals monitor, checking them and recording the results on her clipboard. A sigh of relief parted the doctor's lips, a whiff of fresh air to Monika and Dereck as the doctor turned around and moved to the foot of Tim's bed. Hanging the clipboard on a hook, she brushed the sides of her hair behind her ears with her fingers.

Dereck took the first step forwards, with Monika following as they stepped over to the doctor, daring not to get too close to Tim lest he wake. The doctor's features were plagued by fatigue and dread. Whatever news she was holding back, it ate and clawed its way from inside. Writing on the wall that Monika could read, spelling the bad news.

"I'll have to amputate his arm and leg," Dr. Ellis said, pressing a fist up to her lips, her eyes looking at them both from under her brow.

The doctor shared a feeling of empathy with them for Tim as she looked over at their baby boy. It was more than just a doctoral way of sympathizing; it wasn't just a professional sense of caring that doctors tended to have. They were friends. She empathized and hurt with the wear and tear life had thrown on their son.

A shaken exhale escaped Monika's lips in a quick sigh, holding onto Dereck as her other hand cradled the side of her head. But Dereck, it seemed, would have none of it.

"Is there no other option?" His voice had a way of sounding loud even when speaking with an inside voice. He was projective—a heavyweight, a clap of thunder, that demanded the attention of everyone around him, even if others were in mid-conversation. He always had been the one who led the charge and pursued all avenues of possibility.

Dr. Ellis took in a deep breath as her eyes fell off to the side, looking away from him to Monika. The doctor craned her head, her gray eyes not hiding a definitive "no" to his question, and Monika felt her brows furrowed, cueing the doctor to speak.

"Possibly." There was hesitance in the doctor's voice. "But it comes with a significant degree of risk, as well as permanent aftereffects."

Dereck took a step forwards. "Go on, then."

"It's an experimental radiation therapy treatment." Doctor Ellis breathed out.

"That's only for cancer patients, isn't it?" Monika asked. Flashes of her late mother came back to the fore of her thoughts, out from the chasm of memories within. When life stopped giving and started taking. The last sight of the woman who birthed her into the world, just a hollow shell of who she was before after all the therapy couldn't save her. Before the brain cancer took the rest.

No, not now. She willed those past pains away; this was about her son.

"Traditional treatments are, yes." Dr. Ellis gave a nod, but then shrugged. "But this one uses the Ultra Fission Radiation for recovery. It's a whole different ball game." Her eyes fell again, hands moving like a teacher in a lecture.

"UFR?" Dereck scoffed. "The very same crap that killed more people than the nukes?"

"Do you know how flu vaccines are made? From influenza itself. It's not an uncommon concept." Laura stood her ground, firm but patient. "I've been given clearance by Colonel Winston to use it if parental consent is given."

"That's why you called us," Dereck mused. "You're inclined to this procedure, then?"

"Wait, so he's not going to die then?" Monika felt a morsel of hope as the doctor shook her head.

"Please understand that Tim isn't just a patient to me. He's a friend. I do this with a heavy heart, but the plus side to the risks is a full recovery to well... everything." Doctor Ellis about pleaded.

"A cure-all?" Monika scoffed with nothing short of skeptical scorn; the risks of cancer treatment to her mother had been a gamble, and it only made her dear mother's passing more painful. "I highly doubt it."

"No, it is not a cure-all—but a rapid recovery time for your son's current condition. Think of it like pressing the fast-forward button," Laura corrected, quick and alert. Monika thought it amazing how attentive and awake the doctor was now, like a flipped switch. She was livid now, with her wired features and baggy eyes. "I'd hate to perform the amputation, but I will if you feel that it is a better option. This hospital doesn't have the means to treat the Osteomyelitis, and the infection will progress past the point of recovery by the time we get him to Whitehorse City, which does have such means."

"What are the risks, then?" Dereck asked. "For this experiment watcha-muh-call-it?"

The doctor shuffled through the papers on her clipboard and handed them to Monika. She took the paper and held it for both her and Dereck to read. It was detailed in brief: the *'Ultra Fission Biological Radiation Treatment,'* or *'ULFBERT'* for short. The treatment had an eighty-six percent success rate in human trials, and underneath the brief introduction paragraph were the side effects: *fatigue, skin defects (see back of page for full list), vomiting, diarrhea, hair loss, vision impairment, hearing impairment, taste impairment, increase in UFR levels above the .14 percentage threshold (subsequent euthanizing to follow)*... The list went on and on, and at the end it was noted that *'upon successful treatment, the patient will be required to make weekly visits to the nearest medical facilities for maintenance for the duration of their lives.'*

"We might as well put a stake in the ground and tether him here then," Monika scoffed, looking up at the doctor who shrugged with a "granted" nod.

But what was the alternative? Permanent handicap, or lifelong hospital visits every week? Which was the lesser evil? Perhaps if she knew her son better, she could make a better judgment on what he would want. But that wasn't in the cards; she and Dereck had made sure they barely even knew the man Tim was now.

In such a situation, back in her days as a nurse in Virginia, a decision would have been easy to make. By some detached manner of speculation, in council with a doctor and a cancer patient, she'd be objective enough to see the best course of action. But now? She couldn't find it in herself to come to an objective conclusion. However, her husband, under that thick callous stoicism, accepted the cards where they lay. He took a step back, his face absent as he ran the mental calculations, all the information and variables falling into place, a path for which he found the conclusion at the end. That was perhaps his greatest strength—simplification with the facts.

It was easy for her husband to know what he believed to be the best choice in such moments—when a decision needed to be made, and she couldn't make one herself. After disowning Tim, she and Dereck got back together, and once the Old World had died and the President's last broadcast went out, informing them of the exodus over the Atlantic or the migration north as their only hope for survival, she fell into indecision. But it had been he who decided on going north, and she followed.

Over the last twelve years, he hadn't failed them yet, and she trusted Dereck's strength, despite the roller coaster of their history together; after all, it was his ability to make these choices that brought them and Tim back together. Maybe providence was on their side.

They looked at each other, everything telegraphed in a matter of seconds in a moment of unspoken council. He gave her a nod; she ceded her consent by folding her arms as the doctor handed him the consent form. Monika couldn't sign it; good thing the paper needed only one signature. She took in a deep breath as Dereck took it all into his own hands.

He signed the papers.

Laura picked up the phone, made a call down to the fifth floor, and pressed the nurse call button. In less than a minute, two nurses came into the room and spoke with the doctor for a second before disconnecting Tim from the monitors, rolling his bed out from the room along with the IV and ventilator. She allowed Dereck and Monika to follow as far as they could, stopping them at an electronically sealed door with a hand held up.

"This is as far as you can go."

The two worried parents stopped as instructed, their faces strained. Dereck draped his arm across Monika's shoulders.

Tim's mother leaned into her husband. "How long will the treatment take?" she asked.

"It varies," Laura assured, pointing back the way they came. "We'll bring your son back to the same room after the treatment's… completion."

She didn't want to sound optimistic and say "success" because that would imply a promise she couldn't make. Neutral forwardness was the name of the game, keeping in check cautious optimism. She had seen several doctors make such promises before, doctors who were new to the field and who, out of empathy, gave such assurances to a patient's loved ones. The same doctors would later stand speechless before those same loved ones who cried and cursed: "You promised!"

Laura had learned her lesson about making promises she couldn't keep long ago when a young boy, no more than six years old, stood alone in a euthanizing room. Soldiers stood guard in case the UFR took over and the boy expired before a peaceful passing could be given. It was a memory that stained and lingered and broke her down whenever she gave it privy for too long.

"Will I," he hiccupped, "be," Another hiccup, "okay?" Coughing fit and wheezing.

"Yes, you're gonna be okay," she had strained to say through puffy eyes and quarreling sniffing. Giving lies to the very words she spoke.

The boy, a very bright one at that for his age, seemed to register her conflict. Tears sobbed out his eyes, already fogging over in a silvery sheen as his pupils were transitioning to those of the undead. His veins were a thick gray under his skin, arteries a light purple. His body had emaciated from the effects of the UFR poisoning turning him into a zombie.

He just dropped his head, standing there in place in his underwear. Sniveling and crying with his hiccups, he waited as she approached him. She kept the needle hidden behind her, filled with sodium-thiopental that causes rapid and deep unconsciousness. "I'm just gonna give you some medicine, okay? And it's gonna help you sleep, so I can help you." She had strained to keep her voice normal but couldn't hold back a sniveling sniff.

The boy didn't move. He just remained still, crying in place with his fingers moving at his sides. She thought perhaps he knew what the reality of the situation was and was resigned to his fate, holding onto a sliver of hope that this grownup, this doctor, could make him better. He waited for her, and she gave him the anesthetic that induced deep sleep. After that, she couldn't continue the memory. An intentional mental block, a self-induced blackout, refused to ever remember it.

The gray response she gave to that little boy—crying before euthanizing him after he fell asleep—haunted her. In the end, she resigned to make only one promise to anyone: that she would do her very best. She looked at Tim, the memory shoved aside lest she fall into her chasm of depression, one she had struggled so hard to get out of.

"What's the room number, again?" Tim's father asked.

"Two-thirty-seven," Laura replied.

Dereck gave Laura an understanding nod as he turned them around back to Tim's room. Laura replied with a faint smile and grabbed the doors to close them, parting with as much optimism she could spare as a doctor. The glass was neither half-full nor empty; it was just there, half from the bottom and top.

"Doctor." Tim's father called out and she looked to him. "That's our boy we're trusting you with."

Laura could only give a silent nod.

I will do my best.

Laura caught back up with the nurses and Tim, who mumbled in his comatose state. A tear streaked out the corner of his eye and down his face. She felt her lips smiling, softly. His mind was still active; it was a good sign.

They came to the next set of doors, a nook of the hospital where procedures like x-rays and other radioactive procedures were done. She swiped her key card and the doors opened on their own. Midway down the hall of this little nook stood a man outside a door bearing a red and black fallout symbol.

The man's name was Dr. Saddler, a small old gentleman who stood at chest height with her. A ring of white hair made a horseshoe shape around the balding spot of his head and whiskers formed a five o'clock shadow over his face, filling the gaps between thick sideburns and a mustache that spanned the length of his upper lip. The white hair contrasted with the sunken eyes over heavy bags that traveled down to droopy cheeks.

Laura had found that even the little man's frowns were friendly; the man literally had no mean bone in his body. Except tonight, that friendliness was exchanged with a certain dread.

She knew he had been punching in long hours, getting the ULFBERT machinery installed and the medications for it ordered. Dr. Saddler gave Laura the same friendly reception he always did, altered with a tired smile as she came to a stop before him, the nurses wheeling Tim in waiting behind her. She handed him the papers.

"The parents gave consent."

He sighed, that friendly frown of his forming that inverted crescent of his lips with eyes as still as stone. "Let us hope that tonight the eighty-six percent success margin will include our friend here," he said while signing his name on the bottom of the consent form, authorizing the procedure.

There was a quick *swoosh* of the pen followed by a tap at the end of his last name. His eyes glanced over to Tim. "Serviceman?" he asked.

"One of our finest." Laura offered a smirk with a tilt of her head.

Doctor Saddler's expertise in radiation therapy from the Old World had proven to be of great influence over this new experimental therapy with which they were now gambling Tim's life. She had seen what happened to patients who didn't fully recover. Skin became clammy as their flesh turned to a sickening gray; veins grayed into black tar as their bodies promptly decayed from the inside out. Eyes fogged over with pupils turning to silvery sheens of moons through that fog: eyes of the undead. To put it frankly, dying and becoming a zombie was a more peaceful death than dying during ULFBERT.

A faint voice inside her prompted a wavering doubt. It wasn't too late to turn back now, guaranteeing Tim's survival at the cost of permanent handicap. He was already crippled enough; hell, she was going to fail him for the medical screenings needed to be eligible for military service when they had first met two years ago. It was Colonel Winston, not her Uncle Charles, who had pushed her and Saddler to be more lenient with the standards. She still felt some disdain towards him for that, never being her uncle first, but a colonel.

"These are my patients." She had tried to argue with her uncle.

"And these are dire times," Colonel Winston argued in kind. "People of their expertise and background are a rarity; we need them."

So, Laura insisted on being present during the therapy, despite her trust in Saddler. No, she didn't feel good about it and didn't know if she expected Tim to agree or disagree with the treatment. But there was no going back now, like a vehicle without brakes that had gathered too much momentum and was coasting down a steep decline. There was just one thing to do; they had to ride it out and see where the cards landed.

The ULFBERT-Therapy Room was divided into two rooms, sectioned off by a horizontal wall, the three feet above and below segregated by a thick sheet of glass. Straight through the doors was a thick and air-tight sealed door that lead into the therapy room. Inside rested the device where so much potential as well as suffering rested. It was a large round machine without a center that looked like a metallic donut. A bed protruded out from the donut hole like a tongue.

It was a device originally built for CAT scans but it had been dissected, rebuilt, and repurposed from the original Magnetic Resonance Imaging-Linear Accelerator, MRI-LINAC, devices used in traditional radiation therapy. This modified device came with an arm that would rotate around the bed, where the UF-Radiation rays would shoot into Tim's body. The first of the three stages of Ultra-Fission-Radioactive-Therapy came in the form of external radiation therapy.

The device also doubled with its former CAT scan abilities, all controlled and monitored in the room aft, in aiding control of the treatment with great accuracy and precision.

From here, the sealed door opened and two nurses in radiation scrubs relieved the other two nurses. Laura walked with Saddler to the control panel. She watched as Tim's gurney was wheeled over to the bed of the machine where he was lifted and placed. The gurney was taken back to the former two nurses, and the door closed. Saddler had the controls and monitors up and running, sealing off the door and the three people inside, waiting until a light above the door flickered on in a red glow.

Laura understood the basic mechanics of the treatment, and the external therapy stage was aimed at hitting his body with the Ultra Fission Radiation to promote the growth of UF-Radiation's cancerous healing effects. The arm of the machine began its rotation while Dr. Saddler held his right hand over the knob controlling the UFR rays, turning it clockwise from zero to two, climbing up in increments of twos until the machine peaked at eight. His left hand worked with other controls that she had no understanding of, but she assumed it dealt with the UFR now being beamed at Tim's body.

She bit and gnawed at her nails as she watched, heart pounding against her chest, hoping and praying to whomever might be listening. She looked from Tim to the control panel Dr. Saddler operated from, and back to Tim. If there was a God, truly, she prayed and hoped he made himself known then and there. That ten percent risk of certain death still clawed at her as her teeth clawed at her fingernails.

"Okey-Dokey," Dr. Saddler said to himself, his hands kept still, without further delegation or command at the control panel. The knob was set to eight, and the external radiation therapy was in full swing.

Laura looked over at the screen on the wall to their right, which displayed live, updated x-ray scans of Tim's body. The x-rays moved like a slideshow, showing Tim's skeletal structure, and Laura wouldn't believe it had she not been there. What had previously appeared as broken glass and powder in his left limbs was realigning, small pieces joining back together. It was as if someone had pressed the rewind button, taking Tim back to a couple of weeks ago. Smaller pieces became larger pieces until the appearance of shattered glass looked like cracked glass. The ulna and radius in his left forearm pieced back together, and soon the cracks began to disappear, leaving behind scarring lines where a minute ago they were broken.

The same was occurring within his tibia and fibula. They were rapidly healing back to their original design, and soon, like the long line water makes when running down a windshield and slowly dries, the image of cracked glass faded. It wasn't like a rewind at all, but a fast-forward of restoration, back to their original state. It cleared out the Osteomyelitis but left behind scars from the breaks. They would still be weakened from the damage; then again, Tim's whole body was riddled with scars and damage. However, in just about every sense of the word, he had promptly recovered.

"Und, decreasing UFR rays." Saddler was soft, speaking gradually with the gentle decrease of the knob from eight to six. The old man's eyes were glued to the monitor and x-ray machine. With more speed than at the outset, he brought the intensity of the UFR beams down to zero. The machine's rotating arm had stopped spinning, and the UFR rays shut down. The nurses in scrubs went and checked his vitals and ran a full body check. The last x-ray showed a fully pieced-together Timothy P. Morse.

After a few minutes, that were more akin to a grueling hour of grinding, one of the nurses turned around with a thumbs up. Her voice was neutral: "Vitals are good, no previous physical injuries detected or signs of UFR-Decomposition, Doctor Saddler."

Laura bit her right index fingernail down to the pink, stopping when sharp pains at her fingertip informed her so. The moment of cognitive pain turned back to the instinctual motion of movement, going to the next finger and chewing.

"Gut, gut, Das gut. Oki, initiating decontamination nuw," Saddler said, flipping a switch on the controls.

Inside the room, fans sucked out the air, and presumably everything else. With the fans still going, a mist fell over the whole interior. A thick veil consumed the nurses, Tim, and the machinery. It lingered, and only when the system detected no harmful residual radiation, did the misting stop. The veil faded as the fans cleared the room back into full visual.

An upbeat *ching* chimed, and the red light above the door turned green. Saddler pressed another button, unsealing the door. Inside, the nurses in scrubs proceeded to pat Tim's body dry; the other two nurses moved back to the door, the previous gurney at the ready.

Only when the ventilation finished did the nurse inside open the door and wheel Tim forwards, lifting him from one bed to the other. Saddler took in a deep breath as he spun in his chair, standing back up. He looked at the nurses with a soft wave of a hand towards the door. "Take our friend here back to his room; I'll be there with the systemic shots," he said as they nodded and left.

To Laura, his friendly frown didn't change but did appear less tense. "Stage one completed, and without fault; nuw we run to Stage two. I assume you want to be there with your friend for the rest of the treatment?" he asked.

Laura nodded, and he offered a faint closed smile in return, grabbing her arm for a moment. It was a gesture she appreciated as he nodded and walked past her towards the door.

"Very well; go on and wait with him. I won't be long."

Laura sat beside Tim in-room two-thirty-seven, waiting. Stage one was the most stressful, she would have thought, but worse than that proved to be stage two. If nothing else, because of the waiting and length of time it took, requiring unending hours of vigilant observation. Next to his bed was the IV line along with two monitors. The extra monitor kept track of Tim's Ultra Fission Radiation levels. And, post-external radiation therapy, his was sitting at a heart-pounding eighty-seven percent. Had he arrived in Alyeska with such a high percentage two years ago, she would have had to euthanize him just like the little boy.

"Not again," she mouthed.

Behind her, Tim's parents stood, speechless at his rapid recovery; his face was fully recognizable. ULFBERT came with a promising prospect to put an end to euthanizing professions. In the form of Systemic Radiation Therapy, stage two, of the treatment, ULBFERT was proving not only promising with its eighty-six percent success rate; it was also versatile with its stages in several fields. The rate of patients dying or being euthanized had lowered, and the survival rate went up; good had been pulled out from the bad, and it made her think.

She recalled one time, speaking with Phil, about how she couldn't believe in a God who orchestrated evil in the world. Her mentality had been influenced by a lifetime of hearing about 'hellfire and brimstone,' from her early youth to her adulthood. She thought that kind of teaching was the only one there was. Then she met Phil.

I don't believe God orchestrates evil, Phil had replied. *But I do believe he can bring light out of the darkness.*

It still didn't answer the question of evil for her. But the idea that something so horrible, like UFR, could also be used to heal gave her hope. *Light out of the darkness,* she repeated to herself.

A soft knock came from the door, and Dr. Saddler entered with a stainless-steel tray and two shots full of transparent orange liquid; she stood up to allow him to sit next to Tim.

He offered her a "thank you" smile as he laid the tray on a wheeled stand and sat. His stubby fingers cradled the IV line in his hand with the side port between his fingers, an airless channel to allow extra medicinal compounds, or the orange radioactive liquid, into the line for a rapid dispersal through Tim's body. That was stage two, short and simpler than the previous, kicking off to stage three simultaneously, which was just monitoring UFR levels.

"What are you giving him?" Monika asked, both worried and curious.

"IV fluids, irradiated with UFR's cellular decomposition quality."

"Won't that hurt him?" Dereck demanded.

"Not if his UFR levels are as high as they are now. We promoted the cancerous healing effects; now we just need to lower that before any serious damage is done as a result," Saddler replied, pulling out a handkerchief and wiping his lips dry.

He dropped the spent needle in a box marked for used needles. Both doctors and Tim's parents watched the monitor constantly updating every second with his UFR levels. Holding their breaths, they only released them as the eighty-seven dropped by one percent. Saddler held up a finger, cautioning their optimism in waiting. Five seconds later, the percentage dropped again by one, and still, Saddler held his breath and raised finger.

Six seconds later, there was another percentage drop, then, four and five seconds were both accompanied by another percentage lowering. Until finally, the decreasing rate was consistent with the seconds and the apparent decrease in Tim's UFR levels continued. Saddler let his breath out in a slow rhythm, his breath blowing up strands of his mustache as his head lowered with his upheld hand.

"Nuw," he took off his glasses and wiped his red eyes, "we wait." He replaced his spectacles.

"I'll wait with him," Laura said, folding her arms, her right hand resting on her left elbow, finger pointing to the door as well. "You should get some rest."

Dr. Saddler didn't even attempt to argue. The fatigue was setting in, and the other patients wouldn't benefit from their caregiver faltering with sleep deprivation. Then again, that was the name of the game these days. But after so long, there was no other prompt but to sleep, regardless. The writing on the wall was clear, and there was no point in being modest about it—only humble. He placed his hand over Laura's and gave it a couple of soft pats; distant memories of her late grandfather came from the gesture, setting a soft smirk in the corner of her mouth.

"If an hour passes and his UFR levels have stopped lowering, and remain above the fourteen percent margin, give him a quarter shot of the second needle, a little at a time until we get him back to his original percentage of a point-zero-nine-six-three," Saddler said, holding up his index finger parallel to his face with a soft but firm jerk of his hand for emphasis. "Little at a time. Then, monitor it to make sure it doesn't rise or fall outside the point-zero-one to point-fourteen safe margin."

"I got it," Laura nodded. "Go on now. You're no good to the others if you're passing out."

As Saddler left, Laura took her seat next to Tim and held her hand over his. Across the room, his parents sat. They watched from a distance, never once leaving, save to use the facilities or grab a coffee. She wouldn't leave his side, not until he was awake and alert, and every once in a while, he'd mumble in his sleep. More good signs.

She wanted to tell him she was sorry, wanted so much to take his and Dakota's grief away. She knew their plates had been loaded by a dumpster fire that had just dropped clear out of the sky. She wished there was a way she could help them, but such pains of the soul weren't something she could remedy. At the very least, she could tend to their health. Physical health was something she could nurture. Mental health was a challenge and never a completed science, but it was something she could at least tend to. But the health of the soul was out of her limits—something she had no remedy for.

Faith? she thought. Maybe that was why the three of them were firm believers. Maybe it was faith that nurtured broken hearts and spirits. Phil and Dakota were widows and vilomahs—people who had lost their children. Maybe that was why they were so firm in their beliefs—because faith had saved them.

Thunder rattled the window, and she looked outside over the city of Anchorage to a dismal view of the tall structures and mountains in the distance. Rain started to fall, and she clenched her teeth at the commencing of sirens. The wailing was a distinct indicator of an Acid Rainstorm, an indication of a Protocol Two Acid Rain inbound for Anchorage. Such a storm would shut down the city and lock everyone inside.

She looked behind at Dereck and Monika with a "last chance to get back home," look. She saw only resolve in the faces of the worried parents. They had conviction and weren't going anywhere. Laura, though she was aware of the issues Tim had with his folks, couldn't help but think just how lucky he was. Whether it be Dakota, his parents, or Olivia, he just seemed to attract people and their loyalty.

Soon, the radioactive rain fell, beating against the window, and they were now in lockdown. The hospital, like all other structures and shelters, would be isolated for the rest of the storm. She rubbed her face, sighing deeply as she looked out over the dark city, dreading the long night ahead.

Chapter Six – The Long Night

-October 25th, 2030-

Acidic upheaval burned in Laura's belly, rising to her throat when the glass panel of the window was rattled by a strong gust of wind. She removed the needle from the IV line; another quarter of the Systemic Shot was injected, and she tossed the empty needle into the disposal box. Before too long, Tim's UFR levels continued to lower one percentage about every five seconds. She leaned back in her chair, yawning, as she rubbed burning eyes behind tired lids. Behind her, she could hear Tim's folks resting; the old couple had fallen asleep a few hours ago.

Like a snake charmer pulling her attention from the window, the room suddenly illuminated with bright, purplish-pink light as a crackling clap of thunder shook the whole room. The tray where the last Systemic Shot lie rattled, and a cold chill stormed up her spine in goosebumps, jumping in her seat. She looked outside, over Anchorage.

The city was cast in a bluish saturation from the street, security, and flood lights faded behind the hue of the downpour. Dotted across the buildings were squares of yellow, spotted every so often, third shift workers, unfortunate second-shifters who couldn't be relieved in time. Or perhaps they were the night owls who didn't want their day to end and stayed up, milking time for as much as they could get.

Her heart pounded in a sudden upbeat from Tim's vital monitor; there was a single spike in his heart rate. She turned from the storm, looking to Tim, and his head rolled to face her. For a second, she expected to hear a "hello" but her only response was the steady *beep beep* of the ECG. His UFR monitor revealed his percentage consistently drawing nearer to the fourteen percent safe margin; her fingers fumbled, and she took in a deep breath as her foot started to shake. Time became a blur, and those consistent *beeps,* and the storm pelting the window, created a soothing ambiance. She might have fallen back into doze, fighting against sleep, had her eyes not looked at his UFR monitor once more. A moment of nothingness came, a time delay to process what she was reading. The UFR monitor showed Tim's percentage steady at *fourteen percent!*

A second wind invigorated her; she was hardly able to recall the journey from eighty-seven. It was all a blur. But she croaked out a muffled laugh, joy filling her in relief. She had to be careful in her celebration; they weren't out of the woods yet. She still needed to get his levels back to the original point-zero-nine-six-three percentage.

One milestone at a time. She calmed her breathing, eyes glued to the digital screen.

Point fourteen dropped to a point one-three-nine. Tim was back down in the Green Zone; he was safe, but there was still a chance his levels could creep back up over that *.140* percent or fall below it. Like a pendulum losing momentum and coming to a slow, going left and right, his would go up and down before settling. Administering more of the systemic shots too early could bring that settling down to below zero percent. Patience was key.

For another hour she waited, rubbing her eyes in relentless pushbacks against the returning lull to sleep. The percentage was creeping and crawling down and up. She would administer no more of the Systemic Shot until that number stopped.

Tim mumbled something in his sleep, and she looked over at him. His face was twitching, a subtle flinch to his right nostril and a frown crested his lips. A passing thought of wonder crossed her mind. *Is he dreaming? What is he dreaming about?*

The fact that he was mumbling while comatose was a good sign; his brain was still active after all the blunt trauma it had received. But if he was speaking gibberish in his sleep, she wondered if his mind would register a question.

"What was that?" she asked.

"Phil, it's okay bro. Dakota's not missing, we're not in Atlan… Uh, don't break the colonel's face dude we just got here."

Hearing Phil's name brought him to her thoughts; there he lingered, and she dwelled. It had been nearly three weeks since she last saw him, when she had spent the night with him. A fond smile crested her lips, thinking of how much of a gentleman he had been to her. The restraint he held that night when things became heated, boiling over to steamy and on their way to escalating. Phil certainly wanted her, and she knew she wanted him as well, yet he refrained somehow, when she didn't. Now that she thought about it, she didn't make it easy on him.

She thought it could have been self-control or faith; maybe it was because of his late wife. Maybe a bit of everything. But when things had cooled down, they just lied on his bed and talked all night, sharing their hurts with one another, their stories. When it came time to retire for the night, Phil replaced his old bedsheets with clean ones and let her sleep on his bed while he made a pallet on the floor with his old ones. It hadn't been the way she thought it would go, but it was the best night she had in a long time—a recent fond memory to hold onto, especially over the last few weeks.

Such a gentleman, she thought, pressing her hand to her lips. That longing remained, and her smile became rueful when Tim and Dakota plagued her about how Phil wanted to pursue her when he came back. Had he asked her, she would've said "Yes" without pause.

Deciding not to play the "what if" game, she downed the rest of her cold coffee, zeroing in on the UFR monitor. Tim's percentage dipped to point-zero-nine-six-three. Laura held her breath as four seconds passed. Five seconds after that, it lowered, and her heart hammered. Six seconds later it raised back up where it remained steady.

Stabilizing. She hoped.

Chapter Seven – Providence

Tim's eyes cracked open, just a little. He could hear a man and a woman in a heated but hushed argument; his eyes opened halfway, his vision blurred, and he thought he saw Phil and Dakota in the room. But the room wasn't right; it was the medical room at the base in Atlanta where he had once been on bedrest. Whatever contagious illness had stricken him, the flu or strep throat, he was quarantined in that room while his brother and sister tended to him.

Phil and Dakota's words were hardly comprehensible, but soon he remembered as they exchanged colorful language about their options, trying to find the best way to help him out of his sickness. In the end, Tim didn't remember how they cured him, just that it was a great labor and journey to find what was needed. Yet, that was well over seven years ago.

Phil's voice changed, speaking now with a clear British accent, and Dakota sounded like Laura. Tim blinked several times, clearing out the crusted sleep that clouded his sight, opening them fully. Phil and Dakota were gone and, in their place, he saw Chain and Laura.

Chain's arms were folded, and while his demeanor was very much patient but restrained, his voice was heated in frustration. Laura had the same hushed retorts, heat just as present in her voice, but her demeanor held nothing back, emphasizing by gestures and waves of her hands and arms, shaking her head now and again.

"He's not just your friend, either, and more than that, he's my patient. And if I say he is not fit for military service, then he's not fit." Laura shook her head; there was a finality in her tone that matched her posture, with most of her weight on one leg, arms folded across her chest, and a pensive look on her face.

"Mu'um," Chain shook his head. "All other SRT units are either on Op or in medical care. There's no one else to—"

"There must be someone else; go find them. Ten million survivors in this nation and not one of them—"

"Aren't a top bloke as Tim."

"My answer doesn't change."

"Tell it to your uncle; he's the one who phoned me up. Besides, if Tim knew…"

"Knew what?" Tim didn't even recognize his voice as it came out in a hollow croak.

The effort to sit up was considerable; his whole body throbbed and he either forgot how to use his arms or there just wasn't any strength in them. He fell back, his head landing on the pillows. The bed and blankets would have pulled him back to sleep had his memories not caught up with him; in particular, he recalled the last memory before nothingness.

He saw the ogre of a man fondling Olivia and promising her a horrible fate. He saw Hendricks breaking said man's face in and remembered hearing the exchange of gunfire as Puristans dragged Olivia away. The Lure was captured by the Hair, crying out his name.

Tim wiped his eyes dry; he had been too helpless to save her. He hadn't been enough. His breathing quickened, and sudden alertness flooded his thoughts, pulling him from the lethargy with a sudden need to act.

"Olivia." His eyes widened at Chain. "Tell me you know where they took her!" His breathing escalated in a panting frenzy, his voice fast and hoarse.

"There are people working on it," Laura said, walking over to him, adjusting his bed to help him sit up. Her voice was soft and assuring as if to lure him back to rest. "The best you can do now is rest."

"Fuckin'ell. It most certainly isn't." Chain leaned over the foot of Tim's bed, giving no room or time for the doctor to intercede. Their eyes met. "It's Dakota."

Olivia in peril was bad enough, and the idea that something was wrong with Dakota made him feel helpless and useless as he lied there. "What about her?" he remarked, sharp and clear as Laura grabbed his arm. But she had faded to his periphery, and Chain was holding his full attention.

"Nothing the colonel knows for certain," Laura tried once more.

Chain shrugged, a "granted" response to Laura. "Dunno. Colonel said it was urgent and to come to collect you after you'd been sorted out. Bloody brilliant, this," Chain gave his leg a gentle pat. "Ready to break the other, mate?"

Tim looked down at his left leg and arm. They were usable and healed as he flexed and rotated his arm. Bending his knee, he felt no pain. "Huh," was all he could reply with.

Laura's face receded in dismay, seeing the losing battle she was facing. Tim looked at her, unable to hide his awe. There were questions to be answered later; now, he felt as if there was no time to lose. First thing in the morning he was going to hit the ground running.

"Doc," Tim said, his voice breaking the two-way tie between her and Chain.

Chain had given Tim and Laura some privacy as she started screening him. There was a spiteful silence to her closed lips, save for the simple commands and gestures: "Raise your arm. Breathe in. Breath out." As she examined him, Tim observed his arm and leg with a surreal indifference. His whole body ached, and he was sore as if he had been hit by a train and woken from a deep, coma-like sleep. Every movement was stiff; his bones popped, and each time he bent his knee or elbow, it felt like he was stretching.

Laura stepped back, took out the earpieces from her stethoscope, and draped the device around her neck. A knock came at the door before a nurse came in with Tim's effects folded in her arms: his boots, belt, and a pistol on top.

"I'll go finish up the paperwork while you get dressed," Laura said, leaving the room with the nurse.

Tim hopped off the bed, testing out his balance. Then he paced around the room some, feeling out his balance and any discomfort. He was getting reacquainted with the slight limp in his left leg like he did after Kansas City two years back; yet now his limp had grown more profound and brought a tingle to his hip with each step.

"Hmm," he mumbled, taking it all in. He could walk on it, and if he could do that much, then he was good to go. Apparently, the colonel was of the same opinion.

Minutes later, Tim was fully dressed, tucking his olive drab shirt into his pants and attaching his hip holster before tightening his belt. He bloused his pant legs to his boots and holstered his FNP. There were no magazines for it, which was fine; the fact that the hospital allowed even his pistol to be returned was enough. He ran his hands over his shirt and pants to push out the wrinkles, coming to the thighs of his pants where something crumbled inside the cargo pocket.

What the…?

Fishing through the Velcro and into the pocket, he felt the crumpled letter his mother had written him still there. Aside from the spiteful silence and neutral commands earlier from Laura, she did share with him what his folks had done: leaving the safety of their safe house, signing the consent form, and braving the Acid Rainstorm all night until his treatment was deemed a success. Ending with, *They figured you didn't need them around when you woke up, so they left.*

The alternative to this "ULFBERT" treatment? Amputation. He was grateful for the colonel's and doctor's gamble, but it started with his parents' consent. Had he been conscious and able to decide for himself, he would have volunteered to try the ULFBERT treatment—whatever it took to go after his girls.

"Amazing." That was all he could mutter when hearing of ULFBERT. That was it; he had no words or thoughts, just thinking of the promise such a treatment held. It gave him a humbling feeling to know that, in the end, his experience might help its development out of the prototype stage and into full practice.

A knock came at the door. "Clear," he shouted, folding the letter back into his pocket before Laura opened the door and stepped inside. She met him with eye-to-eye contact now, standing straight but with slumped shoulders. Those hazel gray disks of her irises were looking at him with an analytical benevolence he saw in many good doctors. There was relief in her eyes but disappointment as well.

"Good as new," she noted with a forced smile.

"As good as can be." Tim corrected, still feeling the tingle in his left hip with each step.

Her nostrils flared as she stepped closer, a paper in hand as she gave it to him. Tim looked down, the title reading *DD Form 208.* He looked over the form, skipping over the bulk of the wording—a bunch of mumbo-jumbo he was already familiar with. What he needed to see was the *Approval* box checked and dated with Laura's signature underneath.

Funny, Tim thought. He hadn't even signed his retirement papers yet, but formalities were formalities. "With this," Tim waved the paper, "I get to help Dakota, and I hope to God Olivia as well." He grabbed her shoulder, offering his thanks.

Laura shook her head, shrugging off his hand, and folded her arms. "I'm not mad at you." She leveled her eyes at him, shoulders no longer slumped. "It's just, the last time you deployed and the three of you went out, only two came back. You're supposed to be retired now."

"And kids aren't supposed to be trafficked," Tim sighed, "You do understand that I have to do this."

"I do," she nodded, "Just come back in one piece will ya? You got lucky this time. But even ULFBERT has its limits."

"I didn't need luck, lil' sis." Tim grabbed her shoulder. "God sent me you."

She smirked, arms folded as she stepped closer. Leaning into his chest, she wrapped her arms around him. Tim rested his chin on her head. "Thank you."

Chain was downstairs waiting against the wall, his arms folded, when Tim caught up. Laura branched off from him to her other patients along the way. He didn't relish leaving her in low spirits and wished there was more time to mend such things. But there was a lot he did wish for, and, at best, he got only more problems. Chain shared in his rue as they grabbed hands and hugged only the way guys could. It was a display of intimate friendship in the most callous way, backed by the proverbial, "Good to see ya, Yank," and, "You too, you tea-drinking bastard."

But there was hardly enough good cheer for such banter; instead, pats on the back were greeting enough as they headed for the main lobby.

"What's happened to Dakota?" Tim demanded. His body felt like it was creaking and moaning with each step. Both his left limbs pulsed with a ticklish numbness.

"Not here. It's all tosh." Chain was keeping his eyes locked straight ahead with all his effort to hide the worry and anxiety up front and center: "We'll get sorted out at the colonel's compound. Razor's waiting outside to drive us there."

"I never did get to thank you." There came a silence a moment longer than normal, Tim sorting through the fragmented memories of lying down in the cab of the Blackhawk, air being pumped into his lungs, Dakota broken and defeated next to him. "For taking care of me and Dakota on the way back from Colorado," he finished.

"No need to drip on it, mate." Chain nodded with a smirk. "You may have to return the favor, this time. Things are going mental."

The hall took a turn, coming to a quick end and leading into the main lobby with the front entrance. It was a wide-open space where the check-in counter stood to the left with a packed line of people. Some were holding rags to their faces, others keeping an arm above their chest wrapped in paper towels and duct tape, others had obvious signs of injuries in need of mending or sicknesses to be diagnosed. Then, there were some who looked like they were waiting in line at the ration center in idle boredom. No one dared to make a scene during the long wait and slow reception with the shortage of staff to accommodate—not with the heavy security presence of military police armed with M4s keeping chaos that could erupt from a panicking group on a leash.

A sitting area was off to the right, lining the walls and windows to the outside up to the main entrance. Chairs and double seaters separated the area into squares, with coffee tables between. There, in his periphery, Tim spied his parents as he and Chain came to pass them. Monika and Dereck were sitting and waiting to see him back to health, he figured.

Looking at his mother, all he saw was the front door of his childhood home being slammed in his face. In Dereck, he saw only the absent father. *What ya gonna do, player? You can't forgive others until you forgive yourself, and you, my boy, have one big-ass log in your eye.* Tim's mind rambled in a voice mirroring Dakota's as he looked away from the people who had forsaken him.

The difference between past and present contrasted in a bitter taste in his mouth as his stomach fluttered with butterflies. Coming to the exit doors of the main entrance, he saw a blurred reflection of himself. That was then, and this was now, and he felt inside his heart that gentle whisper speaking to him. He saw in his reflection that the only thing stopping him from hurting was himself.

His first thought had been to just ignore them and walk on with Chain outside to Razor until his parents were out of his periphery. Out of sight, out of mind...only, was that true? Going out into the Wastelands always held the capacity of being a one-way trip.

He clenched his fists, the exit drawing nigh, and the moment became heavy with a do-or-die anxiety that made his stomach churn. Heart racing, his thoughts bounced back and forth between stopping and not stopping, past and present, Rufus and Phil, Phil and Dakota. He didn't know what he was going to do or what he wanted to do, and it was then that his body just reacted, deciding for him. He gave Chain's shoulder a tap just before the exit.

"I'll catch up," he said.

Chain nodded, followed by a tapping of his wristwatch.

Tim turned on his heels and changed direction towards his folks. Monika kept her eyes busy on other things, nervous fingers fidgeting with each other. Dereck maintained that steady, stony appearance that sparked a flare in Tim's nerves and set those butterflies in his stomach aflame. *That same damn stoicism.*

Both his parents looked up at him when he was within spitting distance—faces hopeful but braced for whatever winds may come, a gentle breeze or a violent gale. Signing a piece of paper and gambling your son's future successfully hardly made up for everything. Even now, looking at the two of them, his heart still pounded adrenaline through his body and his fists clenched. He couldn't shake the hatred or wash away the sorrow; he felt there was no way to be rid of it, and it was then he realized that he had no idea what he was going to say or do.

What the hell do I do? he fumed to himself

Worst of all was the splitting feeling of being caught in two directions, at a crossroads with no compass. He couldn't just come out and forgive them. *Could I? At least...* His thoughts mirrored Dakota's voice again, then mirrored Phil's...*forgive?*

His nose started running as he sniffed, and he stopped a good ten feet away. Monika looked up at him, holding her husband's hand. A moment of silence passed before Tim cleared his throat: "They're sending me back out." He broke the silence, and his voice cracked at the start, but he quickly straightened it up in a flat tone.

“We heard,” Dereck replied.

“Will you be okay on your own?” Monika asked.

“I’m never alone.” Tim shook his head, not knowing what to say. He settled then for the simplest of courtesies when helped by others. “Thank you,” he said, his voice holding the tone that came with the ending of a conversation. “For signing the consent form.”

“That was your father, baby.” Monika lowered her voice. “I couldn’t.”

“In any case,” Tim looked at them both, “that’s all.”

“Wait, son.” His father spoke up this time.

Hearing either of them address him as son brought a burning pain, manifesting in tears blurring the bottom of his vision. It took all his efforts to restrain himself, looking at his father who now stood up from his seat. The jaded cloak fell off, and the hard shell around his eyes opened to soft beady ones, the flat line of his lips arched in a frown.

Tim waited, but his said nothing else, and he thought perhaps Dereck didn’t know what to say. Maybe there was nothing more to say, and maybe they both knew what he couldn’t put into words. There wasn’t much else; Tim was done talking. A silence fell between him and them, a good indicator that he didn't have anything left to say. For the moment, the conversation was indeed over.

With nothing else, he turned around and left them, heart still racing as his eyes watered. His nose ran, and when he was out of hearing distance, he sniffed hard, When he was out of sight, he wiped his eyes dry.

Chain stood waiting by an old Fast Back Highlander, and they climbed into the backseat. Razor sat behind the wheel, sporting a pair of prescription eyeglasses, and Chain in the passenger seat.

“Thought you blokes were painting each other’s nails in there.”

“Nah,” Tim shook his head, eyeing his buddy in the windshield mirror. “You know that's our thing; I’d never leave you out.”

Chapter Eight – Reinstatement

Two hours later, Tim was standing inside the observation side of an interrogation room. Colonel Winston, Second Lieutenant Bracket, and Chain were in company, paying witness to Captain Shilling's interrogation of Staff Sergeant Hendricks on the other side of a one-way mirror. The woman had a spark to her, a controlled burn inside, as she poked and prodded at the man. But Hendricks was giving her nothing. The old Marine sat there, cuffed to the table, a force of calm under a swollen and bent-out-of-place nose, along with a shiner, courtesy of Tim. He didn't look comfortable, but his steady rhythm of breaths maintained his composure.

Tim sighed. Five minutes after arriving late to see the captain's efforts, he had already deduced that Hendricks wouldn't break—at least not under legal duress or with bribery. Had Phil been there, Tim had no doubt he'd tell the colonel to shut off the cameras and have all MPs vacate the hall outside.

Waiting for the staff sergeant to crack was bad enough, but at every poke and prod Tim made to the colonel about Dakota, Winston only gave spoonful answers. The control of information flow sparked an irritation that made his temper flare, and the arrival of a new headache shortened his patience. Soon, he found the heel of his foot tapping in place, fists clenched in folded arms as he waited and listened to the dead-end interrogation.

The colonel licked his dried lips and took in a breath. Tim looked at him, interest piqued, hopeful for answers. "Intel suggests Puristans have support from a third party."

"This third party has something to do with Dakota?" asked Tim.

"It seems likely." Winston nodded and gave a radio a single click on the PTT button. Captain Shillings looked back at the glass, shoulders deflating in a slump.

She left the room and came to the observation side without a moment's waste. Tim looked at Hendricks. The Marine's posture was straight, eyes centered on the wall, stoic and emotionless as could be. But Tim knew he was holding himself in check.

"First Lieutenant. You're looking better for wear," Captain Shilling's greeted as she closed the door behind her. She offered a hand, which Tim accepted and shook, and her gaze switched to the colonel. “I can’t get anything out of him.”

“Lemme have a poke at him.” Tim called her attention back to himself.

Colonel Winston nodded his consent. “Go ahead,” he said, then looked over to Chain and Razor. “You two, follow me. Tim, meet us back at the OCR when you’re finished.”

“Will do, colonel,” Tim replied as the colonel and lads departed, leaving him and the captain alone.

Tim stepped through the door the captain had entered, into a short, narrow corridor where the door to the interviewing side of the interrogation room waited. The electronic lock *clanked*, and he entered the room, Hendricks’ back facing him. Tim walked around the old Marine and passed the table where he took a seat across from him. Hendricks' calm exterior was replaced by a perplexed look. Tim noted the man's eyes looked to his arm and leg, and Hendricks was dumbfounded. When he did find something to say, he simply greeted Tim, “Semper Fi, Devil Dawg.”

“Semper Fi,” Tim returned. There was no need to beat around the proverbial bush; he went straight to the point with a simple request. “Where did they take her?”

“I can’t give you that.” Hendricks shook his head, his stoic exterior cracking but a little. He mumbled something under his breath, to himself. Tim wished he could read lips at that moment.

“You could’ve had everyone killed, me killed. You broke the face of that rapey fuck and threatened to kill him. God help her without you around now.” Tim shook his head. “What can you give me?”

“You don’t know what it was like, before the borders were sealed off.” Hendricks’ eyes fell. “You weren’t here; you wouldn’t understand why.”

“Then educate me.”

Hendricks took in a breath and kept his cool, but Tim did notice a light flushing of his face, and his hands, chained to the table, flexed from a fist back to open palms resting on one another.

“After The Calamity, when the borders were unstable and the state was taking in too many survivors, we bit off more than we could chew. Too many people and not enough beds, or food. The first several years was nothing but chaos and disorder, and things only got better when the order was issued and the borders were closed off. Better in the sense that after that we consolidated and reorganized. Even then, we were scraping by." Hendricks' eyes never left Tim's and Tim held the same, neither blinking once. "Lieutenant, the best thing I can say about our group is that we don't want to go back to how it was before; we don't want needless suffering."

"The needs of the many and all that jazz?" asked Tim, receiving a nod in reply. He gave a firm shake of his. "A lot has changed since then. Hell, Hendricks, British Columbia has been reclaimed; did your people ever stop to think about how that much territory gained could accommodate all these extra mouths to feed and bodies to shelter? Instead, you turn to trafficking? And to who?"

"We did." A mean snarl crossed Hendricks' face, and for a split second he looked off somewhere else, perhaps to hide his shame before returning to look back at Tim. "I tried to reason with them about that very idea, but they said it was an unreasonable idea, that we couldn't because of…"

"Your benefactors." Tim finished, receiving a surprised look in return. There was no confirmation, but no denial, either, affirming the former in Tim's mind.

Hendricks sighed, his eyes looking to the mirror. He shook his head at Tim. But he held the resistance; for whatever reason, he couldn't let go of it. "They said outsiders were useful in other mediums and we couldn't keep operating without 'their' help. That British Columbia was, therefore, the right of domestic progeny and not foreign."

"Your superiors sound superficial." Tim pursued his lips in thought. "Who's your benefactor?" He pressed again but received nothing but silence for his efforts. "Hendricks." He shifted in his seat. "I'm begging you, not as an Alyeskan, or anti-Puristan, or anything like that. I'm begging you, from Marine to Marine, please."

America was gone, but the Corps was still very much alive in the two of them: steadfast loyalty between Marines before faction loyalty. Semper Fidelis wasn't just words to say, but a practice, a way of life, something that had been passed down. It was a connection that made him and Hendricks brothers, no matter the distance between them. The cracks in the staff sergeant's resolve widened; no doubt he was expecting that from Tim, but his face showed no contempt. The Marine inside the Puristan shone through those cracks and tipped away from the latter.

"I never wanted this." Hendricks looked to Tim. "Any of it."

"And yet?" Tim shrugged.

"Here we are." The old Marine took in a deep breath and huffed, marking the cessation, at last, of their steady eye contact. "There's a drop-off site, northeast of Fort Liard. Our 'benefactors' pick up the people we traffic there and take them somewhere."

"Where?"

"I don't know. I never delivered outsiders myself; I'm just one who rounds them up," Hendricks replied. "I don't know what our benefactors do to them, or where they take them. Only that they wanted Miss Blundell so much that she took priority over every other target we have; so much that a little over a week ago she was bumped right up to their top ten wanted. Something about her DNA was special."

Tim gave the table a soft pat, looking at the staff sergeant's bent nose. "How's the nose?"

"Busted and clogged." Hendricks chuckled back, "Oo-rah?"

"Oo-rah," Tim replied, standing from his chair and taking his leave.

Before leaving he heard Hendricks' utter "Give them hell Devil Dawg."

In the colonel's Operational Control Room, the five of them stood around the island table of the touch screen display that detailed present-day Alyeska's borders, the Canadian Confederacy, and the Northwestern United States region front and center. Around Alyeska's borders, several black squares were pinpointed, but none of them filled in save for one just north of Fort Liard. There were also filled-in black dots scattered abroad, and over Bellingham was one such dot.

The display also offered a glimpse of the status of the Canadian Confederacy, the main colonies, or strongholds, outlined in red and highlighted, with smaller outposts outlined and filled with horizontal lines. The map stretched far to the East where the Zombie Crisis was taking place in Ontario and Manitoba. Siberian troop movements, supply lines, and all else made a blue line, traversing across Canada and closing in on Attawapiskat. Also in blue was the SRT unit's progression in the Northwestern United States; Phase Vine and Branch was underway to prepare the way for the expeditionary forces of the Army.

Tim thought back to the old days of discovering the New World, where the edges of the maps were being filled in and the unknown was becoming known. The Dead World seemed just like such a map, becoming smaller and smaller. 'Here there be monsters' came to mind as he looked down to Colorado, with no new updates. Colonel Winston zoomed in on the Northwest Territories Province of Canada.

"What are we looking at over here, Sir?" Tim asked, eyeing Fort Liard to the northeast with a filled-in square, and beyond that, a dot; his eyes were glued on Fort Liard, where Dakota would have been just days ago.

"The circles are black site locations the President explicitly forbade any SRT operations in," Winston replied.

"Like Bellingham," Tim thought aloud, receiving a nod from the colonel, looking back to that same dot. Mentally connecting dots, he studied the map over and over. *Outsiders, Puristans, Benefactors, proximity to Fort Liard, Dakota, and Wheeler. Wheeler was an outsider.*

"The non-filled squares are locations we currently suspect to be drop-off sites where the Puristans hand off outsiders to these benefactors of theirs. One location is, as of now, confirmed," Winston said, pointing at the filled-in square between the circle and Fort Liard. Courtesy of Staff Sergeant Hendricks, this confirmed drop-off site was near the black site of Sahtu, just west of the stronghold of Yellowknife.

"So, you believe they've taken Olivia to this Sahtu black site?" asked Bracket. "This is getting a bit out of hand colonel. Hell, we're supposed to be working together to restore the world, not doing this cloak-and-dagger shit."

"Second Lieutenant." Tim leveled his voice at his friend, then looked to the colonel. "What do we got on Dakota then?" he asked.

"Her last known whereabouts were west of Yellowknife, near an outpost called Whati." Winston replied, pointing just south of the Sahtu black site "Damion's people haven't seen or heard of her or a couple of their own. Whati's gone dark, and all signs point to Sahtu. That's our lead on Olivia and Dakota."

What the hell is going on over there? Tim's folded arms dropped, his feet aiming at the door. "I'm ready to get to it then, colonel."

"Not yet." Winston looked at Tim. "First off, Bracket has volunteered to join you. You both are being folded into SRT-Bravo. Tim, you'll replace Razor as second-in-command to Chain. Your rank will remain the same as it was in Alpha, Second Lieutenant. Bracket, military differs from security detail, so you'll be given the rank of private."

"Hell, I don't think there's been a private in any SRTs; good on you mate, already leaving your mark and you've just joined." Razor gave Bracket a pat.

Tim eyed the colonel. "Slug and Dagger?"

"Those two boot necks are attending a two-person AA meeting at the armory," Razor answered for the colonel. "Getting our shite ready."

"Sergeant." Winston hadn't taken his eyes off him. "I don't need to emphasize to you what this means. The last black site you visited?"

"I know." Tim nodded.

The dots didn't just connect to Sahtu as their target location, but all the implications led to and about it. black sites, new breeds of zombies, the Puristans, some third party, people going missing…Every nation had skeletons in its closet, and a line was drawn between the ignorant and those with the knowledge. A silver lining was now being drawn from before they had meddled in Bellingham. It went without saying that ignorance was bliss.

"I've been ordered not to interfere with these sights anymore. I cannot legally orchestrate a clandestine operation."

"So, you're just gonna tell us all this and do nothing?" asked Bracket.

Tim held up a staying hand. *Just wait,* his face expressed to the man. Bracket wasn't one with military discipline, and while the former fireman excelled at security duties, his lack of the former showed.

"No," Colonel Winston answered Bracket. "The President didn't say anything about allowing volunteers to execute a covert operation. Especially since you've all passed your medical screenings and haven't signed your retirement yet."

Tim looked over to Chain and Razor, the former who just offered a shrug with his arms, which were locked in a comfortable fold across his chest. "We've been the dog's bollocks of the SRT Community, fucking corkers, all of us, for the last two years," Chain replied, "You move, we move. It's that simple for us."

"Fucking true." Razor stamped his approval.

Tim gave Chain a smirk and said "Oo-rah" before looking back to the colonel.

"Bracket, you also have been given authorized leave from Captain Shillings. Timothy Morse, Chain, Razor, Slug, and Dagger. You're all reinstated."

Tim stood dressed in full combat kit; it wasn't his usual loadout of a SAW and the weight of extra ammunition. This kit was a lighter load to burden, composed of an M4 carbine and its smaller 5.56 ammunition, a Beretta, one frag, three "bangers," seven thirty-round magazines for his rifle, and two fifteen-round magazines for his pistol. It was still heavy but was not as much as he normally lugged.

He did have his contentions; while he didn't hate the M4, he did like the machine guns. When looking at Slug with a "what the hell?" look, Slug just shrugged. "Chin off it; the op is quick and silent, lasting no longer than a day. Mobility and speed are what we're after, not a knees-up spraying fuck-all everywhere with those dam machine guns you like."

You motherfucker. Tim chuckled, giving Slug a hard pat as he adjusted the sling of his M4. A sensational tingle rode up his left leg and hip, feeling almost like a tickle as he limped about.

Tim was the first one finished, and, waiting on the others, he stared out a window over the colonel's compound as the Lads and Bracket were finishing up. Chain had finished second and come to check on the back straps of Tim's chest rig. Each pull of a strap moved and jerked his body as he stood there, hands resting on his weapon, held in place by its sling, bucking his knees to hold his stance straight.

Bracket was finished next, and Tim checked on his kit. He received an affirming pat on his shoulder from Chain: "Good to go."

Tim returned the gesture to Bracket in kind, his eyes then going back to the window. Outside, a stormy sky contested with a bright, sunny evening, the light and darkness forming a line that spanned down the horizon and out of view. Rain fell in a soft drizzle, and the rest of the compound below was alive and active, people scrambling to get everything locked up for the storm.

A knock came at the door, and Laura stepped inside. Receiving a hailstorm of friendly greetings from the other men, she gave Chain a pat continuing past everyone and stopped at him. Her hands held, with special care, an aluminum box.

"Hey, Doc," he greeted.

"You're probably gonna need this. Had to pull a few strings this morning just to get it ahead of mass production." She offered the box.

Tim took it and opened a little latch holding the lid in place, viewing the contents therein set neatly into foam indentions. Inside was some sort of watch device, and next to it an auto-injector with replaceable cartridges.

"Uh, thanks, Doc. But I'm more of an analog kind of guy… What is it?" He raised a brow at her, receiving a smirk in response.

"A monitoring device," she said, taking the box and setting it on the table, removing the watch-like device. Her other hand pulled up his left hand to strap the device behind his wrist. "It'll monitor your heartbeat, but more importantly it reads your UFR levels. If it starts beeping, then your UFR levels have progressively risen, exceeding the fourteen percent threshold. Should that happen, you'll need to take one of these and inject it into your thigh." Laura pointed down to the injecting device and two cartridges. "Side effects from the treatment, I'm afraid. These aren't as potent as the systemic shots; they're less concentrated with UFR, so one full dose won't lower your levels too far. It should hold you long enough until you can get to higher care from the field."

Tim chuckled, taking the contents from her. "I guess there's no arguing with you on this one, he said, accepting the injector and cartridges."

"No." She gave his shoulder a push with a fist. "If I can't keep you from active duty, then you'll have to start listening to me."

"I guess we have a deal, then."

"Mate." Chain's voice spoke up as he adjusted a helmet and headset. The others were now fully dressed in their kits, following suit, and getting their inner team comms ready. "Wheels up in five mikes," he said, tossing Tim his helmet.

Tim stowed the auto-injector and cartridges in his vest, giving his doctor a thankful smirk and hug before turning to leave. Chain and the others folded out the door behind him and Chain. The joint clambering of their boots falling in sequence sounded like a small marching parade inside the HQ. In their midst, Laura's softer footfalls came behind them.

In five minutes, they were back outside, walking through the drizzle and approaching the ALZ where several Chinooks, Apaches, Little Birds, and Blackhawks rested. A pushback vehicle was towing a Chinook with folded propellers to a maintenance hangar, where, inside, a couple of privates and a corporal were painting motifs on a Blackhawk. The colonel stood dressed in his ACUs, a green beret atop his head. Laura stepped next to her uncle as Tim and the others stopped before him and gave their solutes to their superior officer.

"Ad'ease." Colonel Winston returned the solute.

Tim looked at the old Blackhawk they'd be using, assigned to SRT-Alpha & Bravo roughly two years ago. 'Ol' Faithful' was painted on the nose, with an image of a maiden in skimpy, old, Victorian-style attire smiling and waving to any admirers—courtesy of Razor and Dagger's artistry skills. The old bird had taken them all up and down British Columbia, to Prince Rupert, to the disaster that occurred in Lethbridge, to Bellingham, and to everything in between. It had become an extension of their circle, an honorary member of the family, a home away from home.

"You have everything you need, Lieutenant?" Winston addressed Chain. The latter spared a look to Tim and the others before returning his look to the colonel.

"Aye, Sir."

"Then God be with you, and God's speed." The colonel stepped aside as Slug and Dagger mounted into the bird. Chain and Razor climbed into the pilot and co-pilot seats. Tim sat on the edge, his left foot hanging between Ol' Faithful's landing skid on the co-pilot side and the metal belly. A strap anchored to the inside had a carabiner attached to it; taking it in his hand, Tim secured himself to the bird in case he was to fall. His right foot pushed against the skid to keep his balance, and once he was secured, he gave Chain a thumbs up.

Back outside, a perimeter ring was painted in blue on the ground, and Winston and Laura stood side by side. When apart from one another, it was easy to forget the two were related. But as they both stood there, Winston with his arms folded behind his back and Laura with hers folded across her chest, he saw the resemblance. Laura waved as the bird's propellers started to spin in its awakening, and not long after the landing skids lifted off the ground, they were airborne.

Chapter Nine – Covert Op

-October 26th, 2030-

Tim could see a great deal outside; the Northwest Territories were sliding past him in shapes of different green and black. There was something about sitting with his legs dangling off the edge of a helicopter, buzzing across the night sky and wearing a set of Night Optic Devices (NODs), that he always liked. Maybe it had something to do with his depth perception being thrown off by the NODs, but it was a good respite during the flight. Organizing his thoughts, he smelled the fresh but cold air of the Northwest Territories.

Entertaining memories as he watched the green and black landscape fly by in his night vision, hours passed in radio silence, save for only the most essential of information relayed over the headsets. Then, Chain's voice broke the silence once more, harkening an end to the respite: "Approaching LZ. ETA two minutes."

Tim felt his arms tense and his fingers adjusting his weapon as he climbed out from his thoughts and memories, studying with greater intensity the surrounding area as Ol' Faithful's approach slowed to a hover over their Landing Zone. The sliding green and black landscape came to a still as they hovered. The trees and the mountains were far off as he could see. Down below their LZ, a meadow on an elevated position was cleared of BR-Hostiles and wildlife, just grass surrounded by trees.

In the distance, a white dome of light contrasted with the visual of greens and blacks, and the trees formed a horizon of jagged teeth. The dome light from the Sahtu Facility was a good thousand meters out, give or take.

Tim reached the end of his M4's barrel, activating an IR laser device invisible to the human eye but not with his NODs. Given how the optical devices threw off his depth perception and blurred his vision in a couple meter's radius, aiming down his weapons sites, was a weak link with the NODs. Needless to say, the IR Laser and NODs went together like peanut butter and jelly.

With the green lasers of both his and Bracket's rifles projecting the paths of their aim, they scanned the port side of the LZ, Chain's blind spots.

"LZ clear port side." Tim broke radio silence.

A moment later came Dagger's voice: "LZ clear on starboard."

"Right, then; making descent," came Chain's reply, and Tim pulled his feet up from under the landing skids, resting on the top. "Going black on all comms with Juneau. Only inner team comms from here on out."

Tim gave his affirmation first, followed by an orchestra of "copy" from the others.

The landing skids lowered over the grass and the bird was kept ready to lift back off. Tim and Bracket scanned the port side, Dagger and Slug the starboard, waiting for any hostile latecomers to the noise. The green laser of the IR device held steady as Tim looked between the trees, seeing Bracket's laser, shaky from nerves. But nothing vomited forth from the wilderness.

Both Tim and Slug gave another "LZ cleared," on both sides before Ol' Faithful started powering down. The propellers slowed in their cycles until the bird went silent in rest; they waited for a second longer, listening for any moans, barks, or yelps of monsters or nocturnal predators. But, as with the bird, the wilderness rested in silence. Tim and Bracket disembarked, holding security, while Chain and Razor climbed out from the cockpit seats.

They regrouped at the bird's bow; Tim saw Chain wasn't wasting a single second, pointing to him with a "Tim, take point."

"On it," Tim uttered in a bare whisper, aiming his barrel upwards to not flag Razor as he walked past his buddy to the front of the stack. Feeling the others fall into formation behind him, Razor followed no less than five meters behind his heels as he broke into the tree line, the white dome in the sky behind them.

SRT-Bravo made a clover approach, heading further out and away from the target, then changing course north, and then northwest, masking any lateral movement with distance. So, by the time they came to the Sahtu from the west, they came towards their target in a vertical direction, a separate direction than their LZ. The direction of their travel formed a clover shape when looking at a map Chain resorted to from time to time.

All remained quiet, save for the controlled breathing of each man, the soft snapping of twigs, the shuffling of their gear and clothes as they moved, owls hooting nearby, and coyotes yelping in the distance. The wind moved through the trees like air being blown through a harmonica, playing an ominous tune that was softer than the crunch of leaves under their footfalls.

Night ops were a rarity outside the borders of home given the disposition of the monsters towards the nocturnal setting. Even with NODs and IR devices, contact with the undead was a greater risk, tenfold, at night. Even in the relative security of the middling lands between Alyeska and the Canadian Confederacy, the hairs on Tim's arms and neck were erect. Every fifteen meters, Tim came to a stop, everyone looking around and listening while Razor, who held their six, provided counter-tracking of the signatures of their movement. He brushed leaves over the mud where their boots left impressions, swept the grass pressed down by their steps, and so and so on to prevent any threat from tracking them.

"Clear," followed up the stack from Slug at their rear to Tim, who'd reply with a "Moving" that traveled back down. Then, he'd cross another fifteen meters for the same touch and go.

Eventually, the ambient light of the Sahtu site brightened the vision through the trees so that the black of their vision turned to a purplish white, and the green brightened until it became too bright for their eyes. Tim came to a stop eleven meters from his previous position. He adjusted the nob connecting his NODs to his helmet and raised the device away from his eyes as everyone else followed suit. One by one, NODs were lifted, IR Lasers were deactivated, and a few minutes of waiting in silence passed, their eyes adjusting.

They were in the dome of white light, though outside the visual of their NODs was just ambient light bouncing off the trees, being swallowed by the darkness of night. Tim found that they were in the furthest reaches of the light, where they could see clearly through the trees.

Their movements slowed, becoming more methodical. Sticking to areas where the trees condensed into thick clusters, they moved from thick trunk too thick trunk. They kept their approach vertical and straight. Thirty minutes passed before they crested over the summit of a hill, a position overlooking the southwestern perimeter of their objective, which was now just two hundred meters away.

Tim led the team down the summit, halfway down the hill to a perch, of sorts, formed by a fallen tree collecting eroded dirt and rocks against the trunk like water backed against a dam. With the top of the hill above them, the perch offered plenty of concealment and a good visual of their target area.

Tim removed a pair of binoculars, Bracket doing the same, while the others held security. Looking into his, Tim adjusted the focus of the lens, using a bridge crossing the Great Bear Lake from the south as a reference point. His image came into full focus as he studied the bridge, an expanse that traveled from the southern shore to the black site resting on a peninsula. The bridge accommodated two sets of rail tracks, one for ingress and the other for egress, and was currently under repair.

The place was pretty lit up. Tim traced the ingress rails and followed them up to the southern perimeter of the peninsula where a wall stood, and there was a decent-sized gate. Both blocked any further visuals beyond. The whole place was protected by cement walls topped off with concertina wires, and fixed machine gun nested at every corner. There were teams of three men at each nest: standard gunnery teams, one the shooter, one standing by with extra ammo and barrels, and the third being the team leader. Between each nest were several sentries on patrol atop the wall—riflemen.

"I'm not seeing a way in from the south," Tim mumbled. "Perimeter wall is locked down tight."

Bracket, next to him, repeated as much from the west perimeter, concluding with a "Should we double back and approach from the north?"

"Negative," Chain remarked. "That's not in our time window; the sun will crop up by then."

Tim checked his watch: 0352 hours, Chain was right. Sunrise would be in about five hours. There was no time to make a different approach. *Work with what ya got, make some damn lemonade.*

"Movement to the far west," Razor's voice whispered.

"Nearby?" came a quick reply from Chain.

"Negative, further out."

Tim patted Bracket's back, *I'm on it,* and shifted his position. Settling in and facing the far west, the darkness of the land was pierced by a bright yellow light moving at a steady pace, too fast to be a foot patrol and too far out to raise worries of their detection. Tim aimed his binoculars at the light, seeing nothing but yellow illumination splashing against the trees and masking the movement. Soon enough, sound accompanied the movement with the chugging of a locomotive.

"Train arriving from the east; it'll have to slow down before ingress."

"That's our means of insertion. Tim, take Bracket and Slug and infiltrate. Me, Razor, and Dagger will remain here for ISR & QRF, and hot exfil if shite goes mental." Chain's orders were quick but sharp, not missing a bit of focus in his brisk speech.

"Copy. Slug, take point. Bracket, watch our six," Tim ordered in a hushed command.

In less than ten seconds after hearing the train's chugging, Tim and his team broke off from the others, huffing it down the hill to intersect.

The trek downhill was fast, and the three of them moved with as minimal noise as three men in full kit sprinting could. Their previous approach of slow and steady was neglected for the greater need for speed to reach the point of intersection before the train did; the train was breaking through the trees, coming into view from the west. The carts flew by in slowing momentum, most of them being large storage containers whose doors had more bars and locks than necessary; it looked like overkill for the contents therein.

They were a hundred meters from the facility's western gate, the train slowing more and more, as the head locomotive drew nearer. When deciding it was slow enough to jump on, Tim took the first leap. Latching onto the side ladder of a cargo cart, his hearing and peripheries informed him of Bracket and Slug catching on to the next one. Holding onto bars and edges, he climbed his way to a short catwalk connecting the two carts, panting as he caught his breath. He saw Slug making the same climb from the front of the next cart.

Holding out his hand, his other grabbing onto the catwalk, he helped Slug to the metal walk. They caught their breaths before opening the door and seeing Bracket ingress from the back end of the cart.

"You okay?" Tim asked, wiping sweat from his brow Bracket nodded with a thumbs up, panting.

The train's slowing momentum continued, coming to a gradual stop until the now-muffled chugging faded. A window to the outside gave a bare sliver of a view of the western wall and gate, where a significant force of security stood.

"Bravo Two-Two to Two-One, we've boarded the train, awaiting insertion, Over," Tim relayed to Chain.

"Copy Two-Two. Lie low and wait. Looks like formalities are being accounted for at the head, you'll be inside soon. Over."

"Copy that. Over." Tim looked at his tiny visual of the gate: jeeps with mounted weapon systems, soldiers standing in, over, and under fire lines, several machine gun nests built into the wall, and sentries with binos standing on the ramparts of the wall, perhaps to mark targets for what he expected to be mortar pits behind the wall. He wondered if they expected a host of zombies to swarm them out of nowhere; maybe they preferred to be safer than sorry, or they were worried about the contents of the train. Or, a sickening thought, all the above?

Chain broke radio silence once more. "The train's conductor is speaking with a commanding officer."

"Copy," Tim replied, a soldier coming more into view from his limited visual. An officer in rank.

Tim noted how he was adorned in all black, armed with a Kalashnikov. Instinctively, he suspected the man spoke Russian. Perhaps a representation of a majority, if not all, of the men and women of the black site.

"The CO's on the horn… the gates are opening," said Chain, and soon enough metal grinding against metal could be heard before the starting up of the idle train forwards. The slow momentum of their insertion affirmed Chain's observation; they were in.

Inside the cargo cart, the three of them hid as the lights of the gate shone through the square slits of glass on the walls above, just under the roof. All of them remained dead still. Tim grabbed his radio and gave two clicks on it, code to Chain that they had to go radio silent.

Several minutes passed before the train's slow crawl stopped. *No way is the whole train already inside,* Tim mouthed. He got to his knees, holding out a staying hand to Slug and Bracket, reaching the wall and climbing up to his feet to make use of the window above.

Inside the complex ahead, there was a large metal crane in operation, unloading the containers behind them. Men and forklift operators were getting stationed at a loading dock, no doubt for the cargo carts they were in. Towards the lead locomotive, there wasn't much presence, save for a few men in construction attire moving about, wearing hard hats.

"They're running on a skeleton crew past the exterior," Tim noted aloud for Slug and Bracket.

"Good for us, then," Bracket replied.

They waited until the crane had lifted each of the shipping containers. Then, with each one unloaded, the locomotive pulled forwards for the next in line. The cargo carts closed the distance between them and the loading docks. Tim felt his heartbeat increase the closer they got. Just before the docks where the carts were unloaded were smaller structures, and their shadows seemed capable of hiding their movement, but it was going to be close.

The first of the structures was a steel overhead structure bearing words in Russian, confirming Tim's suspicions. Bracket and Slug stacked at the door, waiting for Tim's command to disembark.

The cart passed under the overhead, and a utility or storage shack between the steel and loading dock was lining up with their cart. It was now or never, and Tim gave the command, "Move."

Slug, on point, took the lead, with enough time for Tim to move ahead of Bracket for the center as his buddy followed up last. Climbing down the connective catwalk, they passed through the shadows between carts and straight ahead of the steel structure above to the side of the utility shed. Beyond the gravel, the ground transitioned to pothole-filled pavement, and a cluster of buildings and warehouses thickened around them, like a self-storage facility.

With every step, and as each unit passed, the tallest structure was always in view, reaching high up to the sky. It sat in the center of the compound. It appeared now as a watcher, towering over the others and observing the comings and goings of the site. This building became their target objective; there, they'd find Olivia's whereabouts.

Pre-existing notions of the place being a black site facility were replaced with the reality of a more industrial-looking complex, complete with a worn but functional network of pipes. There were brick-and-mortar buildings, some as high as five stories, and dozens of smaller utility or storage sheds filling in the spaces between the larger ones. The centermost imposing structure never left their sight, even when moving in the tight shadows of alleys between the bricks and mortar, it stood tall and demanded unending consideration.

Most of the ground was laid over with gravel, but the few paved roads identified the more important buildings. This identification was reinforced by a heavier security force to said building, offering them an overt direction of travel away from the paved roads and through the less watched and more vacated areas. Their movements were more audible with every crunch underneath the sixty pounds of gear. Sweat glued their clothes to their bodies in the cold night, and their breaths puffed out into the cold air.

Slug came to a stop behind a dumpster, holding up a hand for them to stop, and Tim pressed up against his British buddy's right side as Bracket did his. Concealed in the shadows of an exterior wall to what Tim thought had to be an electrical substation they caught up with their breaths. The brief reprieve brought them well-needed time work warmth and moisture back to their arid throats, beads of sweat traveled down their faces.

Slug pied the corner of the dumpster, scanning and surveying, while Tim and Bracket held guard at their three and six. Save for the security presence at the train docks and the gates, they didn't have many run-ins with the skeleton crew. This made Tim feel uneasy; something never came for nothing, and it left an unsettling feeling in his gut. He was sure whatever catch there was to their ease of ingress was coming due and soon.

Slug turned back from his inspection, controlled breaths through his nostrils, and vented out his lips. "We're looking at the back of the Target Building; straight dash across gravel to a rear entry."

"Alright, don't get too excited" Tim patted his buddy who replied with a muffled chuckle. "On you."

When he deemed himself ready, Slug leaned around the dumpster, scanning left, then right, and a couple of quick pants later, said "Moving." Slug broke from cover. Tim, not taking his eyes off Slug, moved up next in line; Bracket, behind him, maintained their six and three o'clock watch.

Tim watched as Slug moved in haste to the back entrance of the colossal structure and the back door of which Slug spoke. Along the back of the building, in a nook of the structure, the door rested up a flight of concrete steps. Next to the steps were dumpsters, under a path to the right of the door. Rails lined the steps and the path above the dumpsters, save for a ten-foot gap for ease of disposing waste.

The gravel transitioned to pavement, silencing Slug's movements as he slowed at the corner of the nook. Tim felt the muscles in his calves, biceps, and shoulder blades tense. Slug's back was to the door as he covered the straight dash. Tim's focus then rested on the door behind Slug, who remained in his periphery below, waiting for the signal.

Shit sandwich without bread. Tim sighed.

No commotion came after Slug's movements, and that unsettling feeling in Tim's gut grew. No longer did it feel like a catch coming due, but now past due with interest. But silence and stillness remained when Slug gave Tim the signal. Tim nodded once. "Moving," he muttered, hearing an "I got you" from Bracket, and he broke from cover.

In a sprint, like Slug, his left leg tingled in stiff motions of his run as he swung his stiff limb forwards. His knee buckled upon landing over the gravel, the many small stones moving and shifting like sand under his weight and throwing off his balance. The transition to pavement eased the tingling as he came to a slow just past the nook, hearing "Clear" from Slug. Nothing became of his dash.

Slug's hand tugged at him as he took cover behind his buddy. M4 at the low ready, he relieved Slug from his watch at the gravel road with a "Hold the door."

Tim, hearing Slug, turned a one-eighty, posting his watch to the door, watching the way he came. All was still and silent. At the substation, Bracket wasn't visible, but he knew the man was there, somewhere in the shadows. He watched, looking left and right; all remained still and silent. Tim gave a thumbs up, and, from the shadows, Bracket started moving, leaving the concealment of the dumpster and substation. Ten yards across, where the gravel turned to pavement, a patrol jeep drove down a service road intersecting the one they were on.

Tim had his weapon canted, compensating the angle of aiming with the slight downward angle of his barrel, ready to engage the targets about thirty meters out. His periphery caught sight of Bracket tensing up. *Don't freeze, don't freeze,* Tim ordered, biting his tongue as if his thoughts could reach Bracket in silent demand.

The jeep slowed, and the men inside looked their way; his periphery caught Bracket still moving. *No good, no good.* They were caught, compromised, and they would need a Hail Mary attempt just to escape from the belly of the beast. His finger at the trigger was about to tug; his rifle was outfitted with a suppressor. But still, the sound of one shot would carry and wake up the sleeping giant of Sahtu. His one chance to save Olivia, to help Dakota, was gone, snuffed out before he could even figure out what he could do for them.

The jeep didn't stop, and Tim kept his focus on the slow-moving vehicle, noticing Bracket was still moving in his peripheries, heading towards him and Slug with a more casual pace. His posture and whole demeanor changed to one of purpose and comfort, moving as if he belonged there, just one of the patrols making his rounds.

Tim thought that might just work. *Don't worry about a one-man patrol, don't worry about a one-man patrol.*

The engine revved and the jeep picked up speed, the patrol continuing with their comings and goings and disappearing around the edge of the structure's corner. Bracket closed the rest of the distance, his calm exterior falling apart like a track runner huffing and puffing as he wiped off sweat above his eyes.

"Holy shit," Bracket vented. Tim pulled at his shoulder, getting him into the concealing safety of the nook as if he were a diver climbing back onto a boat.

Ballsy move, motherfucker. Tim cracked a smirk as they fell back into formation. When Bracket was stacked at their six, he patted

Slug on the shoulder. Slug led the way up the hard gray steps and to a wide metal door. When he tugged on the handle, it would budge.

"Breacher up," Slug called.

Stacked on the door, Tim got behind Slug and removed a mechanical breaching tool from his buddy's kit on his back. *Keys to the city.*

One end of the tool was in the form of a claw, the other end a wedge with a pike poking out at a ninety-degree angle. He observed that the door hinges were facing outwards; normally, such tools would've been used with a sledgehammer, but also louder. Tim instead wedged the clawed end into the deadbolt section, grabbed ahold of the wedge end of the tool, and wrapped his thumb around the pick for maximum leverage as he pivoted his feet at the corner of the landing and door frame. "Claw set," Tim said, then used his body weight and stance as leverage, prying at the deadbolt.

On the first pry, Tim felt the metal bending and the inner mechanics popping with some breaking. At the second pry, the deadbolt gave a reassuring and metallic *POP*. Next, he worked at the handle, setting the claw and going to work, popping it open on the first try. Setting the tool on the ground, he grabbed the handle and pulled the door open.

Slug and Bracket filed in, Slug on point, moving straight left. Bracket followed up, sweeping right as Tim, with his rifle at the high ready, charged in, moving left. They entered a supply room stocked with cleaning materials: racks full of cleaning agents, brillo pads, deodorizers, and so forth. Straight ahead, to the left against a brick wall, rested mops and buckets by an air compressor. All was empty, and following the wall left of their entry was an elevator. Tim backed up to the door, picked up the tool, and closed the door. Slug and Bracket stacked at the elevator where Tim met them, securing the tool back in its pouch on Slug's kit.

"Ready." He gave Slug a reassuring pat as the lad pressed the call button, and a minute later came a chiming and the doors opened.

The elevator went up only one floor, opening into a dark room. The lights were off, forcing them to return to their NODs as the smell of coffee permeated the air. Shades of green and black returned in the shapes of stainless-steel counters, three-compartment sinks, large freezers, and the works for a kitchen. Soft clanks of their boots barely sounded as they moved across a linoleum floor.

Slug led them through the tiny maze of a kitchen, coming to a door with glass panels; bright squares of white light blinded their vision under their NODs. They lifted back up their optics and came to a stack at the door, light shining through the glass, creating a clear barrier of light and shadows. Tim stepped up to look behind the shadows, the square ray of light caressing the front stack of the magazine in his vest pouches.

There in the cafeteria, sitting near a coffee table with mugs in hands, were three officers. Two of them had their backs turned to him, and the third was smirking about something. Tim observed their ranks, using Alyeskan insignias, built using the US Army's rank system: two first sergeants and one captain their conversation wasn't understandable, muffled by the thick doors between them and him.

Their relaxed demeanors and occasional smirks or laughter told of a casual conversation, fruitless for Tim and his team's objective. To the left side of the cafeteria, a door opened, and in stepped a man. All at once, the three men stood straight, giving firm solutes to the individual. Arms were folded behind the man's back, and two silver stars decorated his shoulders. He was a Major General of the Alyeskan Army, typically in command of ten to fifteen-thousand men. If so, Tim wondered where the rest of those soldiers were. The base could accommodate such a force but judging by what they had seen thus far, there wasn't even half of that fighting force present.

"Bit of a damp squid in'it?" Slug mumbled, on the same page with Tim. "Thought there'd be more blokes around."

"I don't know." Tim shook his head, that unsettling pessimism becoming more of a nauseating feeling; a headache was taking root, a slow growth into a migraine.

The major general spoke in a collective calm to the two NCOs and officer in a brief conversation. All at once, the men took their leave, walking briskly past the major general and out the doors, setting hats on their heads. The major general stood patiently as his subordinates took their leave before taking his.

"Him," Tim pointed at the major general.

"Mission adjustment?" asked Slug.

"Affirmative, he's our objective." Tim opened the door.

Following Bracket's example from the outside, they moved in casual strides, rifles resting horizontally at their bellies as they entered the cafeteria and became a presence on camera. They followed out the same doors as the major general and into a hall and the presence of more cameras. For Tim, it was a bit more concerning, seeing not one black person on the base thus far. He worried he might stick out on the monitor like a sore thumb. Surely there were black Russians, though he had never heard of it. It didn't mean there couldn't be one working at the Sahtu facility, right?

Then again, their kits, uniforms, and weapons systems also stood out. He hoped that their "I belong here" casual strides would compensate for their non-black uniform and non-Kalashnikov loadouts. Following the major general down the corridors, at a fork along the way was a sign, written in both Russian and English: '*Security Console*' it read, pointing left and '*Offices,*' pointing right.

Their HVT, High-Value Target, had gone to the offices, but they couldn't pass up the former; it was too good an opportunity to pass up. Tim ordered Slug to deviate left at the fork. The hall broke off into other, smaller sections. But the main console room stood out like a sore thumb, being a large metal door with words printed on it: *'Surveillance Room.'* Stacked at the door, Tim gave Slug the "go ahead." No sooner, he heard his buddy rake his knuckles on the door, and he waited.

The doors cracked open inwards, and without missing a beat, Slug rammed into the door. A resounding "oaf" wailed out from the man behind the door as Slug barged in and Tim followed. Slug held the man on the floor at gunpoint while Tim passed him, halting the advances of the other security officers. Two of them were already out of their seats, their hands going to side arms but stopping when faced with Tim's M4.

"Don't do it, motherfucker," Tim barked, and the two men's hands went away from their weapons.

Bracket followed, holding the remaining three still, with their hands raised.

None of the men spoke a bit of English, and had Phil been there he could have given the instructions in Russian. But sign language with a deadly weapon proved to suffice. One by one, each of them surrendered their pistols, and while Tim and Bracket held the men at gunpoint, Slug patted them down, relieving them of every little object on their persons. Clearing each one at a time, and giving them a shove towards the far wall, Bracket moved his gun to keep them in line. Tim kept his rifle trained on the others while Slug worked.

With all men stripped, Tim and Bracket held them at gunpoint to the wall while Slug secured each man with zip ties to metal pipes on the wall that housed wiring. He then zip-tied their feet together.

"That'll do." Slug stepped back from the men.

Tim walked over to the control panel for the cameras; everything was in Russian on the controls. Unsure what to do, he moved when Slug motioned for him to back away with a "Lemme have a crack at it."

Tim observed each camera one by one, finding no monitor showing or hinting at Olivia's whereabouts. His heart sank with despair that they were in the wrong place, a place they shouldn't have been. Just like they weren't supposed to be in Bellingham when they were, and yet there they had been. Trespassing onto black sites was a bad omen that harbingered devastation. *No.* He stopped himself from entertaining the toxic thoughts as soon as they reared their ugly heads.

Slug double-clicked on the camera monitoring the fork in the hall they took, bringing the footage to full screen. He heard Slug mumble to himself during the process, trial and error until he found which of the controls could rewind the footage.

"Got it," Slug said, and the footage started rewinding, back to where the major general broke right off the fork. He double-clicked on the camera, maximizing the feed over the others as the major general disappeared off-camera. Slug then tapped the right arrow key, the screen going to the next camera following their target.

"You got it?" Tim asked.

"Of course I got it; I'm a fuckin corker."

Aside from being the tech officer of Bravo, Slug had the unique quality of photographic memory, or at least traits associated with it. Although the existence of such phenomena was debatable, the one certainty that Tim knew, even if it couldn't be explained, was that Slug had one hell of a memory. That, and, like Phil, Slug seemed to have an internal GPS built into him. He always knew his cardinal directions, even if inside the maze of a structure like they were in now. These two qualities, used in conjunction with one another, made him uniquely efficient, especially in circumstances such as the one they were in now.

They waited for Slug to finish, and once he had everything he needed, he killed the cameras.

"Alright gents, shall we?" Slug said, taking point at the door.

"On you, bud." Tim nodded as he and Bracket followed Slug, who opened the door and took point.

With the cameras shut down, moving through the building manned by the skeleton night crew came with greater ease. His headache slowly transitioned into a migraine, his heart beating heavier in his chest. None of the cameras have given any hint to Olivia's whereabouts, and there was no guarantee the major general would lead to progress. It all still felt too easy to him, and that catch coming due nauseated his gut.

Slug led them back to the fork in the hall, and from there it was all on him, leading them left and right through a maze in the office section. Doors with meshed glass panels and large windows to the side were like visual landmines. Contact could be received at any second, in which they would be compromised, and the hornet's nest would be firmly kicked awake.

Their progress slowed, pieing off each window and office slower than before. Most were empty, the lights off, but several were lit up and occupied by third-shifters or late-working second-shifters. At some points in the maze of corridors, too many offices were lit, and the way through wasn't feasible without detection, forcing them to double back and for Slug to work out a detour on the move.

What could have been a five-minute walk became fifteen minutes when Slug brought them to a red set of double wooden doors their HVT was last seen on camera passing through. Deadbolts sat above and below the knobs at chest height. The hinges were not visible, detailing that the doors opened inwards.

Tim patted praise on Slug that doubled as a "go ahead."

Bracket's breath hit the back of Tim's neck in tense puffs of exhales through the man's nostrils. Slug counted down from three fingers, the middle lowered, then his index, then his thumb. Hearing a gentle click as the knob turned and unlatched, the door swung inwards as Slug pushed open the door and entered. Tim followed, hearing Bracket's boots behind him as they stormed inside the major general's office.

There was no one inside the office save for the man himself. Dead center of the room was a large, red-stained oak desk facing them, and behind it a wall of glass looked over the expanse of the facility's eastern side. Tim made a quick note of just how large the place was; they hadn't even traversed half of the place from the train docks to here. Now with a view out the eastward half, he could see that the place spanned to the Great Bear Lake, where platforms floated over the deeper parts of the lake. Stationed there was crane-like machinery. It held an absurd appearance like those arcade games with rigged claw cranes.

Staring out the same glass stood their HVT; his posture was straight and firm, and his hands were folded behind his back. He turned, and surprise dressed his features, not out of shock but out of what Tim thought was a look of annoyance. The major general now fully facing them, didn't change his posture but greeted them in Russian.

Tim crossed one side of the red desk with Bracket behind him; Slug remained fixed on the door.

"You speak English?" Tim demanded.

The major general's eyes met his. "Dah." He spoke with a thick Russian accent that was as formal as it was polite. He gave a wave of his arm to chairs on the other side of his desk. "Please sit. I presume we have items to discuss."

Tim didn't move, keeping his weapon on the man, finger inside the trigger guard. One of the major general's hands raised, palm up. His other reached down to a pistol on his hip. Tim watched, eyes stabbing at the weapon, waiting, as the man unclipped the safety strap. His index finger and thump pinched at the slide before the hammer, lifting the pistol from his holster. In slow efforts, the major general laid the pistol on the desk, then gave it a shove, sliding the weapon across to Bracket.

Bracket moved, secured the weapon, and Tim stepped to the left, giving his buddy room to pat down the major general. The latter was still just as calm as he was when they entered, as if this was just a regular routine of his. The patience of the man told Tim this was just hospitality towards his guests. An indication that the man had a choice in the matter felt like an insult to Tim. Such a comfortable demeanor could come from whatever aces were up the man's sleeves. Aces that spoke to Tim as if commands themselves: *You may not harm me, and you will not kill me.*

It was odd and only added to that unsettling nausea in him, the feeling of that catch coming due felt like it would soon arrive. His migraine taking full effect, Tim shoved aside the oddness of the man along with his nausea and headache.

"You are my guests. Please, take my seat," the major general said, lowering his hands and walking around to the office chairs but remained standing all before Tim could utter his command to the major general: "You, sit over there."

Bracket took a seat instead, rummaging through the drawers. Tim stood out of arm's reach of the man, weapon lowered but still at the ready. "Sit."

"I'd rather stand," the major general remarked; there was a sharpness to his voice.

"Then stand. I ask the questions, and you give me the answers. Understand?"

The major general didn't respond, just looked at him with understanding eyes, waiting with a now unenthused look that one might interpret as "Fine, vat are your questions."

"You and this facility are benefactors to a human trafficking group called Puristans, operating in Alaska and Yukon. Yes?"

"I will not confirm or deny confidential information related to this facility's operations."

"The Puristans recently abducted a young woman, Olivia Blundell. She was prioritized by your request to said group of people. She was brought to this facility, yes?"

"I will not confirm nor deny confidential information about this facility's operations or any group associated with our operations."

"Tell me where Miss Blundell is," Tim demanded.

"Forgive me, but I will not divulge sensitive information."

Tim sighed, "Bracket, you find anything?"

"It's all fucked, nothing here." Bracket sighed.

"Bracket, change position with Slug. Slug, see if you can't access his desktop."

Tim saw Bracket and Slug exchange glances out his periphery, but his own eyes never once left the major general's, nor his gun. Slug went to work, sitting behind their HVT's desk and soon muttering curses, and Tim knew why. Everything was in Russian.

"Can you hack it?" Tim asked.

"I need to change the language settings first. Fucking twat, this." Slug's voice trailed off.

"Can you do that from the log-in display?"

"Who's the Tech Sergeant?" Slug waved him off in a bite of frustration, "I'll figure something out."

Tim bit his tongue, observing the major general who still stood calm, patient.

"Petrov" was embroidered over the major general's chest, right under the two silver stars on his chest. From recent memory, Tim heard again Laura's question, "Who's Igor Petrov?" Dots connected in a more unsettling turmoil in his gut: him, Dakota, and Phil raiding the safe house. Phil's sins in Romania were connected, as much as his trauma was, to that very name. The sinking feeling grew that things were getting heavier than they needed to be, too deep and personal. The catch he had been expecting was coming closer and closer. The name Petrov now didn't just mean an antithesis to Phil, but an omen to everyone associated with Phil. The name heralded problems and misfortune for all.

"Igor?" Tim asked.

That registered a change in the major general: surprise. Now the man looked at him, brows raised, and through his calm exterior, there was a brief opening in the curtain: a glimpse to the inside by the look in his eyes. There but for a second, Tim saw the same look that Dakota had, that his parents had, that he had in the mirror. It was grief, dread, and worry: a combustible turmoil of emotions kept in check.

"My name is Valentin Petrov; Igor is my little broter," Major General Petrov corrected.

"Alyeskan military personnel recently disappeared around a Canadian Confederate outpost called Whati. Her name is Sergeant Alice Sousa. Where is she?"

"Dat," Major General Petrov waved a finger at Tim, a change in rock-still expression to one of placid interest returning as he addressed Tim, "I may divulge."

"Where?" demanded Tim, impatience snipping at the back of his throat, to which Major General Petrov's eyes communicated he noted. *Good job, ol' boy.* Tim cursed himself.

"She is accompanying a brigade of my soldiers to Colorado Springs."

Tim took a step back, lost for words, as the major general studied him intently. The heavier security presence at the facility's perimeter, in contrast to the skeleton crew inside, and the ease of movement, made more and more sense. The catch came due, and it brought with it heavy interest, hammering hard in Tim's chest like a hammer smashing out all the air from his lungs.

"Judging by your reaction, I'm assuming you are Sergeant Merlov. Yes?"

Tim's migraine taxed heavier as he glared at the man. "Merlow," he corrected, "How do you kno…"

"Forgive me; such consonants can be hard to pronounce," Valentin explained with a slight dip of his head, a bow for apologies. "You and Sergeant Sousa are both comrades of Sergeant Nilges. Yes?"

"Wha…"

"Sergeant Sousa and my men are on a search and rescue mission for your, how you say, MIA comrade and my little broter, Igor Petrov. Among other inquiries."

The worst thing Tim could have done was let his emotions get in the way of focus. Usually, his training and experience just took over, second nature becoming primal instinct. But he had spent a good deal of time repressing any emotional response, maintaining his composure, collecting the intel and saving it to sort through later. That's what he did, taking in all the information like a sponge, fixated on the objective. One objective was partially met; he knew Dakota's destination and where to go next. But the current objective remained. Olivia needed to be rescued.

"I'm in," came Slug's voice, a lifeline reeling Tim back to the present. "Changing the language setting… Fuckin'ell much better."

"How'd you do it?" asked Bracket.

"The keypad is formatted the same, with Russian and Latin letters. I heard Igor and tried that out."

Tim didn't move his eyes off the major general, but did take note of a scornful smirk on the major general taking in the news and waiting. A few minutes later, Slug came with more good news. "Found her. They're keeping her in a… Harvesting unit?"

"Where is that?" Tim demanded, holding back the unpleasantness that came from the sounds of that. Slug was already on it before the major general would give the same dead-end answer; the Russian's face was the same—calm, patient and indifferent.

"Just outside of here, two structures over. I'm bringing up a floor plan now." Slug answered in the major general's place.

"Can you bring up security cameras on that?" Tim asked.

"One more minute…" Slug mumbled. But five minutes later, he came with more news. "Got 'em. The structure is called the Harvesting Wing. It has its own security camera system, all sorted out from the rest."

"Okay, Bracket," Tim called.

Bracket closed the doors, charged the deadbolts, and walked over to them as Tim hitched a thumb over his shoulder. "You'll stay and monitor the cameras for us and keep an eye on him." Tim pointed at the major general.

"On it." Bracket said, trading places with Slug at the computer.

"You." Tim pointed at the major general, aiming his weapon to the vacant seats. "You're gonna sit there and do nothing. Get on your radio, and have all personnel in the Harvesting Wing vacate immediately."

Major General Petrov did as Tim said, taking a seat and reaching over for his landline. Tim stood behind him, out of arm's reach, barrel ready to execute the man as the major general gave a pause, sensing Tim's weapon before dialing a number. After a moment of ringing the major general spoke in clear Russian, a brief exchange, then he hung up the phone.

"It is done," Major General Petrov said, turning around to face Tim. Before any of them could take the initiative, the major general offered his hands out, wrists pressed together. The man was ahead of the curve, still displaying his act of having a choice that now irritated Tim.

Slug walked over, and, with more zip ties, bound the man, securing him to the chair.

"Bracket. Stay Frosty. As soon as we find Olivia, we're coming back for you to regroup and we'll exfil together. Radio call sign for you is Charlie-Whiskey."

"Got it, Big Hoss. Good luck."

A glimmer of metal caught Tim's eyes; looking at the major general's lap he saw a set of keys, and a key card hung by his belt loop. He reached down and procured the keys. Shuffling them in one hand, he stepped back to adjust them on his person.

"You, too," he said, turning his back to Bracket and stacking on the door behind Slug. Slug released the bolts and took point, Tim following as his buddy's memory and internal GPS led the way to Olivia.

Chapter Ten – Between a Rock and a Hard Place

Slug brought them to a sky bridge linking the central imposing structure to the building housing the 'Harvesting Wing.' Glass panels lined both sides of the bridge, exposing them like sore thumbs. Resorting back to Bracket's 'casual stride,' he hoped on a prayer that detection wouldn't warrant alarm from any sentry on the outside looking in.

Each step felt like the second hands ticking in a countdown to the alarm raised: sentries opening fire on them, guards storming from both ends of the bridge, and either death or capture waiting. For all the worry that scenario warranted in Tim's mind, he kept his cool, laser focus on the set of thick metal doors leading to the Harvesting Wing.

Slug waited at the door, and a key card reader next to the door beeped when Tim pressed the major general's card against it. Metallic clanks and clicks followed by a green light preceded Slug's opening the door, and the two of them entered the structure. Slug scanned left down a corridor while Tim charged right to a little coffee break room where no threats were present; then, he turned heel, both men facing down the corridor.

Like a slow and lethal tour guide, Slug led on, taking left turns and right turns down three floors and down another hall. Their next stop came to another electronically locked door, and another key card reader waited. Tim unlocked the door, and Slug pressed his hip against the push bar, his rifle never leaving a readied position for engagement. Slug charged through into the corridor, and there was nothing to clear left, just a wall, so he broke right, and Tim followed up.

The air had a scent of sanitizer, the kind of smell he'd expect from a hospital. Everything looked clean; the floor was spotless cement with a shiny finish to it. The walls were a light gray and the doors a dark gray. There were no ceiling tiles and the roof was an open ceiling, exposing all the supports and wiring. The hall was vacant, the feeling of moving through a bottleneck never leaving them.

Tim moved to the other side of the hall, five meters between them, heart pounding with each *thump* of their footfalls continuing that countdown of a timer.

"Almost there," Slug whispered.

Tim pressed the PTT button, craning his head, mouth closer to his radio: “Bravo Two-Two Actual to Charlie-Whiskey, we’re closing in on the Harvesting Wing. Over.”

“Copy that. All is quiet on the cameras. Over.”

“Keep us posted. Over’n out,” Tim said, lowering his hand as they came to an intersection of hallways.

Pressed against the right-side corner, Tim could hear the commotion of workers chatting and their steps coming from the right. Slug, across from him, peered down, confirming with a cut motion across his neck that people were coming their way. Their voices became distinguishable, speaking in Russian.

Down the hall towards the voices was a nook along the wall; Tim took point, unsure if Slug saw the opportunity or not. There was no time for verbal confirmation, save for the sounds of Slug falling behind him.

They reached the depression in the wall, and it created an ‘L’ shape indentation, leading to a panel box for electronical maintenance, enough for two grown men to hide in. Counting the steps coming their way from the intersection, there were at least two dozen individuals, all of whom sounded perplexed. The major general’s sudden evacuation of the Harvesting Wing came to fruition.

“Our primary objective is down the way they cropped up from,” Slug whispered, moving into position to take point.

“Copy, on your go.”

Tim waited as the group of people passed on by, Slug making steady sweeps at both flanks. When the threat of detection was gone, he broke from cover and Tim followed. Their way brought them to a long stretch of the hall, windows and doors giving a view inside holding rooms for individuals and captives. Here, they could see many individuals of different colors and ethnicities, male and female, lying comatose inside gray padded rooms on gurneys. They were dressed in hospital gowns, and on the doors listed names on laminated paper.

Cattle being stored for slaughter, Tim thought.

On each door were plaques and grooves to allow the laminated paper to slide in and out. Further down the hall, they came to a trash can filled with more laminated papers. *Previous captives*, Tim thought, looking at the stack. One name caught his attention. *LAFAYETTE, MORGAN.*

The name harkened to Tim, recalling a conversation he had with Captain Shillings a couple of years back, not long after he was folded into the Lure and Hair operation. The captain had shared with him a case when a pair of expecting parents went missing. The name of the soon-to-be mother was typed on the same card Tim now read.

Slug stopped and looked back at Tim. "You good?"

"Yeah," Tim nodded.

"Then crack on, yeah?" Slug gave his shoulder a squeeze.

"Yeah," Tim grunted and continued.

They came to a door whose plaque read: *BLUNDELL, OLIVIA,* and through the glass, he saw the little diva lying still on a gurney, comatose. In her sleep tears were squeezing through restful eyes. Tim opened the door with the major general's key card and rushed over to her while Slug held security.

"Bravo Two-Two Actual to Bravo Two-One. Primary objectives have been located, securing her for transit. Over."

"Copy Two-Two Actual. Be advised, a convoy of some fifty-plus vehicles has just arrived from the southwest. There's a lot of blokes muppeting around outside. Recommend you make haste. Over." Chain's voice replied, a jittering to his tone and Tim could sense the cold was getting to his buddy.

"Copy Two-One. Over'n out." Tim let loose the button and freed Olivia's head from a strap, then pressed the PTT again. "Bravo Two-Two Actual to Charlie-Whiskey, we'll be en route to you, ETA twenty minutes. Over." Tim then removed a needle to an IV line that fed into her left forearm, disconnected electrode sensors placed on her chest that monitored her heartbeat, and relieved her limbs, neck, and midriff of straps holding her in place.

Olivia was fully disconnected from the bindings and sensors, but Bracket had not made a reply. A pause came to Tim, his hand going back to his radio, until the line broke. A brief transmission arrived, riddled with static, lasting less than a second, but filled with banging, shouting, and yelling. The line went out, and a few moments passed as they waited, Tim's heart beating heavier in his chest. Finally, the line broke, and in his headset, he heard Bracket's voice.

"Bravo Two-Two Actual, I've been compromised. Get out of here. I'll make my own way."

"Copy." Tim sighed, nearly giving pause. Scooping Olivia up in his arms, her knees folded over his left arm as his right arm cradled her shoulders. Her head rolled over and rested on the right side of his chest. The added weight of the kid on top of his kit and weapons forced his knees to bend while standing. Tim took a deep breath, looking to Slug: "Get us out of here."

Olivia's added weight was starting to wear on Tim. The adrenaline kept him moving without fail, but he was waning, slowing. Slug had a secondary exfil route working from his memory and internal GPS. Working on the go and making split decision turns, he charged through doors with less certainty, stopping and looking to other doors and down other hallway intersections when indecisive.

The smell of sanitizer left, and the clean and orderly fashion of the Harvesting Wing was now industrialized, smelling of exhaust and gasoline. The walls became cement and dark gray, the doors became a dark blue, the further into the complex they traveled. One such door brought them to a loading bay of a housed railroad workshop that was alive and booming with activity from two trains, parked on the rails before them.

Slug stopped and got to a knee behind a large wooden crate, and Tim fell behind him while Olivia's restful breathing blew in his face. Shadows cut a diagonal line from the nearest corner that offered concealment, and a series of skylights above allowed the moonlight to mix with the yellow lighting of the loading bay, provided enough light to see. Both sets of rails were housing train carts, flat beds, and passenger carts, all being, or already, loaded with supplies, armored vehicles, and an assortment of helicopters with their propellers folded and anchored down.

This is your secondary route! Tim felt himself fume, biting his tongue as he followed Slug's gaze.

Straight ahead, over a flatbed cart yet to be loaded, two storage carts passed, and he saw their ticket out: a large, blue metal door with an exit sign above it, though in Russian.

"Fuckin hard cheese, this." Slug shook his head, "like you've found a quicker way out."

"Not gonna be easy," Tim exhaled, adjusting Olivia in his arms.

"Aldrin?" Olivia mumbled in her rest, moving her head, eyes still closed.

"Shhh," Tim hushed her as her head fell on his shoulder.

Down at the far end of the loading bay, a large, red metal door slid open. From inside, they could see another building joined to the loading bay structure. From the opening doors came a perplexing sight. Soldiers were outfitted with heavy armor systems, large caliber rifles, and machine guns instead of light armaments, some with shotguns and a couple of grenadiers.

A formation of this heavy security force flanked both sides of a forklift, bearing on its forks a giant capsule of sorts. It reminded Tim of a time capsule people buried, but this was an enormous one, and it came with metallic tubes anchored in place around the top and sides. Steam, or very cold air, leaked out, and in fine print on the center front end of the capsule, it read:

Проект Дредноут

Project Dreadnaught

A special cargo cart was waiting for the capsule, and frost spewed out the open side door, revealing an interior of the cart lined with copper pipes and tubing. The structure was reinforced and plated in steel, and mechanics in scrubs stepped out as the capsule was then loaded.

"The hell is that doofer thingy?" Slug mumbled.

Olivia mumbled yet again, followed by stirring in Tim's arms. Tim looked down at her fluttering eyes and mouth gaped in a brief yawn. Sleep crusted the corners of eyes that met his before a weak smile crossed her face. "Hey, Al." A single tear broke from her left eye before her lids fluttered back down.

"Save your strength, hun," Tim whispered to her, tightening his hold as if in a hug.

Slug was about to break from cover before Bracket's voice came over their earpieces: "Bravo Two-Two and Two-One, don't wait up for me. Be advised, home is compromised. I say again, home is compromised. Security has been alerted, you have less than five minutes. God's speed." Then, the line died.

Suddenly, the fire alarm tripped and water poured down over them, a thin veil and a good distraction. Tim stood up from the crate, Slug aiming at the heavier security presence. Their 5.56 rounds would only upset the men in the armor systems, bruise them, and if they were lucky, break some bones. Add the numbers, two against a whole platoon of those juggernauts, and it only ended one way.

The enormous time capsule didn't appreciate the surprise deluge either. It started to shake, the steel structure clanking against the forks of the forklift. The lift itself weighed at least fifteen thousand pounds in deadweight at the rear end, and, from the disturbance inside the capsule, the lift rocked back and forth as if it were made of fiberglass.

From both flanks, the juggernauts backed up, rifles, machine guns, shotguns, and grenade launchers aimed and at the ready. Then to his radio, Tim pressed the PTT button saying, "Bravo Two-One come in, get that bird up and running. Requesting pickup within the complex, I say again, requesting pickup within the complex. Be advised, PZ may get hot, PZ may get hot."

"Copy that, activate IR-Strobes for a quick visual on PZ."

"Two-Two copies," Tim said. Reaching up to his helmet, his fingers searched past his NODs, where he felt the helmet strobe and turned on the Inferred Strobe feature. Same as with the laser, it was naked to the human eye, but with the right optic device, such as the one Ol' Faithful's pilot helmets were outfitted with, they'd stand out like a Christmas tree in the middle of a meadow at night.

"Slug, take point."

Slug nodded, and looked left, then right. His feet adjusted, like a runner before a dash, and when he deemed it the best time, he broke from cover to the flatbed cart dead ahead. Hopping down on the tracks where his shoulders and head poked up, he waited. No commotion, shooting, or disturbance of the loading bay came of it.

It was now or never, and Slug jumped up onto the flatbed cart. Tim's grip on Olivia tightened, his arms like safety belts as the water sprinkled over them. He broke from cover once Slug gave him the go-ahead. The distance to jump was a couple of meters, and in full kit with a ninety-plus pound kid in his hands, he would have landed short of the flatbed had Slug not caught him and pulled him the extra two inches until his boots found purchase on the metal bed.

Across the flatbed, down between the set of rails, Slug helped Tim in lowering the kid. Then, over the connecting coupling between the following two cargo carts, Tim got one leg over the coupling when Olivia stirred in his arms. His focus was on not tripping or falling, but he couldn't ignore the smile on her face from his periphery. Olivia's smile transitioned to a frown as she shielded herself from the water.

"Hat the well, is going on, and what am I wearing?" she asked.

"No time," Tim huffed, tasting salt from the beads of sweat mixing with the drops of water. He got his other leg across the coupling and stepped over to the other side of the loading bay. Olivia held her arms up, climbing over the edge, while Slug held point. Tim climbed up and helped her to her feet, and she took a wobbling stance, leaning on him.

Then shouting came at them, thick with surprise as demands in Russian carried out at them. Tim looked to see a soldier raising his rifle at them, eyes wide, as he pointed to the ground.

Tim snapped his rifle upwards, his speed more than matching the soldier's, who had a head start. Tim's training and conditioning beat the soldiers to the finish line, as he raised his rifle at the high ready, his sights lined up. The soldier, who Tim saw now to be no more than fifteen, had his weapon to the low ready and he started firing. Rounds went stray left, right, up, and down, spraying all over the place; it was a mistake caused by either faulty training, not enough experience, or some combination of the two. Tim placed a single round that pummeled into the kid's chest, where a mist of pink and red erupted.

Tim sidestepped, paralleling Olivia, shielding her until they got to cover as bullets continued in their reckless travel around them. Tim fired another round, striking the soldier in his right bicep, hearing a bullet *whiz* past his left ear. Goosebumps chilled his spine and ran down his arms while a feverish heat fogged his mind with smoke; he let off several more rounds in quick succession, making single-fire feel automatic. After three more of Tim's rounds pounded into the soldier's chest, finally, he fell, landing behind cover. He was either dead or dying.

At the door, he heard Slug wasting no time, getting loud as he shot the locks several times, until they were weak enough to break with a good boot to the door but it still held. More soldiers were arriving, not from their left flank, but from their right. Another good boot later, and the door swung open, Slug charging outside.

More bullets traveled their way as Tim pushed Olivia at the door, returning fire at the gathering soldiers down the loading bay. Olivia let out a cry, and without looking, he somehow knew it was her bare feet landing on the gravel outside. Concrete and wood fragments smacked at his face from the bullets striking the walls and wooden frames of a pegboard. He felt warm blood trickle down from his left ear.

Tim backpedaled out the door, slamming it shut, but it bounced back open. He pulled out a flash grenade, tossed it inside the door, and closed it. A deafening *BANG* left a profound ringing in his ears as he wobbled, running, to catch up with Slug and Olivia.

Slug had scooped Olivia up in his arms to spare her bare feet. They ran as the whole facility came to life. Sirens wailed, mad voices raged on an intercom system, and soon enough, the revving of engines came at them like bloodhounds in hungry pursuit. UTVs, Russian model jeeps, and Tigrs came into view from both their flanks. Headlights all around blinded them, illuminating the nearby world into a gravel stage surrounded by cliffs of blinding lights.

Tim and Slug stopped, their momentum carrying their feet into a grind against the gravel as Slug sat Olivia down.

"Smoke grenades, now!"

Both men removed their two M18s smoke grenades, pulling the pins and tossing them close by. The smoke began to bellow, not yet thick, as the perimeter of Russians condensed. The lights illuminated the bellowing smoke, and soldiers getting their weapon systems aimed at them. Yelling and shouting came from every corner, like a pack of wolves encircling their prey.

Thirty seconds later, the smoke thickened, concealing them. From the collective security force engulfing them, a voice spoke over all the shouting and idle engines. A second later and the voice became familiar now coming over a microphone, projecting over the rest: "Surrender, and you'll be given considerations."

But that was the thing about Tim; he couldn't do it. The smoke was at its thickest now, and Tim held his hand on Olivia's shoulder, keeping her head down and low; if bullets were to start flying, they were more likely to fly at chest height. He and Slug knelt, backs hunched at their lowest, and waited.

"What's your plan now?" came Olivia, her breath puffing gravel dust.

Dammit Chain, this smoke isn't going to last forever. Tim cursed, listening to the same demands on repeat, this time ending with a, "zis is final chance."

The air swirled around them, the smoke and gravel dust dispersed into the faces of the enemies. The concealing veil cleared out in seconds, revealing well over thirty men all around, shielding themselves from the dust and smoke. Then Ol' Faithful's M130 General Dispenser activated, sending out a hailstorm of flares designed for guided missile countermeasures but at the present working as a suppressant to the soldiers. Those not shielding themselves from the dust and smoke were taken by surprise at the big black bird sudden arrival descending in a reckless hover.

It lowered and descended until the landing bars were just a few feet off the gravel. Tim yanked Olivia up, hearing bones popping in painful ways at his hip. He vented the pain in a cry of demand for her to "Get on, now!"

Dagger, in the back, reached out from the inside, grabbing the diva and pulling her the rest of the way. Tim jumped in, detecting Slug following suit. A bullet flew and hit the side of the bird; Tim looked to see Major General Petrov rushing over and lowering the shooter's weapon, shouting at the man.

Ol' Faithful ascended back up into the air as the major general stood shouting at the rest. The enemies, recovering from the blinding dust, smoke, and surprise, lowered their weapons at their superiors command. They were letting them go. In the heat of the moment, Tim's gaze met with the old Russian's, who return the look with a passive glance.

An eerily unsettling message dressed Major General Petrov's enduring placid features: S*ee you soon.*

Tim just scoffed back, "Whatever."

-October 27th, 2030-

SRT-Bravo was well removed from Alyeska's borders and far away from Sahtu as well as any of Canada's settlements. They were in the wild unknown, perched on an elevated hill whose sides were open and exposed. Hills traveled and rolled from the nearby mountains to either side. The peaks were dark silhouettes, shadowy specters looking down on them with indifference, and they left a haunting gloom as cold air swept down from the western peaks over them.

Dagger, Razor, and Slug maintained surveillance with their night optics, forming a three-point sentry-watch from the hill. All was quiet, save for the persistent cries of coyotes to the distant west and the deep haunting bellows of moose to the east. The wind was an ominous presence, sweeping over and under the hills in low moans; gusts whistled here and there through the tree, casting its chill upon them. They were upwind from the coyotes, carrying their scent and presence away from the direction the yelping cries came from.

Tim and Chain sat in the back of the bird, in conversation, while Olivia slept on the cold metal bed, an insulating blanket wrapped around her. The drugs were still wearing off in her system, and they kept the little ball of energy tamed and tired. While she slept, Tim and Chain looked over a map between them, weighed down with magazines. On it, Alyeska was circled in red. Bracket's warning about home not being safe dwelled in their thoughts, preventing their immediate return to Juneau. They felt like fugitives hiding out in no man's land, and Tim supposed they were. Their orders had been to return to base after securing Olivia. Well, objective completed; they had her safe and sound, and Bracket's disturbing warnings echoed in their minds. "Home, compromised."

Canada was marked in a big red X, pretty much a "no go" as far as they were concerned. Colorado Springs was marked with a red star, and there lie Tim's next objective.

Thinking back to the concert, a line from Olivia's song echoed in his thoughts: *Traveling through, this land of woe.*

"It's all mental, but I still say AILA is our best bet. The colonel is dog's bollocks: he'll fold us in with the Identification Protection Department. Well, at least you, the kid, and Slug. No one saw our ugly mugs." Chain waved his hand, pointing at himself, Razor, and Dagger. The wave came to an end with the back of his glove rubbing his forehead.

"That doesn't do anything for Dakota, does it?" Tim shook his head, his eyes hardly leaving the red star. "I have to find her."

"I know," Chain mumbled. "But can you sort the kid out like that, taking her with you?"

"Joseph," Tim mumbled, but he was cut off. He hardly ever used Chain's real name, and never lightly—only when he needed his friend to hear him, to actually hear him. Chain's eyes leveled with his, and Tim saw that his friend understood.

"Timothy, I'll follow you into hell, even to a certified death sentence, if it means finding her." Chain grabbed Tim's shoulders the two locked eyes. "But are you willing to drag a civilian, a kid, into the depths with you?"

"I'm not." Tim shook his head, looking back to his friend. "But what is the lesser evil here? A corrupted general and human traffickers or mindless monsters? You tell me. AILA's Operation Lure and Hair failed. If the Puristans had someone in my security detail, who's to say AILA isn't infected with more double agents as well?"

"I'm not sure," Chain ceded, shaking his head. "Both our options are double-edged swords. Either way, they end with us getting back home and dealing with the Puristan problem. It's now or later, I reckon."

"You're right," Tim nodded: either now or after collecting Dakota, they would have to try and return home. They'd have to deal with the Puristans eventually. It was unavoidable. But some options were avoidable, such as dragging them and Olivia along for the ride into the depths of hell and back. Pinching his chin, Tim shook his head: "I'm gonna hoof it."

"Say again?"

"On foot. I'm gonna hoof it." Tim replied. "You and the Lads get her back to the colonel. AILA can hide her, deep cover from the threats. It's our best option, like you said."

"And you want to go this alone?"

"No." Tim shook his head. "But you're right. I can't drag her into hell with me, and I can't abandon Dakota."

"And we're supposed to do? Say 'Cheerio mate, God's speed to ya,' and let you travel loads of miles on your own? Not even loads—it's fucking rubbish how many miles you'd be hoofing on your own. By then, it's anyone's guess where your sister would be, innit? I don't think so, mate."

"You won't have…" Olivia's voice stirred, her eyes half-opened, and she grunted, holding her waist as she sat up, weak and slow. "To drag me along," she sighed, breathing slowly. The high of whatever drugs she received lingered in her sluggish movements.

Tim took his canteen and offered it to her, and she accepted it with eager gulps.

"Slow sips," Tim warned, but she ignored him and continued to gulp it down, coming to a gagging fit. She held up a finger, got control over her belly, and winced as she leaned forwards. Tim noticed how clenched her thighs were, and though she tried to hide it, a look of shame gloomed her face.

"How long have you been awake?" he asked.

"Around… 'Home is compromised,' I think." She mumbled, holding back a weak but impish smirk. "But I mean it. You don't have to drag me along. I want to help you and your sister." She sniffed, eyes suddenly reddening, fear plaguing her features.

"No, out of the question." Tim shook his head.

Olivia tried to protest with a snap and a wave of a finger but fell short. "It's not your choice," she snipped at him, eyes teary, "It's mine, and I'm old enough to choose for myself. Also, technically I'm not a civilian, either. I was part of a domestic military operation, and I am required for military service until I'm twenty-five. So, on a technicality, I'm an adult not a kid. So I volunteer to help with your military operation for a search and rescue. Sergeant Anal General, Sir."

"Technically, you aren't military personnel, but an asset," Tim snipped back, but he had to hide the laughter he felt from her retort.

She had spunk and she had grit, but without training and experience, he couldn't gamble with her. "You don't know what's out there, kid. You're not going. That's final."

"It's not your decision. It's mine." She raised her voice, falling short again, taking in a tired breath with closed eyes. "Everyone I loved died so I could get into Alyeska. Everyone." She cried, sniffing, and taking a calming breath as her eyes stayed beady. "Now I have a chance to help bring your sister back, and that's what I want to do."

Tim looked to Chain for backup, and though there was some contention on the Lad's face, Tim couldn't believe the look of agreement he saw. Tim shook his head as Chain started nodding.

"Present concerns would be solved with her coming along," Chain offered.

"Are you serious?"

"We establish a COP and sort her out like a private with a gun, holding security and patrol. She stays in relative safety with two others, and the rest branch off to look for Dakota," Chain suggested.

"COP?" Olivia asked.

"Combat Outpost," Chain clarified, looking from her back to Tim. "You know what's out there, and we can use the extra gun. You don't need to be a corker to put down a zombie, mate."

"You know what else is out there that isn't affected by a gun, and even the best "corker" can't compete against it." Tim air quoted with his fingers.

"But you can." Chain pointed at Tim. "We don't need any other bloody corker when we have a top-shelf bloke such as yer'self."

"I don't know how many times I've told you; we didn't beat Inimicus and the Jackle—we survived our encounters." Tim rubbed his forehead, a migraine taking root and fast.

"Don't be a twit," Chain shook his head. "Having another hand manning a doofer could mean the difference between life and death from a BR-Hostile attack. Fucking true, that. Sooner or later, she's gonna be fighting zombies, mate, whether you like it or not."

"Doofer?" asked Olivia.

Tim ignored her, glaring at Chain now. "Sum'bitch." Tim scratched his neck, looking at Olivia, She didn't budge, holding his glance. "You do what I say. When I say it. Do you understand that?

And none of that sassy-ass backtalk; I don't want a debate with you on everything I say. Understand?"

"I do," she nodded.

Chain gave Tim's knee a brief pat, and he clicked his radio. "Gents, wheels up in five mikes. I'll phone up the colonel and inform him of the situation."

"Chain." Tim stopped him before he had a chance to stand and climb into the pilot seat. "Coded message, yeah? Don't know if anyone might intercept it."

"Yeah." Chain cast a smirk with a thumbs up. "I'm on it, Yank; you just worry about shooting shit, alright?"

Razor, Dagger, and Slug returned to the bird. Razor climbed back into the co-pilot's seat, and Chain, the pilot's. Tim saw a pensive look on Olivia's face; her hands were held against her groin. *Oh, Hell.* His heart went out to her, thinking of that rapey brute of a man, Hendricks not there to keep her safe; wondering what he could do or what he could say that might offer her comfort.

Olivia had retreated into herself, sitting there with a thermal blanket draped over her. Eyes locked on the metal floor of the cab, her lips fought to arch in a trembling frown, her breathing had a rhythm of sobbing to it, and tears escaped out her stilled eyes.

He got her up on a seat and strapped her in as the rest of the blokes climbed back onboard.

Then he sat next to her, the regression starting to reverse when he focused on her. Dagger and Slug situated themselves to the fifties on both sides of the bird; Tim slipped out of the sling of his rifle and held it where Olivia could see it. Maybe she didn't need him to say anything; perhaps the best thing he could do was to show her that he still cared.

"Do I still call you Tyrese, then? Timothy?" she sniveled.

Tim sighed, "It's a long story." He motioned back to his rifle.

"It's a long ride."

"And, you're gonna need to know the basics."

The propellers started spinning, and, within five minutes, Ol' Faithful made her ascent. The bird rose into the sky, the nose tipping downwards, and they were en route southbound. Tim showed Olivia basic safety and handling before going into further detail, seeing in the girl the forceful repression of what she experienced. He himself repressed the realization that he was heading back to the same place they had lost Phil. The repressed fear joined in conjunction with his grief, a fear that past events were also bad omens to mirror the future.

Part IV – DAKOTA

Chapter One – Cold World

-October 23rd, 2030-

Dakota had expected to be on her way home six hours ago, until Damion insisted that she “stayed the night.” It had been a polite way of telling her she wasn’t going anywhere, and he had provided her with a small room in an old-world inn within Yellowknife’s walls. Despite sitting around for a ten-hour helicopter transit from the colonel’s compound to Fort Liard, followed by the ensuing twenty-hour train ride from the fort to Yellowknife, she was ready for the track back home—back to Timmy. Now she was lying on the dank, musty mattress.

Damion's words lingered in the back of her mind: “It’s too dangerous to allow train transit throughout the night. Wraiths and draugrs have been breaching walls and defenses of our outposts lately, and we don’t know how. They’ve never shown such intelligence. So, when those gates close for the night, they stay closed until first light.”

Behind Damion, she noticed a tearful reunion with the kid, Wheeler, who had been her charge to escort home, and a much older man. The two clasped in a tight hug, “Picket…you— how’d… man.” Wheeler sniveled in the man’s chest; the latter rested his chin on the kid's head. “I’m so glad to see you, you old crook.”

She had barely heard Wheeler speak the last thirty hours. He hardly mumbled a word unless it was a polite courtesy that came with half effort. She didn’t judge him for that; she was barely talkative herself and returned silence with silence. This had been the first time she had really heard his voice. His face gleamed with a mournful smile that managed to look as happy as it did sad.

Such a shame to hide a sweet smile, she remembered thinking. Her first impressions were brought to their fullest by his voice, which told her that Wheeler was a good kid.

“You’ve seen better days, too, but you’re looking alright now.” The stranger, Picket, had given a withered smile.

Their reunion reminded her of when she was a child and her great uncle had visited from Brazil.

A tingle of pain traveled across her clavicle as she shifted under the covers. The gash the Jackle had carved had yet to fully heal. As if on cue, she felt a sharp pain at her side from where Inimicus had shot her years prior. Those, among other, lesser scars, were but nasty reminders of the monsters—an existential commentary left by the two who left their signatures on her body, permanent reminders that she would never forget them. She reminded herself that they weren't just reminders, but badges of honor, trophies of survival. She wasn't the one pancaked under a boulder or missing her right arm.

Out of boredom, she let loose a raspberry and sat up, clenching her teeth at the extra jolt of pain it brought her. She leaned her head against a window by the headboard. Frost framed the edges of the glass panels. She hadn't seen winter since the last one before the Great Calamity, but she was good without the cold. Only a couple of weeks ago did it start to get colder, and her brows pinched in thought. The night of the first cold storm, she, Tim, and Phil had been the same as Phil's blackout in the White River National Forest. It came to her like an omen, the two occurrences.

Dakota thought it was funny how one thought led to another, going from thinking about her current situation to her brother. Only now, Phil lingered in her thoughts, and with it came the same damnable hurt.

She looked at the frosting glass, thinking that it imitated how she felt inside while the outside blurred in the background. The frost at the edges encased the center that was barely warm enough to stay thawed. Lines of warmth, failing and receding, were flames being snuffed out in the cold.

Moving on without closure was something she had to do with Ron and Sara, to say goodbye without knowing. It was the hardest thing she ever had to do after the dust had settled and the dead rose. Many times, she had to withdraw into a dark crawl space of her mind, where she could cry herself to exhaustion without anyone seeing. She learned to say goodbye, or else she would die herself; she felt that it should be easier now. It wasn't.

What came after this? Who and what were she and Tim without Phil there? What would become of them now, in his absence? Would they sign their retirement papers in the end? Accept that not-so-bright and shiny ending that the three of them had strived for but only two could receive? Tim had been correct; it wasn't fair, but then again, neither were most things in life.

It wasn't fair that before the Old World had perished, her family distanced themselves from her after marrying Ron when she got pregnant out of wedlock. It wasn't fair that she had to say goodbye to her husband and her baby girl without hope for any closure. And it wasn't fair to lose Phil. It was he who she and Tim had starved, wept, bled, grieved, laughed, prayed, and survived with, so close to a modicum of a "happy" ending.

Chapter Two – Saudade

-October 24th, 2030-

The whole night had been a toggle war of dozing off and on, hardly restful. Her ACUs offered not much warmth, but the two blankets covering her kept her from freezing. The cold helped keep her fully awake and alert. When the crest of dawn split open light through the bluish hue of the twilight morning sky and illuminated her quarters, she figured she could get some sleep on the ride home.

She felt the warmth of the golden rays lightly touch her forehead. As the sun rose, so did its warm light travel down in a welcoming feeling over the bed and blankets. She thought then that maybe a couple of hours of sleep was in the cards, after all—if the sun continued in its slow course.

Then, it was as if some unseen force or principality of the unseen realm had sensed her wanting to sleep—it had an antagonistic sense of humor and wanted to get a load of laughter from her misery. Fate dealt its cruel hands, one card after another, and heavy knockings came at her door like the morning crowing of a rooster—right on cue, without a second wasted.

Her heavy eyes lightened, and her heart pumped a bit more as she sat up. Forcing her legs over the side of the bed and into her boots, the two cold little holes sucked the warmth from her feet. She tied her boots as she hollered, "Come in." Looking at the window, she saw the frosting edges now melting; beads of cold water traveled down the glass under the warm yellow ball, not yet too bright to look at. Clouds flanked the horizon and spotted the center in an elegant portrait with the mountains and forest beyond Yellowknife.

The door opened, and an aged man stepped in, the same one who had embraced Wheeler the previous night. His hair was balding in a ring on top, whiting at the sides, receding into little stubbles of thick facial coverings no more than a few weeks past his last shave. He had a slight limp on his right leg, but there was a youthful sense of energy to him.

"Scout Captain Picket, do you have a minute?" he asked with a formal gesture of his smile and hands.

"Of course." She nodded. "What's wrong?"

"It's Scout Leader Wheeler; he dipped overnight. We're combing the outer areas looking for him but need additional help. It would be greatly appreciated."

She nodded before really processing what the request was at its fullest, as if her mind was catching up while her brain operated on autopilot. *Yep, there is always something.*

"Thank you, Sergeant. Meet you downstairs in, say, ten?"

"Five. I'll be there." She nodded.

Picket took his leave as she finished lacing her boots, taking in a breath as she looked back out the window at the crisp morning. The sun's futile attempts to bring warmth only delayed the chill. Only a second's worth of thought passed as she looked out the window, out west. Thinking of Damion's grave warnings about night travel, her eyes settled on the mountains off in the distance and she gazed at the foothills and trees. What was between Alyeska and Yellowknife that was so threatening? What crisis so close to Alyeska could hold so much worry when there was a Zombie Crisis further east?

A second passed, and she focused back on her boots, tying her laces tight and blousing each boot to the pant leg. She set her hair back in a bun as if her commanding officer was about to enter her barracks quarters for inspection. Her uniform, despite being Alyeskan, was set appropriately, according to the Army's standards: laces set correctly, hair in a bun. Ready for inspection.

She sighed deeply; the day was starting at a full sprint, and a gap of time passed as she silenced her uncouth, antagonizing thoughts. One step at a time. Compartmentalizing was the only way she could navigate through a storm.

Meet Picket downstairs. Look for Wheeler.

It was time to get to work, and maybe it was a good thing that Damion had insisted on her "invitation" to stay overnight. Maybe this would improve relations between Alyeska and the Canadian Confederacy, and, just maybe, she could do some good.

They fox-walked over the dried, fallen leaves of the forest floor, chewing the last of her morning breakfast in the form of pemmican. The leaves didn't crunch as much after soaking in the morning dew. But when the day started to get colder, and the shade lowered enough in some places, it sounded like stepping on cracking ice or shards of glass.

The hike in the cold, autumn-like morning tugged at her memories. The sun brightened overhead; any threats that might be lurking in the wilderness were either not around or had yet to reveal themselves. Their objective of locating Wheeler set aside, the hike through the forest wasn't unpleasant, and that pleasantness was luring her back to happier times. Times when she had found peace and joy during the storms of adversity. Times when Tim would stay behind at their base in Atlanta, working on their vehicles, while she and Phil would go into the small nature areas—parks and little bits of thickets in the outer districts of the Highway 285 ring. The two of them had set and checked traps for small game.

It was an odd place she found herself in, concentrating on tracking Wheeler while feeling the saudade of memories—the nostalgia of fond times scavenging and hunting in that old city. Her fondest memory had been when she and Phil had gotten an early start, right at the crack of dawn, and spent the whole day gathering squirrels and rodents from their traps. They had taken a respite on a building that had endured heavy artillery. The corner of it was blown away and left in a decaying state when the undead had pushed the Army out years prior. The structure had been sturdy enough for use for a few years before collapsing in 2022

During the short span of usage, a perch had been a grand spot before the sprawl of urban decay. It was a good view to use for a deer stand over that small section of Atlanta, back when deer had been plentiful in that area. One day, sitting with her thirty-aught-six, while Phil looked around with his binos, they sat with their feet dangling over the edge. The sounds of the vacant city and the moaning of the undead carried over the willowing wind, blowing through the lifeless urban forest. Thunder boomed in the distance like a low note to a massive wind instrument, heralding the incoming precursor storm.

That day had been mellow, a nice day, but fruitless. Phil had known what was troubling her back then. He could see and relate to her trouble; they both had lost their lovers, and they had both lost their eight-year-old children. He could speak with her about that pain because he too carried it as a grieving father and husband.

"You wanna talk about it?" Phil had asked.

"No. Not really." She had shaken her head; the wind blew strands of hair every which way. It was the same response she had given Tim the day prior.

And that was that. Nothing else needed to be said that wasn't already understood. That meant more to her—the fact that her brothers were readily available to listen if she was ever ready to speak.

She tried to force Phil's face away from her thoughts, her and Picket coming to a little creek that stopped her dead in her tracks. The water, no deeper than an inch, rushed over rocks and pebbles. All she could see were those poor stones being drowned under the chaos of the waters. Her feet were anchored in place at the edge of the water as she stared at the flowing current; her breathing was reduced to shaky pants as a nervous chill fidgeted at her spine.

Behind her, Scout Captain Picket caught up; the man was a bit slower, but he still kept up. They both carried Lee Enfield rifles. The rounds weren't as large as the .308 she preferred. But it wasn't a small round either. Her FN FNP pistol at her side, along with her trench knife, offered some security, but even that amounted to little as she remained frozen by the creek.

She could hear Picket take in a deep breath and let it out in a slow, relaxing exhale as he came to a stop abreast of her. He remained there, looking from her to the creek where her eyes remained fixed. All she saw was the water—no matter how deep or shallow, she saw the hazards and dangers of the Great Gulf. There were threats hidden in beauty like wolves in sheep's' clothing.

"You crossing or want me to take the lead?" he asked as a yawn found its way up and out his mouth.

"No. No, no. I'm fine." Dakota mumbled, her voice shook but not wanting Picket to sense her… issues with water, she yawned in kind.

She nudged her right foot closer to the little stream of the creek. Her exhale drew out into a deep sigh as she took a leap and strode over the water. The creek was no more than two feet wide, and she made sure none of the water touched her boots. On the other side and with the water behind her, out of her sight, she did her best to hide the tremors moving across her limbs, passing off what she couldn't hide as being cold.

Picket studied her. She could feel him connecting two and two as if some unknown tension was between them.

"You got a problem with the water, lil' lady?"

She cackled in a soft scoff. "Lady. You certainly aren't talking about me."

She leaned back against a tree, claiming her thoughts away from her panicked self. Drying her eyes and focusing her breath, she didn't feel it at first, but the old man grabbed her shoulder, trying to comfort her. The haphephobia kicked right off, one phobia after another, as she jerked away.

Get a grip. she told herself as Picket recoiled.

"Sorry." He took a step back. "Just want to make sure you're alright. That's all."

"Yeah. Yeah, I'm fine." She nodded, "Space and time is all." She offered a smile, both an apology and thanks.

"You sure you'll be alright?"

"Yeah," she remarked, irritation now snipping in her voice. "How about you take point?"

"You got it, lil' lady," Picket said, offering a quick smirk as he adjusted his rifle and took point.

She scoffed again; being called lady was akin to calling Tim a bookworm when "motorhead" and "movie enthusiast" was more accurate.

She followed him through the thick brush, sticking to the trees where the weeds, bushes, and tall grass were more spaced out. The roots of the trees hogged most of the water and nourishment to not allow much else to grow, so there was a radius of dirt and thin grass around them. The trail never went cold but continued; she swore the kid must have been out all night.

"So, what happened?" Dakota asked.

"Beg'ir pardon?"

"You and Wheeler. That reunion of yours last night? That wasn't just a reunion after not seeing each other after a while. Did it have something to do with him washing down the Liard River?"

She received a chuckle in response, not out of amusement or comedy's sake. Rather, like with Damion's arms folding, it seemed to be a way of coping, some oblivious way of self-comforting. Judging from Damion's dread, Wheeler's somber demeanor, and that heartfelt reunion, something bad was lurking in the northwest areas of the wilderness. Which just so happened to be their heading.

"As a matter of fact, it did," Picket sighed, pushing a big leaf out of his way. Holding it back for her, his face registered that he was on the same page as she. If they were heading into danger, she had a right to know what, exactly.

Ah, a gentleman and a scholar, she thought.

"A couple of weeks back—scratch that, over a month now—we were sent to investigate one of our outposts that had gone dark. What we found though…" He shook his head. "Anyways, we followed a trail to the Sahtu Region, and found this massive… I dunno, complex. We didn't get too far when we were attacked. It came down to just Wheeler and me, and I tossed us both into the river and messed my knee up in the process. The current pulled us apart, and I'm sure you can divine the rest."

"These things? What can you tell me about them?"

"They showed up out of the blue a couple of years back, just a few stragglers from further up north. Nothing a Scout Party couldn't handle. But they've changed over the years… And their numbers have been increasing in the last couple. Drastically." Picket shook his head, "They're unlike any walker, runner, or claymore. Something worse." He stopped, grimacing as he rubbed the same leg he limped with.

"Claymores?"

"I guess others call them satyrs."

"Why claymore, then?"

"Cuz the first one we came across was taken down only by a claymore mine, so we call them that." Picket offered a chuckle. "I wasn't there myself, but I can imagine that one."

She was back on point; the day was waning from afternoon to evening, and the sun was now in its decline towards the horizon. They had run through their evening provisions, having just enough to get them back to Yellowknife by the morning: pemmican, dried fruits, and water.

She cleared a bush, revealing a small opening to a campsite. It was in ruins, and a shower curtain that had been put up for a tent was torn and shredded. The fire hole was out, but still smoked up in a thin flume; everything else was scattered and torn. The rocks over the fire had blood, not fresh or dried, and a set of tracks led away from the site.

"He may still be alive," Picket said. Though he tried to hide it, there was a worried strain to his voice and a wheeze to his breath.

She agreed, unless whatever attacked him had dragged him away or chased after him. Those notions were swayed by the clear imprints of a man on foot going one way and four paw prints leading in a different direction from the site.

"You stay here," Dakota said, "in case he comes back. I'll follow the tracks." There was reason to it, and the old man's knee needed a rest.

"Don't have to twist my arm there," Picket said, wiping cold sweat from his forehead and taking a seat near the fire. "I'll contact Damion and get the flames back up; we won't be able to make it back to Yellowknife before nightfall, and we certainly don't want to be moving around in the dark."

"Sounds good." Dakota nodded and turned back to the trail, wading into the brush.

By herself, in the wild unknown, she found greater focus. All else faded into the background. The sounds of a water current came from the distance as she neared a small river. Her senses were on high alert from the sound of the steady current, goosebumping her skin and weeding out any thoughts that didn't get her away from the water sooner.

Check for Wheeler. If he's there, back to the campsite. If not, look elsewhere.

Clearing the tree, she came to a full view of the river; Wheeler was sitting on a rock deep enough in the waters that the current flowed around him. Socks and shoes rested on the shore, and his pants were rolled up to his knees as cleaned three deep gashes carved across his right bicep.

She was sure he sensed her, but he seemed unaware or just didn't care. Stepping up to the waters, her body stopped just before the current without her conscious consent. Wheeler noticed her and looked at her, Dakota waved at the young man to come to her. Panic rattling at her chest, she thought she'd lose her grip had the comfort of the mud under her boots not grounded her. Her boots rooting into the mud, reminding her she was on land where monsters of watery depths could not touch her.

Taking in a slow breath and a step back, her mind started to boggle with the sounds of the giant electric eel, a Leviathan-Eel as it was properly labeled. *A force of nature,* she thought. Its roar, or cry, whatever sound it was, dug deep into her being and mixed into a chorus with the feeling of apnea when the sea serpent unveiled itself. The monster sounded both like a mournful and verbally active whale. It amped up a thousand percent louder in tone, volume, and pitch. Such a cry drowned everything in that void of the Great Gulf. She saw all around them no hope for land or shore, but a torrential realm of circulating storms and rolling layers of threatening clouds that isolated them on those rigs from a dead and decaying world. She felt hopeless, straying into the abyss that was nothingness.

She saw herself in the depths of the Great Gulf, the mutated Eel sending the three of them airborne, falling back into the water. Only this time, Phil was swallowed whole, and she sunk deeper as Tim disappeared. She couldn't swim back up, couldn't move her arms and legs, and she only continued to sink. Apnea again gripped her as the watery darkness drowned out all light and she saw the Leviathan's silhouette swimming through the deep dark.

There was a seemingly endless void inside her mind, soul, and heart where her demons dwelled. It was a watery hell she couldn't escape, and it nearly toppled her into a panicked fit; this time, her brothers weren't there to comfort her through it. Slow, shaky breaths kept her from falling into the water and losing all control as she steadied herself at the edge of the river.

Realizing her shaking sobs fell in tune with Wheeler's, she looked up, taking a step away from the river. It was then she registered the rhythm of crying; the young man was sobbing. She looked out to him, watching as he punched the river's surface and sent water airborne, startling her as if the drops of water would somehow teleport her back to the Great Gulf. Back to her watery hell.

Suddenly jolted, her shaking voice erupted at the grieving young man. “Hey!”

Wheeler looked over at her, eyes red and puffy with fresh watery streaks running down his cheeks. He had a look of shame and guilt for allowing himself to be seen in such a broken state. It broke her heart. She couldn’t let the young man feel like that, to break down and weep by himself. She leaned forward, her hands outstretched, her left leg taking another step away from the river. As if there was a pit between her and the young man, her hand offered the promise to catch him. All he had to do was take a leap of faith and jump.

“C’mon, bud.” She followed up with a softer tone.

Wheeler looked over at her, fresh blood seeping out the gash of his arm. Tears fell, but his mouth was clenched shut, looking over at her, regarding her with a curious look and coming out from whatever world inside his head he was lost in.

“Just uh… get back over here and lemme look at ya. I’ll patch you up, sound good?” she asked, keeping her shaking fingers open.

He looked around like the water was harmless. But she remained the same, a good five feet away from the river’s edge, waving at him to do as she said. His crying ceased; now he was robbed of the solitude to do so alone, shaking his head as he looked back to the water.

“You have a problem with water, Miss?” His voice calmed a bit.

If I hear that question one more damn time. She sighed, stabbing at him with her eyes, flaring as the waters pried more and more at her. A piece of herself had drowned in the Great Gulf, and a piece of it drowned in her.

“He’s gone.” Wheeler shook his head, looking back to the water.

“Okay. Well, we can’t do anything about that, now can we?”

“What does it matter?” Wheeler shook his head and splashed more water up on the gashes still bleeding down his arm. He had already been exposed; his guts were spilled, in a manner of speaking. It was as if allowing others to see the pains and hurts was as repulsive as being seen walking around naked. There was that same norm to hide the wrongs and ills on the inside, to never let your guts show, and all would be well.

Dakota looked away, taking in a deep breath. She couldn't will her feet forward, couldn't coax him. Shaking her head, her stomach felt like a rumbling sinkhole. Maybe Picket should've come with her.

"Who'd you lose?"

There was no answer as he held a bloodied rag over his arm and pressed tightly over it. His face winced from the sudden pressure.

"I've lost someone too. Recently." Her voice instantly cracked, and her breath shook as she spoke. Wheeler looked at her again, his shoulders slouching, his mouth struggling to remain clenched. "My broder. I lost my broder."

"Yer handling yours better than I am."

She took in a cold breath. "I've had a bit longer to hide it. But don't think that means I'm any better off than you are."

No response came from him.

"It's okay to be sad, Buddy. I'm sad too." Her voice softened, warranting the young man to look back at her. That shameful look of guilt receded, cautious but yielding all the same.

And don't make me stay by the water much longer! Her face now flushed in heat as a cold chill ran up her back from a splash of water against a rock not three meters away from her right foot.

She stretched her hand one last time; after that, she had to get away from the waters Her mind was just about spent. More water splashed near her right foot, hardening her soft look at the young man.

Wheeler nodded, sniffing hard as he rose to his feet, looking at the cold water and then at her. Something seemed pressed at his mouth, maybe words to speak, but they quickly fell back behind closed lips as he stared at her. Uncertainty seemed to grip him, fear of the unknown being something she could relate to; she understood the risk of trusting someone. But her heart went out to the poor kid, she wanted to help him.

"If nothing else, hurry up for me… please?" She breathed out a smirk and waved her hand with a strong press for him to hurry. *Just get over here!*

He stood up and waded into the cold water, the torque's blue flowing surface across the brown of his skin. His feet looked a few hours short of frostbite as he waded through the cold water, either unconcerned or oblivious to it. He reached over and took her hand as she helped him up the embankment. No sooner after he took his leap of faith, she backstopped more, placing as much distance between her and the water as she could. He reached down and grabbed his boots and socks before standing back up and addressing her.

"Bear."

"Huh?" she asked, looking over her shoulder, expecting a grizzly to be coming straight for them.

"She ran off after I shot her. Fatal wound. It wouldn't be proper to let her die slowly. I was fixin on huntin her down after I cleaned this wound up."

Her heart couldn't take much more adrenaline, coming down from the high panic of a grizzly bear warning. She glared at him. He was going to be the death of her at this rate. She shook her head and turned her back to the waters as he followed.

Black bear, she thought, given that he was still alive, with just a single swipe at his arm. Such bears were more timid than their brown counterparts, easier to scare off, but still terrifying all the same. She suspected it was a mama bear, given the fact the thing attacked him. But it was all quick conjecture on her part; she was no expert on bears.

"Must've been a mama bear, because she didn't run when I tried to haze her away. Reckon she doesn't have long to live."

From the inside, she could feel her spirit sigh. The world could be cruel and cold. There was one more thing they had left to do before sundown. She nodded. "I guess we need to track it down, then."

"And the cubs." Wheeler frowned. "If it is a mama, we need to find the cubs, determine if we need to put'em down or not. Even more wrong to leave baby cubs to die without their mama."

That struck deeper than she could hide. She thought of Sara, thought of Phil and his boy, Benjamin. Some bridges could only be crossed once you came to them; there was no point dwelling on it until then. Especially with this.

"Let's patch you first, then we can deal with the rest."

Chapter Three – Traction

Wheeler rubbed warmth back into his toes and feet, the fire at his ruined camp restored and burning with an old, dried log; a thick plume of smoke rose into the trees. A single .303 caliber shot cracked in the distance, and his shoulders jerked as he flinched, receiving a sigh from Dakota, who was cleaning the gashes at his arm.

Sorry, his heart grieved for the bear. Noting that no other shot sounded off, he figured Picket had found the mama bear first. Had the poor girl collapsed when she lost too much blood and her strength depleted? What dread and worry went through the beast's thoughts when she couldn't reach her den in time?

Two more shots cracked in the distance, and tears pressed out through clenched eyes. *I'm so sorry.*

He thought of the mama, just acting out of maternal love and duty to protect that which meant the most. The wild and uncouth was cold and unfair, as was the Dead World around them. The cubs must have been too young, unable to fend for themselves, let alone protect themselves—doomed to a slow and painful death without their mother. Mercy didn't always necessitate fairness.

His father—well his surrogate one—Floyd, would've said "Be happy it wasn't one of dem brown'ens." And Wheeler was. Otherwise, he would've just pissed it off with his shot and more than likely he would be dead or would have suffered more than just the gashes at his arm. All the same, it didn't change what had just happened. What little life remained was like flowers amidst charred and scorched earth, one that was now void of three more lives.

"I'm sorry, mama." He tapped a clenched fist to his forehead in a soft whimper.

This wasn't how he wanted to honor his mama, the very same mother who had laid down her own life to protect that which she loved most.

He grimaced at the gentle patting of a rag against his arm, this one not soaked in water but in rubbing alcohol. The burning spared him from remembering his mother's final moments, and though he didn't hide his feelings, Dakota didn't say anything. Judgment was absent in her features, her eyes were dead-locked on her task. He held his breath at her gentle pattings. The blood had stopped leaking, and no arteries or veins were damaged. *Thank you, Lord.*

"I never got a chance to thank you, by the way," she said, as if noticing he was looking at her.

"Fur what, Miss?"

"Two years ago," she said, and waited.

He searched his memories; two years ago he was further east at the Moosonee Outpost for the Attawapiskat City State. The only thing of major occurrence was the loss of Ethan and Liam of the Danger Unit and… "Holy shit." His eyes widened. *Three survivors. Just outside Morvik's Air Force Base. The flare.* "That was you?"

"I heard from Colonel Winston that you're the one who saw our flare. I dunno how he'd know, though."

"Probably Damion." He now leaned forward. "I reckoned you looked familiar. But I wasn't sure and didn't want to come off weird or anything. After all, you sure were beaten to hell when I first laid eyes on ya. Wasn't sure if you were the same gal. I didn't recognize ya."

"Had it not been for you, I don't think we would've made it past that day." She offered a weak smile, and her eyes fell. "You saved our lives."

Now a humorous thought ran through his mind, remembering the flare he saw two years ago. The rest of his scouting party was heading to their transport, their backs to the east. He didn't know why; maybe it was because he was in the back of the formation that meant he needed to keep tabs on their rear. But whatever the case, he looked over his shoulder, looked due east, and noted how out of place it was in that tamed morning from a vacant and void landscape.

There was nothing east of there, save for the dead city of Morvik, and no scouts were reported to have gone further east than the Air Force Base that day. From the nothingness of the ruined world east, those three people called for aid. Neither she nor her two friends had thoroughly been "put through the wringer" as Floyd had said, upon seeing the three corpse-like survivors waiting for aid.

"Can I ask you a question?"

"Aim and fire."

"What's with that sash?" she asked.

"Oh, this ol' thing?" he asked. "I'm a bit of a comic book junky. Something of a long story."

That his quick way of saying, *I don't wanna talk about it.* But looking down at the sash brought with it all the memories of his late mother. So soon after mourning for the bears, for Floyd, none of the good memories came, and he felt grateful that she didn't pry.

"Where your two friends at?" he asked, looking away from the sash.

She didn't look at him, but took in a deep breath, her focused look deepening into a frown. She slowly shook her head as she sat the rag down and held another dry one to his arm. Pressing hard on it, the sudden pressure sent a grimace over him as the alcohol cleaned the torn flesh.

"Hold that there," she mumbled, holding the rag in place, lifting her hand only when he relieved hers of the task and she started rummaging through her bag. "Tim is back home looking over someone." She paused, exhaling and sighing at the same time. "We lost Phil a few weeks ago."

"Shit." He mumbled. *Another flower gone.*

She pulled out a thread and a crescent needle. Setting the needle between the clamps of a pair of tongs, she let it hover over the fire. The quick, short answers said enough; she was done with talking, and he didn't pry.

When the needle became red hot, she pulled it away, shaking it ever so slightly to cool it down. Taking the thread, and with sharp eyes on the meticulous task, she slipped the thread through the loop head and tied it in place, biting on the string, snapping it, and securing the other end in a knot. Despite the frequent blemishes of pain sparking her features and the brace her left arm was set in, she operated with ease and steadiness, not missing a beat.

Wheeler gritted his teeth and readied himself for what came next.

Dakota took in a breath, slow and shallow, as she moved his hand holding the gauze, readying the needle over his skin. "You wanna tell me why we're out here?" she broke her silence. "Why we're now risking being ambushed by zombies, and Lord knows what else, in the night?"

"Not really." He shook his head.

She chuckled, a cross between a scoff and frustration. "Alright then, clench your teeth." Her instructions were given without ample warning, and he suddenly felt the sharp sting of the needle piercing the swollen skin of the gash at his arm. Clenching after the fact, she pulled the thread all the way through. Pulling together one end of the top gash, she tied it and then clipped it. One down and several more to go, she dipped the needle into a small metal bowl of alcohol and dried it off in the fire.

"Well," she said, ready for the next poke. "You're gonna have to tell me or Picket."

"Floyd," he said, clenching his teeth in time as she stuck the needle into his bicep once more. He winced as he felt the pace of her sewing his skin back together increase. She was no longer holding back, and now, with the momentum of inbound answers spilling out, she worked and listened. The sensational pain was good; it kept the tears and fever of grief at bay, though his bottom lip continued to quiver.

Good old Earl Floyd Jenkins, his father if he ever had one, was a crazy old goon. He always thought of Floyd and himself as Yin and Yang, he was black and Floyd white. Despite Floyd's outward appearance, donning a cap with a Confederate flag upon it, there was no hate in the man, not when Floyd first saved him as a "wee lad." It was the opposite; Floyd had nothing but love in him, put on full display when the old man took his place to die.

Wheeler was at a loss for words; he knew what he wanted to say, but he was unsure of how to say it. His mission had been a failure; his whole team, besides Picket, was gone. The people he had been closest to the last twelve years were taken from his life in just minutes. He didn't know how to process that, this unequal ratio of time. It had all been over two weeks ago, and he was just now trying to process it all. He didn't know how to say it.

The woman was patient, not speaking, and she continued the dauntless task of stitching him back together.

"Sevar—several. Weeks…ago…" He had to stop, sniffing as he wiped his nose off with his other arm's sleeve.

"Take your time."

She had finished stitching the first gash, tying the string and clipping the last stitch of five for the top laceration. Her eyes remained focused. Once more, she cleaned the needle and set it over the flames with a pair of tongs. Determined to patch him up the best she could, he started to break down before her and her eyes remained without judgment.

"Yeh, Yellowknife received word that one of our outposts went dark. So, we were sent to investigate. Our trucks only got so far before the road became impassible, landslide or something. So, we huffed it on foot, and what we found was… It wasn't what we'd expected."

"What?" The needle once more penetrated his flesh, a burning poke that kept the heartache from becoming overbearing. It allowed him to speak.

The area of his injuries was numbing, its radius spreading with each stitch she tied down, a constant prickling of sharp spikes across his bicep. It was an empty outpost; the only signs that people had been there were failed defenses, bullet cases, and blood. They searched for survivors, finding none, not even a body, when sirens wailed from the distance. Sirens, in the middle of a forest, *explain that one to me.* Sirens coming from where they shouldn't be. He paused, taking a moment, but his mind didn't slow.

He had been on point, tracking a mass movement of what he hoped were survivors fleeing the outpost, heading in the same direction where the sirens originated from. He found two columns of railroads, leading them to the southern edge of the Great Bear Lake, the rails traversing over the water to a massive complex. It was a place that should have been rotten and decrepit, but somehow it was well-kept and it appeared that a tiny bit of the Old World had survived.

"You know when the dead first rose, at first glance they were hard to tell from normal people? Now, they look like dried leather tearing over old bones. Well, there were a lot of zombies that looked a helluva a lot like people, a whole mess of 'em swarmed us, young and strong. As if they were recently turned walkers or runners, except… One headshot wasn't enough to put 'em down. No, you had to shoot 'em several times before they'd fall. But you know how hard it is to land a headshot on a moving target."

He saw all his friends—Picket, Floyd, and the rest of his team—forming an over-and-under fire line on the bridge. The underline of scouts fired until they needed to reload, then the over-fire-line would shoot while the under reloaded. It was a system to maintain an unending engagement against the undead up and running without pause. It worked on the older zombies, until the monsters were all dead, there were too many to hold back, or they had run out of ammo.

But that day, the formation bared no fruit; each zombie had cost too much ammunition to put down. Then a horde emerged from behind them, out of the wilderness, cornering them on both ends. His buddies were swarmed in a slow death of chewing and being consumed.

He was no stranger to such a sight, watching people get eaten alive, and it never got easy to process. It was the same story whenever people came back home fewer in number.

"It never gets easy." Tears fell from his eyes, that same story always being a big pill to swallow.

Dakota remained silent, still stitching, but he could feel the news settle on her with some measure of reproach. Like ESP or something, there was a strange shift in her, going from an open ear to one with the sudden presence of tension. Her eyes shook, and, as if she knew something, the shift in her was inwards. She tied up the last stitch at the middle gash and clipped the thread from the needle: rinse while clip in tongs, set over the fire, insert another line of thread.

She was from Alyeska; maybe she did know something, and he wondered if it was a mistake to confide in her. Perhaps she was a wolf in sheep's clothing, playing good cop to meet her ends? Whose side was she on? Was there an agenda behind her company in the first place? *What happened to Floyd?* His racing thoughts echoed what his ears had picked up, his consciousness lingering far behind.

He looked back at her as she now stared at him. "Beg'r pardon?" he asked.

"What happened to Floyd?" she repeated.

He wondered if he should answer that; the present caution he felt made him nervous. There was only one way he could gauge her. Damion took the news of the zombies taking more bullets to put down, headshots included a lot worse than this. Everyone did, and yet Dakota wasn't taken aback by the news. Perhaps she was just that accustomed to such information, desensitized?

"We were trapped on that damn bridge, fixin and just tryin to get away from it all. But somethin' else came." Wheeler felt his breath shake, his body tensing, holding still. He recalled the thick fog consuming the bridge, limiting their visuals. The tallest structure of the complex stood over the fog, still visible. He felt the earthquakes traversing under the wood and metal in the rhythm of footfalls, accompanied by the rattling of heavy chains. The king of the castle sent forth his champion to contend with the intruders and watch from his high tower, that centermost imposing structure at the site.

His heart tremble and his limbs shake with each breath, memory and fear taking hold of Floyd's last moments. There was an enormous arm with beige skin and thick black chains weaving in and out of its flesh: a hidden giant, veiled by the fog, reached out and grabbed Floyd, massive fingers constricting around the old man's head. The hidden monster lifted the man high.

Tears filled Wheeler's eyes; he could still hear his old man's ragged yelling, the crunching of his skull, and that unnatural squish like a grape being crushed.

"I didn't see it; it reached out for me. It wanted me, and Floyd shoved me out of the way." Wheeler sniffed, making eye contact with Dakota. "My father took my place. Now you tell me somethin, what is fair about that?" His eyes glared into hers.

"I can't." Her eyes fell. "Just like you can't tell me what's fair about a parent losing her baby girl."

Damn, was all he could think, but at least she was surrounded by the same forest Floyd raised him, where all those memories were: all the nights he and Floyd and their party spent out in these very same trees, the very same camping spot. They stayed out in the wild for a week or two, clearing the Canadian wilderness of zombies. They cleared zombies all around Yellowknife and all over the Northwest Territories, for that matter. It was the same wilderness where Floyd taught him everything he knew.

Wheeler felt more connected to the memories out here than inside the city. And, if he was being honest with himself, and to answer her previous question, he had to see that facility again—to gather any intel he could about the place, then report back to Damion so they'd have something about the place. The objective was to evacuate other outposts near that place of death back to the city state. Something had to be done.

"I'm sorry." Her voice was gentle.

It should've been me. He sniffed hard.

"My broder." Dakota said, tying the string into a knot. He heard the snip of a pair of scissors, his third gash now stitched together. "The last I saw him, he was at the feet of a big monster. That one armed bastard took him from me and Tim." She sniffed hard, letting a tear fall.

"I don't know how to do this again," he croaked.

He never got over losing his mother; it just became a weight he could bear. Some days were better than others. He didn't think he'd ever feel anything like it again. Yet now, here he was.

Dakota's hand fell on his shoulder, and he looked back, eye to eye. He found not some wolf in sheep's clothing, but that same empathy she bared before. Still, he wondered why news of strange zombies didn't surprise her much.

"I'm sorry, hun," she said, moving his other hand to hold another gauze pad over his arm. He did so as she started wrapping tape around the pad, then tucked and tied it in place.

"Thank you."

Twigs snapped before she could reply, and a two-rhythm whistle came out from the darkness deepening around them. From the same direction, the mama bear's tracks had gone. Wheeler then pursed his lips and returned the same two rhythms of whistling back out. His now-patched arm reached out, his hand over Dakota's rifle.

"It's just Picket," Wheeler said as the man emerged forth from the dark, the ugly deed finished.

"Found the mama's litter nested at a babysitter tree about half a mile or so northeast." He held a stilted face, internalizing what he had done, what had to be done. The proper order of things. "They weren't fully weaned." His face darkened, and Wheeler understood—mercy could have a darker side.

Had to be done.

Dakota didn't get much sleep; it was becoming more normal by the day. Almost a familiarity came with it, one that was comforting. The lack of sleep was no worse and perhaps a bit better than what she had gotten from her time in Atlanta. Staying up and keeping watch straight through the night was preferable. The cold air soothed the heat from swelling thoughts, those thoughts that made concentration a constant struggle. The need to keep the fire burning lest they freeze to death reinforced her focus.

Maybe it was Wheeler's story of younger draugrs, and now wraiths, taking headshots like bullet sponges and not going down. The Revenants had been a startling enough discovery: younger zombies eating older zombies. Even the President had her and Tim sign confidentiality agreements in knowing such things. But these zombies Wheeler came across didn't sound at all like Revenants. It left an unsettled feeling in her stomach, knots that made her nauseated. From the shady dealings of the country to some secret agenda, things were getting deep, and it was a short, shallow end before she and Tim would become loose ends to tie up.

She was supposed to wake up Picket an hour ago but decided the silence and solitude of being up alone was more soothing. She knew she wouldn't be able to rest—maybe get some sleep, but no rest, no matter how groggy her head felt or how tired and heavy her eyes were. She perched against a tree, its branches curving up and over her in a natural awning, and she looked out at the stars and moon, laced by tattered slivers of cloud clover. She found respite. Picket and Wheeler's snoring intertwined with the popping and steady rhythm of the fire, and the nightlife hooting of owls and other nocturnal animals was medicinal.

She felt so out of place, like a stranger in a foreign land, and she guessed she was. With Phil gone, with the space between her and Tim, she felt… hollow. Who was she without her brothers? She didn't know; her identity had been so intertwined with her brothers, the three of them together, that it scared her.

"What do I do with this?" she asked, barely a whisper.

She wished for Phil's guidance, his wisdom, for Tim's unyielding resolve and support. But she was left with nothing, far removed from her boys. *Wasn't even supposed to be here,* she thought, shaking her head. There was no point in thinking about what should've or could've been, despite the simple reality that she would've been back on her way home. She couldn't change her circumstances, only make something out of them.

She reached into her coat pocket and removed her compact Bible. It was the same book she found in a pew twelve years ago after a blustering conversation with Phil. At the end of her rope, mourning, scared, every fiber of her being stressed and strained, it seemed like all the lights of the world were suddenly and silently smothered when the bombs blew. That night, she cried out to the Lord. With nowhere else to turn, she opened the proverbial door and found light waiting outside. It brightened her dark.

She wanted, so desperately now, for that light to shine away the darkness looming over her. She opened to one of the many bookmarks coming to the book of 1st Corinthians, then flipped over to the next bookmark she had placed in 2nd Corinthians. She read chapter five, verse seven. One of her favorites.

"We live by believing not by seeing," she read. *Is it not about what you feel but rather the truth the word reveals?*

Even then, nothing was resonating with her. No matter how hard she tried, she couldn't find the moment when it felt as if the Scriptures were speaking to her. At that moment, she feared that she could read the whole book and nothing would harken to her or help her. It was feeling more and more like a dead end, and that scared her; the pain and grief just wouldn't go away, and she was tired of hurting.

God, she prayed, looking out at the majesty of the night sky. *I know one day you'll make everything right. But right now, I need some help, here. I'm struggling. I don't know who I am without my boys.*

Some moisture pressed through her closed eyes, but not enough to form beads of tears. She sunk to a place where rock bottom turned out to be quicksand and felt as if she were sinking into deeper, darker places.

Please, Lord. I need something.

Chapter Four – SOS

-October 25th, 2030-

Dawn glistened over the horizon, and the dark gave way to light; the night passed in silence. Save for the morning chirpings of birds and the gentle whoosh of the crisp wind blowing over a dew-frosted morning landscape, all was still and quiet. The fire had survived the night, keeping a thawed radius around the site.

Dakota's joints and rump had gone stiff from the forest floor. There was a pronounced crick in her neck that pinched her nerves, adding a sour temperament that welcomed her waking eyes. She took in a deep breath as a cold breeze pushed past her. Strands of hair clumped by her sweat swayed from where they had freed from her bun. Her clavicle, shoulders, left arm, and forehead all ached, adding to those pinched nerves.

She looked over at Wheeler and Picket, who were already awake. Not two hours ago, she had woken Wheeler, when her body demanded she sleep. Now both were up, and it came to her that they were letting her rest for as long as time allowed. The old man was digging into a piece of pemmican, and Wheeler stood looking over the distance. A pensive scowl dressed his face, his weapon resting in his hands. She followed the direction of his gaze, looking at the horizon, seeing nothing but trees and the fog of morning under them, veiling the foliage underneath.

"What is it?" she asked.

"Word came from Yellowknife. Another outpost went dark overnight," Wheeler said, not looking away from the horizon.

"Whati outpost," Picket chimed in after swallowing a bite.

"Is it in that direction?" she asked, reading the writing on the wall. These men were going.

"Less than a few hours hike," Wheeler's voice fell into a mumble. "We can be there before noon."

"Okay, then." Dakota reached for her rifle, leaning against the tree to help stand up.

Picket dumped his fork into the food packaging, rolling it up and stuffing it into a cargo pocket of his pants. "Back to it, then," the old man sighed, standing up. She could hear the popping of bones as the old man stood.

"Finally," fumed Wheeler.

"Wheeler, take point, quiet and…" she said, but as she spoke, he turned before she could finish. She grabbed him by the shoulder and spun him to get eye contact. "Hey, slow is steady, and steady is fast."

Wheeler nodded, and she freed him of her grip. There was a sudden cocky twerk of his head and a wired smirk. "I'm on it, Miss. Can we go now?"

He didn't wait for an answer, taking point and spearheading through the thick brush between the trees. She sighed, shaking her head at the sight, adjusting the sling of her rifle, and followed up center as Picket guarded their six.

Wheeler brought them to a set of railroad tracks that guided them the rest of the way to Whati. The steel tracks and timber ties held no uniformity of design. They lacked the visual symmetry that came from the layers of inspections and policies of the Old World systems but lacked none of the quality of a reliable rail system connecting Whati to the rest of Canada.

A wandering thought came to her, curious as to how expansive the railroads across Canada were.

Through the thick veil of the forest's trees, gray contrasted between the brown trunks and green leaves that hadn't fallen. The closer they got to that gray filler, the more the trees and brush cleared into an open field spotted with tree stumps. That gray sight came to full view in the form of a concrete wall, standing around seven feet high and encompassing the Whati outpost. Watchtowers were positioned at each corner of the short wall but were vacant of sentries, and nothing but silence came from the vacant sight.

Never a good sign, she mouthed, looking from tower to tower, another cold breeze rustling past them.

"Stick to the tracks." Picket spoke just loud enough to be heard, but not loud enough to be carried and projected by the wind.

She looked at the spaces between stumps. The ground wasn't full of grass and weeds and brush; the vegetation rooted out to just bare soil. The outer edges of the open perimeter were riddled in craters, some deeper than others, with splayed remains of charred flesh and limbs strewn about. The path of the craters formed a funnel shape to the tracks that led to a wooden gate set in a steel framework with the rusted metal forming an 'X' across the thick timber. Only, the gate was left open, not fully, but just enough for a few rows of people standing shoulder to shoulder to squeeze through.

They followed the tracks and passed the last bit of craters a few meters away from the rock bed that flanked the rails. Together, the three of them stacked at the door, Dakota and Wheeler peeking through the opening crack while Picket watched their six. Both pied the angle every way to see only more of a vacated settlement. She thought of the story of the Roanoke Colony, when a supply ship arrived from Europe only to find the place empty. A wooden post carved with the word "Croatoan" was the only clue, and the inhabitants had never been found.

She patted Wheeler's shoulder and inched forwards with a simple "I'll take point." As he nodded and shuffled behind her, the rocks on the tracks moved and crunched under their boots. It was a subtle and ignorable noise if things weren't so silent, but it now carried with the wind like a blow horn, a pencil drop to shout out their presence to anything inside.

It was the ulna bone in her left forearm that had an oblique fracture to it. Holding her rifle in the standard position didn't hurt too much, but it came with a certain dread if or when she pulled the trigger. She had anxiety about the pain of the force and recoil of a shot, pain that was situated on a countdown, an inevitable adversary.

She bit down the worry, focusing on each angle and every sector she scanned as they passed the wooden gate. Being the first one through, she broke to the left, her weapon at the high ready. They found nothing but an empty train yard and loading bay as they passed the gate. Well, not nothing. The smell of lead, iron, and blood warmed the air inside, instilling a nauseating spell and contrasting with the crisp air, drying her throat. The tracks, ties, and gravel were the first signs of the carnage; blood and tattered clothes were strung out, and the signs of slaughter continued up to a parked locomotive at the loading bay.

Picket and Wheeler followed up behind her, but the old man made a gagging noise and nearly dropped himself. There were three main principles to operate on: speed, surprise, and violence of action. If you lost one, you lost them all. They came to a standstill, and Dakota grimaced under her breath, eyes not leaving her twelve as Wheeler aided a now-vomiting Picket.

"Wheeler?"

"He's got this thing with blood."

That was a new one: mission adjustment when on target with a hemophobic. Her eyes were still scanning, ears tuned to the rapturing silence of Whati. "Alright, Picket. Keep your head down and eyes closed. Wheeler, guide him. On me, ready?"

A few seconds after the man's vomiting spell past, the two shuffled into position. They responded with a double "Ready."

She led them up the tracks, over a short flight of steps, and onto the loading bay, walking beside the locomotive. The machine was modified to a great extent, distinguishable from the trains she was used to seeing.

The entire train station was caked in blood and tatters of flesh. Shredded clothes and shoes were left in bloodied piles of red fabrics and soles. Rifles, shotguns, pistols, and other small arms were scattered over the crimson-painted bay, bent and broken. In some places, the blood pooled into puddles where the fate of the poor souls to have perished were sealed; their bodies would have been completely consumed and now inside the stomachs of monsters, dissolving in acid. They were reduced not to ash but to a more undesirable end. The thought of being eaten and digested always sparked a cold tremor up her back, one she was accustomed to taming. Her stomach churned at the sight and reality of it all, but nothing compared to Picket; his capacity to operate was hindered by his hemophobia.

The train looked to be operational, but there was no telling until they saw it for themselves. She climbed up the side path of the locomotive, Wheeler helping Picket along the way behind her. She opened the door, and Picket climbed into the conductor seat, eyes opening with a pale face.

"Either of you know how to operate this thing?" she asked.

"All Scout Captains and Leaders are required to." Picket raised his hand, index and thumb erect, the other fingers folded down. His voice croaked in an effort to maintain his composure. "We both can man it."

"Okay." She nodded, backing up to the door, feeling the cold breeze prick at the back of her neck. "Give this thing a full body inspection; see if you can get it up and running. We'll high-tail it back to Yellowknife."

"And you?" asked Wheeler.

"I'm gonna take a look around for any potential survivors or threats."

"By yer'self?"

"There's only three of us, and that train is our most essential asset. Your friend there needs help and protection if he can't go outside. That leaves two of us here, at a minimal, but with an unsecured sector around us." Dakota sighed, pinching her hand at her forehead. "Unless you got a better option."

Wheeler backed down, looking away.

"Minimal engagement only; don't shoot unless you need to. Capeesh?"

"Aye," Wheeler said, backing up to Picket. "It's a small outpost, but fur one person it can be large. Keep yer guard up, Miss."

Dakota nodded, holding a hand over her radio, turning the volume to its lowest setting. "Radio silence. One click to see if the other is okay. Two clicks to tell me to get back to the train and get the hell out of here."

Picket replied with a thumbs up, and the young man gave her a nod, tuning down the volume on his own. She climbed down from the train and around the front, facing the rest of the outpost. Above her, cable lines traveled from the train station deeper into the outpost, and she had a thought.

What would be a community today without some kind of intercom, or warning system?

The cable lines traveled deep into the outpost; the outer districts of Whati were a mashup of residential structures that looked more like slums. It was a patchwork of corrugated metal, wood, and tarps—anything that could create a barrier for shelter. Walls of stacked rocks formed barriers between the little plots of shacks; the sense of property ownership was still prevalent, even in the modest and humblest of structures. Some were destroyed and ruined, others missing a wall or a roof. The deeper into the outpost she went the more the structures became solid and permanent: remnants of the Old World informed her that Whati was a pre-existing community. Old houses and shacks of the original Whati now had busted windows and broken-down doors.

One such house was missing its front door and the frame where the deadlock would have been. Wood splintered and shattered where the three sections of hinges had previously been screwed into the frame, and the deadbolt locked across. On the front porch, ten lines were carved into the wood, ending in ten lines of blood, disappearing into the darkness within.

Flexing her hand and fingers, the entryway now looked like the mouth of a hungry giant—one now in a fatigued stupor after its meal, oblivious to her presence. It was a sleeping giant as she crept by in slow strides of silence.

Another house had its window busted open, and rows of shattered glass lined the frame like jagged teeth, dried in red. The bottom of the panels and house siding underneath drooled dried blood. Two bloodied handprints flanked both sides, a failed escape that risked blood and injury over dying. Those two handprints smeared back inwards in a long streak of being dragged inside, forever silenced in the dark.

The cable lines continued, passing more houses, more sights of grave endings suffered. What troubles and tribulations had these people survived after the death of the Old World, only to end up as food in the end? If the relative safety that was supposed to be the province of Northwest Territories could be compromised so easily, then, she wondered, in the end, how vulnerable was Alyeska?

The cable lines came to an end at an open area past the housing district. A slight elevation of Whati brought a view of the big lake the original community was built on. She felt a tremor rise to her knees; her breath started to shake as she stared out at the body of water before her. But her wits were still about her, suppressing the panic sparking up her back before it could reach her thoughts.

A long time ago, she'd painted it as beautiful; the rays of sun sparkled over the tamed waters. But inside, the waters were anything but tamed, housing the demons lurking within and the troubled thoughts that hammered against her non-stop. Looking away from the wide-open waters was enough of a remedy, and she trained her eyes back up to the wires. They came to an end at the center of the community, at what she thought would constitute city hall.

Fencing had been set up around it, the kind of fencing used as quick barriers. It was a vain attempt to hold the position from which the cable lines originated. Several sections of the fencing lay toppled over. The pavement between the chain-link fence and the building looked like people had scattered confetti of brass cartridges all around that now sparkled in the rays of sunlight breaking through an opening in the overcast sky.

A wide building with stairs led up to a set of double doors. The right flank of the steps protruded outwards to a wider section of the structure, just a few steps short of being flush with the base of the stairs. Three windows were set about that right side, the bottom panels barred by boards of wood. Sandbags poked up from the bottom panels, and the barrels of three machine guns settled in the large nest of sandbags from within.

To the left of the stairs was situated the same, though the boards had been ripped off and the twisted barrels of the machine guns laid outside the breach in the perimeter. The roof was decked out in solar panels along with another compromised machine gun nest. Blood streaks trailed down the windows and roofing where the gunnery team met their demise. The blood streaked down around the three windows as if the structure was mourning in red tears for its loss.

Stepping over and around one of the many breaches in the fence, the soft clattering of brass casings crunched between her boots and asphalt. Getting her other foot to the others side of the barrier, her rifle was at a low ready as she listened for any disturbance in Whati's graveyard ambiance.

Even in her slow, careful step placement, the brass casings rattling against the concrete from each step taken, further disturbing the silence. It was a consistent rhythm of discord that any nearby predator would know not to ignore. Yet still, with each pause and low ready waiting she gave, she heard only silence in response.

Whati was too deep in its lethargic stupor to wake up for seconds. Letting out her held breath, Dakota crept to the stairs, her boots constantly stepping on and skittering the hollow brass cylinders of spent bullets. That soft chorus of high-pitched, clinking metal made her teeth clench together, cursing them.

Giving pause here and there, her heart hammered behind her chest; she could count the pulses at her carotid arteries when her feet finally came to the first of the wooden steps. They were due for replacing; the screws needed tightening, with every step up came a painful wail from the wood and screws.

She reached the door that had been barricaded; there was just enough space to squeeze in as if something had clawed a hole through and shoved the barricade aside. It was barely enough for an adult in full kit to fit through. She ducked and weaved in and around the obstruction, and the smell of crimson putrefaction flooded her nostrils from her inhale. The rotten iron smell contaminated her lungs and sent her into a fit of coughing. Once inside, she stood up, raising her head a bit too soon and striking her head on wood, forcing out a "dammit" through gritted teeth. Lowering her head, she continued.

The inside was dim; ambient light from the veiled sun blared through the boards of wood in horizontal rays of gray illumination. Specks of dust floated like contaminants in water over the brown dried blood waxing the floors. Some spots were not fully dried, puddles of grime thickening in a sticky coat. Rags of tattered clothes clung to the floor. From inside the neckline of her shirt, she pulled up her neck gaiter, raising it over her mouth and nose to filter out the smell with her breath. It did little to filter out the smell, but it made an improvement all the same, and she'd take what she could get. Set in a diagonal position from the entrance, a door rested, labeled 'Communication Console.'

Winner, winner, chicken dinner.

The inside was empty of threats, and after entering the console room and finding it empty, she closed the door and wedged a chair up under the handle. Ambient gray light flooded this room as well, with boarded windows set before the console controls. She let out a sigh, relieved when finding that the place still held power, only at the cost of the microphone being busted.

She cursed the broken mic, looking around the room for a replacement. She found nothing, save for a Morse Cod Dial inside the last drawer she checked. The little device was covered in bloodied fingerprints and came complete with a cord that connected to a switchboard. The last receiver on the dial was connected to being to Edzo Outpost. Three other plugs offered her the option to attempt communication with Yellowknife, Edzo, Gameti, and Wekweèti.

Her bun had come fully undone, and her hair was falling around her face and over her eyes, blocking her sight. Sighing, cursing, and grunting, she pulled her hair back into a half-up ponytail with the half-down held back and out of her face behind her ears. Some strands of bangs managed to evade her efforts and dangled over her eyes in clumped, sweaty strands.

She blew one such strand away from her nose where the hair itched. Rubbing the sensation away with her sleeve, her other hand grabbed a piece of paper detailing communication history: check-ins, responses, and requests, etcetera listed. She scrolled down to the very last timestamp, reading: "0100 Whati Outpost to Yellowknife, hourly check-in. All seems secured."

Dakota grabbed a wire and removed it from its place on the switchboard labeled "Yellowknife," and she set the wire into "Whati Emergency Alert." She sat down on a chair with the Morse Code dial under her index finger. Taking a moment to piece the series of taps together in her head, she then wrote out the taps and spaces with her left hand on the back of the communication history sheet. She cackled, briefly, thinking of how quicker Phil would have been at Morse Code; he wouldn't have even needed to write it out first.

With her message written out for quick reference, she dialed first, ensuring comms were still functional. Sending a series of taps and spaces out, she heard the message being relayed on the intercom system outside. Satisfied, she continued, short and simple: "Any Survivors to Train Station."

Her radio went off, Wheeler's voice coming in soft and level: "Dakota, you got your ears on? Over."

"Affirmative. I thought I said radio silence? Over." Her right index finger hovered over the dial, ready to repeat the message. The heel of her foot bounced up and down in a restless motion, with her toes pinned to the floor. Taking a glance up at the boarded windows before her, through the slivers of view between the centermost boards, she saw the graveyard that Whati had become. All was silent and still; there were no signs of life.

"Is that you operating the emergency broadcast? Over."

"I am. Over."

"I think whatever attacked this place is still here; we're picking up hoots and whistles over by the station. Picket says the locomotive is functional, just needs a little TLC before we can get it operational. Over."

"Whatever he needs to do, just watch his back and yours. I'm still trying to contact any survivors. Over."

"Copy that. Standing by, Miss. Over 'n out."

She tightened her grip on the dial. *Please, at least one person.* She begged and hoped, re-tapping her message, praying that whomever was still breathing would hear her orders. A hoot, like an owl, came in through the busted glass in front of the console. A spike of goosebumps ascended the center of her back.

C'mon, come on.

A whistle came in response from somewhere deeper in the outpost. Again, there was a hoot nearby, followed by another whistle that was further away. She then understood that the zombies never left and now were searching for the source of the noise disturbing their lethargic rest. Even worse, Dakota understood the hoots and whistles were the zombies communicating. They could coordinate with one another!

Immediately, she dropped the dial and disconnected it from the switchboard. She grabbed her radio, her thumb slamming the PTT button as she did so. Yet as she was about to speak, a hoot came from outside, right above her window. They had found the source. Above her, the rhythm of something moving on all fours came from above the old wooden roof and shingles in slow, steady *thumps*. Dust knocked loose, snowing over her and filling her nostrils and throat, threatening the silence with a sneeze or a cough. She climbed down underneath the console, waiting.

There had been no warning, and a cough-sneeze ruptured forth, disturbing more of the silence. She tried to muffle it, covering her face with the fold of her elbow. An itchy scratch remained in her throat, demanding relief but receiving none as she held it all in. Silent as a mouse, she turned her radio down, trusting Wheeler to make the best decision he could in her radio silence.

She stowed the radio back in her pouch before something heavy fell on the roof, then another, in a sequence of steps. Something was moving. Puffs of dust fell, giving a trail to the path of the movement above, towards the building's entrance outside her room. The thing huffed and the silent thudding of bare feet landed on the cement outside. The pacing picked up, footfalls slapping against the hard floor at a rapid pace going away but not fading out.

Her heart sunk upon the sound of a scream waking up the whole settlement. At first, she heard her baby girl screaming, her baby Sara crying out for help from the monsters swarming her. Somewhere nearby, there was a child—a survivor. Dakota pulled herself out from under the console and looked out the boards covering the shattered glass panel, out over Whati.

Movements between some of the shacks and housing caught her eye, too fast to register any detail other than a pack of anthropomorphic beings in full sprint.

The movement on the roof above her shifted, an aggressive shuffling of feet turning a one-eighty. Dakota removed her radio, turned the volume up, and keyed the PTT button: "Wheeler, a little girl is running for her life. I'm trapped and can't move. Near the Whati communication console. Can you assist? Over."

More dust fell over her, some getting into her eyes. She blinked at the invasive feeling, an irritating itch. The presence moving about on the roof let out a loud howl. Dakota rubbed her irritated eye until the itch stopped as the footfalls on the roof charged right above the windows and stopped.

"Copy that, Miss. I'm on it," Wheeler replied.

Whistling came soon after from above the window.

Immediately following, there was a ruckus at the front entrance as the failed barricade and breached windows with the machine gun nest suffered more bombardment of flesh. It was a rough, feral pursuit of food: bloodhounds following the scent she left behind. Outside, she could hear the already failed breaches break even more and several pairs of bare feet slapping against the wooden floor on the other side of the door. A second later, the knob turned, and she readied her rifle as the door cracked open, stopped by the chair wedged under the handle. Hoping her silence would be enough to make them lose interest, another childish scream cried from the outside, carving into her soul, and she could feel her feet turning towards the door. She didn't want to wait.

There was one thing she could offer the little girl, and she pulled the trigger. Her ears rang, and the force of the recoil felt like the shattering of bones in her left arm. The bullet pierced through the crack, and something yelped and cried from behind it. The sound of the thirty-caliber had become an epicenter of noise, waking the whole outpost.

The reprieve at the door was short-lived; bodies now smashed and bashed against it from the other side, the wooden barrier arching inwards in a pronounced bulge, inches away from splintering and breaking. Faint glimpses of the monsters on the other side revealed two to three hurling their whole forms into the wooden obstruction while one retained the added pressure to it. Teamwork made the dream work.

Immediately, Dakota jump-climbed onto the console, grunting at the added stress to her broken arm. Situating herself into the angle she needed, she held onto a ledge above the windows and proceeded to ram her boots into the boards. There were hard, steady kicks in sync with the barrage of smashing flesh against the door behind her. She could hear the *cracking* of wood before her, the boards in front starting to free themselves from the screws bearing them in place.

Behind her, the door hinges moaned in a metallic warning for her to hurry up. The door frame succumbed to the endless volley of tackles. The boards over the window continued to bend and break at a lesser rate.

"Come. On. You. Piece. Of..." She gritted with each thrust of her boot.

One board busted and broke, falling free outside. Her right hand grabbed ahold of the next board above. She hurled herself out the window as if on monkey bars, right on cue with the sound of the door breaking open and the rapid scraping of claws against the old wooden floor. She could feel the claws reaching out after her but falling short of her neck and face. Then, the sling of her rifle stopped, freed from her arm but tangled around her neck.

Something popped as she hung by the strap, coming to a jerking stop, her feet kicking against the building's side as she looked up. Clammy, pale hands and fingers pried at her weapon sling, stock, and barrel, pulling her back up like a fish on a hook. Her own hands wedged between the sling and the skin of her neck, offering just enough room for shallow breaths to sustain her. The sound of claws scraping disappeared as the horde ran around to the outside. Hound dogs collecting their game.

The other zombies didn't reach out after her like mindless wraiths or draugrs but worked on the other boards to the windows left and right. All were striving to be the first one over that finish line—to claim their kill and food. Dakota let out a cry as she removed a hand from between the sling and her neck, now wheezing in a desperate struggle for breath. Her head was swelling from the lack of air, and her freed hand patted against her chest until her fingers located the cold, wooden handle of her trench knife. Faster than her thoughts could run, her fingers unclipped the safety strap and yanked out the blade, raising it to cut away the strap choking her.

There came a snap and the motion of the sling grinding against her neck, leaving behind a burning sensation as the strap unwound itself. She fell several feet, landing in a single, hard bounce that sent the blade of her knife against the cap of her right knee. It was similar to how it felt cutting through thick leather as her knife slit through fabric, flesh, and the bone of her kneecap. At first, it felt numb; then, there was a burning heat blazing behind the rythm of the cut before the pain and blood came. Her cry screeched out in a croaking rasp at the pain came at her in full force.

An uncontrollable shake shot up her spine as if a blackboard was being scratched. It was "Croatoan" carved into her bones in a single linear gash. Dakota's chest flared, swelling and pausing from her own will of repression. Adrenaline spurring her forwards, her training drilled into instinct as she acted in absence of conscious thought. She rolled over, pushed up with her good arm, got her good leg under her, and hopped up to her feet. The pressure on her fresh, bleeding knee was like a two-hundred-pound weight had thrown on her. The pressure across her clavicle suddenly became minuscule from the trauma to her knee.

The zombies were already out the front door, charging at her. One zombie was already closing in on her. The safety strap to her pistol was unclipped, and she yanked out her .45 caliber, placing three rounds center mass in the thing's chest. The zombie went from full Olympic sprinter to a twitching contortionist, shriveling on the ground and landing face-down at her feet. Dakota took one limping step back and placed a round in the back of the thing's skull.

She didn't know what to think after the .45 round split open the cranial plate of bone at the back of the thing's head. She was speechless at the sight of the zombie pushing himself back up and reaching for her leg. She limped back several steps, the rest of the pack now leaving the building's entrance and coming at her left flank. The zombie before her now stood in a disoriented wobble like a drunken stupor.

Fuck this. She shook her head, turning heel, and took off in a limping sprint.

Chapter Five – Tooth and Nail

Every pant for breath stabbed at her side, the cold air drying her throat and chilling her lungs. The only warmth she felt was the blood leaking out her knee and down her leg. The cut felt like a cotton shirt being ripped open, little by little, with each forced bend from her running. Sweat clung to her skin, gripping at her clothes, chilling her on the outside against the cold air.

One of the "Olympians" as she dubbed them because of how they ran had caught up to her. The monster dove at her, going for her legs. She had enough warning to leap in her next step with her left leg. Gaining enough air and distance, she evaded the tackle, landing on her right leg. The pressure folded her knee as she stumbled. Her arms caught against a street pole, keeping her sprint in full gear.

Dead ahead was a red brick-and-mortar building that spanned three floors, its front door still attached and left open. She went for it, taking the front steps two at a time, the door yielded no resistance upon her impact. There was a splintered gash in the door where the deadbolt should have been. She cursed, slamming it shut, and got bare glimpses of at least four dozen Olympians five yards away and closing in.

A wooden wedge for a door jamb lay nearby, and she kicked it over to the front door and guided it into place, ramming it home at the base of the door. Her boots made moist sounds; each step came with a familiar stickiness to it, and her spine shivered in an unzipping tremor of goosebumps at the base of her skull. The door opened a few inches, the jamb catching and holding it shut. Barrages of flesh came from the other side as before.

The putrefaction stung at her eyes like salt, and her nostrils wretched from the foul stench; she paced down a narrow corridor offset by a flight of stairs to her right. She could hear the monsters now flanking the building, coming to a metallic rattling, the kind belonging to a chain-link fence.

Flashlight in hand, she moved, and the white light splashed a swaying circle moving and swaying in tune with her steps and breathing. It illuminated the walls smeared in bloodied handprints. It looked like the walls were sweating bead of read sweat. She turned a corner where there lay the upper half body of a man, mostly eaten, save for his left arm and chest. Ribs, spine, and some organs stuck out from his missing half. Her torch shone on his left hand, where there glittered the metal of an AK 74. She holstered her pistol and got down to her good knee in a pained effort.

"I'm sorry," Dakota said, relieving the corpse of the weapon and bandolier around his chest. There were only two magazines found among the pouches. She removed the AK's magazine, finding it half-full, and there was one round still in the chamber. She replaced it with a full magazine, thirty rounds plus the one hot'n ready.

She moved with the AK at the high ready, her flashlight pinned between her hand and barrel; her broken ulna was begging for relief. She scanned for threats, navigating through the tomb of brick and mortar. Passing bodies and limbs, her mask over her face filtered the smell. The moaning and creaking of the wood made silence hard with each step.

The front door was never given rest from the bombardment; there was a continual presence of battering. The wedge held, but the hinges would give in due time, so she hastened her progress, abandoning stealth for speed and coming to another corridor. In the back half of the inside, the bloodied gore wasn't so present. The sound she had been dreading finally arrived—the front door shattering and smashing open, the square piece of wood falling flat in a splashing impact at the front.

The zombies sought her out like bloodhounds, and she turned a one-eighty, firing round after round into the monsters, bottlenecking the corridor behind her. Flashes of gunfire illuminated the mass body of undead cannibals glaring at her in lustful hunger. They climbed over one another, clawing at the walls and the ones who suffered her barrage of gunfire. Red and pink sprayed out from the front of the column: headshots made easy.

She fired until her back thumped against a surface, and her heart fell in her chest, thinking it to be a wall. The obstruction gave in an inward swing, and she nearly tripped backwards on her heels but caught herself, emptying her magazine at the nearest Olympian. Then, she slammed the door shut. There was a deadbolt at chest height, and she charged the bolt before the door pounded and bent inwards.

The room was adjoined, and another door was adjacent to the one she entered, from which a single zombie emerged. He seemed less feral than the others, with a wider build, as he entered the room. He closed the door behind him and charged the bolt, and there was a deep quality to his eyes that glowed in the darkness, contrasting with his pupils focused on her.

Dakota ejected her empty magazine, charged her last fresh one, and racked a fresh round into the chamber. She didn't have time to fire before the large zombie picked her up and hurled her against the wall. Back and head striking the hardwood, her breath cut short and her thoughts blurred. All but one thought had been robbed, just one simple thought: *Get that weapon up and running!*

As fast as she had been shoved into the wall, she was pulled from it. Her boots left the floor, and gravity became non-existent as she was flipped upside down. The roof was all she could see before her back came pummeling down against the floor.

The zombie dropped at her, yanking her legs apart as she kicked, hands fighting to get her rifle out from underneath the arch in her back where it had landed. His salivating maws closed in at her throat with gaping teeth, and she cried out in a dried wheeze. Her right leg found purchase between her and the monster, getting her bleeding knee pressed against his chest and pushing him back. Her right hand found her pistol's grip, yanking it out, and she emptied five rounds center mass.

It jerked as if shot by arrows, coming to a rigid enough stop for Dakota to aim down her sights at his face. She pulled the trigger three times.

The monster moved at the last second, suffering only one bullet that splattered his left eye, ending in a resounding crack of the socket behind it. He dropped to his knees with a double *thunk* and face planted on the floor with a fleshy splat, between her knees.

Dakota gasped; the air had been knocked clear from her lungs, leaving her with short, hollow breaths that came and went in rapid succession as she holstered her pistol. She got her primary back up and steadied up to her feet. Her heart fell in her chest from the *cracking* at the door where a jagged horizontal rift widened from the unending bombardment. The windows in the room all had iron bars on the outside, save for one where the bars bent and twisted outwards. The glass shattered and blood trails followed down the wall from the window seal and over to the room where the big one came from.

Limping over, she used her AK's barrel to clear out the remaining glass shards. A quick, one-second look outside told her the chain-link fencing at the sides hadn't yet been breached. She got her bad leg out first when two large hands clamped at her shoulders. She leaned forwards and jolted her head back like a battering ram, charging the back end of her skull into the assailant's chest, feeling the sternum between his breasts. She was replied to with an "OOMPH," the arms holding her with that familiar rigor mortis grip of wraiths and draugrs. She was yanked back in, and the monster spun her around to face him, the One-Eyed Bastard.

She jabbed his throat with the barrel of her AK, getting his hands off her to hold his throat. Shuffling back and choking, a fit of rage burned from his red eye. The door barely held together, that vertical crack now a splintering hole. She pulled the trigger, but the beast was still within arm's reach, swiping the barrel as a bullet shot off to the side.

She didn't have time to respond; the one-eyed Olympian raised his leg, and she felt his foot thrust against her chest between her breasts. The bottom window seal met the center of her thighs, and her left arm prevented her from falling backwards. Her whole clavicle pulsed with the back of her head. Staggered, she could only watch without time to dodge as the brute shoved her chest with both hands, throwing her outside.

She tumbled out backwards, shards of glass digging out a line of cuts across her mid-back. With a hard bounce on the dirt, she landed. A dry wheeze puffed out her mouth; she was struggling to breathe as she looked up. Pressing her elbows to the dirt, her vision blurred with a ringing to her ears as she pushed herself up.

The only singular thought she could hold to was to get up and move. Crawling over to a tree stump, she did just that. Her knees and legs shook, a ringing in her ears fading in and out with the faint thuds coming her way. Looking back to the window, she saw the blurred image of the large zombie closing the distance. She turned and bolted as fast as she could manage.

The overcast sky had deepened into a dismal array of clouds, and the smell of rain was in the air, cold and refreshing with a chilling breeze that felt like autumn's waking breath. Her hair clumped in thick strands, from which beads of sweat traveled down her face and neck. The cold short breaths of air she managed to take in contrasted with the heat of her lungs flaring behind her chest. Her core ached, and the constant effort of trying to catch her breath was taxing; it occupied too much of her mental space.

Behind her, the Olympians had caught up; the chain-link fencing was now breached, flanking the brick building and chasing after her. Yet not one of them would pass up the big one, the Alpha of their numbers. Never once did he let them swarm her but kept at a slower pace, a cat playing with his food. Never had she met a zombie with intellect or a personality—*and this sucker has both.* She turned a corner around an old bed and breakfast turned ration center, when Wheeler's voice broke over her radio.

"Dakota, we have the girl. She's safe inside the locomotive. Found a truck and are coming to you. What's yer location?"

Thank God! She cried out. *Just a little longer.*

Between her and the train station, an old warn building rested, left rotting and decaying even by the former people of Whati. She entered the side door, and inside the building was little more than a long corridor that spanned the entire length. Windows stood at waist height to the right, and a series of connected rooms stood to the left.

She swung the door but didn't have time to close it before one of the monsters charged in. Slamming the door open, the force of the battery hurled Dakota down on her back, AK up and running.

She fired two rounds into the monster but came up short as he picked her up and slammed her back down, up once more, and down again. He was like a fisherman smacking his game against a rock to kill it or knock it out. She felt something warm trickle down the back of her head. The barrel of her rifle was stuck between their bodies as he went in for a third pounding into the floor.

Her lungs couldn't keep up; breathing was now a commodity. Dakota gritted her teeth, set her tongue flat against the bottom of her mouth, nostrils flaring, and pulled the trigger. Ten rounds were let loose, and bullets zipped out from her rifle, going in random directions down their collective lower halves.

The monster cried out, the warm thickness of blood trickling down over her right leg, seeping into the fabric of her pant legs and the open gash on her knee. The monster let go of her, backing up to his leg, the blood pulsing out from a damaged artery. She backpedaled, pushing her boots against the floor, gaining two feet distance out of arm's reach. She took the opportunity and placed two more rounds into its chest. The Olympian staggered back, flinching more than anything, and two more of the zombies reached the door, catching their shot-up friend and tossing him aside before diving after her.

The first one missed Dakota as she put more distance between her and them. The second one dove further, landing at her feet, his hands clenched around her right leg, not waiting to sink its teeth into her calf. She cried out in pain. That first one, who fell just short of her legs, regained his composure and fell on top of her, wrestling for her weapon. Seconds felt like minutes as the serrated teeth dug into her leg, pulling at her muscle tissue. She cried out in an incoherent babble of curses, head-butting the zombie on top of her. She received only a second's worth of her weapon freed from his grasp.

Her calf felt like a chunk was being ripped out, and she aimed and fired four rounds center mass, dropping the third one to the floor. That first one, now recovering from his staggering and flinching, was limping towards her, his blood still pulsing out his leg. She aimed her weapon point blank at the zombie biting into her leg, and four rounds later, he was dead. She snapped her barrel over to the limping zombie and placed a single round between his eyes. His head snapped back as he fell dead, and she emptied her remaining bullets into his chest for good measure.

With shaking legs and hands, she struggled to get her back to her feet, using the wall to help her limp over into the nearest room. Dropping her AK by its sling and yanking out her pistol, she aimed out the door now clogged with the Olympians, backing up inside until she could slam the door shut and charge the deadbolt. Holstering her pistol, she emptied the spent magazine and loaded the half-full one.

The door barely lasted a second, coming just a breath away from ramming into her face as the Alpha thrashed in. She pulled back the action, loading a round into the chamber before his hands again grabbed her. One was over her weapon, and the other pulled her hair. But he didn't bite her; instead, he dragged her with him as he stomped to a single window and threw her face-first through the old glass panel. Time slowed, and the nicks, scrapes, and cuts from the glass registered at the same time she landed in a coughing fit on the dirt below. Blood traveled down her cheeks and lips, and there was a pause between already shallow and wheezing breaths. Her broken arm felt numb; she was surprised it hadn't fallen off.

Dry croaks of desperate inhales clawed at her throat, her limbs moving in a crawl away from the structure. Her vision blurred at her peripheries, the only clear sight being a thicket ahead of her. The trees were spaced out, traveling down a sloping drop ten meters from her. Behind her, she heard the Alpha's feet land outside the window, and she rolled over and aimed her rifle at his legs, the only target she had time to zero in on. She got five rounds out at the thinner targets; they moved in aggressive strides at her. Four missed their mark, and the fifth splattered at the ankle, obliterating the bulge of bone there.

The Alpha closed the distance before a sixth round could be issued. His balance was thrown off, but he was undeterred as he grabbed her by the hair and pulled her up to her feet; her half-up ponytail came undone as clumped slivers of sweaty hair dangled at the sides of her vision. She felt a tree against her back, her head pulled to the side, and the monster's fangs dripped in saliva. The cat, now done playing with his food, had foul breath that seeped into her pores.

Dakota grimaced, reaching for her pistol. The angle she was pinned at made it just out of reach. Olympians closed in around her and the Alpha but didn't join in; they were like hungry wolves waiting for their leader to get his fill first. Stars filled her vision, and she built up enough umph, taking a fool's chance. She leaned into his bite, his teeth breaking through flesh, and he missed her jugular and instead bit into where her neck met her collarbone. Fangs ripped through skin and broke the scabbing over the gash from the Jackle over her left clavicle.

An empty cry issued forth as she arched her back, freed the tree, and pressed one foot against it. Wrapping both her arms around the Alpha, she kicked off from the tree. The monster's ankle gave, his balance compromised, and both went tumbling down the hill.

The fall freed her of the Alpha, separating from him down the hill as momentum and gravity took them into two different paths of rolling. Dakota barred her right arm diagonally over her face, instinct prompting her to keep her broken left pressed against her chest. She raised her legs into as much of a fetal position as she could offer, creating a roll cage with her limbs.

They smashed into trees, broke against rocks, and at some point, Dakota's left side struck what felt like a stone. A boney *crack* came at her midriff, and she rolled over the rock and continued downwards. She felt the trunks of small trees in the thicket smack and prickle her body. Something managed to get through the gap of her roll cage and smack her ear, flaring it in a pulsing irritation that kept her awake in a fresh wave of adrenaline. But even her body couldn't produce as much as normal, the spike in alertness quickly fading.

Her tumble slowed at the base of the hill, her momentum losing energy as she came to a motionless stop. Arms spread, she lay on her back. The struggle to breathe took up all her mental space now; all systems were committed to the most essential that was now failing. Dakota's vision of the cloudy sky above was a blurry one that spun to the left and out of her sight, then rewound for another spin. The urge to vomit came strong upon her, the acidic taste in her throat.

She sensed movement. She could hear it now, halfway down the hill, the mass of monsters not giving up the chase. They were persistent buggers. Then, closer to her, was more movement. It sounded like a dog shaking himself off from a bath with grumbled snarls and growls. She picked up the sound of gradual limping over the bed of rocks and the laboring of breaths. She tilted her head, looking down over her chest rig and bandolier, the tips of her boots erected at the sky. The Alpha glared at her with his right eye, limping on his shattered ankle as red crimson pulsed out through the many bullet holes, his body covered in scrapes and bruises.

Her arm fumbled, forcing whatever she had left in her to roll over onto her belly, and a spurt of vomit shot out, nearly choking her. She had to swallow it back down to breathe. She tried to push herself up, but it cost too much. Settling on sitting up against a stone where she could see clearly out of one eye, the Alpha drew closer, and his horde neared the base of the hill.

Using her right arm and the stone, she climbed to her feet, her left arm against her breasts. Standing felt foreign, and her knees shook like Jell-o; the stone was like a walker keeping her standing. Her right hand moved to the empty pistol holster on her right thigh; it wasn't there, it was lost somewhere on that hill.

Rolling her eyes, she glared at the monster who was now holding his side. The deep red of his right iris seemed to pulse, beating bloodlust at her.

"You started it, fucker," she mumbled through a faint wheeze.

The Alpha paused, and his demeanor changed into something that seemed to resemble a slight grin. It was an odd and disturbing look that made her wish he would instead glare again—a look that said: "challenge accepted."

She found her trench knife still secured in its sheath, and she removed it and wielded it in her right hand as the Alpha came into arm's reach. She came at him with a sharp jab, bringing the tip of her blade to the Alpha's throat, giving all her reserves of strength into this last attack. The blade carved through the skin like rubber and dug down until it stopped at the bone of his spine. She yanked the blade out, now dripping red. The Alpha limped back, flinching from his now-sudden struggle to breathe, hands clenched around his throat. She came back with another jab at his temple, until he caught her blade midair and charged his elbow into her sternum. Her lungs seemed like they were both swelling and withering, reduced to raisins inside her chest; she couldn't breathe.

The beast grabbed a wad of her shirt, vest, and bra strap in one hand and the other he placed around her belt. He heaved her clear into the air above his head in an arc of movement, throwing her down upon the ground. Puffs of dirt went airborne around her, mimicking the outline of her splayed self.

The last bit of oxygen in her body was depleted into a thin wisp of warm air that was swallowed by the cold chill, without more to renew. She was fading; her vision blurred, and all was going numb. The cold of the outside was no longer a present chill. She was done, staring up at the deep red eye of the monster, his left eye dripping crimson over her face.

The last bit of her energy she used to keep her knife clenched in her fist, but she was unable to swing or jab with it. She just held onto that blade as all seemed to come to a standstill. Sleep gripped at her like the pulling down of a window sheet. Disturbed only by a single rifle report, a bullet *snapped* through the air above her. The side of the Alpha's face splattered upon impact: more of his blood over her. The monster took a step back, dazed as though in a drunken stupor, the bullet making contact with good effect.

Her vision blurred in and out, like in micro-naps of sleep. She was missing a few seconds here and there, seeing real-time in a slideshow of events without the in-between. A truck rammed into the monster, throwing him a yard back. Wheeler was pulling her up into the bed, and the world rushed by them as the horde caught up, chasing them.

Her sternum was already broken, making it easier for Wheeler to pump air back into her lungs. He wasn't sure if her condition qualified for CPR, but she wasn't breathing, and her face was paling. There wasn't much response from the woman. Vivid flashbacks of the day he first saw her two years ago came to the fore of his thoughts. Beaten to hell and back. He pressed his hands over her chest, lacing his fingers and giving her chest compressions.

He had never given CPR before, though Liam and Ethan of 'Danger' had made it a requirement for all soldiers of the Canadian Confederacy. He recalled the steps as he leaned upwards, his shoulders directly over his hands. His balance was hard to keep with the quick, bumpy ride and frequent sharp turns Picket took to evade the horde. Their roars were a constant reminder of death just two seconds away from a bad decision or a drop in speed.

Twenty or thirty compressions? I can't remember!

He started anyways, getting to twenty and tilting her head back with her chin. Pinching her nose as he puffed air into her mouth, he prayed air was being sent to her lungs. He waited for the breath to dispel, and her chest fell. Picket took a hard turn, forcing him to brace himself, feeling the rubber grind over the rocks of the railroads.

Bouncing and jerking without hope of a straight even line of travel, he gave her bloodied lips another breath and continued with the chest compressions.

He gave her another twenty, hearing an idle mumble leave her lungs—wheezy at first, hard to hear, as he pressed his ear to her lips, asking her to repeat.

"It's tirty." She barely uttered, breath pausing and not coming back.

He continued his compressions up to thirty, followed by another two breaths. Rinse and repeat, until finally, her shallow breath returned without pause. It was a slow and gradual rate, and some color returned to her paling features, eyes fluttering.

She sat up in the bed, Wheeler bracing her for another sharp turn from Picket. The truck's shock system did not agree with the bumps and jerks of the terrain. The woman's eyes started to close again.

"Hey, hey," Wheeler shouted at her, her eyes half-open.

She held up a hand to wave him off, "I'm still awake." Her voice was calm, the kind of calm that came from a place of physical weakness.

Taking in seven seconds of breath, holding, and releasing them for eight, she wasn't all there. She was dazed and looked like someone sick with pneumonia, completely disoriented.

The back window of the cab slid open before Picket warned them of another sharp turn. Wheeler covered Dakota with his body, bracing her and himself before the turn nearly smacked her head against the side of the bed. She kept her left arm to her chest, and her breathing continued as he gently released her from his brace. Either too hurt to express any emotions, or just calm enough, she looked at him, offering a weak smile, and patted his knee. It was a "Thanks."

"We got problems!" Picket shouted.

"Dammit, can we not just have good news?" Wheeler shouted, removing his belt and wrapping it over her right knee. The pant leg was torn open and soaked in blood. He pulled the belt tight at her mid-thigh. The force of it winded her and she croaked a rasped grunt. "Sorry," he offered and secured the belt in place, but he wasn't, really. The fact that she could respond to the pain was a good sign.

The truck came to a hard stop, and there was not enough time for Wheeler to brace the two of them as they both smacked against the back of the cab's windows. The truck groaned and wailed; Wheeler recognized the sound of low-power steering fluid wailing from the front. Picket brought the whole vehicle to a ninety-degree turn, losing the much-needed speed and giving them a view of their way out of Whati. It was completely blocked by more of the monsters flooding in from the open doors of the train station.

That's a big problem!

Picket had them driving back into Whati, the two hordes joining into one massive body of monsters in hot pursuit. Grabbing an AR-10 from the open rear cab window, Wheeler set the weapon into Dakota's hands, giving her arm a soft pat: "Hang in there, we're gonna make it out of this."

He looked back at the train station disappearing around the corner to a supply structure; the locomotive disappeared from view. In the last bit of visual, he saw no zombies swarming it, the doors still looked closed, and he silently prayed that the girl was still hidden, tucked away, and safe inside.

Picket made another sharp turn, hitting the main street of the outpost. Movement meant staying alive, but they were running out of room.

Chapter Six – Final Protective Fire

The wind blew her hair to and fro, strands poking at her eyes, blocking her vision as she held onto the sides of the truck bed. The Ford took another hard turn, sliding her and Wheeler around like pinballs, and she shoved the arch of her boot against the side of the bed wall to catch herself from sliding. Over the tailgate, the Olympians flooded the roads behind them, their heads, necks, and shoulders vertical over their hips, in full sprint.

A loud *POP* shot a ringing sound to her ears, a disorientating wave of a concussion from the audible force released in one deafening boom, followed by another. Picket was shouting something that only registered in an indiscernible call for attention. She leaned over the side of the truck to look at their direction of travel; their speed and trajectory slowed from the flat tires.

She looked ahead, given no chance to brace for the abrupt stop of the truck; the tires locked into a skid over the dirt road, and her head smacked the cab rear window. She collapsed to her right side, and blood ran down the left side of her face, leaving streaks of warmth down her temple and cheek.

With one hand, she grabbed onto the side of the bed, then lifted her boot, climbing up over the side and rolling over. Her right hand held a tight grip on the side as she swung down in a pendulum motion. Her boots ground across the gravel, hand still holding on before the angle forced her thumb's release, and she fell flat on her rear.

Wheeler was at her side before she could get back up, his hands pulling her to her feet, both staring at the horde. She turned around, seeing the cause of their sudden stop; they were cornered against the lake with no road or path left for the truck to squeeze through. It was the proverbial end of the line.

The grill of their truck came to a stop the side inches from a flatbed truck blocking their way. Upon the flatbed of the truck were piles of sandbags in the form of a gunnery nest, held in place by metal bars; two gun barrels rested over the edge and her eyes widened with hope.

That could work. She prayed the weapon systems were still functional.

Wheeler released her, hands held out in case she fell. But she had enough in her to keep a steady stance for the five feet between her and the technical's flatbed. At least, she had enough to wobble in a labor of limping, getting one boot onto the flat front tire of their truck, freeing her hands upwards. The stretching sent scores of tightening pains across her abdomen and chest. Hands clenched around the metal frame of the sandbags, she pulled up and rolled over the edge into the mobile nest.

She heard a door slam shut from their previous truck before Wheeler came jumping over into the nest in just a fraction of the time and effort it took her. Picket ran over to the driver's door of the flatbed. The engine cranked and rolled but with no commitment to finish.

Using the sandbags, she climbed up to her feet and looked out at the vast open lake behind them; they were separated by a mere five yards and a wall of large stones and mortar. She could feel the panic settling over her, a small spur of adrenaline from an already depleted tank keeping her eyes open. She turned from the lake, settling behind one of the two weapons, the sight of the rock barrier forming something of a mental barricade between herself and that panic.

When her hands clamped around the control grips of the weapon, she felt centered; a calming focus came over her when she looked down at the weapon system. She was unable to hold back a cruel grin when she saw the Mark 19 Automatic Grenade Launcher.

There was a tactical plan known as Final Protective Fire, prearranged for military units in danger of being overrun. It meant directing all lines of fire at the enemy forces to impede their movement. Throwing all that you had at them. She removed a flare gun from her vest, and fired it into the sky, forming their Final Protective Line. It was all or nothing.

Dakota readied the Mark 19, and cracked open the top cover, seeing a 40mm round was ready to be fed into the bolt face, before slamming it back down. She readied the iron sight point blank at the torrential wave of flesh and bones coming their way. She couldn't hold back an eager smirk, ready to put on the hate. Making sure the safety feature was off, she yanked back the charging handle to feed the next grenade into the bolt face. Both hands clenched the control grips of the

Mark 19 and she pressed her thumbs against the trigger, unleashing hell at the horde.

The Mark 19 sounded off in a satisfying *thunk, thunk, thunk*, and the following explosions against the face of the horde became a pleasant melody to her ears. Thirty yards back, a thick veil of gray smoke and pinkish-red mist covered the hordes' decimated front wave. The following wave emerged through the carnage of red smoke and mist. She let loose another volley of three round bursts, one round each to the left, center, and right. Another cloud of smoke and pink mist plumed, veiling the face of the horde, now twenty yards away. She ducked after each explosion from the pebbles, dirt, and other debris hailing down over the flatbed.

She fired another volley, but only two *thunks* came before the grenade belt ran empty, sounded by a metallic *clank* right before the latching of the action to the machine gun next to her. Wheeler got the other weapon system in the nest, an M1A1 Fifty, up and operational, and now held onto the grips. He relieved the absence of Dakota's Mark 19 with barrages of hate at the horde.

Dakota shuffled around, looking for another ammo can. Boots kicked away spent casings and empty ammo cans as she looked. Her heart pounded at the sound of the same *clank* of an already empty machine gun. She feared that they were black on ammo, stuck and cornered against the lake.

In just a few passing seconds, the simple desire to get the mobile bunker operating, to even a minimal capacity, had become an insurmountable task. All the ammo cans she found were empty, spent brass casings clanking across the steel of the flatbed. It wasn't too much to ask for, she thought, but then again, Murphy's Law had to be taken into consideration. And, like she so often heard from Phil, "Murphy was a fuckhead!"

Picket climbed out the passenger side door of the truck; she needed no explanation or wasting of time for the bad news. The truck wasn't functional, and now she was starting to hate this *mobile pile of junk nest*. Picket rummaged about behind them before tossing up onto the bed two ammo cans; the heavy *thunk*s of the metal boxes landed on the steel bed and brought relief. She opened one can, full of .50 caliber rounds, and kicked it over to Wheeler. She grabbed the other, different in size, and stepped back to the Mark 19. She heard Picket climb up into the nest with them and aid Wheeler in reloading with a shiner for a left eye and blood streaking out the right corner of the man's bottom lip.

Dakota yanked out the empty ammo can from the mounted weapons tray. She dropped the new one and pulled out a belt of grenades, sliding the first link through the feeding channel. Raising the top lid and made sure the 40mm explosives were set in place, she closed the lid and pulled the charging handle. Without losing a moment, she heard that comforting sound commence once again: *thunk thunk thunk.*

The debris and concussion-inducing waves from the forty Mike Mikes were disorienting and taking a collective toll. She could hear the fifty-cal burning through ammo on full auto. She tried to yell at him, the machine gun's barrel glowing red, but there would be no hearing her.

Brass rounds split through the air into red-hot dotted lines, almost like tracer rounds, pummeling through the zombies, two or three birds with one stone at a time. Pink and red sprayed about the horde, breaking through the veil of smoke and bloodied mist. Picket fell between the Mark 19 and M1A1, too close to either weapon's danger ends than she would've liked. More ammo cans spilled out, falling from his arms, and the old man paused for a minute, holding his left shoulder, favoring something.

That same metallic *clank* sounded off, like the chiming of a bell, the tolling of the hour, signaling the old man that it was time to get back to work. Her Mark 19 was again dry, and her left arm seemed to relish in the relief from the ending vibrations of the recoil traversing over the oblique fracture there. Right on cue, Picket was at her left now. She raised the lid and kicked away the empty ammo can as the old man dropped a fresh one into the tray. Then he disappeared behind her, over to Wheeler, while she loaded in a fresh belt, latched the lid, and charged the handle. An unending ring throbbed in her ears, barely hearing Wheeler's voice crying out for a new barrel as his current one bent downwards, glowing red and yellow.

Picket and Wheeler fumbled around in her peripheries, removing the old spent barrel, the former taking off his coat to yank out the piece of hot metal. A metal rack behind the truck's cab held a rack full of barrels, one of which Wheeler now secured into the weapon system. The lack of double coverage made it impossible for the Mark 19 to hold back the unrelenting waves of the horde.

"GUYS," Dakota shouted, barely able to hear her voice over the ringing in her ears; her tone conveyed a simple cry of demand for them to "HURRY THE FUCK UP!"

Her wish was their command. A second later, the fifty was up and running, returning its volley of red-hot brass into the horde. Wheeler was now practicing more restraint in controlled bursts of fire. An empty ammo box smacked her ankle from Picket's shuffling, and she bit down on her bottom lip from the ringing-sharp pain traveling up her calf while the man took her water canteen from her vest. He went back over the Wheeler, and there was a boldness in the man as he stayed near the death machine's dangerous end and poured water over the barrel. Steam sizzled upwards in warming ribbons of vapor.

Their complete twelve-o'clock visual became obscured; she couldn't even tell if there were any Olympians left in the wake of the carnage. Splatters of fleshy chunks and dismembered limbs rained down like heavy hail, and pink and red came down like soft rain, putrefying the air around them. The world fell behind the lens of a pinkish-red hue, with smoke clouding all else in between and her peripheries.

Then she saw why the mobile nest had failed as the Olympians now charged at them from both flanks. The frontal wave was annihilated, and she thought *Decoy!*

The monsters encircled them, encompassing them from their 9 o'clock to their 3 o'clock. Neither weapon system could accommodate for the direction of fire to their left, right, and front all at the same time. She couldn't even adjust the turning knobs under the Mark 19 to redirect her fire in time.

An Olympian came from their right flank, climbing over the grill and clambering over the cab. Picket and Wheeler both took up their Lee Enfields and unloaded several .30 caliber rounds into the monster, ensuring that the thing wouldn't get back up. Then, from their left flank, another emerged, climbing up the back end of the nest. She caught one of them in her periphery, forcing her to free her left hand from the turret to her pistol. She grimaced when, again, she felt an empty holster.

Reaching over to Picket's holster, she yanked out his Glock and aimed the barrel at the monsters now within arm's reach. She emptied five bullets into the top of the skull, blood splattering across her left side and dampening the soot and dirt on her shirt, hand, and neck as the thing fell backwards, dead.

Their position was no longer defendable; near the far end of the flatbed lay, in a dried puddle of crimson, an M1A rifle, much like her beloved M14. She holstered Picket's Glock before reaching with her left arm for the rifle. Her arm wasn't reactive; impairment of some kind prevented her from grabbing the rifle and she grabbed it with her right instead.

She swung her legs over the sandbags behind her, bending her legs upon impact and falling over. Both Picket and Wheeler landed and fell. Wheeler helped Picket to his feet as she crawled, trying to get back to her feet, and fell again. Picket and Wheeler covered her, shooting at the monsters swarming their flank, now at her six.

More Olympians came at the two men's six, and after her next failed attempt to get her feet under her, she gave in to her collapsing. Falling onto her right side, she aimed her rifle at the monsters and fired. The zombies fell upon impact but were still alive, crawling for Picket's legs. Wheeler leapt over to her, pulling at her left arm, shouting "C'mon!" A dried-out cry issued involuntarily from her in response. Getting her feet back under her, Picket emptied several rounds into the zombie's heads behind him. She could hear more at her six.

Robbed of time for proper aiming, she pressed the stock of the rifle between her right side and arm, firing from the hip to the nearest hostile. Three rounds splattered the center mass of the beast, splintering his ribs and sternum as he jerked in a twitching fumble, face down. She emptied another three to the back of his head for good measure.

The sudden presence of rapid *thwoops* came in continuous rotations, en masse. The noise came from up high, reverberating through the sky from the north. An unmistakable chorus of helicopters converged on their location.

"Thank God!" her heart cried out.

The zombies now thickened at their flanks, the three of them backed up side by side to the rock wall. Her weapon locked back on an empty magazine. A bandolier lay nearby, and she favored her left arm against her chest, getting down to a knee, searching the bandolier for another. Praying it was the same size, and finding a single magazine inside, she removed it and let out praise to see that it was the same as for her rifle. She shoved in the fresh mag, pulled back the action, and was back up and shooting.

The three of them backed up to that wall between them and the lake. The cost of ammo per monster made any resistance too much of a burden. The back of her thighs and knee contacted the rock and mortar wall, lining a slope that traveled down to the lake, paved in slabs of stone.

She felt like she was falling backwards, her body shaking now as she rested the barrel over her left elbow to steady her iron sights at the nearest threat as the rest of the horde encircled them. The zombies climbed over one another, a wall of sentient flesh that swallowed the truck and mobile nest. They were just a few yards from them.

But out of the sky, like hellfire rained down from above, missiles descended from the heavens, leaving flumes of vapors in their wake. The projectiles arched down in a judgment of hellfire and brimstone upon the thick of the horde, annihilating the collective body of the zombies with extreme prejudice. Splendid balls of fire and smoke erupted, and debris again hailed down. It was as if heaven had sent forth angels to protect them as four attack helicopters flew overhead.

Two transport helicopters followed and came to a hover over them. Gunners on both sides operated machine guns picked off the survivors of the horde. Her vision became tunneled by the explosions and sensory overload. Her M1A locked back on an empty magazine; she was again black on ammo, and she dropped the weapon and took out Picket's Glock from her holster.

The zombies, too close to the three of them for the helicopter gunners to take out, were four in number, theirs to contend with. Among the last of the Olympians, she saw him, the Alpha, standing. He was a foot taller than the rest. His deep red, right eye glared at her, and his crippled body submitted to his will as if there was no hindrance in his corporal form. He stepped forwards when one of the lesser of his pack lunged at her. But the Alpha pulled the lesser one away and threw him towards Picket and Wheeler. The other two, respecting their leader's wishes, joined the first, ganging up on her friends.

Dakota understood then; the Alpha saw her as belonging to him. He shared a kindred disposition towards her with Inimicus—the prizing of prey. But he wasn't as durable as the latter, and it went both ways; he was hers as well. She offered the same look he had given her earlier: *challenge accepted.*

Dakota offered a prayer for her two friends as the Alpha made the first move. She had her trench knife already in her left hand and Picket's pistol in her right.

She got off three rounds by the time the Alpha closed the distance. The first one missed its mark; the monster was able to move with a sudden burst of speed, but not enough to avoid the next two rounds puncturing his belly and left side without any registry of pain in his face. The only cue of damage done was the splattering of blood and flinching from the bullets.

He wrapped his hand around her pistol, and her left arm finally gave into her commands, moving as she willed it, but with rigid movements as she rammed her trench knife into his chest where his heart should have been. He only grimaced as he forced the barrel of her pistol toward the bottom of her chin.

Dakota's eyes widened, trying to force the barrel away, grunting and cursing. She searched for any weak spots in the Alpha shanking him with stiffened jabs with her knife. But he took each shank, even as blood started to drip out over his bottom lip. His other hand grabbed her hair and pulled her head back, and she felt the cold touch of the Glock's barrel under her chin.

A look of pleasure crossed the monster's face; the clammy flesh of his finger forced inside the trigger guard, over hers, pressed against her index. She could feel the inner movements of the pistol and cried out as if her will could dictate reality. The firing pin sent forwards into the brass round loaded.

Click. Her gun misfired, the bullet defective.

The Alpha's look of pleasure regressed to one of scornful contentment, twisting the gun out from her hand and throwing it aside. Her blade now jabbed into his neck before he pulled her with both hands into a head butt; she faded out for a second. Coming back from the sensation of falling backwards and against the rock wall, the edge of a stone dug into her lower back. She felt sharp stabs against the back of her hips and spine. She caught herself in a spasm to right her stance. The Alpha had blood leaking out both corners of his mouth and a gash at his neck; he heaved in laboring breaths and the deep glow of his eyes dimmed. He was diminishing.

The taste of iron filled her mouth as she dared a weak, charging step at the Alpha and plunged her blade into the temple of his head. Warm, thick liquid ran down her wrist from the blade, dampening her sleeve and traveling down to her elbow. Goosebumps covered her arms and neck as the monster's blood leaked down to her armpit, seeping into her shirt and the wing of her bra; a sudden urge to vomit came about her.

She yanked the blade out and rammed it in harder again until the guard splashed against his bleeding temple in a moist splatter. The Alpha grabbed her by the shoulders and heaved her up, slamming her down on the top of the rock wall. The tip of the occipital bone of her cranium smacked the mortar between two rocks.

The air left her lungs without time to replenish, feeling like they were being pulled through her chest. She was unable to catch back her breath or recover from the dazed blow to the back of her head. Her eyes locked onto the Alpha as he reeled back a fist and gave a hard jab to her nose, blood splattering down her twisted nostrils and over her lips, cheeks, and forehead. Feeling weak and complacent again, she was numb to the pain now and near unconsciousness.

Fast as lightning, she saw that the numbing effect was the key to her survival. The Alpha reeled back for another jab, and she craned her head as his fist pummeled the rock. Her limbs shook and her muscles were weak, but she couldn't feel any of the pain now. Using the numbness, she constricted her arms and legs around the Alpha's punching arm, pressing the bottom of her boots against his chin but not before he opened his mouth and bit into the steel of her boots. She saw his fangs crack and break. Seizing the opportunity, Dakota continued her barrage of shanking into his side.

She saw an ordinance box lying sideways with its contents spilled out, a single claymore left behind. She looked back at her foe freeing his teeth from her boot, and he again lunged down after her. Saliva dripped over her neck and chin. Once his face was within reach she rotated the blade in her hand and brought it down between his eyes. The blade slit through the front cranial, digging in halfway before stopping, stuck. He paused due to whatever neural damage had been dealt. That was the sweet spot, the frontal cranial between and above the eyes.

The Alpha's grip on her waxed and waned, and she freed herself from his grip, pulling back her knees to her chest. With all her remaining strength, she kicked the handle of her knife, sending the blade deeper until the cutting edge broke off at the hand guard. The steel was fully cemented into his flesh and bone. With her other boot, she kicked against his chest, embedding a bloodied boot print against his sternum, kicking him back.

Her heart pounded, and she felt a small pulse of adrenaline course through her, a second wind coming to her. It was enough for her to roll off the wall in a hard thud to the ground but in arm's reach of the claymore.

Her eyes widened as she sat up against the rock and mortar, using the wall to stand with claymore now in hand. The clacker, a detonating device, had already been wired and was ready to use with the ordinance.

She looked over to see Wheeler ramming the stock of his rifle into an Olympian's face, sending it to the ground. Picket stomped on its chest, striking the thing's head to the floor and disorienting it just enough to keep it steady for two rapid gunshots to the face. The other two Olympians, recovering from previous blows, again converged on her friends, not ready for the attack.

"Get over the edge, now!" she cried, spending whatever air she had been able to suck into her lungs. Unleashing her orders in a dry wheeze, she did not wait to make sure the two men complied. Dakota sat the claymore in a nook of the wall where the mortar had withered and chipped away; it was enough to hold the explosive in place, front towards the enemies.

The last of the adrenaline wore off as she slid over the wall and used gravity to pull her down to the other side. She took half a second to ensure the det cord was still connected to the clacker. The Alpha, now regaining himself, clawed at the blade stuck in his head. His stance waned as if disoriented, and he was glaring through the blood streaming down his face.

She cried out thanksgiving to God when her periphery registered her two friends rolling over the wall behind cover. Falling back down, her back to the wall, her feet pressed against a ledge of one of the rocks paving the slope. The four zombies were not a full meter away as she pulled the trigger of the clacker down to the bottom, hearing its famous *clacking* sound. Then the world silenced to a deafening ring from the explosion unleashed point blank upon the monsters.

The wall and slope trembled and shook, and she bounced in place from the force of the blast. Her ears were now "Fully shot to an overwhelming shit" as she once heard from a Ranger in Regiment. It was as if little people were inside her ear canals, banging on her eardrums with hammers. She waited there for a moment, even as Picket and Wheeler started to pick themselves back up and get eyes on the threats. But she was spent; she was done. There was too much damage for her to even organize or think about. All she knew was that she felt sick with nausea and her entire being throbbed; the only saving grace was the numbness she felt. Wheezing breaths in and out her parted lips and, bent nostrils whistled with some of the inhales and exhales.

Wheeler stumbled over to her, coming between her and the sight of the lake. The rock wall no longer separated panic from focus, bringing her to a full state of suffering in body, mind, and soul. Wheeler blocked out the water as he took a knee before her.

"…id we get 'em?" she managed through shallow breaths, that faint whistling through her broken nose.

He offered a faint smile, just barely, through a swollen lip. He nodded, holding a hand on her knee, patting it. "Ma'am, I'm grateful as all could get out that I saw yer flare that day."

She smiled back the best she could, attempting to crack a huff of laughter in response, if the muscles to her lips could even move as such. Lifting one hand up to his, his fingers locked in place as he helped her to her feet, allowing her the sight of their victory. The horde was no more; those four remaining Olympians lay in crippled ruin, the fronts of their bodies charred and steaming in a gory display of their defeat. It was as if the state of decay had been fast-forwarded and scavengers had picked away at their chests, leaving behind unrecognizable flesh, bones, and organs. The heat inside their bodies contrasted with the cold air rising in flumes of steam.

The Alpha, his bottom jaw missing along with most of his neck and chest, blinked with his one eye. Blood pooled around him; his right arm ended in a stump just above the elbow. His dark, crimson eye blinked again, staring at her, death taking its slow, careful time. She felt her feet stagger and stumble backward just staring at the beast. Her eyes now looked down at a broken nose, nostrils flaring in a forced exhale.

I win.

Above them, one of the hovering helicopters had ropes thrown out the sides, men fast-roping out of the bird. Soldiers were dressed in all black, wielding Kalashnikovs. Blood now drying from the cold air down on the left side of her face, she fell back against the wall. Getting a firm spot on a flat surface, she focused now on her breathing. The sight of water down below gripped her when Wheeler left to help Picket.

Time passed in what felt like hours. She faded, coming back too to the sound of Wheeler's voice: "Hey, hey." Wheeler gave her a gentle shake awake. Her eyes opened, and he was again between her and the water. Picket was sitting right next to her, breathing heavily.

"You did good, Buddy," she wheezed, giving his swollen, bloodied cheek a soft pat. "Real good."

"What happened to minimal engagement only?" he asked, and she couldn't fight back the chuckle in her response, nor the gut-wrenching pain that came from the contractions of her diaphragm, cutting her laughter short.

His radio went off, and she couldn't tell what was being broadcast. But she got her answer as Wheeler picked up the radio and pressed his PTT button, standing up to look at the surrounding area. The accent wasn't Canadian or American; she thought it sounded like Russian. But it could've been North Koreans at this point, as long as the Olympians were dealt with.

"I could not understand yer last, say again?"

It was Russian. All was made clear as she suddenly heard the transmission clear in one last effort to push back the gripping unconsciousness. Phil's lessons to her, and Tim's, came to fruition; she understood a few words. "They're asking for effect on target," she mumbled, a sudden intake of air sweeping her further into unconsciousness.

"Good effect on target, but we need medical assistance ASA-Fucking-Now. Three wounded. Two are in critical condition."

More Russian came in response, but she understood the simple "Affirmative."

She did the math herself; respiratory was active, and she guessed her radial pulse was under thirty. Unable to check it herself, even if she could, she doubted she could stay focused long enough to count past ten before dozing off. She could follow commands, though. For however long she was conscious, according to triage, she predetermined herself of delayed priority.

Time seemed to skip; she came to when she was being carried by four men over the wall. Her arms were around two of their shoulders while the other two cradled her legs. They treated her with careful ease to get her lying on a stretcher; over the ringing in her ears, she picked up the sounds of mounted fifties letting loose—not too far, but not near, either. A circumference of gunfire descended from helicopters above them, creating a safety net of a perimeter around the Final Protective Line. The perimeter was reinforced with a couple of squads of infantry. Picket and Wheeler beside her, and two men carried Picket while Wheeler walked with the aid of another.

They were taken to a helicopter, a red cross painted on its side, as the men loaded them into the bird. More came to a hover above, more men fast-roping down. The finish line was crossed, and this new valley was now behind her.

Whati was reclaimed.

Chapter Seven – Revelation

Dakota sat at the edge of a vinyl recovery couch in the nurse's office of Whati's schoolhouse. A Russian medic, Sergeant First Class Petrenkov, was tending to her wounds.

Already the medic had given her first-degree burns on her neck some ointment, cleaned and stitched the gaping wound at her right knee, removed the shards of glass from several areas of her body, cleaned and wrapped some gauze around her lower and middle back with medical wrap, cleaned and dressed the bite at her right calf and neck, and redressed her whole clavicle where the scabbing had been peeled away. Her left hand was now in a cast, and her already broken ulna would now require more time to heal. Her left eye had been given some ointment, and the sergeant had even shaved the left side of her head so he could stitch the laceration there. He had given her some antibiotics for anything that may have seeped into her wounds as well as a shot of penicillin and a tetanus booster. Her shirt had to be cut off as she was unable to raise her arms, and now she was sitting there in just her bralette, wrapped in bandages from the bottom of her bralette down and above. The wrap doubled as compression to offer some relief and support for her broken ribs. Cold air seeped through the gaps of the boards over the broken windows, snipping at the bare skin of her back and neck. Wheeler shielded her from most of the chill as he stood behind her, helping her lean back as Petrenkov's hands braced over her upper thigh and lower hip.

Had it been Phil or Tim, she'd have felt comfortable, but her phobia never went away among strangers. Repressing any irrational instincts to punch or kick, she let the man do his job. The sergeant looked up at her from under his brows, features bearing a solid look, and she gave him a nod, clenching her teeth.

"Tree." The word was all too quickly followed by the jerking motion of him setting her hip bone back into its socket.

Her whole body tightened, and she cried out in a muffled grunt that transitioned to a slow, fuming exhale. She clenched her eyes. Wheeler now held her entire weight as he sat her back up straight.

"Tvo, one." The medic shrugged with a nod, patting her shoulder as he set the earpieces to a stethoscope over his ears. He took the circular bell of the device and sat it at her upper back between the straps of her bralette. He said in a gentle voice, “Deep breafs, Sergeant.”

She took in a deep breath. “You already listened once.”

“I like to do one at start, and one at end, to see for any…. Uh, changes.”

She humored him and took in a deep breath, despite the sharp pains stabbing her sides. It felt as if her ribs were poking at her lungs. Holding each one for as long as she could before letting it out, each intake was only a short whiff, and she couldn’t hold it for very long.

“You took too much damage,” Petreknov muttered, shaking his head. A frown dressed his face that she noted with unease. He moved the bell again, and again she breathed as deeply as she could.

“What is it?” Dakota asked through a prolonged exhale of pain.

He moved the bell once more and didn’t speak, and she again took in a breath, studying his face for any changes. But none came as he set the bell over her sternum and listened. She coughed upon her last exhale, a faint spell came over her, and her pain renewed from the force of it.

“You are lucky. One of our men has hard time rememberin medicine from home. So, I prepare for his negligence,” the sergeant said, digging into his bag and procuring from inside it an inhaler. “Nov, he learns lesson. Hov you say, Albuterol?” he asked.

“Sergeant?” Dakota asked again, accepting the inhaler. This time, Wheeler gazed at the medic with an inquisitive look. Out of her periphery, she noted the guard posted at the door tensing up in his stance.

Sergeant Petrenkov pulled out a collapsible tube of ointment, along with two bottles of pills. “Pain relief for concussion and broken bones. Antibiotics for the next two weeks. Ointment for svellin and skin over broken bones,” he said as she accepted the items.

She clenched the inhaler, ointment, and bottles tight before stowing them in her left leg’s cargo pocket. A quick jab of pain struck her side, forcing her to pause. Pressing her right hand against the bed to steady herself, she waited for the hurt to subside and stared at her knees. She saw the right pant leg cut off and removed above the knee, and her knee dressed in bandaging.

"As I say, too much damage," Petrenkov said once more, but she noticed the medic wasn't speaking to her, but to the guard at the door.

"Petrenkov," she said, looking up at the man from under her brows, beads of sweat collecting at her eyebrows. "What aren't you telling me?"

He cradled her bottom jaw in his palms. She looked up, wincing at the new pains it brought her. He pressed his thumbs to her swollen nostrils; the gentle touch was enough to force her teeth to clench.

"Last thing to do," he said.

She waited for the countdown, "Dree," Petrenkov started, and she braced for the surprise resetting as he did with her hip. But it didn't come after three, and as he continued down to "tvo," he again surprised her and set her broken nose back into its natural setting. "One." He finished, and she barraged him in cries of grunts and curses.

The medic took a step back. Smart of him, as she felt the need to punch his own nose and break it. But upon closer inspection, the sergeant's nose bore that distinct deformity from past damages; it was crooked even, complimentary to his cauliflower ears.

Still, she couldn't breathe through her nose, but seeing it no longer crooked at an angle from her inner peripheries was a better sight; it was normal.

"You've seen better days," Wheeler chuckled, still next to her. His injuries had been dressed, other older wounds redressed, and he was in fresh ACUs.

"I know." She was muffled, her voice sounding congested from the lack of air flowing out her nostrils. "You should see the other guys."

"I don't know vat dat means," Petrenkov mumbled. "Zey are zombies, not guys, and are dead," he said, pulling out some gauze pads, medical wrap, and antibacterial cream. "But my…" he waved his hand. "Instructor alvays told me, scars don't take from beauty. Zey add to it. Now this vill burn," he said, pouring some rubbing alcohol on a rag and without warning, cleaning the cuts over her cheeks.

She closed her eyes, feeling her hand tighten around the inhaler and bottle of pills in her cargo pocket. Two more soldiers walked inside, bearing a gurney between them; they moved with all urgency while being as careful as they could. On the gurney, the small form of a little girl lay in the center.

At first, Dakota didn't see the child, no more than ten years old, but she saw her daughter. Only when the first soldier blocked the image moving past her and the sight of the girl returned, the illusion of her little Sara was replaced by the little girl of Whati; some other mother's baby girl. At that moment, Dakota wanted to weep, her heart bleeding out through her lips in a pitiful smile. The little girl from inside the locomotive had survived. Her skin was pale and her breathing was shallow but present; she was sleeping.

"I'll have to hurry zis up," Petrenkov's voice now sputtered. Eyes looking from the child back to Dakota, there was a sudden haste and hurry now in his eyes.

"Here, lemme do that; you help the girl," Wheeler said, relieving the sergeant of the rag and rubbing alcohol.

The medic rushed over to the child, and the same soldier who had stood guard by the door walked over to Dakota and Wheeler; he had with him a fresh pair of ACUs, urban digital camo with the shirt sporting only sleeves in the camo, and a solid gray center. New boots sat erect on top of the pile of folded clothes, along with a new pair of undergarments and socks. She couldn't lie; she was ready to ditch her bra, still feeling that blood soaked wing of the one she wore. Thinking about the zombie's vile blood made her nauseated.

The soldier gave a tip of his head in a greeting with more business to conclude while Wheeler finished cleaning the cuts on her face—rather, the half of her face not covered with bandages. By proxy, the use of her left eye had to be surrendered while the tape held the gauze in place. Once done, Wheeler helped her to her feet. Each step was met with a pronounced limp from her hip.

"Zese are for you, please dress yourself and zen follow me," he said, offering her the clothes.

She frowned, accepting the offering, and limped over to a corner of the room with a privacy curtain set in a track on the ceiling. She grimaced as she pulled the curtain, then remembered all her handicaps. Closing her eyes, she called out, "Hey, Buddy."

"Yeah?"

She sighed, "I need some help, please."

Wheeler helped her walk down the hall, moving in a steady rhythm with a limping right leg and a casual stride in her left. She was dressed in clean clothes that weren't torn, bloodied, or burnt. Every step was an anxious endeavor due to the pain from her broken ribs.

They followed a group of three men down the bloodied halls of the school. The general of their rescue cavalry had called for her, specifically, and Wheeler joined, leaving no room for debate, adding that she needed help to walk from the nurse's station to the front office. It was a quick walk but prolonged by Dakota's slow pace. Arriving at a meeting room, one of their escorts opened the door and leaned in. A quick exchange passed between him and a man who stood over a table, arms clasped across his chest looking down at a map spread out over the old wood; he bore the ranking of major general.

Dakota saw from over her escort's shoulder other men inside, all situated around the table and bearing insignias of commanding ranks. They were armed only with pistols at their sides; no vests, rigs, or other gear adorned them, and not one of them was less than twice Wheeler's senior, either salt and pepper hair or fully gray in color.

The major general nodded to their escort and spoke something back; there was a leveling calm to his voice. It was a tone of confidence that didn't pass into arrogance but of calming focus; it made her think of Phil. He could almost be mistaken for her brother had his accent not been so thick. The escort nodded with a straightened stance and saluted the major general, and Dakota and Wheeler were prompted to enter the room as their three-man escort took their leave.

"Sergeant Sousa," the major general greeted her now in plain English, his accent carried over heavily.

The very sound of his voice speaking her name with such familiarity made the hairs on her neck erect; it was as if they were former acquaintances meeting again for the first time in years. She stopped several feet from the edge of the table. Her eyes stabbed into the man, looking around her; something inside her was warranting caution.

She counted the men in the room; there was the major general and the five other commanding officers along with a couple of other NCOs. She looked for alternative escape routes, but there was only one way inside the room, and it was behind her with Lord knew how many possible hostiles beyond. Several windows, with busted glass and wooden boards, lined the wall behind the major general, and there was a table between her and him. She looked for the nearest soldier, a guard right past the door. He had only a pistol, but a pistol and a hostage could work though it wasn't ideal. She could feel her heart pound harder in her chest, understanding the situation was a no-way-out scenario.

The major general held up an open hand, and she felt more unease as he seemed to read her like an open book: "Recover yourself, Sergeant. You are not among enemies here."

"How do you know my name?" Dakota demanded.

"It's okay," replied the major general with a comforting assurance to his tone.

Just a ruse probably, she thought, hearing shuffling behind her, looking over her shoulder again at the guard posted to the door. Hands that once were folded behind his back were now at his side, left hand over his pistol grip.

"What and how I know isn't important. What is important is time," the major general gestured to the table. "Please. We are short on that."

She limped over to the table, favoring her left hand; she hated looking so weak in the presence of strangers—possible enemies. She elected instead to stand behind the only empty seat at the table, no matter how much her hip begged her to sit or her ribs cried out for rest.

She wondered why she felt so uneasy around these men. She had no direct relation or connections with those of Russian descent living in Alyeska, save for the occasional "hello," "thank you," or "goodbye" over the last two years. The only link between her and any Russian was through Phil, and that was indirect. But that had to be why. It was a connection, all the same, and one that brought with it a plethora of emotions and baggage in the face of Russians, especially one bearing the name Petrov. It was like water and oil; they just didn't mix, a lasting illness of disposition that survived past the First and Second Cold Wars.

The major general mirrored her, keeping even with Dakota as he stood across from her and poked at his chest. "I am Major General Petrov."

That name lingered in her thoughts; it was distantly familiar, and she knew it was only through Phil that the name wasn't completely foreign to her.

"I'm assuming you need me for something?"

Major General Petrov nodded with a bit of a smirk. It was not one of condescension for her pitiful façade of hiding her pain. She felt as if it was one of approval; he liked her. What was worse was that the man seemed friendly enough, but such things were also efficient façades: false lure into openness in which he could take advantage of her compliance—should she lower her guard.

Major General Petrov broke his stance, leaning over the table, fingers spread, as one hand pressed down over a couple of sheets of paper and slid over to her. She looked down to see two pictures, cast in dark frames of black, the images coming into focus from within the borders. The first picture was of the Jackle; his face wasn't recognizable save for the skinless features of his muscles, flesh, tendons, and bones that made that nausea in her gut worse. She saw the flattened snout with shattered teeth and mushy spots where his eyes used to be. The other picture showed Inimicus; the fiend was missing his entire right arm and shoulder and his flesh was scorched. Dakota's eyes stabbed at the latter.

"I know you have history with zese two," Major General Petrov spoke, his voice lowered just a touch. "I'm on orders from President to hunt zese monsters and kill zem."

A chuckle parted her lips in response, a scoff that relieved her need to cough and clear her throat bringing a fresh wave of pain from her ribs. This time, she was unable to hold back the pain, leaning forwards on the table, forehead against her fist as she held her side. A tear escaped from the pain, one that she quickly dried. It was as if the major general had just reached the punchline of an ill-favored joke while she took a drink.

"Excuse me?"

She didn't like how she must have looked at the present in her broken state, now close to an emotional breakdown, with Phil suddenly weighing heavy on her thoughts. Now, add the shock and surprise she felt from the idea of people hunting down Inimicus and the Jackle? Body, Mind, and Soul were all compromised; she was at a game of poker with no play or ace up her sleeve. She hated it.

There was no reproach or change in demeanor, save for a soft expression to the stoic exterior. She could see he did not judge her reaction but made note of it. It made her feel like some kind of study, something she didn't relish, as she shook her head at the man.

"We would greatly appreciate your assistance in zis endeavor. Your experience and expertise would help me to keep my men safe durin zis operation."

She felt Major General Petrov continuing to read her like a book. He pulled the chair behind him to take a seat. His fingers laced as his elbows rested on the table. "I understand your skepticism, Sergeant. I've read up on you and you're brozer's exploits." He nodded. "Very impressive."

"What? Have you spoken with Tyrese as well?"

"No."

"Why just me then? Why not get the whole package deal? Tyrese has just as much experience as I do. If not more!"

"I will tell you. It is as I said, Sergeant. Time," Petrov replied, the beat of his words never falling off-beat with one another as if he was a teacher addressing his student.

Her nerves started to pinch in a growing dislike for the man.

"Fortunately for me and my men, you are moment of opportunity, at the right place at the right time, before my men depart for Colorado. You would be most valuable asset."

Dakota looked down at the map of Canada and the US. A significant amount of travel lines and routes were marked for soldiers and asset logistics, all the way from the Sahtu Region down to Colorado Springs. That feeling in her gut became more unsettling; she felt light as if her bones were hollow, and she would just float down like a leaf if she fell.

"You're serious about dis?" She asked.

Major General Petrov nodded, just once and slowly, eyes staying on hers. He was unmoving and unflinching.

"You want my advice when it comes to these two?" She slid the pictures back to him. "Don't go after them."

"That's not an option, Sergeant."

"If you read about our 'exploits,'" she quoted with her fingers, arms still folded across her chest, "Then you'd have gathered that we only survived because we fled; we didn't go after them." Her voice was raising with each word, with the memory of that big one-armed bastard kicking Phil's body over that dusty road; it was still too fresh. The fiend's face had been placid in pleasure over a victorious hunt while he was choking the life out of Tim.

"We've tried everything." She shrugged, sneering, not at the major general, but at his request. She thought it was arrogant. "Explosions, stabbing, burning, shooting, drowning, blunt brute force. All at point blank range in so many ways I'd rader count the grains of sugar. We've blown holes out of their bodies and thrown them in a lava pit."

She wanted to scream "FUCK!" but bit her tongue, restraining herself. Her thoughts fell into turmoil. *A damn ordinance package comparable to a nuclear explosion didn't do jack shit, except take my brother from me. What the hell do you want me to do? Throw their asses into space?*

Wheeler grabbed her shoulder, her mind racing in heated self-council. She then took the offered seat across from the major general. Trying her hardest to hold back her bottom lip from quivering, she looked back at the picture of Inimicus with a loathing intent; she didn't like killing, but she supposed she'd enjoy watching him die.

Major General Petrov remained still an endless well of patience within as he held unwavering eye contact with her, and seldom did he blink.

"Zere is somezin you haven't tried, which I hold to my disposal, Sergeant." The major general nodded again, once. "It holds promise, yet all the same, I would still very much like your assistance. To improve mission success and better the chances of survival for my men."

Dakota leaned on the table with her elbows. "My brother is expecting me home. I don't want him to worry," she said.

"What if I promise to inform him of your attendance with us?"

Dakota hardened her look at the major general. She studied the map again, this time not focusing on Colorado, but on the Northwest Territories. She was looking with intent at Whati, Yellowknife, and to the northwest, where the Sahtu Region was marked. The major general and his forces came from that direction. They were dots, and everything from Wheeler and Picket's stories of their ill-fated mission connected the dots.

"You were quick to get here."

"We were," Major General Petrov nodded, a "granted," she observed.

"This wasn't a rescue; this was a cleanup."

He nodded again; his lips remained in a flat, horizontal line that offered no reaction for her to study. But a brief flinch of his eyes upwards said enough, a reaction that read, "The gig's up." Yet he didn't seem to mind. She couldn't get a read on him.

"It is," he ceded. "But zat doesn't rob your rescue of merit. I'm glad we found you and your friends in time."

She thought of Bellingham, of the Revenants, and now of Whati and the Sahtu Region with these "Olympians." The confidentiality agreement she and Tim had signed before, the mention of black sites, now this cleanup—it all made sense to her though she couldn't prove it, and she didn't expect Major General Petrov to confirm or deny her theory that the Olympians were BR-Weapons. Ones that had broken out from the Sahtu black site.

"General, I implore you. Get rid of these BR-Weapons you've been producing and don't go after Inimicus or the Jackle. Dey only bring death and ruin. I know. I've dealt with them from the start." It was all she had left to argue.

Feeling now like a deflated balloon, bereft of life or strength, she felt a fatigue grip her. It was fatigue she had only felt only twice before, a weariness of the soul that almost killed her when The Calamity occurred, and the world was reduced to ruin and rubble. The second had occurred when she realized, and accepted, that she would never find out what became of her husband and daughter.

Her face flushed, and she felt her eyes becoming heavier. "I don't make zose decisions, Sergeant. I only execute zem when delegated to me," Petrov remarked.

She sensed Wheeler tensing up behind her. A glance, and she saw now he was the one with white knuckles over clenching fists. He had gone inside himself, and she reached over and lay her hand over his.

Hang in there.

"What if I…" Major General Petrov waved his finger, looking for words… "Sweeten the cooking pot, as you might say."

She leaned her head back, wondering what on earth he could offer her. In her heart, she had already signed her retirement papers; it was the first thing she would do when returning home. Once she got back, she was done.

Had she been the one who created them? Was it her job to get rid of them? No, but she wondered if she could wash her hands clean of Inimicus and the Jackle? What if signing her papers would then doom others who were more ignorant of the two titans, who lacked her experiences? Despite her disbelief that the two brutes could be put down, she felt as if she and Tim were the only ones equipped to deal with them. As if the three of them were wardens of the titans, so to speak; she was baffled by the sudden responsibility she felt.

Staying on the same line of thought with Dakota, the major general then slid a third sheet of paper to her, another photograph of a darkened image set in blackened borders. The shadows were thick over the black and white picture of a silhouetted man standing among the rocks of Garden of the Gods in Colorado Springs. Pikes Peak and the other mountains formed a devilishly dark backdrop of a wall behind the silhouette. The picture was taken far away, the lens unable to focus in on the figure who was but a dark gray blur. Clouds were dark above the man, all coming together to create what she felt was an ominous image of an unstoppable force.

"Right after your operation in Colorado, I was ordered to dispatch a recovery team who verified Inimicus and Jackle's survival. Before zat team discovered the monster's survival, zey came across unidentified person. Zen few days later an elite SPETSNAZ team was sent in for search and rescue. I would be down zere now if not for this tragedy in Whati. So, I am sending my right-hand man ahead of me with a brigade of soldiers to Colorado Sprins to establish foothold while I finish here."

"And this man?" Dakota asked.

"I believe you must have your own zeories of who it is, yes?"

"Sergei," she mumbled, pressing her top front teeth down on her bottom teeth, focusing her breath through her nostrils.

Another hostile she wouldn't mind getting her hands on. Another link connecting to Phil. He seemed to be at the center of this, and despite remaining unspoken, there was something else going on. Another agenda of the major generals, of the presidents.

From under the table, the major general brought up a laptop and sat it in front of him. He typed a few keys, moved the touchpad mouse, and made a few clicks before spinning the monitor around to face her. On it was an audio recording, no more than a few minutes long, and the major general played the file:

"Oscar Charlie Romeo to…" Dakota recognized the call sign and the woman's voice, one of the Alyeskan Air Force Operators in Winston's OCR and that sent a sinking feeling into her gut.

"Hello," came a young woman's voice, eccentric and wild.

"SRT-Alpha, this is Oscar Charlie,"

"Oh, hi. Sorry. We need…"

"Go ahead…"

"What?"

"Miss, there is a few-second delay. Calm down and listen clearly before you speak."

A few seconds passed.

"My name is Autumn, me and my friend are sick and hurt and need you to send help, please."

Five seconds passed.

"Oscar Charlie copies Alpha. Do you know your medevac request?"

Another five seconds before: "Okay, I have it here; it's written down, but, uh. Gosh, I don't get it."

Five seconds later: "That's okay, just say it slowly word for word."

Five seconds passed: "Okay. It is…Line One: One-Tree-Sierra-Delta-Charlie-Niner-Six-Zero-Niner-Niner-Niner-One-Zero. Line Two: GEO-Viasat sat Phone, Tree-Four-Dot-Five-Four-Six, SRT-Alpha. Line Three: Two Charlie. Line Four: Alpha. Line Five, Two Alpha.

Line Six: X-Ray. Line Seven: Charlie, Green Smoke. Line Eight: One Alpha, Break, One Bravo. Line Nine: None, Mountainous Region… Did you get it?"

Five seconds later: "Standby. Your nine-line request is as follows. Line One: One-Tree-Sierra-Delta-Charlie-Niner-Six-Zero-Niner-Niner-Niner-One-Zero. Line Two: GEO-Viasat sat Phone, Tree-Four-Dot-Five-Four-Six, SRT-Alpha. Line Three: Two Charlie. Line Four: Alpha. Line Five: Two Alpha. Line Six: X-Ray. Line Seven: Charlie, Green Smoke. Line Eight: One Alpha, Break, One Bravo. Line Nine: None, Mountainous Region?

"Yes, Ma'am."

"Alpha, your MEDEVAC has been approved, standby for ETA. Over… Alpha, is everything okay?"

"Oh, God."

The young woman cried, cutting off into static as a raging thrash of a roar made the speakers vibrate and the whole file ended in a static shake from the force of the familiar voice. The Jackle's voice.

The major general's face was still as stone, unflinching and expressionless. Folding his hands, he laced his fingers on the table again as he continued to study Dakota.

"Sergeant, this girl doesn't have much time and I don't need to explain what all zis implies. I'm not asking you to operate and fight. You've done enough of zat. No, I just need you advise Colonel Reznov for any and all concerns regardin Inimicus and Jackle. To be consulate, yes? In return, ve'll capture zis Sergei, search for your missin comrade and pray we're not too late in savin this young woman." There was fatigue now to his voice, his hand partially shown, his cards laid out perfectly in order and in place. She sensed a few cards were still hidden—aces up his sleeve. He was ready for her answer and done with the conversation.

Dakota had a strong suspicion that she was being asked for her involvement on the basis of a smoother and cleaner transaction. This meeting was simply a polite gesture of the major general. Compliant assistance always went further and was more efficient than forced assistance. But he had been right; the implications from that 9-Line MEDEVAC said enough for her to make up her mind then and there.

Line Three detailed two wounded who were of priority care. One of those two she believed was the girl on the recording, but the other? *Certainly not Sergei, but...* And she wanted to cry, wanted to break down at that very moment, wondering if Phil had indeed survived and left behind—if he had been down there this whole time, in need of urgent medical care? All the while she and Tim were playing the self-pity game.

But she didn't cry; she could do that later. For now, she held herself inside a stoic shell while faced with Petrov's audience. The major general's patience was now no longer an endless well, and she understood what came after this polite gesture of his. In reality, she didn't have a choice, and she didn't need one. She would go willingly either way.

"I need one thing before we go," she said, mirroring Valentin's eye contact: firm, still, strong in her regard. This was ending only one way, and compliant assistance was the safest approach.

"Yes?"

"Him," she said, hitching her thumb at Wheeler. The young man took a step back, shaking his head. Before the young man could reply, she looked right at him, softening her expression just a little. "And the other man. Picket's his name."

The major general didn't flinch, but there was a slight movement in the muscle between his ears and his eyes. The unpleased look quickly faded back behind his unreadable exterior.

"It vill be done." The major general leaned back in his chair and gave a quick shout; not a second later, the doors opened as a man stepped through the door and gave the general a solute. He bore the silver eagle rank of colonel pinned to his collar and the name "Reznov" was embroidered over the left pocket of his coat.

"Do you have everyzing prepared, colonel?"

"Dah, my men are ready."

"As is our specialist, and a couple of extra personnel. Our Canadian friend here and his senior pupil, mmm, Picket, yes?" There was a change to Major General Petrov's tone when addressing Wheeler; Dakota sensed a bit of reproach to his tone.

"Yes, Picket," Wheeler confirmed.

"Ve make accommodation, Sir." Colonel Reznov nodded.

"Why the hell am I going?" Wheeler whispered to Dakota in a hiss. "My place be here, Miss."

"Just go with it," she hissed back, looking at this Colonel Reznov.

"We're ready den." Dakota held out her hand and Wheeler helped her to her feet.

It felt weird to regard the man as colonel, given Colonel Winston and Stacey. But as this Colonel Reznov nodded and took his leave, she and Wheeler followed, bidding farewell to the major general. Wheeler assisted Dakota in her limping, and with a faint whisper he added: "I don't want to go to Colorado, Miss."

"Do you trust me yet?" Dakota asked.

The young man gave it a second's worth of thought, then sighed a "yeah."

"Then trust me just a bit longer."

Chapter Eight – Stick-Up

-October 26th, 2030-

Dakota sat in the coach wagon, facing out the window, her right leg stretched out over the whole seat, her left arm resting in a sling as her shoulder leaned on the glass. A strained cough came from the seats across from her. Wheeler stepped over, handing Picket a canteen. Picket didn't look all too well as he sipped the water. He was tired, sore, and favoring his bruises along with a couple of broken ribs himself. But the old dog could still walk and talk; some would call that a win. A bit of guilt tinged at her for dragging the old man along as well.

"You okay?" she asked, her voice ending in a short cough.

Picket gave her a thumbs up as Wheeler sat across from him, checking on his bandages. The angle at which she looked soon brought a tingle of discomfort, forcing her to look back out her window, and the pain faded. Outside, the veil of a rainstorm blurred the world, and the tracks formed a bend, allowing a view of the expanse of the entire freight as far back as her visual would allow. There was cargo, coach, fuel, and flatbed wagons, the latter hauling Tigrs, BTR-80's, cargo trucks, and attack choppers including Havocs and Mil-Mi-28.

The train had arrived from the Sahtu, and she felt impressed by the commitment of troops, supplies, and vehicles committed. More than that, all that was being transported had been divided by weight and into two separate freight trains. It had been her "good fortune" to be on the first freight, hauling the bulk of the coaches; light infantry was spearheading the way into Colorado to establish a foothold. The three of them had been allotted their own coach, one she felt was more like a detainment coach with its bars over the windows.

Despite the impressive arsenal and expansive force the major general had provided, she still thought it wouldn't be enough, even after considering the apparent crippled state she had last seen the two tyrants in. She just didn't believe they could be killed by conventional means; anything short of a nuke felt ineffective.

Back in 2017, a few months after The Calamity, she, Phil, and Tim had caught wind of the Exodus Event to Europe or Canada, and she thought it best to get to the coastline and hitch a ride over the Atlantic. The three of them fled through southern Missouri on their way to the Atlantic seaboard and suffered their first encounter with the Jackle.

That skinless Behemoth, in his prime, had taken on a full US Army Armor Company of four armored platoons. In all, there had been fourteen M1A2 Abrams Tanks, Two HMMWVs, an M113A3 troop carrier, and an FMTV Cargo truck, and the monster had devastated the whole company. Of the sixty-two men in the company, no one survived. The only solace for the ill-fated company's efforts was that one of the Abrams's main guns was still functional. It was enough for Phil and Tim to land a headshot on the Jackle and sent the beast fleeing.

That day had been a hard one though the three of them found no shortage of weapons, ammo, and provisions looted from their brothers in arms. There wasn't enough time to bury the men; a horde of the undead less than a click north of their position was closing in on the location, drawn by the commotion of the skirmish. They wouldn't allow the bodies to be eaten either, so they loaded the fallen, and supplies, in the back of a semi that Tim had gotten operational the day prior and continued on their way to the Atlantic. They stopped at an open field the next day to bury the dead.

So, as she stared at the jeeps, cargo trucks, APCs, BTRs, and attack choppers of the Siberians, she was vastly underwhelmed. She thought about how hard it would be to dig enough graves for a brigade. It didn't matter if the major general arrived with the other freight train and the rest of his division.

The tracks straightened, the back of the freight fading from sight to parallel the endless forest of southern Alberta, passing like a rapid slideshow. The sun was setting, twilight bluing the sky that deepened over the western horizon she faced. Mountain peaks and treetops formed a double row of jagged teeth under the sky. The hungry mouth of the Wastelands consumed the foolish who willfully leapt into its void.

Sometime during the night, the train slowed to a stop, and there was shouting outside as men walked around in hurried strides. Boot stomps thumped the roof over them as sentries took defensive positions. Out the east side window, she saw a far, open field, and between her and that expanse of land, another set of railroads laid. A minute later, one of those Tigrs passed by their coach on another set of tracks.

"Huh, well ain't that clever?" the old man asked in a low mumble. "Why did we never think of that?"

She was an oblivious spectator to whatever had interested him so.

"Thought of what?" asked Wheeler.

"That Jeep there. It's a dual-mode."

"What's that?" Dakota asked.

"They attached a Hi-Rail to it, allowing it to drive on railways," Picket said, pointing at the front of the Tigr. There was an extra set of wheels with grooves down the round sides, much like train wheels: a perfect fit for the truck to mount the railroad ahead.

"It's scouting ahead, then," Dakota thought aloud, connecting the thoughts to Picket's intrigue. She thought harder about the implications; if they were scouting ahead, then they were close to the furthest reaches of the Canadian Confederacy's railroad system, which, according to Wheeler and Picket's knowledge, went as far south as the US-Canadian border. "We're close to the States, then," she concluded.

"Southern Alberta and northern Minnesota, I'd reckon." Wheeler wiped his nose, confirming Dakota's suspicions.

The dual-mode Tigr passed fully from view, and they remained in place for a good hour or so. After which the train picked up speed, moving now at a slower rate, pressing on into territory she, Phil, Tim, and the Lads had only recently charted.

It would go on like this for the rest of the night, moving slowly, and stopping. Waiting, and then moving again. At one stop rifle reports were registered, and shouting came from outside. Her body tensed and her senses were put on high alert from the unending *POP POP POP.* Out her window, she saw tracer rounds shot out into the night.

The tracers came at every fifth round, glowing red projectiles spearheading and disappearing into the western darkness, showing the other gunners and riflemen where to direct their fire.

The soldiers keeping guard over the three of them were ordered outside. One shouted out a final command for them to stay put and exited the coach wagon's door, joining in the defense efforts.

Dakota only saw opportunity.

"I asked you to trust me," she huffed, getting up to her feet, and she limped in a brisk pace to the door the man had just exited. The next wagon ahead was a cargo wagon. "You and Picket were just loose ends to the general," she said.

"What are you talking about?" Picket looked confused. "Bryce here was of diplomatic importance and shit."

"Until he got back home," Dakota clarified, "He got back home, and we'd gone MIA at Whati, where the general was 'cleaning up his mess.' It wouldn't be hard to say KIA from zombies in a report, and from what I saw, those things in Whati don't leave any remains behind like the others." She yanked open the door, and the pressure of the pull at a wrong angle pained her broken ribs.

"Fuckin'ell." Wheeler cursed.

Dakota looked left, right, up, and down, hearing boots over the roof above and down around the old rocks around the railroad. "The Sahtu black site, Whati, those zombies, all of it. You two would've just been loose end witnesses. You weren't going home; you'd be going to your executions. Probably me too, after serving my purpose."

"Are you sure that you're not betting our asses on a theory? What are you doing anyways, lil' lady?" Picket about shouted.

"Hijacking this train."

The sounds of boots went to the back side of the coach's roof opposite the end they were on. Dakota limped across a metal catwalk set over the connective coupling holding the coach wagon to the cargo wagon. The door to the cargo opened smoothly without a metallic whine; its hinges were well-oiled.

Picket and Wheeler followed behind her. Across the cargo wagon was another door set; a glass panel gave a view of a flatbed wagon ahead. A couple of Tigr jeeps were anchored in place. Past that was the back end of the freight locomotive head.

Dakota wiped some snot running out of her nose with her shirtsleeve. Resting her left hand on Wheeler's shoulder, she pointed back out the way they came. "Disconnect this wagon from that one."

Wheeler looked to Picket, then back to her. Uncertainty kept him rooted in place.

"You have to trust me," she begged. "Please."

Picket fumed out his nostrils, undecided. But Wheeler caved, making a choice, and he ran back to disconnect the wagon. The old man pointed a finger at her; there was no choice. They were all gas and no breaks. "You better be right on this."

Among the storage crates was a weapons locker containing AK-74s, a couple of AK-12s, and other weapon systems of Russian make she wasn't entirely familiar with. She grabbed one of the 74s and passed it to Picket—and another to Wheeler once he returned, his task completed. The cargo wagon successfully disconnected from the coach wagon. Picket had opened a munitions crate with magazines of different varieties inside. Dakota looked and found the appropriate size and caliber for their weapons systems.

She loaded the polymer magazine filled with thirty rounds of 5.45x39mm rounds. She preferred thirty-cal munitions, but the smaller rounds would do for the time being. Picket grabbed two magazines, tossed one to Wheeler, and she took a spare and stuffed it in her cargo pocket.

"Alright, on me, gents," she said, pulling back the action, making sure a round was in the chamber, and pressing up on the door. Picket stacking up behind her, Wheeler took a position on the other side of the door, pulling it open.

If it all played out right, she wouldn't have to shoot. Lord willing, she didn't want to put her busted arm through any more damage. The door slid open in a metallic protest, and her teeth clenched at the noise it made. Wheeler stopped opening until there was just enough room for them to fit through. She stepped over the coupling system of the locomotive and onto the flatbed wagon. There she had a better visual; men were forming a fire line on the gravel below and over and under a fire line facing west, gunners were on the wagon roofs, a triple-layered firing position holding off those unseen threats now visible as silhouettes running at them; they weren't quadrupeds.

Draugrs, she deduced. More tracer rounds shot out from the machine gun nests above. The threats numbers were diminishing, and their window of opportunity with it.

Her efforts sped up, looking back to her twelve. She stepped over straps and chains anchoring the Tigrs in place, around the grills, and down the driver's-side flanks. She stepped over the next coupling system and onto the locomotive itself; it was just a dark mass of metal.

Two narrow paths branched off, flanking around the head of the freight train: one for the conductor and one for the engineer to get to their stations.

She pointed to the path flanking left while poising herself to the right.

"Picket, check your watch," Dakota said, looking at her own, studying the red bar of the second hand in its rotation. "Sixty seconds from my go. Breach the door. We'll ambush them at the same time. Ready?"

"Ready," Picket said, eyeing his watch.

"Three, Two, One. Go." Two lines passed the five. 00:07 Seconds was her time. Whatever Pickets was at, he gave her a thumbs up. They were synced, and they split at the flanks, pushing to the objective. She moved with a fox-walk approach, her boots pressing over the old, rusted metal with barely a noise as she reached the conductor's door.

She checked her watch.

Thirty seconds left before breach; she peered through the glass to see two men inside. One was manning a radio, the engineer she assumed. The back of the conductor's head was also visible as he manned the break operating station.

She checked her watch again. Twenty seconds until breach.

Her second hand closed in on 00:05, trusting Wheeler and Picket were in place, and in two seconds she opened the door and breached the tight confines of the locomotive. She heard the other side-door yank open and Picket grunt quiet demands. Unable to keep her gun out of arm's reach, she held it at her hip. Circumstances provided a situation where she couldn't miss if either of the men were to try something.

Wheeler disarmed the conductor and engineer of their pistols as Picket took over the engineer's station. Dakota backed up, guiding both men out to the flatbed wagon with Wheeler behind them. She wanted to shout at the young man, being that they both were facing the dangerous ends of each other's weapons at the same time as their captives.

But there was no time for it; the conductor and engineer both saw the situation for what it was—two guns on the men from two separate angles. They had no leverage in the situation, and when she could she took a step back, clearing Wheeler's line of fire, she waved the barrel of her rifle to the ground below, gesturing for them to "get off."

The engineer and conductor climbed down. The gunfire of their defense efforts trickled, the sounds of snipers picking off the remnants of the threats to the west. Men shouted from the other wagons, sounding off with one another as the draugr threat dissipated; their voices were less alarmed and more informative.

"Go help Picket get this thing running, and now," Dakota snipped at Wheeler.

She didn't look away from the two men, keeping her eyes and weapon aimed down at them. Her left forearm begged for relief, threatening to lower the barrel under duress. Her aiming faltered, and waned, the iron sights lowered from the conductor's center mass to his legs. Her arm became disobedient, but the two men below her remained still and silent.

The locomotive started forwards, and on the radio the engineer had left inside the operating station, she could hear Colonel Reznov's muffled voice shouting out at them. He was unaware of the hijacking, his voice fuming in frustration. But the train was going, with the flatbed and cargo wagon in tow, leaving the other one-hundred-and-ninety-seven wagons and rear locomotive behind them. Warning shots fired over their heads, more tracer rounds. Dakota leapt back on the flatbed wagon and ducked behind the back end of a Tigr. She looked over at the coach wagon, seeing no threat emerge from the roof or inside.

Oh, they're pissed off now. She couldn't help but grin and laugh.

Once they had made enough distance outside of the Russian's range, Dakota made a quick sweep over their commandeered freight train. But there was no one on it save for the three of them.

It wasn't long after that the dual-mode Tigr came into view the further south they went. Picket slowed the locomotive and kept the lights of the train blinding at the back end of the Tigr.

From the little Jeep, the passenger door opened. A man stepped out, holding a radio in one hand, raising both arms, demanding with flaying movements, "What the hell?" She climbed down the locomotive, camouflaged by train lights blinding her targets and approached them in surprise with her weapon raised. Wheeler had crept around to the driver.

In one brief transaction, they had ambushed both men without firing a single shot. She barked at Wheeler, "Get him out," and her buddy yanked open the driver-side door. The man behind the wheel obeyed Wheeler's commands as he stepped out, leaving his pistol on the dashboard.

Wheeler climbed back up onto the locomotive, keeping the men at gunpoint, and hollered, "I got them, you go ahead."

Dakota lowered her weapon, her left arm thanking her as she limped to the driver's seat of the Tigr and climbed in. "Alright, gentlemen. Heading off," she said over her radio, closing the door and putting the Tigr into drive. She sat her radio in a cup holder and eased into the accelerator.

"Copy that, I'll keep an eye on these men until you get this thing moving, ol' timer." Wheeler's voice came over his radio.

"I'll keep it under twenty miles per high, lil' lady," Picket replied. "Just make sure you give me a warning if we have to stop. I'll need more space and time to bring this big sucker to a still."

"Copy that," she replied, but it wasn't long until she passed out of radio range from Picket.

She kept at a slow and steady pace with the high beams on for what she prayed would be a clear journey straight to Colorado. The rusted steel rails disappeared under the hood of her ride; trees absent of foliage framed the railroad's flanks in a wooded tunnel. A map sat on the passenger seat, and she pulled it onto her lap. With the cab lights on, she looked down at the laminated paper to a pre-outlined route of a railroad map back to Colorado Springs.

Hang in there, Buddy, she thought in silent hope and prayer. *I'm coming back for ya.*

Chapter Nine – Wastelands

-October 29th, 2030-

The last two days had been a relay of Dakota scouting the railroads ahead of the locomotive, keeping a steady 25 to 30 miles per hour. Wheeler and Picket followed behind by a few miles with their stolen assets. Through the night and day, they went, not wanting to waste the head start they had gotten on their angered escorts further north.

As night gave way to the dawning sun glimmering over the eastern horizon, a cold stretch of barren Colorado plains was illuminated. This marked the third day of their venture, and, finally, they were in the state.

Time felt very much like it was ticking down to catastrophe: monsters and Sergei ahead of them and Siberians behind. But for the time being, the last two days had taken it easy on her broken body. Eating MREs when she needed nourishment and filling up on water when thirsty, hunger and thirst were kept distant by prolonged sedentary activity. Burning no calories and sweating no moisture, she made little less than a dent in their commandeered provisions.

Here and there, she would stop, and inform her new friends, or they would inform her, of a need to refuel or relieve themselves. Taking turns, Wheeler at one point switched positions with Dakota so she could sleep a wink. She was woken by Picket when her assistance was needed.

Now they were only a few hours from their destination, and there were butterflies alive in her belly along with a nauseating feeling when the landscape became more and more familiar. The last time she had been in Colorado never parted from her thoughts. At the very best, the events that had transpired and the cost of it all remained in the back of her mind but was never absent.

The city of Colorado Springs wouldn't be hard to miss; in place of tall buildings, the metro area and districts would be a crater the size of a nuclear indentation on the earth. "God's thumbprint," she had heard a guy in SRT-Foxtrot call such things. The hole in the earth was left in the wake of her, Phil, and Tim's arrival to this desolate place barely three weeks ago. Like the city, they were broken and empty in the aftermath. Being back in the same place now, Dakota chuckled.

Where she and Tim had left a piece of themselves behind, it seemed now that the Wastelands had imparted a piece of itself in them.

Checking the date on the dash of the Jeep, she saw that it was October 29th.

Happy Halloween, she mouthed silently, absent of enthusiasm.

The sunrise to the east brightened, the morning dawn transitioning to early afternoon, illuminating the mountains off in the west. The Rockies appeared as light blue waves across the darker, western reach of the sky. Above the peaks stood the highest one; only its summit appeared snowy, an illusion made by the white rocks of its peak. The bottom of the chief mountain was hidden behind the waves of the lower mountaintops.

Pikes Peak gloomed, a watchful sentry in the backdrop. Waiting to see what they decided to do and where they should go, it was an eerie spectator, observing from afar and casting its shadow over the area. To such giants, a small Jeep and the small freight train traveling across the frosted dew of the late morning must have seemed like ants wading over a frosted patio.

She was back in the abyss, she felt—Dante's Inferno, dubbed the lowest pit of hell, a frozen lake. Upon her return to that abysmal place where she last saw Phil, it seemed as much. Of all the three-hundred-and-sixty-five days on the calendar, they just had to come back right before Halloween.

The route of the first freight train continued south. Just outside the dunes of rubble and seas of debris were the remains of Colorado Springs. Dakota waited at the next rotary switch. The rails split, one going southwest and the other southeast. She informed Wheeler and Picket when they came in radio range that they would need to stop. When the locomotive came into view, it slowed in its approach and came to a grinding halt over the rusted tracks. The two men disembarked, Wheeler hopping down to the ground while Picket stood on overwatch.

"What are we doing?" the young man asked.

"We're splitting off from the route." Dakota pointed southwest. "I want to be out from the line of travel of Colonel Reznov."

Picket eyed the rotary switch, hands on his hips.

"There's some WD-40 in the Jeep." Dakota hitched her thumb over her shoulder at the Tigr.

"We're gonna need all of it, then." Picket shrugged.

He hadn't been wrong; they ended up using the whole can of lubricant, along with a crowbar. The rusted joints of the switch loosened, the rail axis and the workings of the switch moving slowly. The lever moved the railroad tracks to merge with those bearing the southwest approach.

Dakota climbed back into the Tigr, taking with her a good deal of pain that dwindled into discomfort from the exertion. Pushing forwards, she left just enough room for the train to pass, then disembarked again, walking back to the switch with Wheeler hopping down from the locomotive.

She contemplated not sabotaging the switch, being both an asset on their way in and out of the area. Wheeler even advocated as much. But they had the Tigrs as well, coupled with the fact that the silvery sheen of the tracks where their stolen train passed left a trail of breadcrumbs for Colonel Reznov to follow straight to them. She shook her head, and together, they sabotaged the switch after turning it back to its original southeast bearing.

The level of debris and ruins coating the area from the shockwave of the blast had expanded further out than she expected. The tracks were cluttered with obstructions so much that the Hi-Rail attachment to the Tigr *clanked* and *clacked* more and more. The Jeep shook and jumped as if she were driving over potholes, fearing the vehicle, and worse, the train behind her would derail. When the Tigr's two front wheels had lifted, she had enough.

Everywhere she looked, buildings were collapsed, near collapsing, or, like a passing warehouse, still standing, albeit on its last legs. Everywhere, in between battered wood, chipped stone, and broken glass, all manner of human materials littered the ground. The ground that remained visible was charred and cracked, void of vegetation, and almost impassible up to the warehouse.

Off the beaten railroad path, just north of the city limits, a railway workshop stood, brittle and waning like the warehouse. It wasn't ideal, but beggars couldn't be choosers. The workshop sliding doors had been left open the rails were still intact up to the inside and beyond. She waited there, keying her radio twice every other minute. When Wheeler and Picket came back within range, hearing her two clicks, they called over.

"We're now entering… what looks to be an old suburb," came Picket.

"That will put you about twenty minutes north of my position. Stop at the workshop; you'll see it soon. We'll set up shop there. I don't think the rails will accommodate us beyond that point." She pressed her radio against her forehead. "Over," she added, struggling to keep her eyes open from the sudden sharp pain at her side.

She took out the bottle of painkillers and downed a couple of them; they were measured in 10 milligrams each. Picket replied with a "We'll be there in two shakes of a lamb's tail."

Why a lamb's tail? Never mind, she mumbled to herself, keying her radio. "Copy that. Over'n out."

Stepping out of the driver's door, AK in hand, she climbed up on the hood and surveyed around her. There were no immediate threats in the area, nor the sound of any. She was in some kind of industrial district northwest of Colorado Springs. There, in silence, she held watch, waiting for her friends to catch up.

Fifteen minutes later, her ears perked at the sound of the train slowing down but not yet within visual. The tracks behind her came around a bend that was hidden behind the dune of a collapsed structure. Any threat was bound to be drawn by the locomotive's chugging. Yet nothing came of it; the surroundings remained silent, save for the low moan of the wind creeping over the desolation around her.

The locomotive came into view around the bend with the other two wagons following, slowing down in its approach. It finally came to a metallic screeching of a stop, ten yards behind the Jeep. Picket and Wheeler climbed out and down the metal beast, weapons held at the low ready as they met up with her, looking at the wide-open doors of the workshop.

"Just big enough to fit three links in," Picket whistled.

She gave Picket a pat, soft on the shoulder, taking a step past him. "Single stack on the door. Wheeler, take point. I'll follow up center. Picket, watch our six."

"Sounds like a plan, Stan." Picket's nostrils flared in an exhale, with Wheeler hurrying passed her to the front.

They formed up to the left of the open door, and Dakota felt a pat on her shoulder from Picket when he was ready. In turn, she patted Wheeler's shoulder, informing him they both were ready.

Once the young man was good to go, he passed through the wide opening, cutting right, sending out a wave of irritation from Dakota as she rushed in to cover the left. Picket followed up and watched center. All was empty inside the big open space for trains to park. To the right was a series of doors, one dangling sign indicating a 'Break Room.' Grated stairs to the far end on the right led up to a catwalk, to what she assumed was the workshop supervisor's office. To the left were crates, wooden pallets, and other miscellaneous items of abandon.

"Okay." Dakota lowered the iron sights of her weapon under her vision. "We take it room per room, slow and steady. Ready?"

"Ready," Wheeler and Picket both replied.

An hour later, a complete sweep of the place had been finished, and all entry points were either secured or barricaded. The hardest part was in closing the large sliding door they had ingress from. Without the electrical means to operate the door, she looked around for manual overrides, until an idea crossed Picket, and he motioned for them to follow.

Back at the Tigr, he stood by a winch at the Jeep's grill and pointed at the metal doors.

"With any luck, they won't snap off and the door will just slide shut." He shrugged.

"Well." Dakota let out a breath through her nostrils, the Co2 visible as it dissipated into the air above. "Unless you got a better idea, Wheeler, I'm game."

"Nope, just fingers crossed we don't break it."

She climbed into the Tigr, disengaged the Hi-Rails, and, with four-wheel drive, repositioned the vehicle opposite the large sliding door. She flipped the red safety guard over the in-cab winch control, turned the key to disengage a security lock, and pressed a little metal stick left. It gave slack to the metal wire as the two men pulled it out and over to the big sliding doors. They found a spot to wrap the wire and hook it in place. Wheeler kept tension on the hook, and Picket gave her a thumbs up: “Alright, give it a go!”

She pressed the stick to the right, the winch at the front winding, and the slack tightened. Wheeler freed his hands when the slack was no more, and the winch gave a tight pull. The Tigr jerked forwards at the sudden tension, just by a hair, as she let up on the stick, pressed her foot against the brake pedal, and again pressed the stick to the right. The door moaned and creaked, rusted protests in cracks that made her certain the wheels or tracks of the sliding mechanics would snap right off.

The Tigr’s brakes locked in place and pulled towards the door, wheels grinding against rocks and rubble and catching on the nearest rail tracks that chalked the tires. The Tigr, now locked in place, pulled more on the giant door without giving. The large piece of metal shook and rattled. Rust broke off and came down like poisoned snow as the joints and wheels were freed from their twelve years of sitting. An unpleasant metallic *SNAP* shot through the air. Dakota flinched, and the guys jumped as the snapping sound rippled outwards, echoing through the silent ruins around them.

In compensation for that loud broadcast, the metal doors jerked. Wheeler and Picket covered their mouths with the sleeves of their coats to avoid the snowing rust. The tension on the Tigr and door loosened; the winch was now reeling in the wire as the door moved. Metal ground against metal until it closed shut on its tracks.

“Alright. Disengage!” Came a shout from Picket, reduced to a holler from his covered mouth.

She let up on the stick and pushed it to the left, offering enough slack for Picket to free the hook and unwrapping the wire from the door. Wheeler guided the wire into the winch as she shifted the stick back to the left. Thunder rumbled over the mountains, and with a cautionary glance, she saw storm clouds rolling over the mountains, like a fog gushing over the sea to the shore. Lightning flickered above the peaks; a drizzle fell over them.

"Let's hurry this up!" shouted Wheeler as Dakota reeled the rest of the winch back in place.

Dakota parked the Tigr behind the workshop, an employee parking lot with four trucks that had long since been sitting in forgotten abandonment. Rain now fell over the metal roof, creating a soothing ambiance that threatened to lull them to sleep the moment they sat down from their labors.

Dakota thought the rain to be a Godsend as it would wash away their scent and cover their tracks, at least against the monsters. She took solace in knowing that any wraith, draugr, or satyr, along with Inimicus and the Jackle, would seek shelter during the storm.

For the first time in over a decade, she faced the threat of both humans and monsters in unison. Not since the Falling Lines Event and Exodus Event did that familiar feeling of being hunted on all sides strain her nerves. Yet, for the time being, the only concern would be Sergei or potential forwarded units from Colonel Reznov.

As the night settled, she searched the cargo wagon, finding more weapons and munitions. Trading out her AK-74 rifle for an SVK, she readied that thirty-caliber round she favored so much. She removed a plate carrier from a vest and filled its pouches with seven, 15-round magazines for her new weapon. She grabbed a new pistol holster, and over her right thigh she holstered what she thought looked like a modernized 1911 Colt.

Phil would've known what it was called, but all she cared about was that it was chambered in a .45 ACP. It had extra stopping power compared to the other pistols chambered in 9mm.

It felt like Christmas morning, Wheeler took up an SVK like herself, and Picket held onto the same AK-74. She added to her kit a small coyote bag with enough MREs and water to last a day away from their temporary COP, along with other odds and ends. The bags added a little under forty pounds, per her estimations.

By then, the sun was lowering, and with the little light of day remaining, they bunkered up in the supervisor's office on the second floor. The stairs barricaded and a rope to the grated floor for a quick descent offered enough comfort for them to at least sleep in rotations.

Yet despite all that, Dakota knew she would not find rest even if she could sleep.

The supervisor's office was joined to a meeting room. Despite the glass fogging over and frosting at the frames, they had a good visual outside the workshop to the north, west, and south. Dakota had found a map pinned to a peg board in the meeting room; it detailed the railroad system in and around Colorado Springs. She took it and laid it over the meeting room's oblong-shaped table. Picket was to her right, Wheeler to her left.

With the pre-sighted map stolen from Colonel Reznov's scouts, and the old railroad map sitting side by side, Dakota traced her fingers north on the former. "The second freight train had another locomotive, without a doubt. Colonel Reznov probably used it to backtrack the whole train where they could circle and continue heading south," Dakota said, tracing her right index finger back up to the Montana-Alberta border where they had ditched them.

"They would've had to backtrack at least to Milk River Outpost to get that rear locomotive in the front," Picket said.

On the map, an old town called Milk River sat, the old town transformed into an outpost of the Canadian Confederacies railroad network.

"About how long would that have taken?" she asked.

Picket's brow furrowed, and he shrugged, "Depends if they were hauling ass to catch up or not. Factor in the amount of weight they're hauling, the terrain, and so on and so forth… I would figure the rails could safely accommodate a speed around fifty miles per hour. Around a four-hour round trip to get back to where they were. Then there are those two fellows we left on the side of the railroad who they would've stopped to pick up along the way."

"Assuming they weren't dead by then," Wheeler added.

"I figure maybe seven, eight hours behind us." Picket shrugged, looking at Dakota.

"You're the reason we're here…"

"To save our skins," Wheeler interrupted.

"For which I am grateful, if we were in danger. However, I still wanna know why we're here and what we're in for."

She sighed and nodded. It was a long story, but they had all night. She checked her watch; with night setting in, it would cost them a good seven to nine hours off their timetable. Unless it were absolutely necessary, nighttime operations in the Wastelands couldn't be conducted. She expected Colonel Reznov and his men to be as wise and to lay low if they hadn't already arrived in the remains of the city.

She pulled up a musty office chair and sat. The leather of the seat was rotten and moldy, soaking through her pants making her grit her teeth. She kicked it out from under her and took up a folding chair instead.

Picket and Wheeler sat down across from her, and she looked at the young man.

"You remember my brother I told you about?"

Dakota was on the second watch after Wheeler woke her up for his relief. She sat in the meeting room while her companions bunked down in the office. Their weapons and equipment were ready to be hauled up upon the first sign of trouble; she hoped the Colonel would lay low for the night, but worst-case scenario thinking was the name of the game.

The fogged and frosting windows offered limited visuals in three of the four cardinal directions: north, west, and south. Rain tapped on the metal roof and glass; that lulling melody was unending, prying at her eyes to close as she sat on an old wooden chair.

From the cargo wagon, they had found more than just supplies and weapons. There was a radio scanner that, in optimal conditions, ranged a good fifty miles of detection range. The relative flat ruins of Colorado Springs, courtesy of the GFOABs—she expected to reach as far, with the scanner. That kept her awake, her unending search for any radio communication, and an unending search for the hope of Phil.

"C'mon, Buddy, I know you're out dere." She sniffed, turning the volume up an increment. *Say something.*

She had a CB radio, rated for thirty miles in range, and with the new terrain as it was, she expected to reach that far. Pressing the PTT button and wiping her eyes, she spoke clearly and steadily for the umpteenth time that hour. "Phil, if you can hear me, it's Dakota. Please respond. I say again, Phil if you can hear me, it's Dakota. Come in." She pressed the radio to her forehead, clenched her eyes, and waited.

Only static responded as it had for the last four hours; it was Picket's turn now to take the watch, but she elected to remain on duty. The response of static, indicating no sign of Phil, no sign of his presence, seemed to her an audible heraldry for the Dead World and gloom that surrounded her. She lowered the mic back to her lips.

She hoped for the shame of the reality that they had left Phil behind if that meant he was still alive. If such rueful feelings meant hugging him one more time, she'd gladly accept them.

Please respond, she begged, and then it came—a break in the static.

It stuttered at first, incomprehensible. Her eyes shot open, beady but drying fast, and she leaned further into the mic, pressing her ear closer to the receiver.

She had taken the bait of hope, hooked to a fishing line with given slack, and now despair would reel her in closer to its grasp. Her heart was racing, and the very same guilt and shame clawed at her as her ears sharpened, anticipating Phil's reply. But the signal was weak on the scanner.

If he had heard her signal and she couldn't get clear feedback, then he had to be somewhere outside that thirty-mile radius of her broadcast but within that fifty-mile radius of her scanning. In the darkness of night, blurred by the limited vision of her windows, she could see nothing but pitch blackness disturbed by the occasional flicker of lightning.

"Phil, Phil, come in. Say again your last."

Her lips threatened to smile, and hope shone too brightly in her voice. That fishing line gave slack, allowing her to pull and tire herself out before reeling back in closer to the grips of despair.

She heard labored breathing coming over the line, rasped. Hope departed as she was pulled out of the water and into the hands of despair when she realized it wasn't Phil. It wasn't his voice. The line cleared; the message now came without the disruption of static.

His words erected the hairs on the back of her neck and shivered her spine with goosebumps: "Not my face."

Part V – All Hallows Eve

Chapter One – The Hunting

A loud crackling thunderclap jolted Dakota awake, her right eye crusted in sleep, the other still blinded under her bandaging. A second later, a hand fell on her shoulder, and she jerked forwards, right hand making a quick grab for her pistol, but stopped as the face of Wheeler came into focus, walking around her as silent as a fox, hands raised.

"I'm sorry," she sighed, her right eye slowly closing back into rest as she leaned back into the seat.

"I didn't mean to give you a scare." His hands lowered.

She shook her head. "Just on edge, I suppose." She looked back at the door to the office. "Picket still asleep?"

"Yeah." Wheeler sat on the desk next to the radio receiver and signal booster and wiped his nose. "The man's tough, but don't let him trick ya; he ain't getting no younger. I don't know how he's managed to keep up at this age."

"Just how old is he?" She raised a brow.

"Hell, I dunno." He gave her a single nod upwards, fingers motioning to his face. "It's been a minute since we let those air out, don't ya think?"

It had been more than a while since she let her wounds breathe or swapped out the bandages. The task fell to the back of her mind, taking less priority, considering the other things she had to do. Then there was the fact that she couldn't do it all on her own, and she exhaled deeply knowing, what offer came next.

"Do you need a hand, Miss?"

She considered it. Bending and moving her arms at even the normal angles they were designed for made her skin sweat and her eyes water. That alone had become a laborious task, let alone everything else that needed nurturing.

She leaned forward and untucked her shirt from her pants, lifting it as far as she could, stopping when her ribs demanded her to. Clenching her teeth, from the discomfort as the young man helped her remove her shirt. It was just as much of the pain as it was her phobia of being touched. Taking in breaths as deep as she could manage before sharp jabs at her right side made her flinch, she was robbed of her next deep breath. Wheeler was gentle as he began to unwrap the tape and removed the bandages around her waist. After that, he removed those around her neck and shoulders.

"You're a good kid, Buddy." She patted his leg. "Thank you."

"I reckon we both have things to be grateful for, Miss," he said, wadding up the bandages into a ball and tossing them aside.

Anxiety clenched at her teeth. Her fist pressed against the top of the desk, and she distracted herself from the panicked thoughts by looking out the windows. There was thundering and lightning outside, illuminating the thick fog that had settled over the land. The veil of thick gray blocked the housing, small businesses, and nature at a curtain of visibility exceeding, at the most, thirty yards.

Her thoughts threatened to drift to those oil rigs in the Great Gulf—lonely structures in a void of chaos. The workshop suddenly felt very similar inside the storm.

"Any activity outside?" he asked.

"Nope, all's been quiet." She bit her cheeks on the inside.

He helped her get her shirt back on, her hand favoring her side. She lifted her right leg, and he rolled up the pants leg past the knee in gentle folds. Revealing the gauze and wrap over where her trench knife had carved, red had seeped through the layers at some point and dried.

"You recall what you said to me before?" he asked.

"I've said a lot of things."

He laughed. "No offense, Miss, but you don't really talk much." His eyes focused as he unraveled the medical tape around her knee. The peeling feeling was a sensation of relief. "We're down here because of your brother, right?"

Dakota took in a deep breath and nodded "yeah." The wrap and bandages at her calf were removed, balled up, and tossed aside. Next came the gauze that was sticking from the dried blood; she felt a tingle as he peeled it off. There were little specks of fresh blood from where parts of the scabbing had been removed.

"Well, I'm not one to pry if it ain't my business. I figure yer not either. But if you need me to listen, I'm an open book, Miss. Just remember what you said to me. It's okay to be sad."

When her knee was uncovered and the stitches allowed to breathe, Wheeler leaned back. The rest she could get herself, the first being the bandages covering half her face. The cut there never stopped throbbing; it would recede but pick up again in rhythm with her pulse. She found the coldness of the air to be a soothing contrast to the heated throbs that went from her head to her toes.

She took out the inhaler and took in a deep breath through her right nostril. The left was too swollen from where it had been bent to allow air passage. She didn't breathe in as deeply as she could; if she did, she would have been sent into a coughing fit that didn't mix well with broken ribs. She held her breath for five seconds before slowly letting it out through her mouth. When fully deflated, she put the inhaler to her lips and breathed in a puff of the albuterol. Taking it all in, she held it inside for a few seconds before releasing it in a slow exhale. A couple of weak coughs followed.

Dakota rested her head back in the chair, right hand searching for the pain meds and antibiotics. Coming to a shaking stop, she held her breath as her ears focused on the disturbance of silence from outside. She limped over to the window, peering out into the darkness as the rain was letting up.

Thinned by the distance between the source of the sound and themselves, muffled through the fogged glass, came harrowing screeches and wailing moans of hunger pains. Brows furrowing, her right eye focused on the fog from which those moans echoed forth. It was as if the thick gray veil was sentient, yearning for their flesh to devour. Silver sheens of moonlight shone through an opening in the overcast, purplish night sky. Those silvery sheens contrasted with the grayness of the fog, revealing the blurred outlines of shapes moving in the dark.

Her heart pounded looking at the figures: wraiths moving at their shambling pace, among which draugrs hid and blended until stimulated by the promise of food. She hated how there was no distinguishing factor until something triggered them, hated how the things sprinted in full pursuit.

"All entry points are locked down; I'll tell Picket we need to keep things around here quiet." Wheeler disappeared out the door, silent as a fox, parting with, "That ol' man's joints will pop and alert the whole damn mess of 'em."

Dakota hefted up her SVK, backing up towards the far wall from the windows, where the shadows were thicker. The moonlight kept all things illuminated well enough, and out of her elevated vantage point she could see the moving bodies of the undead. She wasn't looking at the zombies but searching among their number for something bigger.

Amidst the orchestra of moans and screeches rose a low gurgling rose, a deep and congested snarl that rattled through the air over the moans, demanding silence. With that rattling snarl came the unmistakable, and, she thought, crude sound of metal grinding against concrete.

Here and there, fading in and out through the fog, she saw pulses of light. Little bursts of brass-yellow lighting moved in a pulse-like rhythm in the dark behind the silhouetted zombies. Her own heart was banging in her chest, hairs on the back of her neck erect. Remembering the last time she had seen the fiend, she recalled what he had taken from her and Tim. Hate filled her heart, calmed her breath, and narrowed her focus.

She had her thumb pressed to the PTT button but hadn't initiated the break in radio silence. Stopping when her eyes detected quick movement from the outside, her eyes widened as she dove out of the way of an incoming projectile. It blew out through the veil of fog like a cannonball. The counterweight back end of a forklift broke open a hole in the meeting room. The heavy relic of machinery plummeted through the wall and onwards through the workshop's roof.

Wincing, with her right hand holding her side, she got a knee under her, then a foot, and she stood back up. That rattling snarl transitioned into words, hate seething with each syllable as he spoke: "I SEE HEW."

Then she heard Wheeler break radio silence, the sounds of the two men rappelling down the rope to the first floor. She got back into the supervisor's office when a mass of glass shattered, bricks crumbled, and metal tore from a breach in their perimeter. The floor under her shook; she thought it would collapse and she hurried to the railed walkway outside. Looking down, she saw Inimicus bringing down a crude mixture of twisted rebar and reinforced cement in a hammer strike. The giant mallet looked as if it was ripped out from a building.

Wheeler kicked Picket square in the chest, sending his friend out of harm's way; the force of the kick sent the young man in the opposite direction. Inimicus's hammer crashed down against the train instead of her two friends, and the mass of cement and rebar grazed down the side of the locomotive, dealing a scar in the metal beast.

Dakota limp-sprinted to a joining catwalk running adjacent to the one she was on. Standing high above the train, taking in quick notes as she lined up her sights, she saw the fiend's arteries illuminated under his skin—the source of that pulsing brass-yellow color. His movements were slower, groggy, and laborious, but deadly all the same. He had his hammer back up, readied for another strike at Picket who was recovering from Wheeler's kick. Dakota's sights met the center of the monster between the shoulder blades. The monster's right side showed twitches of movement as if instinctively trying to use a right arm that was no longer there.

She pulled the trigger and clenched her teeth from the recoil traveling up her broken arm and fading out passed the shoulder as if needles had been stuck in her left shoulder blade. The bullet made impact at the spine; the monster jerked forwards in a quick spasm. Fresh pink blood misted out from the entrance wound.

Inimicus turned, coughing up pink blood, now dripping out his scorched flesh of a bottom chin. The rotten flesh of his upper lip was fully cauterized from lip to nostrils. Skull bones shone bright white through the charred, fleshy tissues, but he wore a cynical smile as he looked at her. Joy sparked in his eyes turning his back towards Picket and Wheeler. She supposed the two men down below were more like mere fawns of interest. Inimicus was a hunter, and she understood, just as Phil and Tim did, that Inimicus viewed her and her brothers as buffalo or some other trophy hunt.

"You want your trophy?" Dakota hollered at him.

Inimicus glared back with a gleeful grin, his bloodshot eyes never moved from her. He took a step in her direction. Behind him, she saw Wheeler on a knee, aiming his rifle at the fiend. Inimicus, fully aware, gave an uncaring kick with half the effort he usually gave in his attacks. But it was enough to send the young man airborne. She watched Wheeler bash into the coach wagon of the train and fall somewhere between the loading bay and tracks.

"PHESS AWF," Inimicus sneered at him now, his voice irritable as he looked back at her.

"Picket?!" Dakota yelled down. The old man was out of her line of sight, but she could hear his shuffling. She didn't need to say anything else; he got the message, replying with a simple, "I got the kid."

Dakota took a step back, glaring down at the monster. "Come and get it then fucker!"

With as much speed as a white-tailed doe needs to cross twenty yards in a matter of seconds, Inimicus's face tightened upon her challenge. Invigorated by a second wind, he squatted and kicked up off the ground in a single leap, hurling himself up to the catwalk, coming to collect his prize.

Dakota ran. She made it to the other side of the catwalk and workshop where her options were to dead ends at her left and right. But one offered a window. Behind her, she could hear the careless tearing of metal, the protest of the grated catwalk supporting Inimicus's weight. Dakota took off towards the window.

It was a six-by-nine window, composed of seventy-two glass panels, each one a square foot. Old and brittle, she aimed and fired her rifle, bullets weakening the glass before she hurled herself into it.

Glass dug into her forearms and fingers as leapt out into the thick shroud of fog, now with only five meters of visibility. She landed on an awning composed of corrugated metal, traveling down at a forty-five-degree angle. It cushioned her fall, slowing her momentum as she slid off and fell ten feet to a hard thud in the mud.

She dared not bend her knees before landing, at least her right one, using her left to absorb the impact. Directing the speed and momentum forwards to her left arm and shoulder, she rolled to a stop. She was free of injury, but nothing short of absolute pain seethed with every breath. The painkillers' effects were waning. Her body throbbed with pain, more and more as she tried to climb back to her feet but fell into the mud.

Her body would not yield, demanding a hiatus. Inimicus came to a cratering land, denting the mud around him in a two-foot radius, falling to a knee soon after catching himself with his hammer. He, like her, was suffering.

She watched the pulses of the brass-yellow light intensify, and vomit spewed forth out his mouth and onto his hand, burning and steaming against the cold air. Wraiths and draugrs making their approach around them endlessly continued in their moaning and screeching orchestra from the deep of the fog, not yet in sight.

Dakota tried to get up, to flee, but again fell back down into the mud. She rolled over and tried to crawl, and the mud rose to her chin, but her broken body yielded no obedience. Falling face-first into the mud before rolling over on her back, clumps of mud were sticking to her hair and face. Her chest rose and fell in rapid pants. She had hoped that she would have enough in her to lure the fiend away and survive the night. But now, all she could do was aim her SVK and dump every one of her bullets into the monster's face.

Inimicus reacted to every impact; out of the ten rounds she had left in her rifle, seven found their mark. Each one landed a critical strike on the monster and slowed him, but he continued coming closer and closer. Her body seemed to be more submissive, arms and legs willing to get back up to her feet. But now Inimicus was upon her, towering over her, and he kicked her back down.

Dakota spasmed as she lay broken. Her right hand went for her pistol, but Inimicus stepped on it, pinning it into the mud. He raised his hammer, and she noted his displeasure as he looked down at her. There was a shake of his head. "HUW TISABOINTING." To which she responded with a raised middle finger.

Gunshots came in rapid succession, cracking overhead. One after another, each one made its mark against Inimicus's chest, splattering up a line to his neck and face. The monster took one step back, then another. The sound of boots splashing in the mud came up from behind her. Her right hand now freed, she unholstered her pistol, raised it from the mud, and joined in the attack. She and her unknown savior barraged Inimicus, who was now shielding himself with his one arm and hammer.

The form of her savior was now in her far right periphery, his rifle locked back on an empty magazine. Lowering his rifle, he removed a familiar revolver from his waist. She took note of the monster's weakened midsection and the poor balance of his stance. She zeroed in her sights on Inimicus's right knee and fired the last two bullets of her pistol before the gun jammed in a misfire.

The two rounds found their mark, making enough of an impact to throw off the monster's stance. *Funny*, she thought. Had this been the situation two years ago, she believed the fiend would have killed them by now. *He's getting weaker.*

Inimicus fell to a knee, using his hammer to catch himself, leaving his face wide open. Her savior aimed the antique revolver and fired two shots that splattered into Inimicus's left eye and right jaw. The monster fell into a gagging fit, catching himself on his fallen knee. More of the brass-yellow plasma spewed forth before he gave one last glare their way and turned to flee, disappearing into the shadows.

Heavily, Dakota was panting; her whole body and clothes covered in mud, and she throbbed all over. She let her head fall back against the muddy ground, splashing the wet dirt as she looked to her savior.

Moonlight shone through the break in the clouds. The calming rays of light veiled the figure; he was dark as a silhouette until her turned to face her. It was a man dressed in all black, wearing a mask, bone in composition, looking down to her.

"He'll be back," Sergei said before turning his back to her. "Leave, now."

Chapter Two – Canto XIII

Dakota didn't leave; a second wind came to her—new energy no matter how faint or little, and she threw it all into her legs. Limping, arms flailing, her right hand could barely hold her rifle. She used the trees, cars, piles of rubble, and anything she could to steady herself, shuffling from point to point, one small goal at a time.

She chased after Sergei, following him into the scorched woods where the remains of the trees were twisted trunks of coal void of foliage and had ashen branches. A vaporous fog soon emerged, hiding the tree roots, twigs, and the ground. The gas rose to her knees and came with an odd smell as she gasped and huffed for each breath; Sergei fled deeper into the barren woods.

In one great croaking demand she told him to "STOP," but he didn't. In some bewildering way, Sergei moved in a casual limp that outpaced her hurried spurts of shuffling that should've caught up to him. Coughing fits began to take root with each of her inhales and exhales. The man's form then changed from a normal human's form to that of an ethereal spectre, a sentient scarecrow walking on elongated wooden stilts, the same said of his arms protruding out the sleeves of his coat. He moved with rough stiff movements at the joints, the sound of cracking like that of snapping twigs with every move.

Her vision narrowed, and her peripheries faded from her vision as if she were in some kind of tunnel. The trees around them grew grow; the dead, burnt trunks framing upwards, the ashen limbs of branches forming an antagonizing arch that blocked out the night sky. Distorted faces of rigid lines, resembling Sergei's mask, emerged from the burnt bark of the trunks. It was as if the pattern of barks moved and twisted to form Sergei's "face" en masse now, glaring at her. The trees had faces that cried out when she leaned on them, protests of pain in the form of a screeching ring to her ears, bringing shivers up her spine.

"You break and tear at me." The words echoed back at her from the stilted form of the madman she couldn't catch up to. The mouths of the trees moved to enunciate each syllable as she fell against the next tree. Her head moved with the rhythm of her now panting breaths. "Are you without pity? Leave me be, lest I choose not my face," he continued.

Dakota wouldn't leave. For though the words came in some hyperbolic mystery she couldn't discern, she didn't hear the voice of Sergei, but Phil's voice. The echoing effect then came from all around her, his voice now hammering at her from the many mouths of the trees, thick red crimson bleeding through the cracks in the bark.

Sergei and the trees continued to speak with Phil's voice: wishing for her to go home, bury Phil as she knew him, and move on. But the sound of Phil's voice brought out a stoutness of loyalty she couldn't deny—the kind of loyalty that would prompt a mother or sister to dive into the fires of hell after a beloved. Dakota had heard his voice; she knew he was here, and he needed her help. She wouldn't let him go, and she'd swim into the deepest pits of Dante's Inferno, all the way to the frozen lake's bottom, if it meant reaching him.

"NO!" She fell on a tree, both hands holding onto to bark as she screamed into Sergei's face before several sharp wheezes disoriented her. Hard sniffs followed by bloodied sniffs down her nose and into her muddied mouth. The salt of her tears entered at the cracks of her lips and brought moisture back to her dry mouth.

"I'm no Virgil; I can't bring you back if you don't."

Sergei came back into view, far down the tunnel of funneling trees with his face upon them. The fog diminished, and suddenly she found herself closer as if the distance and time were cut from existence and she teleported within arm's reach of the madman.

What Sergei didn't know was that she was Phil's Virgil; she came to bring him back. Instinct took over and her SVK was now at the high ready, sights aiming down, and in a hoarse bark she ordered him to "STOP!"

He obliged but refused to raise his hands. His back faced her, rising and falling with heavy rasps. Everything in her moved to pull the trigger. But something provoked restraint, something inside her kept her from shooting the man. Perhaps it was the familiarities she had seen in Sergei's stride that reminded her of Phil's, or maybe it was because she heard Phil's voice. Whatever the case, Sergei was her ticket to her brother.

"Where is he?" she growled.

Sergei's head turned over his shoulder, and the left eye of his mask looked at her. In that black hole of an eye, she saw a glimmer of moonlight, shining on the pupil within; the cold air of his breaths rose out through the rigid mouthpiece and floated up into the air where the coldness of the world ate the warmth.

In a low voice, he spoke, absent of emotion, “I killed him.”

His words cut straight and sharp into her guts, tightening her heart and crushing her soul.

“No.”

Her shoulders fell, eyes watered, as she realized she had spent her second. Wanting to pull the trigger, and wanting to give up, she fell to her knees. The darkness enveloped her, and she closed her eyes, sobbing, with no will to move. Sergei continued with his flight and disappeared into the darkness, leaving Dakota broken and weeping as she collapsed on the ground.

She didn’t know how long she had been there; the last sense of time was when her watch beeped once, signaling midnight. When she felt like she had enough strength to sit up, she remained lying. That vaporous fog had fully dissipated, and the world returned to normal; the trees were no longer damned souls bearing Sergei’s face nor funneling the woods ahead. Everything was back to how it had been, the world outside and the pain inside.

Dakota waited, wondering to herself, “For what?” Perhaps to muster the will to keep going. Yes, that had to be it. Thinking of Wheeler and Picket spurred something in her, an ember to keep her from giving up. The two men’s statuses were unknown, and the training workshop was compromised by Inimicus. She needed to get back to them; they needed to restore their defenses and figure out their next move.

But she continued to lie there, just like that night, eleven years ago in Atlanta when giving up hope on her baby girl and husband. In a darkest hour when her heart couldn’t go on with not knowing.

“Dakota?” Phil had been the one to find her inside a school’s nursery. She had laid down on a musty, pink bunny, and given up.

It had been Phil who brought her back to their armory turned base; there, with Tim, they kept her going until her will returned. That had been the start, for her at least, when those two men became her brothers—became her everything. Only now, there wasn't Phil to find her, calling out her name, and Tim wasn't nearby to help.

"Dakota?" She heard but didn't respond. She sniffed as a tear escaped her eyes. "Dakota?" he continued, and she roared out for whatever evil was toying with her to stop. Rolling over, gritting her teeth against the pain it brought to her right side, she got her rifle ready to aim and shoot.

Only it hadn't been a trick. She sat up when she saw two men rushing towards her. At first glance, she didn't recognize Tim, or Slug behind him. Several times she blinked in disbelief— another trick of the fog perhaps. It had to be a trick; Tim was moving without a broken arm or leg. Her thoughts were proven false when Tim fell to his knees before her, grabbed her by the shoulders, and looked at her. She realized it wasn't a trick, and she couldn't help but think that in her darkest hour, God had sent her who she needed the most.

Hope was an odd thing; she dared not to hold on without some measure of caution. Tim was supposed to be thousands of miles north, back home. It didn't make sense to her, and she thought she was seeing things again. So, it was only when she grabbed onto her brother's shoulders, she knew it was indeed who she needed the most. She broke down and wept with a bitter smile. She fell into his chest, grief, and joy tugging at her from both directions. His arms tightened around her and his chin rested on her head. She felt him push at her, softly, his hands now cradling her head as his thumbs caressed her bruised cheekbones and, already, she knew. They couldn't stay there.

"Let's go, Ranger girl." His voice was comfort immeasurable.

She nodded, holding onto his wrists as he helped her back up to her feet.

Chapter Three – Sister's Keeper

-October 30th, 2030-

Slug kept ahead of them, reaching the door to the breakroom, holding it open for them by the time Tim carried Dakota through. Along the way, Dakota's limping and hopping made her hard breathing a rattled wheeze. When Tim saw it was taking all her effort to just stay conscious, he stopped helping her walk and hoisted her up in a fireman's carry.

Tim lowered Dakota down on a bench, slowly, mindful of her tender side. Slug stomped across the breakroom to a red emergency exit door and gave it a couple of good pushes. The door was latched and held.

"Alright, I'm gonna hook up with Dagger for patrol. You two good?" asked Slug, holding a thumbs up. He was already backing away from the emergency exit to the way they had entered.

"Yeah." Tim gave him a nod.

"Copy." Slug frowned and left.

Tim caught a brief exchange between the Royal Marine and Olivia wanting to enter the room.

"C'mon, I can help 'em." The girl stomped her foot.

He could hear Slug closing the door, cutting off further protests from the kid. "If the answer was no before, what makes you think it's any different now?"

Tim stomped over to the door, yanked it open, and glared at Olivia. "You want to help, get into that coach wagon there." He pointed at the train. "Get a cot set up, some MREs, and water. That oughta keep you busy, and if you finish with that, go find Chain."

"Aye, aye, Sir Asshole, Sir." Olivia gave him a middle finger salute before departing to the train before he could say anything else.

Dakota grimaced from behind him, a weak cackle. "I think you're stuck to the hip with her by this point."

"She's a handful; that much is for sure." Tim snickered and closed the door, pacing back to his sister. He unclipped his radio and set it on the table next to them along with a first aid kit.

"You gonna fill me in?" she asked, waving a finger from his left arm to his left leg.

"You first." Tim returned the gesture but motioned at her from head to toe, ending with a quick, "Lean forwards."

She did, and he helped her untuck her shirt and remove one sleeve at a time. Dakota winced at the slightest movements. Tim's heart ached at the bruises, swelling, scrapes, and scratches all over her body. "First, let's get you fixed up; then you can tell me all about it."

"You shouldn't have to help me do this." She shook her head, eyes falling to the floor.

Tim grabbed her shoulders. "Look at me."

She looked up, meeting his eyes.

"I was being selfish before. I let you grieve alone and was an ass while you took care of me."

He felt some relief when she smiled, "You're still an ass," she laughed faintly, "but you're my ass… eh wait, that didn't sound right."

"I meant what you knew." Tim chuckled, giving her a wink.

"Buddy." He felt her eyeing him as he opened the first aid kit. "You were dealing with more than just losing Phil."

Tim couldn't say anything to that, but he still felt resolute. He had taken her for granted, up until the point they went on their own ways; that wouldn't happen again. No matter what demons escaped the closest.

With careful intent, Tim patted clean dirt and other debris from her cuts, scrapes, and stitches with rags he wetted from his canteen. Then, even more gently, he pressed disinfectant wipes against them. All the while, Dakota hissed through clenched teeth, ending only after the application of antibiotic gel and dressing of the cuts and stitches.

After dressing her knee, he lowered her leg and rolled her pant leg down. "Do you want your face dressed up, too?" he asked, watching as she reached into her pocket, removed an inhaler, and held up her index finger.

She took in a puff, breathing in all the albuterol, and held her breath a couple of seconds before exhaling. A couple of weak coughs followed.

"No, thank you," she said, stowing away her inhaler and procuring a couple of pill bottles. Tim took the bottles and read the milligram count for the painkillers and antibiotics before giving her two of each and the remaining water in his canteen.

"I'll get you some more when we get you to the coach," he said as she downed the pills with a couple of gagging sips. Her breathing was heavier now, and her head fell back against the bench's backrest. That made him worry more.

"You good?" he asked, receiving a shaking grin in response.

"Not in the slightest." She chuckled.

They were in the coach wagon, Dakota refused to fall asleep on the cot Olivia had prepared. Instead she sat munching on an MRE and sipping water, they brought each other up to speed on their eventful last few days.

"ULFBERT, you said?" she asked, after another puff from her inhaler.

"I know." Tim looked at his left arm for a brief second, just to make sure it was still healed and not a figment of his imagination.

"And Ol' Faithful?" she raised the brow over her one good eye.

"We stashed her at a rendezvous location, call sign Foxtrot Romeo, a few mikes west of here, inside a tennis court. Well hidden," Tim said, then sighed in response to her persistent probes at his left limbs.

Dakota never stopped when he told her about the treatment, going from arm to leg, leg to arm, even after he shooed away her hand like a fly. This time she was poking at his thigh.

"Never mind that." Tim waved her hand away. "You said you heard Phil's voice, but Sergei claims to have killed him?"

She shook her head, blinking then nodded. "Yeah,"

"Which one is it, then?" Tim bit his bottom lip, more in thought than asking.

"I don't know." She shrugged. "Hope for the best, plan for the worst?"

"The best we can do right now." Tim shook his head in agreement. He pinched his nose, fingers falling to the sides of his chin. "Right now, the Lads are holding security. Wheeler and Picket are monitoring comms. You need to rest."

"And you?"

“I’m not leaving your side,” he remarked, quick and sharp.

The door nearest the flatbed wagon opened, and Olivia entered. She leaned against the wall with an MRE she was picking from. An AK-74 dangled at her side from its sling. “You two are just adorable, you know that?” She smirked.

“Good hell.”

“Thank you.” Dakota smiled at her, pointing at the cot.

“You're welcome.” Olivia brightened and smiled back to her. “I brought you an extra blanket,” she said, untucking a rolled woolen blanket pinched between her arm and side.

Tim took it and lay it at the head of the cot, then looked at his sister. Dakota sighed and gave in, laying her head on the rolled blanket. He then tucked her in, doubling up the blankets before lowering to a knee next to her, holding her right hand in his, and patting her cheek. “Tomorrow, we’ll look for Phil. Then we'll get the fuck out of here.”

Dakota was lights out midway through, and he felt as if he were smiling and frowning at the same time. The moment he became aware of it, he tucked his sister’s hand under the blanket.

Not two feet away from sat Tim. Pinching the bridge of his nose, he felt another headache setting in. It came with all the familiar discomforts that preceded an inevitable migraine. He opened his eyes when Olivia walked over and sat next to him.

“She gonna be okay?” the diva asked.

Tim nodded. “Did you talk to Chain?”

“He said to remain on standby if you needed help with her.” She nodded to Dakota. “Pretty banged up.”

“Ranger tough; she’ll be fine.” Tim looked to his sister, then back to the kid. He saw the same kind of regression he had seen in her from the back of Ol’ Faithful; he felt a silent tension that seemed to take root inside her that she couldn't seem to talk about. And the kid was a talker, which worried him; nudging her shoulder with his elbow he asked, “How you holding up?”

Olivia stretched her arms, fingers fidgeting with one another as she shrugged. Two years ago, he wouldn’t have pressed, even if he saw the girl repressing something. To have her calm down would have been a wish granted back then. But now it made him worry. The last two days she had been someone else; she wasn't the same happy-go-lucky Olivia Blundell as before.

"Olive?"

She licked her dried lips and bit her bottom as if to hold it back. Her face tightened and strained before her features caved in and her eyes watered.

Oh hell. Tim's heart ached, taking a chance, and wrapping his arm around her

She pushed back; it was clear she didn't want to be touched, and at the same time, he could see she needed something to hold her together—some kind of compressing comfort and maybe a reminder that not all men who lay hands on her would harm her.

Olivia squirmed, but he held her tight, and soon she caved further. Her pushing hands now held her face as she sobbed. Her tears dampened his shirt as she broke apart, and he held her together.

Tim lulled her with an unending, "Shh," resting his head over hers. They stayed like this for a while, Tim letting her soak his shirt with her tears until she had tired herself to sleep. By then, Tim moved to the wagons bench across from him and laid her down to sleep, covering her with a couple of blankets.

"It's okay now," he whispered to her, folding the blanket under her chin so it wouldn't cover her mouth.

Tim didn't catch a wink. Instead, he stayed up all night with the others on a shift rotation made by Chain. All was clear and silent, and occasionally Tim limped over to Dakota and hovered his fingers under her nostrils when it looked like she had stopped breathing. Fear was replaced by relief when he felt her breaths brush against the skin of his finger. Then he'd sit back down, across from Olivia. She moved and mumbled in her sleep. Somehow prone to covering her face with the covers, he'd uncover her face time and time again.

Several hours of this passed, and all the while he sorted through and processed everything that had transpired over the last couple of days. Sahtu, Major General Petrov, Dakota, Phil, and Olivia. On and on. He felt as if he were drowning, reaching out for anything to pull him back above water, and something did. In the form of a crumpling sound from his right cargo pocket he reached in and pulled out his mother's letter. His other thoughts returned to him as he looked at the paper, crumpled, folded, and creased all over. But still legible, still waiting to be read.

He glanced over to Dakota. She had been right before, and he felt as if he had been hurting her. He couldn't do that anymore; that path led only one way, and it hurt those around him. It had been a miracle they were back together again, and he didn't want to take that for granted anymore. His migraine was now in full effect, but he could still feel that gentle voice inside, giving him those soft pushes to do that which he didn't want to do. What he feared to do.

Tim unfolded the papers and read the first line once more. "Hey Baby. I know it's likely you won't read this."

This time, Tim read on.

Chapter Four – Scarecrow Terrace

-October 31st, 2030-

Click click, sounded off from his radio.

Two seconds of silence followed before another *click click.*

On and on it went, pulling back the curtains of sleep as Tim woke with a nauseating feeling of dread that came with those audible pairs of clicking. His eyes were crusted over with sleep, staring with sharp intensity at the radio.

The intervals of two clicks, followed by a two-second silence, rinse and repeat, was a silent alarm, warning system that would continue for as long as the sender was able to, or until the receiver replied with a double click from his own PTT button.

Understanding the presence of danger, Tim's eyes scanned the inside of the coach wagon; Dakota stirred awake in his peripheries. His hand found his radio on the seat beside him and gave the double-click affirmation.

Tim shook Olivia awake, and Dakota was now sitting up. Grimacing flashed across her face holding her side with tender care. Both Tim and her looked to the coach wagon points of entry, fully aware.

Olivia was slower to respond, sitting up as she rubbed her eyes, bloodshot irritability on her face; she was not a morning person. "What is that?" she asked.

"Nothing good." Tim clipped his radio back on his vest; the silent alarm continued once more, then ended. He had a growing fear of their buddies on watch being captured or executed, a signal flame snuffed out in the distance.

His M4 was leaning against the seat and the window, not a foot away. Grabbing his weapon, he rushed over to the coach door. Outside, he looked left, performing a quick one-second scan. *No one in sight.* He looked right.

Wheeler came running out from around a corner in a beeline to the coach. Tim stepped out, keeping more than a meter's distance between his raised rifle and Wheeler as he covered the young man's approach.

Wheeler brushed past him and into the coach as Tim closed the door behind him, Dakota had Olivia down under the windows as Wheeler stepped over to her, holding the kid's AK-74.

"What are we looking at here, bud?" Tim asked.

"I don't know," gasped Wheeler. "Chain put me on patrol with Slug and Dagger, and we were ambushed. Everyone's been radio silent since."

"Ambushed by who?"

"Soldiers in black ACUs," Wheeler said. "Colonel Reznov's men, if I had to guess."

"Slug and Dagger?" Tim demanded, a quick snap in his voice, but Wheeler only shrugged. "We're quitting this place then, falling back to Foxtrot Romeo," Tim said, walking over to the door.

Behind him, he heard Dakota spur Olivia back to her feet, and his radio went off with Dakota's voice echoing from behind him. "SRT-Bravo, to anyone left, rendezvous to Foxtrot Romeo, I say again, rendezvous to Foxtrot Romeo."

"The Blackhawk?" Olivia looked at him, then around at the coach wagon, waving her arms around. "Why don't we take the train and plow through it all?"

With counting fingers, Tim replied, "It's too big a target, easy to find, slow at first, we can't turn this thing around, and we don't know the condition of the rails beyond, sweetheart."

Tim removed his pistol from his holster and handed it to the kid.

She grabbed the gun, tucking it in her arm before pulling the action back. A warm feeling of pride came to him when seeing she had made sure the chamber was hot'n ready.

"Bravo's helicopter is ten mikes west of here. Too rough of terrain for the Tigr; we'll have to hoof it on foot. Wheeler, take up the rear. Dakota and Olivia, hold the center. I'll take point."

Turning back to the door, he listened as everyone fell into formation. When Dakota's hand patted his shoulder, they were ready, and he opened the door. Stepping out to their nine o'clock, his iron sights never left his field of view, looking low then high.

The whole place was dead, with no sign of the Lads or Picket, nor any hostile. The fact that there was no sign of threats breaching the workshop told him they were setting up isolating and blocking positions outside the building to keep them from egressing the location. If that was the case, then they had a very narrow window before such positions were fully formed—but it was a gamble and their only move.

Tim double-timed his efforts, hearing the whistling wheezes and huffs of Dakota keeping up behind Olivia. He strode cross the wide open of the loading bay to the employee breakroom dead ahead. The door gave, and Tim broke left, hearing Olivia follow straight behind him; Dakota broke right with Wheeler behind her.

We gotta train these kids up. He shoved the thought aside, studying the room that was clear of threats. The emergency exit door was still closed.

Rushing through and around the old tables and chairs to that emergency exit, the lot of them formed another stack at the door; Tim counted off the pairs of feet behind him until he knew everyone was stacked behind him. Then he waited for another cueing pat on his shoulder.

"What?" whispered Olivia.

"Pat his shoulder, now," came a hushed snip from Dakota.

Tim felt Olivia pat his shoulder, and he shook his head and opened the door.

Outside was a fenced-in area with housing construction equipment on the building's west side; the Tigr Jeep was over in the southwest corner. So close, but too far out of reach. Tim moved to the nearest point of cover leftwards out the door and checked behind the door that swung open outwards.

Clear.

Olivia was beside him and Dakota along with Wheeler to the right, taking cover. The place was a miniature maze, one that took precious time to move through with that methodical clearing of every new sector they came to, moving five to ten meters at a time.

They came to the gate leading out of the maze, but when seeing the chain and padlock on the ground Tim's heart beat like a hammer. The outside ring of rust completely encircled the inner shine steel to the metal link, the core of the link. They hadn't even heard the cutting, the moaning of rusted hinges opening or closing, or the rattling of the chain links.

Fuckers are good, he seethed through his teeth in an exhale.

It felt like it had already been too late. Tim shoved the gate open and no sooner he heard the clanking of something hitting the cracked and weed-infested cement under them like the sound of a soup can clattering. He leapt out and sidestepped behind the safety of the outer fence before the loud *BANG* disoriented his world and lingered in a ringing to his ears.

Dakota stumbled out through the gate, holding her head, and Tim pulled her clear of the gate's fatal funnel. Neither Wheeler nor Olivia came out, and he pied the gate, looking back inside.

Tim was greeted by the *WHIZZING* of several rounds flying overhead, forcing him back from view. More bullets continued to pass overhead, yet not one was shot at the chain-link fencing.

Both he and Dakota ducked as the rounds continued to suppress them. Tim took a knee, his other leg pushing against rock and soil, his back flush against the chain links. He dared an angled look back inside. Olivia and Wheeler were picking themselves off the ground, stumbling and falling. Tim aimed two meters off the tip of his barrel from Wheeler, returning fire; his voice sounded muffled in his head, trying to form words he couldn't discern.

The kids were just in arm's reach, but the unseen forces had fire superiority. A cascade of hellfire then descended on him, and bursts of machine gun fire ripped the chain links across from him. Barrages of lead tore through the metal at head's height, and he got the message.

Tim covered his head from the debris of bullets striking a pile of wood pallets next to the gate. Dakota shielded herself. Tim returned more fire as Dakota reached for the nearest kid she could grab. Men in all-black ACUs filled the area like a pack of wolves, grabbing and detaining Olivia, then Wheeler. Tim and Dakota watched, their efforts in vain as the two kids were dragged away from the fight and out of sight.

More machine gun fire continued to rip through the fencing, a gradual dissension of the fencing's height behind them. It was one that would force the two of them to their bellies, making for suppressed targets, easy to flank and capture. They both knew this, yet Tim didn't want to leave. Not wanting to abandon Oliva, nor flee from an inevitable defeat, he cursed at himself for her second capture under his protection. A fire burned in him, one that he couldn't vent as the suppressing hellfire continued to chip away at the fence, continued to force them closer to the ground.

Dakota pulled at his arm, and he yielded; there was nothing more to be done. While they still had room to stand, the only thing they could do was retreat to fight another day. He yielded to his sister, taking a flash grenade, pulling the pin, and tossing it through the gate while Dakota hurled a smoke grenade where a creek merged with a nearby thicket down a slope five meters away from them.

The loud *BANG* left a slight tingle ringing in their ears as they put the workshop behind them. The shooting died down, giving them a window of escape before the suppressed gunfire broke out again. They broke for the slope, sliding down mud to the creek where the waters barely crested over the soles of their boot, making a splashing impact as they limped-ran for the thicket. The bank of the creek was more of a ditch that rose to their waists. Dakota's smoke grenade bellowed in concealment as they disappeared into the cloud of smoke.

Back at the workshop, they could hear engines revving and men in pursuit. More bullets *popped* and *cracked* overhead. The water deepened, covering their boots entirely, and the creek transitioned to the metal ring of a rusted culvert underneath a street. The flanks left and right rose in small slopes of dirt and brush to the road above. They climbed up the junction and onto the road, following it deeper into a neighborhood where the remains of Dead Traffic were thick enough to warrant the caution of Ankle Snatchers; those zombies who were stuck and remained under vehicles, pinned by the deflated tires.

They waded in deeper, until the Dead Traffic congested not just the streets but the front yards of the houses as well, until the thickness was too dense for any Tigr to drive through. Debris sent airborne from the GFOABs flooded the space between cars and houses, blocking out all visuals of the ground below. It made stealth impossible as they waded deeper into the sea of ruin.

Foxtrot Romeo was nestled in an old neighborhood park, complete with a bicycle trail encompassing the playgrounds and ball game courts. Now it was fully consumed by withered, tall grass and trees; the only court not fully concealed was the park's tennis court. The fencing still stood around the faded blacktop of the tennis court.

There the Ol' Faithful rested, the tree canopies spread wide, and the trunks spaced out provided a wide-open area to maintain a decent visual for any mindless hostiles while offering plenty of obscurity to any threat that could reason. The area was a double-edged sword.

No one else had made it to the bird. Tim yanked open the pilot door and clambered into the pilot's seat, donning the radio headset over his ears as Dakota walked over and stood guard outside the door next to him.

"Scanning all frequencies," Tim uttered, listening without speaking. Leaning back against the seat, he stared through the cockpit's windshield and fence past to the trees beyond.

Crows cawed in the near distance; the cold breath of autumn's wind swept through the trees and chilled them. There were distant clatters and noises from the Dead World falling apart in its decaying state. There was no clear consistency of noises, moaning, footfalls, or anything indicative of zombies approaching.

"Anything?" asked Dakota.

Tim heard nothing from his first scan, only the static. "No," he sighed, unplugging the headset, and turning the volume down to a low setting for them both to listen while they waited. He adjusted himself so he could sit sideways, his left leg dangling out the pilot's seat and his right against the ledge.

Dakota slid open the side door and took a seat on the edge, her feet resting against the landing skid. "I should've known they'd find us there."

"They weren't zombies; they were people." Tim shook his head, "It's been a long time since we've had to contend with the like; you did the best you could with what you had."

"I still should've known better,"

Tim reached over and held his hand out. A second later, he felt Dakota's hand meet his halfway. He held her hand and gave her a soft squeeze. *Don't beat yourself up.*

"They would've needed a place large enough to house three thousand plus personnel. And a place to keep prisoners," Dakota thought aloud.

"Only thing is, the city is mostly scorched earth and rubble." Tim pulled his hand back and rubbed his forehead. "I say we wait here for another hour, give Chain and whoever may still be around more time. If it's just us, we'll need shelter come sundown."

"There." Dakota pointed with the barrel of her rifle.

Tim followed the direction of her gesture. At Ol' Faithful's eight o'clock, standing just over the canopies, was a brick structure. Possibly a school. They wouldn't need the whole building, just a small section of it that they could lock down with a primary and secondary method of egressing. From this distance, the old building looked sturdy, and its elevated position offered a promising prospect.

"Yeah," he agreed.

An hour passed, and nothing changed. All remained silent, without a soul in sight. It was a depressing reminder of how fast they could feel alone, isolated in the Wastelands. How quickly things could feel like they did before they knew that there was an Alyeska or the Canadian Confederacy to the north. It felt like they were floating on a raft in a sea of desolation.

On a piece of paper, Tim wrote out a code: Juliet Zulu Bravo Oscar Oscar Alpha Quebec Golf Oscar Lima Golf Charlie X-Ray. Then he tucked it away on the dash where it could be easily seen. He then risked a break in radio silence, giving out a single chiming click with his PTT button, a simple 'come in' request.

Silence was the only response they got, and he tossed the handset down, turned off the power to the radio, and climbed out of the pilot's seat, adjusting the sling of his rifle while Dakota slid the side access door closed.

"Ready?" Tim asked, grabbing the pilot door to close it, then stopping when the radio on his vest went off. It had a lower range than the birds, and excitement reared its teasing head from the sudden hope he felt about Bravo's proximity. One of the Lads radioed in that they were close to their rendezvous.

In response to Tim's last request, single click had come back: *I read you*, it meant. But then it clicked again, the line stayed activated, and background noise from the sender came in distorted static. Dakota stepped next to him, waiting, listening, as her radio had received a stray bullet from their fleeing. The more they listened to the background noise, the more they could register the sound of someone crying in the background, a man who sounded hysterical in desperate prayers in another language.

Then labored breathing came over the line, drowning out the other pitiful one. The breathing was rough, deep, and raspy as gibberish uttered forth. The sender's voice was far too close to the mic, making more static that came at their ears in stabbing discomfort. Then the line ended.

Tim grabbed the handset and pushed the PTT button. "Say again your last." He requested.

The line went off again, and that rasped breathing drowned the pitiful voice, the person now removed from his prayer and begging. But the heavier voice bellowed in a furious roar: "Make your face quiet. NOW!" before a splattering smash and an agonizing wail issued forth and the line died.

"Sergei," Dakota muttered.

The line clicked, gurgling coughs dying out in the background as the breathing continued.

"He's just wasting our time." Dakota grabbed his shoulder.

"Dammit." Tim set his radio back in place, turned down the volume, and looked at that tall, brick structure. "Lead the way then, Ranger Girl."

Slow was steady, and steady was fast. Moving fifteen meters at a time, they would come to a stop, look, and listen. Between them and the school was a labyrinth of a neighborhood, complete with dilapidated housing, some reduced to cinders, and more withered, tall grass that offered concealment for all types of threats, both radioactive and natural. There was Dead Traffic where Ankle Snatchers could be anywhere. But the worst of it was the smell.

Putrefaction of recent decay permeated and tainted the air. Dakota had her gaiter up over her nose. Tim didn't have one as the smell stained his nostrils, much like how a can of sardines holds the stench long after the contents are removed. The closer they got to their objective, the more the school felt like a bad idea.

That putrid smell intensified until it bogged down the air and felt like it had slimed over Tim and Dakota's sweating skin. It stuck to them, congested their nostrils, and filled their lungs. After passing through a thicket and into a grove, they came to a peculiar spot. The ground was scorched, houses had collapsed, and from the ruins sprouted trees. The twisted limbs of the branches climbed up into the waning sunlight, now just barely dimming the sky, approaching its descent to dusk. From those burnt limbs hung the bodies of men.

These weren't old, rotten corpses hanging by their necks; their flesh was in the early stages of decomposition. Men hung upside down, low enough to suffer the fate of being feasted upon by wraiths and draugrs. Legs traveled down to the stumps of waists or chests, past which all else had been eaten. Others had been hung higher up, left to die from blood loss, their arms bound behind their backs. They were left to watch their comrades endure a slow death before their own demise would follow. The higher-hanging men had bled out through gashes at their necks, their faces locked in a twisted look of despair. A few persistent wraiths lingered, reaching for more of the lower-handing stumps out of reach.

The zombies paid Tim and Dakota no mind, enough so that the duo could put blades through their skulls. The burnt grass and charred dirt were soaked and caked with the dripping remains of the dead, which stuck to their boots as they moved through the bloodied grove.

This wouldn't be the only site of sacrilegious disregard for human life; several more would be found along the way. It was never more than five men, scout teams, hanging in the same way, left to die. Two or three were suspended higher, to watch their comrades be eaten alive, before expiring from their own injuries. That putrid smell was carrion, and it only intensified the closer they got to the school. But it was too late to turn back and course correct, to find another structure for shelter.

Tim's message for Bravo had told them to go to the school, and night was closing in fast. The gates of hell it, seemed, had become their only place of refuge. Tim and Dakota moved in sync with one another in that same slow, steady rhythm.

He knew when she was about to stop, and he did so three meters before she did, making them spaced-out targets to any would-be shooter. Watching their six, he waited for the sound of Dakota's breathing to pick up. It would rise into a huff when she was ready to push on, and when that huff came, Tim knew it was time to go.

Eventually, Dakota sounded off for "contact front." Tim spun around to get a visual, both pressed to either side of a sedan, resting on it to steady the aim of their weapons. Tim's line of sight came into focus at several more bodies, stripped down to their underwear, forming a dam of sorts by blocking the street ahead. Blood coated the old pavement in a thick pool that trickled down to a nearby storm drain.

Zombies were on the mass of carrion, peeling away at the meat and bones like a flock of vultures scavenging from rotten carcasses. The rancid smell, along with the gluttonous slurps and moans, made him sick. Jealous crows cawed from the utility lines above, waiting for any scraps left behind; only zombies never left anything.

"We can't go that way," Tim mumbled.

Sudden movement, the flapping of wings, got their attention. One of the crows had departed his post on a streetlight, cawing as he flew westwards. Tim followed the bird and stared at the sight of a person standing just over the tree line in a 'T' pose. He patted Dakota's arm and pointed towards the motionless individual. It bore Sergei's signature, and with it, a scenic reroute to their objective.

They crossed the street, leaving the blockade of carrion and zombies to their three o'clock. They moved between a set of houses and through a small alley of backyard fencing shrouded with vines and weeds. The 'T' posing individual was now concealed behind the canopies of dead trees. The night closed in with every passing minute, a dreadful countdown.

The street they came onto was packed with Dead Traffic crows chimed in with an unending chorus of cawing, in concert with the distant cries of coyotes. The chill of the wind swept over the rusted vehicles, telegraphing with it the endless moans of the dead: a eulogy for a dead world.

Dakota came to a stop, and Tim took a position at her six. He heard from over his shoulder, "We've been made. Pack of hostiles due south of our position. They are coming our way, no draugrs sprinting at us, all wraiths," in a hushed voice.

"Copy." Tim returned in kind.

He felt her hand reach back and swat at him, and he turned and faced her in a northward direction. He saw her eyes fixated on her ACOG scope. Whatever visual she could see, magnified by her optic, Tim couldn't make out. He could barely distinguish the bend of the road beyond. He moved to Dakota's right side, getting a better angle, and then he saw it.

In both yards, flanking an intersection with another road heading west, were two figures mounted on poles. Like with the one before, these were 'T' posing, deathly still and far out of reach from the wraiths below. They were scarecrows, Sergei's modus operandi, and, he feared more so—*Phil's.*

The sun dimmed to a ring of red and its rays no longer scarred their vision. The sky was a thick cloud-covering painting, what would have been a beautiful sight on any other day. Shades of red, orange, and pink stretched north and south. The coating of warm colors made a canvas across the entire horizon.

When Tim was a boy, his mother would tell him such beautiful sights were a gift from God—paintings to inspire awe and enjoyment. Only now, behind the backdrop of dead trees and twisted branches silhouetted against the reddening sky, it was more of a canvas detailing a malevolent maniac's madness.

The closer they got to Sergei's handiwork, the slower they approached. The two scarecrows at the intersection looked like sentries guarding the entrance into what they realized was a cul-de-sac. The hanging men's faces were covered with rotten burlap sacks and were both dressed in the same all-black ACUs of Alyeska's Siberian Forces. Trees and underbrush formed an arching canopy over the entrance, giving it a gate-like appearance.

The first scarecrow had 'Petrov' embroidered on the right-side chest of his ACU top, along with a single silver bar pinned to his collar, the ranking symbol of first lieutenant. Tim harkened back to his conversation with the major general. Looking at the body, he nodded in dreary understanding, *Igor.* Tim stared up at the sack covering the body's face; a hole had been ripped out, spanning down the side of it, veiled by a shadow too deep to see the face underneath. He suspected he didn't want to see the corpse's rotten face nor the carving on the forehead he was sure was present.

"The major general's brother." Dakota's voice affirmed Tim's thoughts.

"And the same one who Phil encountered in Romania," Tim sighed, "Dammit it all to hell; what is going on here?"

This was another worry to ponder, though for a later time when they weren't being hunted or out in the open. When Valentin Petrov received news of his brother's demise, what recompense would follow from a man willing to send three thousand plus infantry and all the assets Dakota had mentioned on a single errand? What then?

Tim looked over at the next scarecrow when Dakota started to say something. She didn't get far, as her voice trailed off, coming to a sudden stop while Tim inspected the other sentry. He didn't even register Dakota's sudden paralysis, her transfixion on the cul-de-sac before them. He assumed she was scanning the dead end for more threats while he inspected the other sentry. 'Lossif' was embroidered on the right side of the ACU top, a single golden bar at his collar: *Second Lieutenant.*

Tim looked at Dakota; she was still locked in place, and her weapon was not raised. He stepped abreast of her, getting a better angle through the arching gateway of vines and vegetation. Looking down the dead end, her paralysis met his own. They had found the rest of the missing Wolf Pack, and more.

Spaced out in the front yards of twelve houses that formed the cul-de-sac, hung the men. Their arms stretched out to their lefts and rights, tied to wooden posts in that 'T' pose he had seen earlier. Dead trees, grass, bushes, and underbrush filled the spaces behind and between the houses, completely enclosing the whole area with a rampart of dead wooden limbs.

All the scarecrow's heads were covered with burlap sacks. A total of twelve men were MIA and yet here there was a thirteenth.

That thirteenth body held him and his sister in their frozen state, straight down to the centermost house; his body hung, facing them, not dressed in all-black ACUs. He donned a black and red flannel, blue jeans, and hiking boots with a burlap sack covering his face. Arms bound to his scarecrow post at the wrists so tight, the hands would have lost blood circulation long ago.

They walked side by side to their brother's body like timid dogs unsure whether to approach their abusive owner offering attention. Slowly, and in disbelief, their eyes never left Phil's body. The other scarecrows faded into obscurity at their peripheries and vanished until all but two remained to either side as his motionless body towered over them. The red sun set behind his hanging form, and the shadow of the house stopped just at the edge of their brother's wooden post.

It was the same gut punch that Tim felt when the Death Notification Team stepped up to his porch all those decades ago with the news of Rufus's death. The same "knowing" without ever being truly sure when he watched his father drive off later that day, never to return. The same emptiness and dread filled him as he and his mother lowered an empty casket into the ground. The isolating and foreign feeling of leaving for recruit training. Guilt and self-loathing overtook him as they did when confronted with the sight of the dead baby in her mother's arms in England. Tears streaked down his face, very much like when his mother had slammed the door in his face. It had all boiled up in the very same moment of darkness where he was helpless and bereft of hope. That very same day, he was on the edge of a bridge staring down at the I-95 traffic.

His crying eyes hardened, and he felt in his soul that he just wasn't enough. Tim cried out to God in a silent lament as his eyes fell to his boots, gazing into the past to the same yellow footprints Rufus once stood on: shoes he could never fill, shoes he didn't deserve. In the present, a small puddle of reddish water rippled between his boots. Then and there, he felt as if the Lord had abandoned them, had abandoned Phil.

Anger filled the void where hope and joy once prospered. It was an uncontrollable rage, like what he felt when confronted by his mother and father in a sudden reunion three weeks ago. At that moment, Tim felt lost and forsaken.

Tremors quaked the ground, reverberating up through the soles of his boots to his feet and fading past his ankles. With each tremor came a ripple in the puddles. A familiar presence soon filled the air as the tremors followed in twos; it was the pacing of a pair of feet belonging to an old nemesis. A cold, downwind gust of air telegraphed familiar growls as the cold of the world stabbed his hands, neck, and head.

The sun was lowering under the wall of twisted limbs, dilapidated roofs, and corpses of the scarecrows. He turned to face the direction of the wind, needing to get a visual of the Jackle coming their way. They were stuck like mice at a dead end of a maze with the Minotaur closing in on them. Tim turned, facing the intersection as the growls intensified, deepening, and becoming more discernable with a congested rattle to them.

Tears fell out the corners of his eyes, down his cheeks, and along his jawline, dripping from the stubble of his chin as he blinked the rest away. His subconscious caught it before his conscious did, a small change in the scene that kept him still. Something was wrong with two of the sentry scarecrows, or rather, something was different than before. His confusion lasted only a millisecond before conscious thought caught up to the subconscious. He was staring at the vacated scarecrow post where Lt. Petrov's body had been mounted.

"We're missing one," his grieving voice croaked, dry and level in a flat tone.

His sister had barely turned around next to him when a spark flickered at the base of the dead vegetation arching over the intersection. The flames traveled in a direct path like they would over a trail of flammable liquid, leaving behind the fire to feed on the dead bushes that made perfect kindling. There was no time to get out when the fire had blocked the way. Two fiery arms stretched out past the houses, wrapping around the rampart of dried, dead vegetation in an infernal embrace. Flames like hungry teeth consumed them in a wild dance under the red sunset.

"We walked into a damn trap," Dakota cursed.

Tim looked back to Phil's body, the array of red clouds, and the crimson sun above, with the dancing flames reaching up to the heights of the former. Phil's wooden post was stained in brown-red that pooled at the base. The sight of it dug in deep and scarred his eyes. Tim felt it claw into him, staining his soul. It was a spotted canvas now dripping red in blood. There was no time to get Phil's body down, no way for two crippled people to get their brother's corpse out of the trap and save it for burial. Tim looked to his brother, ashamed, and searching for answers only Phil could give. But only silence harkened down from the watchful sentry.

I'm sorry, Buddy, his heart cried out.

Dakota's hand pulled him away from the sight of the hellish fury as the flames spread inwards, feeding on the houses. Waves of smaller flames moved across the front lawns, ending at the sidewalks and eating the mailboxes. Glass cracked and shattered from the inferno's heat, and the fire popped and sizzled.

The tremors intensified, heavy thuds shook the ground under them, and at that moment, Tim caught movement from inside the wall of fire; there were shuffling figures ingressing towards them. He raised his rifle and aimed at the first he saw; his UFR monitor on his wrist then started to beep. His breath soon felt heavy, and weakness gripped him at an accelerating rate as he watched the vertical movements of humanoid shapes, set aflame, shambling towards them. From between the houses, out the front doors and broken windows, the dead arrived from every angle. They were demons sprung free from the Third Ring of the Seventh Circle of Hell, whose gates were now wide open, spewing out flame and death upon them. If God had indeed abandoned them then Hell embraced them.

"Dis is FUBAR!" Dakota's voice cracked, her tone shaken and broken to a state he had never heard before, and it broke his heart. His breathing reduced to panting, and his knees shook as the beeping from his wrist persisted; holding his weapon became a daunting task as his strength waned and weakened.

They stood back-to-back, and the Jackle's voice, now in hearing distance, rattled like iron chains, mingling with the popping inferno and the hunger moans of the demons. The Behemoth's footfalls came closer and closer, the tolling of hell's bells heralding their annihilation.

They wouldn't lie down and wait for the end. The flames fueled the duo; the writing on the wall was as simple as it could ever be. Tim gritted his teeth, raising his weapon, and aimed down the sights of his

M4, sweat coating his skin. He sensed Dakota doing the same behind him, softly grunting in pain as she struggled with her broken arm. He wasn't sure how long he could stay conscious, the unending beeping at his wrist a countdown of his coming blackout.

They fired, and for each demon killed, two more took the place of the fallen. The line of hostiles pushed in closer, crossing the front yard thresholds and onto the pavement of the street that held back the flames from reaching him and Dakota. Though like fiery veins, fire traveled over the pavement by way of the weeds sprouting from the cracks in the street. Veins of ember burned at their feet.

A passing thought came to Tim as he zeroed in his sights on the next, nearest demon's head:

Happy Halloween.

Epilogue

-The New Storm Approaches-

Colonel Reznov kept his hands folded behind his back; he had to restrain himself in some way as he stared out to the south. Through the wall of glass panels, the darkening of evening was lit by the inferno making its way north, burning what kindling and fire fuel the Godfather-Of-All-Bombs hadn't destroyed. Flames of red and yellow raged over the desolate landscape, illuminating the horizon, spreading and crawling up the mountains and to them. Those warm colors of fire transitioned to shades of purple at the flanks of the inferno and faded in the blackened night sky to the west. The plume of smoke reminded him of the Karymsky Eruption four years ago on the Kamchatka Peninsula. It was a wide chimney of smoke, pluming and rolling in layers of ashen grays that rose and disappeared into the darkening sky.

He couldn't help but think of this as a culminating event after Sergeant Sousa and her comrade's hijacking of his locomotive and freight. His entire brigade left stranded in Northern Montana. The dominoes had fallen since then, each one larger than the former. As the saying went, "Shit rolls downhill."

He shook his head and turned his back to the giant window, facing a table where a map of the Colorado Springs metro area was spread out and weighed down by bricks and ammo cans. Red lines were marked, digging lines, to prevent the wildfire from reaching the Air Force Academy.

He had been frowning ever since Sergeant Sousa had betrayed them, and now that frown turned into a snarl. If he were to lose any of his soldiers because of her betrayal, or this fire… well, he didn't know exactly what he'd do. But his heart throbbed with pulses of adrenaline from the anger he felt at the thought of his men dying, needlessly at that.

They had just recently secured the entirety of the Air Force Academy north of the desolation of Colorado Springs. Instead of manning their posts, fortifying, and setting up countermeasures for any monster attacks, most of his forces were now committed to digging trenches or holding security for those diggers. Three thousand men were meant to hold this Forward Operating Base, or FOB. *Three-thousand, one-hundred-and-fourteen exactly.* And now, he had to commit twenty-four-hundred of them to ensure those dig lines were set up. Two hundred were running search and rescues, scouting ops, and QRF for the former two. Three hundred were non-combatant personnel and hadn't seen any combat experience, being technicians, mechanics, and performing other essential duties. That left just one-hundred-and-fourteen combative personnel to hold down the fort.

Then there were the several MIA soldiers not yet accounted for. He bit down on his bottom lip, figuring that by now those men were beyond hope: no flares, medevac calls, or distress signals of any kind to call for help.

He had wanted to tell the major general that he didn't want Sergeant Sousa or her two friends with him. He wanted to inform his superior that the three assets could also double as liabilities; now his suspicions were proven to be an understatement, at best. The only reason he had put a capture and detain order and not a kill order out on her was because there hadn't been any casualties because of her deviance or the fire. But teams were MIA and there were wounded; there were plenty of wounded.

They had suffered sprains, lacerations, bites, fall damage, and on the list went. All were treatable, but out of the hundred wounded, forty-seven were suffering from a most peculiar condition. Men on night watch reported strange happenings, shooting at hostiles who weren't there. Some of the men cried out about Baba Yaga, and others about demons, and on and on. This mass hysteria got a few of his other men shot by those shooting non-existent threats. Men had to be detained, and he had heard their terrified screams over the radios; the medics reported that the afflicted were suffering from extreme hallucinations.

It was supposed to be a simple errand, Reznov thought, rubbing his forehead, fingers pinching the bridge of his nose. Just establish a foothold and await the major general's arrival. Now, such simple orders were a daunting task to complete.

"Sir." A voice called behind him, a welcome distraction.

Colonel Reznov turned to see Lieutenant Sanders dressed in casual fatigues tucked into her uniform. The English threw him off; he had been given a few officers and non-commissioned officers of American-Canadian descent under his command.

"Apologies," he said, seeing the lieutenant holding a radio to him.

"Staff Sergeant Jarvis," she explained.

Among his English-speaking non-commissioned officers, Staff Sergeant Jarvis had proven to be a great investment in his brigade. The man had an affinity for science, botany in particular, in which the staff sergeant held a Master's degree from the Old World. Now, reassigned from his platoon to figure out this outbreak of hysteria, Jarvis's updates were on Reznov's list for immediate attention.

Reznov accepted the radio and pressed the PTT button. "Da, Staff Sergeant Jarvis."

"Colonel," exclaimed Staff Sergeant Jarvis. "I think I found something; you'll want to see this."

"On my vay." Reznov gave the radio back to the lieutenant and took his leave.

A lounge area of the academy had been repurposed for the medical ward, and an adjoining office space was given to the staff sergeant. Walking past his injured men strengthened his resolve. The medics were overworked and understaffed; his brigade didn't have enough people, it seemed.

Along the way, a timer went off near a soldier laying on a cot. The man's left arm was set in a tourniquet; his right was held in a brace. Reznov took a minute and loosened the tourniquet, seeing that blood wasn't pulsing out. Then, he held a clean rag to the wound and waited until one of the medics arrived, a skin stapler in hand.

"Spasibo." The medic thanked him, her eyes focused on patting the laceration dry as she began stapling the wound closed.

"My pleasure," Reznov said, continuing to Jarvis's office. The doors had broken off their hinges when they had first tried to use them. So, Reznov stepped straight inside, where staff sergeant gave him a wave to enter without looking his way. The staff sergeant's eyes were stuck to a personal microscope, that, to their great fortune, he brought on his own accord.

"Fascinating," the staff sergeant murmured. The low tone of his voice did not indicate if he was addressing Reznov or himself.

"Vat are we looking at?" Reznov requested.

"It's a mutation," the staff sergeant murmured again with that same kind of voice. He pulled away from the device and procured a personal book of his. *Field Guide to Herbs and Plants*, Reznov read along the spine.

Jarvis scrolled through several clusters of pages, back a bunch, then forwards a couple of pages, until he found what he was looking for. "Lactuca Virosa, Bitter or Wild Lettuce, some call it. But here, it's clearly not the same plant anymore… altered by UFR contamination?"

"And you suggest zat zis…Lactuca Virosa is behind the mass hysteria?"

"Well," Jarvis shrugged, scratching the stubble on his cheek, still reading from the same page, "The original plant was and still is known for its mild sedative effects and hallucinogenic properties. In conjunction, we have reports on the size and mass alterations of BR-Sea-Hostiles by UFR contamination, if they are to be believed."

"Zey are," Reznov affirmed, quick and sharp. Jarvis had never crossed the Pacific, had never seen the mutated sharks, whales, and many other hostiles of the sea—those that had been hunted before the Submarine Net had been established. He never saw the destroyer that was gripped by the tentacles, its main weapon systems destroyed, the ship saved only by depth charges. "Zey are very real," he affirmed.

"Then, is it too much to believe that plants can suffer drastic alterations as well? I mean, sea monsters, zombies, and BR-Weapons aside."

"Zen vy have we not seen such before?" he asked.

"Colonel, I can point out a whole plethora of indigenous and evasive plant species back at the Mainland State that have been altered and mutated by the UFR. All with differing degrees and results. Most are docile and go by unnoticed. As long as they provide us with oxygen, food, and materials, no one gives plant species a second's thought. Until something radical like this is found, attention is rarely given."

The staff sergeant did have a point; Reznov ceded with his silence.

"I don't think any species back home has undergone such an extreme alteration like what I'm seeing here. This could very well be the first discovered BR-Plant-Hostile. Lord, I'd hate to see what afflictions the Toxicodendron genus suffered."

"Never mind vat it is, I vant to know, if so, zen how is it causing hallucinations? And how can I protect my men and vomen from it?" Reznov hurried him on.

"This way," spoke the staff sergeant, rolling on the office chair borrowed from the colonel's office on the freight train. Jarvis skidded over to an old glove box. It looked to be a sand blaster whose structural integrity had been reinforced by recent welding and adhesives for the glass—a contained and sealed box.

Inside was a rooted plant and a can of cold spray that he believed read *Gum Remover*. "What is the common denominator of each episode of hysteria and hallucinations? They occur during the coldest hour of the night or morning. So, I had the men you assigned to me go out and they reported this…" The staff sergeant slipped his hands into the glove compartment.

Inside the box, he grabbed the spray can and pressed down on the nozzle; the cold air ejected from the can in sharp contrast with the humid temperatures inside. Then the colonel understood what the staff sergeant was doing.

"Grab that temp gun and point it at the plant. Hurry," Jarvis remarked, quick and sharp.

The colonel grabbed the temp gun, aimed, and pulled the trigger, looking at the little screen. At 0 degrees Celsius, the plant blossomed in his periphery and a vaporous fog quickly filled the box.

"Interesting," Reznov noted.

"It only makes sense, given recent temperature drops, that such an occurrence hasn't been noticed. Though this specific genus doesn't grow in Alaska. If the freezing temperature of water triggers this kind of effect, then Lord only knows if the same can be said for the other BRP-Hostiles back home. It would be wise to suggest a national observation study in case any similar triggers by the cold may exist in other mutated species back home."

"I get back vith you," Reznov said, giving the staff sergeant back a firm pat. "Keep me updated on further studies."

The Colonel had his quarters set up in the former Dean's office of the Air Force Academy. Along the way, he had sent an order out to all the commanding officers of his brigade, halting any further night ops. Silently cursing himself, he continued to his office.

He had known better, and in his hubris, he thought his brigade could handle night ops. There was a reason that night ops were severely limited in standard operating procedures nationwide and were authorized only for special operations. If Staff Sergeant Jarvis was correct, monsters weren't the only threats at night to worry about. He had made a bad call, and his men were paying for it. But there was something else pricking at his thoughts.

At the desk sat all the intel and maps—everything on SRT-Alpha and Bravo from their departure at Bonner's Ferry, Idaho, to the recovered and again MIA status of the three survivors of Wolf Pack. He had spent all his free time re-reading everything connected to this desolate place over the last week since the major general had assigned him this operation. What pricked at his memory was foggy and needed clarification.

He understood Staff Sergeant Jarvis' conviction that the mutated wild lettuce might be causing the mass hysteria—he had seen that vaporous fog in the glove box. His mind was on the common denominators of all the information he had of hand: hallucinations, shooting at non-existent threats, vaporous fog, nighttime, wild vegetation.

Two packets of reports were at the center of his attention, one from Sergeant Sousa and one from Merlow of SRT-Alpha. Taking a seat, he cleared a spot on the table, sat the two reports down, and flipped through the pages. He flipped past a report on SRT-Alpha and Bravo's expedition to Bonner Ferry, their voyage through Montana, Wyoming, and Colorado. He stopped, in both reports, where both sergeants spoke on behalf of their late comrade Sergeant Nilges; both accounts lined up with one another nearly perfectly.

Both SRTs took shelter at a rest stop. Sometime in the middle of the night, Sergeant Nilges abruptly went outside and never came back. Both sergeants went on record saying that their late comrade had blacked out and went AWOL in the forest. In the wild, he was attacked by an unknown assailant. In the accounts, he read a quoted radio command later received—Sergeant Nilges ordering them to "Stay out of the forest, stay out of the fog."

Reznov's sat phone rang, breaking his concentration. Without thinking, he retrieved the phone and answered the call, eyes still skimming the report.

"Da."

"Colonel Reznov." The voice wasn't one he recognized; there was a cold malice to it that came across calm as a lamb but more vicious than a Siberian Tiger. In the background, he could hear the crying of men. *My men!*

His attention was pulled from the debriefs and fully to the phone. He could hear the same pitiful pleas he heard from those suffering hallucinations. Yet, these pleas didn't come from a place of hysterical terror but from one of fatigue from pain.

Reznov could feel his knuckles turning white from his grip on the phone.

"Sergei Cultivascú… Or Sergeant Nilges," he muttered, holding back the sudden hatred staining his thoughts. "Vatever cause you have for war against us, be sure zat zere is no personal vendetta on the men you have vith you. Come, let us reason togezer, that zey may live and go back home to zeir vives and children. I pray you."

There was a long period of silence, a pause with interludes of heavy breathing: the kind that spoke of an injured man, and his eyes fell back to the paper, where Tim and Dakota detailed Phil telling them that this "Sergei" had taken five headshots without flinching.

Then Sergei broke his silence. "There can be no peace between lambs or wolves, no covenants between wolves or lions. We are not of one mind, and there can never be any peace, no negotiation, no reasoning."

"Zere is no reason for you to kill the people trying to save you!" That staining hatred came out now, deepening his voice. He could feel the phone move from his tight grip as he pressed the plastic tighter against his face.

More silence, then: "I will be paid, in full, for the grief Wolf Pack caused us, on account of our brothers in arms, who they needlessly tortured and slaughtered. We will be paid in full."

Reznov felt himself shiver, not out of fear but because of what came next after such a statement. A spike shot up his spine, hearing a guttural growl from the line, then a fiendish bellow. But the latter came not from over the phone, but as a muffled echo from the window.

"Vat have you done?"

The line cut from the other side. Colonel Reznov shot up to his feet and rushed to the window. Staring out over the Air Force Academy, fire still burned in the distance. Explosions rattled the earth at the eastern perimeter, and the radio on the desk behind him came to life. A legion of distressed men crying of security breaches, zombies, and a skinless titan renowned for its brutality and merciless slaughter. The newly installed sirens came to life, harkening to the two-thousand-plus men digging those ditches to the south, calling for aid, and he thought, an alarm clock for the sleeping giant that was the Wastelands. Their folly came to him in full understanding of Sergei's devices; he was coming for Autumn.

Standing there, he heard from the radio one of his American-Canadian officers: "BR-Weapon has been identified, the Jackle has breached the perimeter. Say again, the Jackle has breached the perimeter!"

Reznov stood, shock giving him pause as he took solace in the knowledge that if Sergei wanted Autumn Nector back, he wouldn't find her here.

Acknowledgements

There are so many people to thank for their aid, advice, and other means of help in the completion of this book; to who I am much grateful and indebted.

WEEKS Book Three started as a side project with no intended direction back in the Winter of 2009. Right after I wrote Books One and Two. Only few close to us know how hard that winter was for us; an arduous season where an arduous story was contrived and written. With the continued support and enthusiasm of my family and friends my writing has grown into what it is now, and me into the author I now am. To my immediate family and close friends, I am the most grateful! Of which, some require more specific gratitude.

My father in Heaven, thank you for the gift of writing you've given me. I don't know where I'd be in life without my passion. Thank you so much, for always being by my side; there aren't words to describe how awesome you are!

My little brother. This whole thing started with just the two of us, in addition with a couple of our friends, all the way back in 2008. But you have remained by my side and an influence on WEEKS of which I cherish a great deal. You are as much a part of this as I am!

My dear mother. Your continued support and nurturing nature helped in ways I cannot describe nor thank you enough. From reading the very first draft of WEEKS in a spiral notebook to the book it is now. You've been a continual foundation I can retreat to and share ideas with. I cannot thank you enough!

My old man. Your knowledge and skills with many things mechanical and construction and things of that nature have been a blessing. You've always been ready and eager to help me. There's so much here that your insight and knowledge have been of great help; not to mention your continual support and interest in this book.

My Gmama Flora. You've to been a continual source of support as well as a peer editor for my earlier drafts. You've given me much support and interest in my work and I am most grateful!

My Gmama Bonnie. I was grateful you at least got to see my first two books released. You always worried about my future security and pushed me to take care of myself especially financially. This dream is a risk, but not one done without considering your advice. I love you and I miss you dearly, we all do.

My big Sisto. I know “Sisto” is not a word, but it’s what I call you. You’ve been there a good deal for me and offered support and feedback that I took to heart. Thank you for your support and enthusiasm!

My brother Charvell. I never would’ve guessed we’d become family after our first meeting. I treasure you and the person you’ve grown into. Not only that but the support and enthusiasm you bring to any and all creator endeavors is the center of many ‘our hanging outs’ that I look back on and forwards to with fondness.

My fellow in Pen and friend, author Ben Kerr. I am very grateful for our chance meeting. Not only are you a talented writer, but you’re an excellent critic whose talent for writing helped to better this book. Only authors can understand how special that is, so thank you for your critiques. I know my writings become better since knowing you.

My Friend Jennifer, who after I released Book One, has been of great support. Straight out the gate of me being a published author, you’ve been nothing short of enthusiastic, and supportive. I am glad to have met you.

There are many more to thanks to give and not enough pages in this book for me to give. If you are one of those people who has helped me in the past and are reading this, I am indebted and humbled. Thank you for your help!

About The Author

Jasyn T. Turley was born in Wyandotte County, Kansas City, Kansas; and lives in Independence, Missouri. He is an independent author and full-time custodian. He holds an Associates in Arts degree from MCC KC Community College. He started WEEKS Book Three back in the winter of 2009 and has been continuously working on it, and its sequels, since then. He has more science fiction and fantasy books in the works that he plans on releasing in the future. You can learn more about Jasyn, the series WEEKS, and future projects at https://turleybookinn.com

Check out his other books:

WEEKS Book One & WEEKS Book Two

Coming Soon
WEEKS Book Four

Visit: www.turleybookinn.com for updates

A special request from the author: If you enjoyed this book, and/or the previous installments, then I sincerely ask that you leave an honest review as it would greatly help me grow in both writing and business. I cannot stress enough how helpful reviews are so please be sure to do so.

Scarecrows don't pick
their faces

$15.00
ISBN 978-1-7334027-6-7
51500>
9 781733 402767

Made in the USA
Monee, IL
12 April 2023

31210725R10266